Theatre History Studies

2023 VOLUME 42

Edited by
LISA JACKSON-SCHEBETTA

PUBLISHED BY THE MID-AMERICA THEATRE CONFERENCE
AND THE UNIVERSITY OF ALABAMA PRESS

Copyright 2023
The University of Alabama Press
All rights reserved.
Inquiries about reproducing material from this work should be addressed to the University of Alabama Press.

Template Design: Todd Lape / Lape Designs

Essays appearing in this journal are abstracted and indexed in *Historical Abstracts* and *America: History and Life*.

MEMBER
CELJ
Council of Editors of Learned Journals

Cover Illustration
John Rice, *Charlotte S. Cushman as Meg Merrilies [in Terry's "Guy Mannering"]*, Folger Shakespeare Library Shelfmark: ART File C986 no.4 (size XS); used by permission of the Folger Shakespeare Library

Cover Design
Todd Lape / Lape Designs

Editor
Lisa Jackson-Schebetta, Skidmore College

Associate Editor
Jocelyn L. Buckner, Chapman University

Editorial Assistants
William Davis-Kay, Skidmore College
Erin Einzig, Skidmore College

Book Review Editor
Ariel Nereson, University at Buffalo—SUNY

Editorial Board
John Fletcher, Louisiana State University
Felicia Hardison Londré, University of Missouri-Kansas City
Ron Engle, University of North Dakota
Meredith Conti, University at Buffalo—SUNY

Consulting Editors
Wendy Arons, Carnegie Mellon University
Nic Barilar, University of Wisconsin-LaCrosse
Matthieu Chapman, SUNY Purchase
Will Daddario, Independent Scholar
Shannon Epplett, Illinois State University
Lisa Fitzpatrick, Ulster University
Sara Freeman, University of Puget Sound
Miles P. Grier, Queens College, City University of New York
Brian Herrera, Princeton University
Shelby Lunderman, Seattle Pacific University
Sarah Marsh Krauter, Bike City Theatre
Laura Mielke, University of Kansas
VK Preston, Concordia University
Olga Sanchez Saltveit, Middlebury College
Max Shulman, University of Colorado Colorado Springs
Daniel T. Smith Jr., Michigan State University
Patricia Ybarra, Brown University

Past editors of *Theatre History Studies*
Ron Engle, 1981–1993
Robert A. Schanke, 1994–2005
Rhona Justice-Malloy, 2005–2012
Elizabeth Reitz Mullenix, 2012–2015
Sara Freeman, 2015–2019

Please note: there was no issue published in 2013.

Theatre History Studies is an official journal of the Mid-America Theatre Conference, Inc. (MATC). The conference is dedicated to the growth and improvement of all forms of theatre throughout a twelve-state region encompassing Illinois, Indiana, Iowa, Kansas, Michigan, Minnesota, Missouri, Nebraska, North Da-kota, Ohio, South Dakota, and Wisconsin. Its purposes are to unite people and organizations within this region and elsewhere who have an interest in theatre and to promote the growth and development of all forms of theatre.

President
Shawna Mefferd Kelty, SUNY Plattsburgh

Vice President
Cason Murphy, Iowa State University

Conference Planners
Jeanmarie Higgins, Penn State University and Jen Plants, University of Wisconsin-Madison

Associate Conference Planner
Brandon LeReau, University of Georgia

Internal Communications Officer
Julie Burrell, Cleveland State University

Treasurer
Tony Gunn, Brigham Young University

External Communications Officer
Macy Jones, University of the Ozarks

Accessibility Officer
Catherine Peckinpaugh Vrtis, Independent Scholar

Graduate Student Representatives
Mackenzie Bounds, University of Washington and Tyler Everett Adams, Ohio University

Immediate Past President
Chris Woodworth, Hobart and William Smith Colleges

Theatre History Studies is devoted to research in all areas of theatre studies. Manuscripts should be prepared in conformity with the guidelines established in the *Chicago Manual of Style* and emailed to Jocelyn Buckner at ths.editor@matc.us. Consulting editors read the manuscripts, a process that takes approximately four months. The journal does not normally accept studies of dramatic literature unless there is a focus on actual production and performance. Authors whose manuscripts are accepted must provide the editor with an electronic file, using Microsoft Word. Illustrations are welcomed and should conform with the instructions listed on the style guide on the website: http://matc.us/wordpress/wp-content/uploads/UAL-Press-Guidelines-Revised-2013.pdf

This publication is issued annually by the Mid-America Theatre Conference and the University of Alabama Press.

Subscription rates for 2023 are $25.00 for individuals, $35.00 for institutions, and an additional $10.00 for foreign delivery. Subscription orders and changes of address should be directed to Accounting Specialist, University of Alabama Press, Box 870380, Tuscaloosa, AL 35487; (205) 348-1564, phone; (205) 348-9201, fax.

Any single current-year issue or back issue is $34.95 each if ordered through the Chicago Distribution Center. (*Please note: there was no issue published in 2013.*)

Theatre History Studies is indexed in Historical Abstracts and America: History and Life, Humanities Index, Humanities Abstracts, Book Review Index, MLA International Bibliography, International Bibliography of Theatre & Dance, Arts & Humanities Citation Index, IBZ International Bibliography of Periodical Literature, and IBR International Bibliography of Book Reviews, the database of the International Index to the Performing Arts. Full texts of essays appear in the databases of both Humanities Abstracts Full Text and SIRS.

CONTENTS

List of Illustrations {ix}

Introduction {1}
—LISA JACKSON-SCHEBETTA

PART I
Studies In Theatre History

"Check One, Two, Three": Dispatching Sonic Labor in Richmond's *In the Heights* and *Nuestras Historias* Exhibit {7}
PATRICIA HERRERA AND MARCI R. MCMAHON

The Actor's Life and State Funding for Theatre in France: "We Are the State" {27}
—CYNTHIA RUNNING-JOHNSON

"She Is No Longer What She Was": Charlotte Cushman, Melodramatic Femininity, and the Maidenly Mode of Singing in Daniel Terry's *Guy Mannering* {49}
—ALEXANDRA SWANSON

PART II
Care

Introduction to the Special Section {75}
—MATTHIEU CHAPMAN AND MILES P. GRIER

"Humane Care": The Rhetoric of Premodern Care in *The Tempest* {85}
—ROBERT O. YATES

CONTENTS

"Not *Another* Essay on Care Work in Academia!" {95}
—JESSICA N. PABÓN-COLÓN

Responding to Crises of Racial Capitalism with Care and Resistance {104}
—KATHERINE GILLEN

Access Intimacy as a Philosophy of Care in Post-Pandemic Academic Theatre {110}
—CATHERINE PECKINPAUGH VRTIS

There Are No Small Parts, Only Fractals {116}
—SHERRICE MOJGANI

Beyond Polite Words: Understanding Trans Erasure and Exploitation in Academe {120}
—KARA RAPHAELI

A Path Out of the Desert: Enduring and Educating in the Time of COVID {125}
—SHANE WOOD

Who Cares If We Like Them? The Problematics of "Likability" in Production and Progress {131}
—JOSHUA KELLY

When We Gather in the Clearing, A Cardinal Croons {138}
—JOHN MURILLO III

PART III
Essay From The Conference

The Robert A. Schanke Award-Winning Essay, MATC 2022

Present Perfect Tense: Revolutionizing Dramatic Narratives through Living History at the Oconaluftee Indian Village {147}
—HEIDI L. NEES

PART IV
Book Reviews

Casey Kayser, *Marginalized: Southern Women Playwrights Confront Race, Region, and Gender*
—REVIEWED BY CHERYL BLACK {161}

CONTENTS

Theresa J. May, *Earth Matters on Stage: Ecology and Environment in the American Theater*
—REVIEWED BY SHELBY BREWSTER   {163}

Chelsea Phillips, *Carrying All Before Her: Celebrity Pregnancy and the London Stage, 1689–1800*
—REVIEWED BY MEREDITH CONTI   {166}

Sean Metzger, *The Chinese Atlantic: Seascapes and the Theatricality of Globalization*
—REVIEWED BY ZACH DAILEY   {169}

Jake Johnson, *Lying in the Middle: Musical Theater and Belief at the Heart of America*
—REVIEWED BY MICHAEL DEWHATLEY   {171}

Noah D. Guynn, *Pure Filth: Ethics, Politics, and Religion in Early French Farce*
—REVIEWED BY WHIT EMERSON   {174}

Alexis Greene, *Emily Mann: Rebel Artist of the American Theatre*
—REVIEWED BY NANCY JONES   {176}

Gretchen E. Minton, *Shakespeare in Montana: Big Sky Country's Love Affair with the World's Most Famous Writer*
—REVIEWED BY FELICIA HARDISON LONDRÉ   {179}

Donelle Ruwe and James Leve, eds., *Children, Childhood, and Musical Theater*
—REVIEWED BY BRET MCCANDLESS   {182}

Henry I. Schvey, *Blue Song: St. Louis in the Life and Work of Tennessee Williams*
—REVIEWED BY TOM MITCHELL   {185}

Soyica Diggs Colbert, *Radical Vision: A Biography of Lorraine Hansberry*

Mollie Godfrey, ed., *Conversations with Lorraine Hansberry*
—REVIEWED BY LETICIA L. RIDLEY   {187}

Christin Essin, *Working Backstage: A Cultural History and Ethnography of Technical Theater Labor*
—REVIEWED BY CHRISTINE WOODWORTH   {191}

Books Received   {195}

Contributors   {197}

ILLUSTRATIONS

SWANSON
Figure 1: John Rice. *Charlotte S. Cushman as Meg Merrilies [in Terry's "Guy Mannering"]*. {50}
Figure 2: Measures five through ten of "Oh! Rest Thee Babe." {56}
Figure 3: Measures eleven through thirteen of "Oh! Rest Thee Babe." {57}

Introduction

—LISA JACKSON-SCHEBETTA

As I complete my four-year term as editor of *Theatre History Studies*, I revisited my first volume. I submitted volume 39 to the press in September 2018. It was in print and in your mailboxes in December 2019. The world then changed in unimaginable ways three months later, in March 2020.

As I have written before, one of the most exquisite pleasures of editing this journal has been the generosity of the colleagues with whom I have worked. Authors and guest editors have invited me to engage with them in the intellectual, aesthetic, and developmental dances of their ideas, arguments, and craft. Scholarship is an intimate thing, borne of and limned with our interests, curiosities, convictions, and passions. Writing is personal, too, and experimental, a deeply internal journey to create sentences that render our thoughts into words. Writing history adds to these dynamics additional, multiple ethical exigencies. It is high stakes. It is also, I believe, infused with generosity, or *can be*. That is, we write and publish for others. At our most cynical, we might say we write and publish solely for the machine of academia and personal advancement. And while I do not deny that writing (like history, like writing history) is instrumentalized, gate-kept, and lorded over in our field, we also write *for each other*. Whether we mean to or not, we inspire, teach, and move one another with our writing.

I have learned a great deal from every author who has submitted writing to me over the last four years and from each guest editor with whom I have had the privilege to work. I have learned about topics and methods, as well as processes and professional and personal convictions. I have learned from each and every peer reviewer who donated their time, labor, and generosity to authors'

LISA JACKSON-SCHEBETTA

work. I have learned from Ariel Nereson, book review editor; Jocelyn Buckner, associate editor and incoming general editor; and Sara Freeman, immediate past editor. These three women have been inspiring, visionary, and supportive constants. I have learned from my colleagues at the University of Alabama Press: Joanna Jacobs, Dan Waterman, Sara Hardy, and Penelope Cray have been patient, thoughtful, rigorous stewards of my work, and—by extension—the work of each contributor in each volume.

All of these colleagues have made me a braver historian. They have unsettled what I thought I knew. They have humbled and moved me. And, they have taught me how to read the work of my fellow historians with greater generosity. I look forward to taking this with me, and I hope you might, as well.

It is my pleasure to present you with volume 42 of *Theatre History Studies*, the fourth and last volume of my term as general editor. The three articles in the general section offer an array of sites and insights, methods and provocations. The special section of this volume, "Care," brings together a selection of curated, critical responses to our field—its recent and long histories, as well as its possible futures. The Robert A. Schanke Research Award-winning paper from the 2022 MATC conference interrogates time itself. Taken together, these pieces, along with our Book Review section, amply represent both the multiple ways this journal serves us, as scholars and laborers, and the journal's consistent dedication to history and historiography, a unique and increasingly imperative site/practice for our world.

Patricia Herrera and Marci McMahon open the general issue with a breathtaking performance and theatre history that takes up place studies, museum studies, sound studies, and race studies. Urging us, from the outset of the article, to listen for the "sonic labor of Latinx Richmonders amidst public performances of white supremacy," the authors mobilize the "sonic dispatch" as both "practice and theory." Herrera and McMahon examine public performance and orality in Virginia Repertory Theatre's production of *In the Heights*, the Valentine Museum's *Nuestras Historias* exhibition, and local Latinx Richmonders' daily lives to document the ways in which history and theatricality illuminate, enact, and refute marginalizations of people of the global majority.

Cynthia Running-Johnson contends that French theatre professionals—as artists, laborers, and citizens—must repeatedly navigate their relationship to "the state." What is it to be employed by the state while simultaneously interpolated as the state itself? Running-Johnson details how theatremakers in France struggle to define themselves in relation (and in resistance) to the state's constructions of belonging. Running-Johnson's study reminds us that theatre funding, central not only to production but also to the lives and experiences

INTRODUCTION

of artists and audiences alike, is an oft-overlooked yet vital aspect of theatre history.

Alexandra Swanson takes us on a deft and detailed journey into constructions and subversions of femininity in melodrama. Marshaling musicological, historiographical, and performance studies methodologies, Swanson crafts a close examination of the repertoire of Charlotte Cushman's performances of Meg in Daniel Terry's *Guy Mannering*. Reading the score, vis-à-vis the body, Swanson unsettles established narratives about melodrama as well as celebrity, character-type, and feminist history.

As we gathered in Cleveland in 2022, a highlight of the MATC conference was our ability to award the Robert A. Schanke Research Award to Heidi L. Nees. Examining multimedia installations in museums, Nees asks, "But *how* does a site like the Oconaluftee Village achieve and communicate tribal perspectives given its foundation in linear notions of time presupposed on notions of progress?" Nees's fundamental question demands that we, as historians, rethink the ways in which *time*—a foundation of our discipline—is so often, so readily, and so unquestioningly normalized through Western constructions. The paper is published here in its conference form.

The special section of this issue, guest-edited by Matthieu Chapman and Miles P. Grier, presents a different kind of study in/of time. Chapman and Grier originally conceptualized the special section (before and in the early months of COVID) as focused on racecraft in the early modern world. As you will read in their unflinching introduction, that special section could not be realized for a variety of reasons, ranging from the personal and professional toll of the pandemic on scholars (and, in particular, on scholars of the global majority, women, and disabled communities) to ingrained institutionalized racial biases that continue to plague and crush (the field of) history in theatre and performance (and beyond). Chapman and Grier pivoted to create a curated section, "Care," in which they invited scholars to capture their moment, their ways of working, and their experience as scholars, humans, and citizens in 2022. The result is not only a documentation of our field—and the ways of working it demands, denies, and supports—but also a call to create an archive of our field in the midst of a global pandemic that has thrown (yet again) into sharp relief the ontological and epistemological violences upon which our field and professions continue to rely. The archive created by "Care" demands we *attend* to our most recent histories (alongside the long histories that have shaped them) in order to *tend* the work of making *change*.[1]

May you revel in the work of the authors in volume 42, even as you work to attend and tend your field(s).

LISA JACKSON-SCHEBETTA

Notes

1. The special section's format resonates with the format of *Theatre History Studies* volume 41's clutch of pieces on dramaturgy and historiography, as well as with other journals' recent intentional moves to increase the variety of formats available to scholars, not only in response to the challenges of COVID-19 but also in thoughtful engagement with the ways different formats allow for different kinds of research, conversations, and provocations. See, for example, the recent special issues of the *Journal of American Drama and Theatre*, edited by the American Theatre and Drama Society: "Asian American Dramaturgies," edited by Donatella Galella (vol 34, No.2), and "Milestones in Black Theatre," edited by Nicole Hodges Persley and Heather Nathans (vol 33, No.2).

Part I

STUDIES IN THEATRE HISTORY

"Check One, Two, Three"
Dispatching Sonic Labor in Richmond's *In the Heights* and *Nuestras Historias* Exhibit

—PATRICIA HERRERA
AND MARCI R. MCMAHON

As you are tuning into this essay, we invite you to take a moment to listen to the *In the Heights*'s song "Benny's Dispatch."

"Check one, two, three. Check one, two, three."[1]

Hear the palpable sounds of Latinx and Black, Indigenous, and people of color (BIPOC) fighting for their rights and pushing against the legacy of slavery and racism.[2]

Sonic Dispatch 1: The Unveiling of the Maggie Walker Statue

"Atención, yo, attention."

In summer 2017, six hundred people witnessed city leaders pulling back the tarps covering the statue of African American entrepreneur and civil rights advocate Maggie Walker. The ten-foot bronze statue stands tall facing Broad Street in Jackson Ward, or "Black Wall Street," the very site that historically functioned as the dividing line between Black and white Richmond, Virginia.

As the crowd collectively counts down 5, 4, 3, 2, 1, the roar and applause grows. Singing the lines "Facing the rising sun of our new day begun, Let us march on till victory is won," from the song "Lift Every Voice and Sing," the community members resound Richmond's fraught racial past.

Amid this reclaiming, family members recall Maggie Walker's voice and well-known words of resilience: "Unite head, heart, and hand. Be strong in words. Stand firm in what is right. Have faith, have hope, have courage and carry on." These celebratory sounds of Black community members inspire and reimagine resilience, refusal, and reparation in a space where Black people were not always welcomed on Broad Street.

Sonic Dispatch 2: Virginia Repertory Theatre's *In the Heights*

"Honk ya horn if you want it."

That same summer, Virginia Repertory Theatre, a couple of buildings down the block from the Maggie Walker statue, produced the Tony Award–winning musical *In the Heights*, with lyrics by Lin-Manuel Miranda and book by Quiara Alegría Hudes. As audience members, we hear the voice of Spanish-speaking radio disc jockey Oscar Contreras who runs WBTK AM 1380 Radio Poder, Richmond's primary Latinx radio station, directing audiences to turn off their cell phones in Spanish first and then English.

As if we were quickly scrolling from one radio station to another searching for the right music, we hear a mix of prerecorded Afro-Latinx musical genres open the show—salsa, the bolero "No te vayas," a merengue, a pop-infused piano riff accompanied by an egg shaker, and the popular Spanish rap song "No pare, sigue sigue."

We then hear Oscar's voice inviting listeners to a party at the pier: "Yo mi gente, pull out them kiddy pools, and call me up with the sizzling summer scandal. Tomorrow is the fourth of July. You know, cuatro de julio. And we are kicking it off with a celebration. La fiesta is tonight with fireworks at the marina. It's going to be caliente." Oscar's invitation in Spanish affirms the inclusion of Latinx communities in Richmond. His voice perseveres, disrupting the exclusion of Latinxs often rendered inaudible in the city's white supremacist legacy.

Sonic Dispatch 3: The Valentine Museum's *Nuestras Historias: Latinos in Richmond*

"I'm on the microphone this mornin'."

After the first act of Virginia Repertory Theatre's production of *In the Heights* concludes, we walk out of the theatre to the lobby. As we wait in line for the restroom, we see four panels featuring the bilingual Spanish and English exhibition "*Nuestras Historias*: Latinos in Richmond" that recently opened at the Valentine Museum, nearby the theatre.[3]

The panels recall the stories, objects, photography, and voices of Latinx people from more than sixty interviews. These personal testimonios proclaim the journeys, dreams, and experiences of Latinx Richmonders.

We hear snippets of sounds from the exhibit: the gossiping of women in a hair salon, the ringing of church bells, and the claves from the Richmond music group Bio Ritmo. These sounds permeate the listeners' ears in the day-to-day realities and resilience of Latinx people, amplifying their contributions in Virginia's historical memory.

The above sonic dispatches amplify the palpable synergy produced by cultural agents from the global majority in the former capital of the Confederacy laboring to revise Richmond, Virginia's fraught racial history. The "sonic dispatch," we contend, makes audible the BIPOC labor of wielding sound to create and sustain strategies of refusal and resistance to white supremacy. The Maggie Walker statue unveiling, Virginia Repertory's production of *In the Heights*, and the Valentine Museum's exhibition *Nuestras Historias* all took place as the Charlottesville neo-Nazi "Unite the Right" rally occurred in summer 2017. As the unveiling of the Maggie Walker statue occurs, Virginia Repertory Theatre undertakes its first Latinx production, *In the Heights*, since 2009. Simultaneously, the Valentine Museum curates *Nuestras Historias*, its first dedicated exhibit about the Latinx community. While the institutions that activated these Black and Latinx productions may not be directly working together, we hear across their works a shared activist synchronicity laboring to make visible and audible the history and lived experiences by the global majority in Richmond.

Inspired by the song "Benny's Dispatch" in *In the Heights*, this essay listens to sonic dispatches as a theory and a practice that makes audible the sonic labor of Latinx Richmonders amid public performances of white supremacy. We hear and see BIPOC cultural agents, like Benny, dispatching sound to navigate the rifts of racism. As a Black taxi dispatcher, Benny uses a two-way radio to communicate to drivers alternative transit routes to surpass traffic congestion. He not only leverages his voice on the microphone to facilitate safe and expedient navigation, but he also uses his voice to uplift the community amid daily economic pressures. Working within a predominantly Latinx neighborhood, Benny has developed sonic skills to navigate across cultural, linguistic, and spatial differences. Benny uses sound to elevate the community when he invites drivers to welcome the character Nina—an aspiring first-generation Puerto Rican college student who returns home from Stanford—by honking their horns. The cacophony of honks over the radio brings a smile to Nina's face, affirming her connection to Washington Heights. When Benny uses his taxi dispatch to communicate to drivers on the ground, he also works with the community to transcend the blockages of circulation, communication, and mobility. Cultural agents like Benny dispatch sound to redress power imbalances created by neoliberalism, asserting BIPOC humanity and presence amid forces of gentrification.

Even as Benny's sonic dispatch supports the Latinx community, he confronts the legacy of colorism. When the character Kevin Rosario, the owner of Rosario Car and Limousine, disparages Benny's relationship with his daughter Nina because of Benny's Blackness, the musical reminds us of the ongoing work of racial equity within Latinx and BIPOC communities. The Hollywood film version of *In the Heights* not only eliminates the character Kevin's racism toward Benny but also does not cast any dark-skinned Afro-Latinx actors in the main character roles.[4] In doing so, the film version reifies both the Latinx community's elision of Blackness and Hollywood's white supremacist practices.

We hear and see Maggie Walker as a historical predecessor to the character Benny in Virginia Rep's *In the Heights*. The Maggie Walker statue that now stands tall in Jackson Ward involved almost two decades of efforts started by Black community members, and other Richmonders, including Maggie Walker's family, museum, and public art representatives. The organizing labor of these multiple communities activates the city's memorialization of the legendary Black civil rights leader and entrepreneur. Just as the Maggie Walker statue inspires and reimagines resilience and reparation in a space where Black people were not always welcomed, Benny's dispatch is a reminder of the ongoing BIPOC labor needed to fight racism and go beyond Richmond's Black and white binary to integrate the Latinx community into the city's history.

Composed as a series of sonic dispatches, this essay "listens in detail" to Virginia Rep's *In the Heights* (June 23–July 30, 2017) and the Valentine Museum's *Nuestras Historias* exhibit (July 2017–May 2018) to amplify how Latinx cultural agents navigate white supremacist paradigms.[5] As a dramaturgical listening practice, the sonic dispatch amplifies the aural contours and textures produced by Latinx bodies that labor, on the one hand, to negotiate neoliberalism and, on the other, to disrupt the perpetuation of social injustices.[6] We claim both negotiation and disruption as sonic strategies produced by Latinx bodies to resist, survive, and thrive amid white supremacy. In the first sonic dispatch, we offer a listening practice that hears the Afro-Latinx diasporic sonic textures of *In the Heights*. While the Broadway musical has Afro-diasporic elements in its soundtrack, we do not claim the work as an example of Afro-Latinx theatre.[7] Afro-Latinx theatre affirms the lived experiences of the African diaspora in Latin America and the Caribbean, including the movements, musics, cultures, and spiritual practices arising from the entangled histories of enslavement and colonization.[8] Afro-Latinx theatre addresses the lack of representation by elevating Black Latinx histories and lived experiences and the prevalence of colorism as a normative practice throughout the Américas. By listening in detail to *In the Heights*'s Afro-diasporic sonic textures, we hear the soundscape as both pushing against traditional Broadway musical conventions and negotiating a neoliberal, American Dream success story.

In the next section, we listen to Virginia Rep's *In the Heights* as a failed sonic dispatch, produced on the heels of Lin-Manuel Miranda's success and celebrity with *Hamilton*. The production capitalized on the vocal virtuosity of Oscar Contreras, a well-known Spanish-speaking radio disc jockey in Richmond, to reach Latinx audiences without laboring to commit to or invest in the Latinx community. We claim Virginia Rep's "failure" as one shared by many white theatre companies unable to reach their potential BIPOC audiences by not investing in those communities or demonstrating allyship. By contrast, in the final section, we hear *Nuestras Historias* as a multipronged sonic dispatch calling Richmonders to listen differently to the experiences of Latinx communities in the city. Through collaborations that were developed over several years, the exhibit sustained an authentic engagement with the Latinx community that both valued and recognized their labor and contributions in the city. By featuring the contributions of many Latinx Richmonders, including Oscar's sonic labor as a radio broadcaster, *Nuestras Historias* resulted in creating a more inclusive history of Richmond. The Valentine Museum was also committed to developing long-lasting relationships with the Latinx community.

Listening to the sonic labor of Latinx cultural workers demands an autoethnographic practice that pumps up the volume on our different positionalities, enabling us to listen to these sonic dispatches through an intersectional ear.[9] Patricia, a first-generation American of Ecuadorian descent born and raised in Crown Heights, Brooklyn, understands firsthand the social and political realities of Afro-diasporic neighborhoods in New York City. She has extensive experience cocreating community-based public history projects, including museum exhibitions, docudramas, and digital archives that amplify the civil rights issues of Richmond. She also served as one of the oral historians and advisory board members for the *Nuestras Historias* exhibit. Marci, a white woman from San Antonio, Texas, has spearheaded the institutionalization of Mexican American studies curriculum at a Hispanic-Serving Institution in the South Texas United States-Mexico borderlands. As part of this work, she has mentored generations of Mexican American undergraduate and graduate students with a community-engaged curriculum that includes Latinx theatre and performance. With our firm commitment to Latinx equity and social justice, we understand the power and possibilities of theatre and performance as vehicles of social justice.

We make a double call. First, we call on theatre and performance studies scholars to listen to the labor of Latinx artists and cultural producers navigating the "Great White Way."[10] White American Theater (WAT) has historically excluded or tokenized global majority theatre workers while still relying on their labor to meet a quota of representation and diversity. When BIPOC bodies are included in the theatremaking process, WAT erases their contributions. Because of these pervasive racial disparities, BIPOC theatre artists coalesced in June 2020, inciting an industry-wide anti-racist movement with their social media manifesto "Dear White American Theater," which quickly went viral. In their manifesto, they "demand[ed] proper credit for [their] work and legacy, and an end to the culture of theft and extraction," proclaiming "We are not only our bodies."[11] In this same vein, our essay elevates the "Dear WAT" call to hear Latinx cultural workers beyond the extraction of their bodies as labor.

Second, we call on Latinx theatre studies to tune in to the understudied frequencies of sound in cultural representation, claiming the sonic as a counter-performative register that troubles neoliberalism.[12] Visual representation of BIPOC bodies on the theatrical stage has dominated Latinx theatre studies because of WAT's historic erasure of bodies of color. We heed Jennifer Stoever's concept of the sonic color line, which conceptualizes race as not only a visual construct but also a sonic one.[13] Riffing on Cherríe Moraga's "theory in the flesh," we analyze sound in the material body, tracing out the political vibrations of sonic labor performances of resistance and survival.[14] This sound theory in the flesh is a move that pays attention to sound in performance, how sound is an enactment of the body, and how sound shapes fleshy bodies.[15] Likewise, Daphne Brooks and Roshanak Kheshti turn to sound as a theory and method for understanding fault lines of power.[16] Thus, by claiming sound as a register of representation, we do not discount the political importance of visuality in Latinx theatre studies. Instead, we pump up the volume on the sonic labor of Latinx cultural workers who create strategies of refusal and resilience at multiple registers beyond the visual.

Afro-Diasporic Sonic Dispatches in Broadway's *In the Heights*

We want to first position *In the Heights*'s Afro-diasporic sonic dispatches as pushing against Western Broadway musical traditions, making audible the sonic labor of Latinx cultural agents. *In the Heights* was conceived, developed, and produced from 1999 to 2008 during a time of increasing neoliberal policy, anti-immigrant rhetoric, and racism. Miranda first workshopped *In the Heights* at Wesleyan University in 1992 during the "Los Angeles rebellion," a response to the "not guilty" verdict in the Rodney King police brutality case. Two years later, Miranda continued to develop the musical during California's Proposition 187 in 1994. Over the next decade, rising fears over the ethnic immigrant "other" accelerated in the aftermath of 9/11 in 2001. These neoliberal anti-immigrant border policies targeted Arab Americans, other communities of Middle Eastern descent, and Brown/Latinx Americans. Quiara Alegría Hudes joined Miranda to write the book in 2004 during increased border violence and militarization. The *In the Heights* film (2021) reflects the heightened anti-Latinx rhetoric and policies during Trump's presidency, specifically its attempts to end Deferred Action for Childhood Arrivals (DACA).

While these political moments are not specifically named in the musical, we hear *In the Heights* pushing against the loud anti-immigrant sentiment through an Afro-diasporic soundscape.[17] *In the Heights* narrates a story of a Latinx community in Washington Heights aspiring to attain an American dream. Audiences witness how their dreams are deferred, due not to a lack of hard work but to the neoliberal forces of gentrification that displace longtime residents from the neighborhood. Even as the musical and film do not center Afro-Latinx experiences, we hear in the musical score by Alex Lacamoire a sonic counter-narrative that amplifies Afro-diasporicity. The opening song centers two Afro-diasporic percussion instruments: the clave and the güiro. We hear the 3–2 or 2–3 beats of the clave and the rasping sound of the güiro holding down the rhythm of the song even when other sounds, like birds chirping, cars passing, and cars honking gradually get louder. The clave and güiro infuse the musical with Afro-diasporic textures and contours, dislodging Broadway's Western musical conventions. Miranda and the Broadway cast produce a sonic world where hip-hop, reggaetón, and salsa push against neoliberalism to claim spaces of belonging. We further hear the labor of claiming and affirming Afro-diasporicity through syncopated songs and raps in Spanish, English, and Spanglish, including the Piragua Man who speaks in English with a Caribbean inflection, yelling "ice cold piragua! Parcha. China. Cherry. Strawberry. And just for today, I got mamey!"[18] *In the Heights*'s Afro-diasporic sonic dispatches push against Western Broadway musical traditions, making audible the sonic labor of Latinx cultural agents.

The American Dream "bootstrap" narrative of success at the heart of Latinx-authored musicals such as *In the Heights* has led critics to argue that the Broadway musical form, even when authored by Latinx playwrights, does not have the ability to disrupt comfortable neoliberal narratives.[19] As a work embedded in the Western musical form, *In the Heights* purports a linear, assimilation narrative of immigration: one that upholds the view that as long as the immigrant works hard, they will achieve the American Dream. Yet when we listen closely to the sonic labor of *In the Heights*, we hear the political work of the musical pushing against the American Dream myth and the white supremacist neoliberal paradigm.

Disembodied Sonic Dispatches in Virginia Rep's *In the Heights*

Catering to neoliberalism's drive to profit from Latinx stories without meaningfully engaging with the community, Virginia Rep produced *In the Heights*, directed by Nathaniel Shaw, on the heels of Lin-Manuel Miranda's success and celebrity with *Hamilton*. Virginia Rep's production capitalized on the vocal virtuosity of Oscar Contreras, a well-known Spanish-speaking radio disc jockey who runs WBTK AM 1380 Radio Poder. Hosted by a religious nonprofit organization, Radio Poder is one of the few Spanish-speaking radio stations in Richmond, serving educational programming, including immigrant legal rights, home ownership, financial resources, language classes, and other programming to enhance self-empowerment and resilience.[20] The production employed Oscar's sonic labor to stand in for Latinx representation and his connections to call in Latinx Richmonders to the theatre.

In the summer of 2017, we saw the Virginia Rep production of *In the Heights* three times. We were impressed by the quality of the production, yet what continued to linger was the overwhelming, traditional, older white subscriber audience each night, even though it was peppered with racial diversity. On the first night, we heard the production trying to bring in Latinx communities with a preshow bilingual recording in Spanish and then English, welcoming audiences to the show and reminding them to turn off their cell phones. Immediately, Patricia recognized Oscar's voice. By using the voice of a popular Latinx radio personality, we acknowledged that the theatre was trying to make inroads with the Latinx community. We were also hopeful that the bilingual preshow welcome would require non-Latinx and non-Spanish-speaking audiences to attune their ears to ethnic and cultural differences.

We heard Oscar's voice inside the theatre as a sonic dispatch, calling us to commune with other Latinx Richmonders in a theatre that has historically

SONIC LABOR

served a white audience. Prior to *In the Heights*, Virginia Rep (formerly known as Barksdale Theatre) had produced only two Latinx plays: José Rivera's *Boleros for the Disenchanted* during its 2009–2010 season and Karen Zacarias's *Legacy of Light* during its 2010–2011 season.[21] These two productions were part of Virginia Rep's planned "three-year Hispanic Theatre Project," with the aim to "produce one play from the rich treasures of Hispanic culture." Additionally, according to founding artistic director Bruce Miller, "all three of the plays will be presented in English, with super-titles for Spanish-speaking audiences."[22] Yet, per our research of online reviews from this period, we did not find evidence of this occurring. The theatre thus tried to build a Latinx audience, yet as Nathaniel Shaw, Virginia Rep's then artistic director in 2017, speculates, the company did not meaningfully engage the Latinx community, and the white subscriber audience had little interest in seeing lesser-known Latinx plays.[23] As a result, Virginia Rep's productions of Rivera's and Zacarias's plays did poorly at the box office and the third production never materialized. Six years later, Virginia Rep returned to producing Latinx theatre with *In the Heights*, capitalizing on Miranda's success with *Hamilton*. Unlike Virginia Rep's two previous Latinx productions, *In the Heights* had record-breaking box office numbers: not because the production increased Latinx audiences but because white Richmonders were interested in being "in the room where it happens."[24]

Virginia Rep's technique of having a known Latinx community voice make the preshow announcement is not new. This convention has been routinely used by predominantly white American theatre companies as a way to authenticate their staging of Latinx works. For example, Edward James Olmos recorded the preshow announcement for the Mark Taper Forum's fiftieth anniversary revival of *Zoot Suit* in 2017. And a 2020 digital staging of *Fefu and Her Friends* by Season of Concern Chicago hired Lourdes Duarte, a noted Latina television news personality, to introduce the show, moderate the talkback, and read the stage directions. Virginia Rep, utilizing this convention, capitalized on Oscar's well-known voice in Richmond to make inroads with Latinx communities. While this might not have been Virginia Rep's only outreach strategy, their use of Oscar's voice served as a symbolic gesture in the absence of a meaningful investment and commitment to Latinx audiences, which are necessary to create inclusive theatre spaces.[25]

After the bilingual preshow welcoming, Patricia was surprised to hear Oscar's voice again. This time, the production used Oscar's voice as a DJ in the opening of *In the Heights*, where audiences hear various Latinx radio stations playing different musical genres, including hip-hop, salsa, and merengue. This opening is

PATRICIA HERRERA AND MARCI R. MCMAHON

standard for every production of *In the Heights* and consists of snippets of various songs, some of which we later hear in the musical. We first hear salsa, then the bolero "No te vayas," then merengue, then a pop-infused piano riff accompanied by an egg shaker, followed by the popular Spanish rap song "No pare, sigue sigue." The fast-paced movement between these sounds evokes the illusion that we are hearing someone scrolling through radio stations searching for the right music. These Afro-diasporic musical styles index the different Latinx communities that coexist in Washington Heights. We then hear Oscar's voice inviting listeners to a party at the pier: "Yo mi gente, pull out them kiddy pools, and call me up with the sizzling summer scandal. Tomorrow is the fourth of July. You know cuatro de julio. And we are kicking it off with a celebration. La fiesta is tonight with fireworks at the marina. It's going to be caliente."[26] Oscar's voice in this moment serves as a linguistic and cultural marker of Latinx identity to Richmonder audiences. However, only audiences who can understand and speak Spanish can catch this audible difference. While Oscar's voice offers the potential to activate Latinx communities in Richmond, we observed that night that most audience members did not register Oscar's voice. By layering Oscar's voice in the opening of the musical, Virginia Rep, once again, co-opts his cultural capital to diversify their traditional, older white subscriber audience.

When the show was over, Patricia recognized Oscar outside the theatre, and we were eager to talk to him. He informed us that the next day he would be doing a live broadcasting on Radio Poder's Facebook page to promote the production. That Saturday afternoon, while we were culling together our notes and thoughts on the two productions we had seen thus far, we tuned in to the live feed and heard Oscar greeting his listeners in Spanish in front of the theatre: "Hola, mi gente, estamos aqui en 114 Broad Street." The close-up selfie camera angle, along with his voice, creates an intimate connection with his listener-viewers. With his warm greeting and his notation of the theatre's location, Oscar attempts to convince his followers to join him in seeing one of the few Latinx musicals productions in Richmond. As the camera zooms to the promotional poster outside of the theatre, he explains with excitement the story line of *In the Heights*: "Hay dos Latinos que son protagonistas que viven en un barrio en Nueva York. Uno de los personajes es Abuela. Muchos se van identificar. ¿Quizás tienen una abuela como ella? Los otros dos protagonistas: Nina, es puertorriqueña y Benny un Afro Americano que quiere ser parte de la familia. Usnavi es dominicano."[27] To help his audience connect with this Latinx musical set in New York City, he tells his listeners that "perhaps you have a grandmother like Abuela?" Oscar appeals to his listeners by centralizing the abuela, the matriarch in most Latinx families. He also underscores the racial and ethnic identity of the

SONIC LABOR

various characters (Nina is Puerto Rican, Benny is African American, and Usnavi is Dominican), highlighting the pan Latinx representation in the musical.

Oscar moves into the theatre lobby where there is a display of the cast's headshots, making an unfamiliar space familiar. As we get a close-up of their headshots, he calls out their Latinx-sounding surnames. He pauses on Vilma Gil, stressing that she is of Cuban descent, one of the earliest Latinx communities to migrate to Richmond, and has performed in previous Richmond productions. Oscar's dispatch of Gil's cultural and professional background is significant as the majority of the actors, with the exception of the ensemble, were hired from outside of Richmond. Oscar then moves inside the theatre, inspiring his Latinx listeners to imagine sitting at the theatre. He tells his audience that he will focus only on the theatrical seating because it is illegal to show the set. The camera shot, along with his voice, attempts to convince his Latinx listeners to attend the performance: "This could be you. You could be here. Aquí estamos esperándolos." Instilling a sense of coming together as a community, he informs his audience members in Spanish that there are discounted tickets for community organizations and families, and he even offers free tickets for those who can arrive three hours before the matinee. Through the mediums of radio and live streaming, Oscar uses his physical presence and Spanish-speaking voice to demystify the elitism of theatre, breaking down the linguistic, cultural, and economic barriers that have made theatre inaccessible to Latinx and Spanish-speaking communities in Richmond.

Oscar's assertion of his physical presence and voice on his Facebook live feed affirms and validates the Latinx communities' right to be in the public space of the theatre. Oscar was able to approach the promotional process creatively due to the nonprofit nature of the radio station and the station's already firm commitment to listening to the needs of local Latinx communities. Virginia Rep's connections with Latinx organizations were mostly through a cross-marketing, neoliberal strategy, which does not equate to long-lasting relationships with the Latinx community.[28] Oscar, however, had the artistic license to go beyond the press material and created a multipronged approach to programming that included interviews with the actors and using Radio Poder's live stream FB to promote the show outside of the theatre. Through the nonprofit station, Oscar leveraged his voice and role in the community to try to initiate a relationship between the Latinx community and Virginia Rep. Yet, Virginia Rep's use of Oscar's sonic labor remains muted and contained within the walls of the theatre serving the white audience. Since Virginia Rep does not labor to commit or invest in the Latinx community, Oscar's sonic dispatching alone cannot build a Latinx audience.[29] Virginia Rep's "failure" with the *In the Heights*'s production to sus-

{ 17 }

PATRICIA HERRERA AND MARCI R. MCMAHON

tain relationships with the Latinx community is one shared by many white theatre companies unable to reach their potential BIPOC audiences by not investing in those communities or demonstrating allyship.[30]

Community-Engaged Sonic Dispatches in *Nuestras Historias*

We hear *Nuestras Historias: Latinos in Richmond* at the Valentine Museum as a sustained, authentic engagement with the Latinx community that values and compensates Latinx labor. The exhibit opened in July 2017, a month into the Virginia Rep production. Centered around more than sixty interviews conducted with Latinx people in Richmond, *Nuestras Historias* dispatches Latinx life through personal testimonios (both textual and sonic) and material artifacts, including photography, transmitting a multisensorial diversity of Latinx experiences in Richmond. By including the voices of Latinx immigrants from Cuba in the 1960s alongside more recent immigrants from Guatemala and El Salvador, the exhibit dispatched diverse Latinx experiences as a result of intentional collaborations with Latinx communities and businesses throughout Richmond. A collaboration between the Valentine, Richmond Public Libraries, Sacred Heart Center, and University of Richmond (UR), *Nuestras Historias* was the first bilingual exhibition in Richmond to elevate the journeys, dreams, and complicated relationships of diverse Latinx communities in the city and nation. The *Nuestras Historias* exhibit was the first time that the Valentine, which has been collecting, preserving and interpreting Richmond's four-hundred-year history for more than a century, dedicated an exhibition to Latinx communities. While the Valentine, similar to Virginia Rep Theatre, has a mostly white subscriber audience, the museum intentionally worked with the Latinx community to create the exhibit. Through collaborations that were developed over several years, the exhibit functioned as a multipronged sonic dispatch calling Richmonders to listen differently to the experiences of Latinx communities in the city. In doing so, the *Nuestras Historias* exhibit pushes against the neoliberal machine and American Dream myth in stark contrast to the lack of outreach and grassroots organizing demonstrated by the Virginia Rep production.

The genesis of the exhibit began in Patricia Herrera, Laura Browder, and Lazáro Lima's Latinx-themed courses at University of Richmond (UR) through a series of events for their linked classes funded by an NEH/ALA grant to commemorate five hundred years of Latino history. Herrera, Lima, and Browder organized screenings of the NEH-produced documentaries *Foreigners in their Own Land (1565–1880)* and *Peril and Promise (1980–2000)* and also curated two

SONIC LABOR

events: "Latino Lives, American Dream: Young Latino Fiction" with award-winning Richmond-based Latina author Meg Medina, and a community conversation at the Valentine, "Latinos in Richmond: Breaking the Black and White Binary," the first discussion of Latinos in Richmond ever hosted at the museum. The work the professors conducted in these courses served as the incubator for the large-scale, ambitious *Nuestras Historias* exhibit, which became a collaboration between several institutions throughout Richmond. As a result of the UR professors' groundwork, Richmond Public Library applied for an NEH Common Heritage grant that would be used to fund both the exhibition and the digitization of the objects, documents, and other materials that tell the story of Latinx in Richmond.

Nuestras Historias directly involved the Latinx community, from the curators to the team of interviewers led by Latinx academics in collaboration with community members. The choice of curator for the exhibit amplifies the community-engaged process central to the grant partnership. Through an interview process that valued Latinx experience over hiring someone who only had a museum studies degree or museum exhibition experience, the Valentine hired their first ever Latinx guest curator, Wanda Hernández, who came on board as a part-time curator to help build the museum collection and participate in conducting oral history interviews. Along with a Latinx guest curator, the Valentine Museum created an advisory board of majority Latinx members who were leaders in the Richmond community. Hernández came to the team as curator with not only a museum lens perspective but also extensive knowledge and networks within the Latinx communities in Richmond as a result of her community organizing work and her concentration in Latinx studies at Virginia Commonwealth University (VCU). As a result, Hernández was able to tap into both her personal and her professional networks to reach out to and create a relationship of trust with Latinx community members for the oral histories that became central to the exhibit. The Valentine Museum valued Latinx labor and leadership, from the curator to the work of UR professor Herrera, along with the museum's Latinx advisory board. The collaborative interview process that was undertaken by community partners stood in stark contrast to Virginia Rep's instrumentalized neoliberal strategy. To initiate the interviews, Herrera, Lima, and Browder focused on establishing relationships with the community, organizing a series of events focused on the diverse experiences of Latinx, the state of Virginia, and the city of Richmond. Herrera and Browder, in collaboration with their students in their 2016 team-taught course, developed the group-interview process/template that the grant partners took in producing the material for the Valentine exhibit.[31]

PATRICIA HERRERA AND MARCI R. MCMAHON

Informed by the interview process that Herrera and Browder developed with their students, the partnering organizations launched two events, *Cuentos e historias/Stories and History*, which took place at both Sacred Heart and the Valentine, in which the Latinx community was invited by Latinx leadership involved in the project to voluntarily share their stories and bring material objects that represented their experiences in Richmond. These events brought in more than fifty participants to share their experiences in small-group oral history interviews. The partnering organizations reached out to the Latinx community through their professional and personal networks. For instance, Sacred Heart Church invited the Latinx community to their interview event by using flyers and church announcements in all their programming, from their ESL to leadership courses.

For the Valentine interview event, Hernández reached out to her personal and professional networks, including her VCU Latinx sorority, as well as the Central American community in Richmond, and invited members of Latinx-owned businesses, such as Sabrosita Bakery and Kuba Kuba, to join the interview events. As part of her networks, Hernández formally invited Oscar to be interviewed for the exhibit. Along with excerpts of the interview, the exhibit displayed Oscar's Radio Poder headphones and microphone. By including this equipment, the exhibit acknowledged Oscar's extensive role and labor in dispatching essential day-to-day news to the Spanish-speaking Latinx community.

The exhibit prominently featured the racial and ethnic diversity of Latinx in Richmond. Upon entering the exhibition room, the first image visitors see is a large window-sized scrim of Hector "Coco" Barez, an Afro–Puerto Rican percussionist and former member of the group Bio Ritmo who spent a decade playing with the renowned award-winning hip-hop group Calle 13. "Coco" has been an active player in the bomba community within and beyond Richmond; bomba, one of the oldest Afro–Puerto Rican dance forms, comes from the roots of enslavement. Not only are museum attendees visually immersed in racial and cultural multiplicity, but they are also immersed in the multivocality of Latinx Richmonders. The exhibit included three different listening areas where we hear Latinx multivocality permeating the listeners' ears conveying the day-to-day resilience and realities of Latinx people. These listening areas are the result of interviews with community members and found sounds that amplify the contributions of Latinx people in Virginia's history.

In the entryway of the exhibit, a lamp speaker hangs over the museum visitor, immersing their ears in a sonic collage of Latinx voices and environmental sounds of Latinx spaces. We first hear a group of women laughing waiting to get their hair done at Christy's Beauty Salon. As the laughter subsides, we hear the

SONIC LABOR

jingling of a door opening followed by the ringing of church bells. Here, belonging is created by affirming religiosity and faith by Latinx in Richmond. When a Latinx Richmonder says, "Nobody for a second should think that we come from somewhere else . . . that we have less loyalty to Virginians," we hear the use of sound to claim citizenship and belonging in response to anti-immigrant narratives. We hear the rhythmic pattern of the clave from Bio Ritmo rehearsing and the voices of children playing at La Mancha, a neighborhood in Southwood. This sonic collage is further layered with personal testimonios of economic struggle and of working forty-hour weekends and with utterances of encouragement with órale to the recitation of a poem in Spanish and English at the first Latinx Graduation at VCU in 2016. Collectively, these sounds do the work of affirming the active participation and contributions of Latinxs in Richmond.

Just as the sounds in the first listening area allow us to travel through a multivocal collective memory of Latinx past, present, and future in Richmond, the second listening area moves participants through a variety of geographic locations. This section of the exhibit amplifies voices from Latin America, including Guatemala, El Salvador, Brazil, and Mexico. Through headphones, museumgoers listen to a two-minute excerpt of different Latinx voices of all ages that anchor the belonging of Latinx community in Richmond. We hear the recording of community members saying "My name is_____. I am from_____. These are our stories" in different languages, including Spanish, English, Spanglish, Purépeche, and other Indigenous languages. This multilinguality sonically marks different inflections, rhythmic patterns, and tonalities within the Latinx community, acknowledging the multiethnic transnational heterogeneity of what it means to be Latinx. The *Nuestras Historias* exhibit's emphasis on multivocality was extended into the museum's programming through bilingual brochures in Spanish/English and exhibit tours in Spanish. Unlike Virginia Rep's unsuccessful attempts at incorporating Spanish supertitles in their Hispanic Theater Project shows from 2009 to 2012, the Valentine's implementation of cultural and linguistic differences in their permanent museum programming helped to welcome Latinx communities into a predominantly white museum space.

While the second listening area works to fade out the fixed, monolithic notions of Latinx people, the third listening area sonically dispatches the labor of Latinx activists in Richmond. Through the archival sound recording of the late Reverend Ricardo Seidel, a minister and advocate for immigrants and Latinx throughout Virginia who led the initiative for Spanish-language mass in Richmond, we hear the honoring of Latinx activist ancestors and their legacy. The exhibit commemorates Reverend Seidel, who conducted the first official Spanish mass in Richmond and is thus remembered fondly for creating a permanent place where all Latinx could gather and worship.[32] The exhibit displays a large portrait of Reverend Seidel along with a sound recording of him leaving a message to his family on the same night he passes away. After putting on the headphones, a beep followed by a static sound transports us to a time where landline telephone recording was a technology and mode of communication that is now virtually nonexistent. With the hope of recovering soon, Reverend Seidel says: "Hi Michael, Carmen and Isabel, children and your mom also. I want to thank you for your prayers. I'm feeling gradually better. . . . Thank you so much for your friendship, and your concern and your prayer. God bless you all. I love you all very, very much. Take good care." In the transcribed text, we infer Reverend Seidel's gentle and kind voice full of gratitude with the words "thank you," "god bless you," "I love you," and "take good care." This transcribed text does not fully capture the range of emotions that we hear on the sound recording. Through the headphones, we hear the slight quivers in Reverend Seidel's voice as he strains to stay upbeat and exude hope between each word, even as he conveys love and gratitude. The interplay between his voice and the image of him calls back his flesh and bone into the world of the living, mobilizing museumgoers to continue the labor of advocacy for Latinx people.

We can hear, see, and feel the different community engagement approaches between the Valentine's *Nuestras Historias* exhibit and Virginia Rep's *In the Heights*. In contrast to Virginia Rep's transactional use of Oscar's labor, *Nuestras Historias* materializes Oscar's sonic labor by displaying his radio headset and microphone, tools he uses to dispatch pertinent information to empower Latinx people. The Valentine Museum demonstrated its commitment to the Latinx Richmond community not only by producing the exhibit itself but also by employing a Latinx community member to curate the exhibit in collaboration with other Latinx-vetted spaces. In addition to making space for Latinx leadership, the museum created bilingual programming, removing language barriers that have historically prevented Latinx communities from connecting with predominantly white spaces. The combination of these efforts demonstrates how the Valentine was committed to developing long-lasting relationships with the Latinx community.

Final Dispatch

With these sonic dispatches, we urge White American Theater (WAT) to listen differently to the experiences of Latinx and BIPOC communities fighting to dismantle a neoliberal economy.[33] We recognize that these two nonprofit organizations, the Virginia Rep and the Valentine, have different missions, models, and commitments to community engagement. Yet when we listen to them together, we hear *Nuestras Historias* as a sonic dispatch by, for, and about Latinx communities that more loudly affirms their racial and ethnic multiplicities during a pivotal moment of mobilization in Richmond's history. Even when the unveiling of the Maggie Walker statue took place a city block away from Virginia Repertory Theatre, the theatre company's production of *In the Heights* neglected to be in conversation with Latinx and BIPOC activists. When WAT uses recognizable Latinx voices without meaningful engagement, it becomes a symbolic gesture that does not equate to the investment in and commitment to Latinx audiences that is needed to transform and make American theatre fully inclusive. By contrast, *Nuestras Historias* played an integral role in documenting Latinx lived histories of oppression and resistance, amplifying their sonic labor. We thus return to our second call, urging Latinx theatre studies to tune into sonic labor as counter-performances that move the conversations about Latinx Richmonders beyond a Black and white binary. With sound-making practices, *Nuestras Historias* amplified the Afro-diasporic histories of Latinx Richmonders. If WAT wants to map out a more equitable future filled with hope, possibility, and justice, they must synchronize with the global majority movements that have already labored to make visible and audible their histories and lived experiences.

Notes

1. Each sonic dispatch in our opening begins with lyrics from the *In the Heights*'s song "Benny's Dispatch." Lin-Manuel Miranda, Quiara Alegría Hudes, Andréa Burns, Janet Dacal, and Carlos Gomez, *In the Heights Original Broadway Cast Recording* (New York: Sh-K-Boom Records, Inc., 2008).
2. Moved by anti-racist movements, we use the term "Black, Indigenous, and people of color" (BIPOC) to center Black, Indigenous, and people of color alliances, amplifying these communities' shared histories of resistance to white supremacy. With the term, we signal the contributions of multiracial and multiethnic communities, including Latinx, Asian American, Pacific Islander Americans, Middle Eastern Americans, and others, in the shared fight against antiblackness and Native invisibility. See The BIPOC Project: A Black, Indigenous, and people of Color Movement (website), accessed June 24, 2022.
3. For a virtual tour of the *Nuestras Historias* exhibit, see Google Arts and Culture (website), *Nuestras Historias: Latinos in Richmond*, Valentine Museum, Richmond, Virginia, July 27, 2017–May 28, 2018; accessed April 14, 2023.
4. Ari Shapiro, "The Dark-Skinned Afro-Latinx Erasure in *In the Heights*," *All Things Considered*, National Public Radio (website) June 16, 2021, accessed June 24, 2022; Maira Garcia, Sandra E. Garcia, Isabelia Herrera, Concepción de León, Maya Phillips, and A. O. Scott, "The Pain of Being Erased," *New York Times*, June 23, 2021, C1.

5. Alexandra T. Vazquez, *Listening in Detail: Performances of Cuban Music* (Durham, NC: Duke University Press, 2013).
6. We draw on Ross Brown and Mladen Ovadija's theories of sonic dramaturgy that focus on the function and meaning of the processes of creating and arranging sound. See Ross Brown, *Sound: A Reader in Theatre Practice* (Basingstoke, UK: Palgrave Macmillan, 2010); and Mladen Ovadija, *Dramaturgy of Sound in the Avant-Garde and Postdramatic Theatre* (Montreal: McGill-Queen's University Press, 2013).
7. See Daphne Sicre, "Afro-Latinx Themes in Theatre Today," in *The Routledge Companion to African American Theatre and Performance (CAATP)*, ed. Kathy A. Perkins, Sandra L. Richards, Renée Alexander Craft, and Thomas F. DeFrantz (New York: Routledge, 2019).
8. Derived from these intersecting fraught pasts, Afro-Latinx theatre attends to the back and forth movements across national borders and racial divides. See Petra R. Rivera-Rideau, Jennifer A. Jones, and Tianna S. Paschel, in *Afro-Latinos in Movement: Critical Approaches to Blackness and Transnationalism in the Americas*, ed. Petra R. Rivera-Rideau, Jennifer Jones, and Tianna S. Paschel (New York: Palgrave Macmillan, 2016).
9. "Pump up the volume" comes from our essay "¡Oye, Oye!: A Manifesto for Listening to Chicanx/Latinx Theater," in *Dossier on Chicanx/Latinx Teatro*, ed. Brian Herrera, *Aztlán: A Journal of Chicana/o Studies* 44, no. 1 (spring 2019): 239–48. For more on the concept of "intersectional ear," see Elías D. Krell's "'Who's the Crack Whore at the End?': Performance, Violence, and Sonic Borderlands in the Music of Yva las Vegas," *Text and Performance Quarterly* 35, nos. 2–3 (2015): 95–118.
10. Alberto Sandoval, *Jose, Can You See?: Latinos on and Off Broadway* (Madison: University of Wisconsin Press, 1999), 10.
11. WNET Group, "'Dear White American Theater': Over 300 Theater Artists Call Out White Privilege in Industry," AllArts (website), June 10, 2020, accessed April 17, 2023.
12. In *Modernity's Ear: Listening to Race and Gender in World Music* (New York: New York University Press, 2015), Roshanak Kheshti brings economies of labor and neoliberal paradigms into the conversation with music and sound. As Francis Aparicio also reminds us, both the visual and the sonic function as counter-performative sites that trouble white dominant narratives. Frances R. Aparicio, *Negotiating Latinidad: Intralatina/o Lives in Chicago* (Champaign: University of Illinois Press, 2019), 136.
13. Jennifer Lynn Stoever, *The Sonic Color Line: Race and the Cultural Politics of Listening* (New York: New York University Press, 2016).
14. Cherríe Moraga, "Theory in the Flesh," in *This Bridge Called My Back: Writings by Radical Women of Color*, ed. Moraga and Gloria Anzaldúa, 2nd ed. (San Francisco: Aunt Lute Press, 1983), 23.
15. Marshall, Herrera, and McMahon, "Sound Acts, Part 1: Calling Back Performance Studies," *Performance Matters* 6, no. 2 (2021): 1–7.
16. Daphne Brooks and Roshanak Kheshti, "The Social Space of Sound," *Theatre Survey* 52, no. 2 (2011): 329–34.
17. For further discussion of the various ways *In the Heights* engages neoliberalism by catering to or critiquing its discourses, see Elena Machada Saéz, "Blackout on Broadway: Affiliation and Audience in *In the Heights* and *Hamilton*," *Studies in Musical Theatre* 12, no. 2 (2018): 181–97; Elena Machado Sáez, "Bodega Sold Dreams: Middle-Class Panic and the Crossover Aesthetics of *In the Heights*," in *Dialectical Imaginaries: Materialist Approaches to U.S. Latino/a Literature in the Age of Neoliberalism*, ed. Marcial González and

Carlos Gallego (Ann Arbor: University of Michigan Press, 2018): 187–216; and Gabriela Cázares, "Resisting Gentrification in Quiara Alegría Hudes and Lin-Manuel Miranda's *In the Heights* and Ernesto Quiñonez's Bodega Dreams," *American Studies* 56, no. 2 (2017): 89–107.

18. Miranda, Hudes, Burns, Dacal, and Gomez, *In the Heights Original Broadway Cast Recording* (2008).
19. Patricia Ybarra, for instance, contends that even when Latinx-authored musicals are on Broadway, they cater to neoliberalism. Ybarra suggests that while singing along to *Hamilton* is pleasurable, it does not carry the same ethical imperative as Latinx theatre that engages with neoliberalism to disrupt simplistically clear and happy immigration narratives. Patricia A. Ybarra, *Latinx Theater in The Times Of Neoliberalism* (Evanston, IL: Northwestern University Press, 2018). See also Donatella Galella, "Being in 'The Room Where It Happens': Hamilton, Obama, and Nationalist Neoliberal Multicultural Inclusion," *Theatre Survey* 59, no. 3 (September 2018): 363–85.
20. Dolores Inés Casillas argues that Latinx communities use Spanish-language radio to navigate racial and linguistic profiling; radio "crafts a distinct aural public sphere where citizenship is not a (quiet) formality tied to pen and paper but a personal subject matter voiced publicly by callers and experienced collectively by listeners." Dolores Inés Casillas, *Sounds of Belonging: U.S. Spanish-Language Radio and Public Advocacy* (New York: New York University Press, 2014), 6.
21. Virginia Repertory Theatre was created by the merger of Barksdale Theatre and Theatre IV in July 2012, forming one of the largest performing arts organizations in Central Virginia.
22. Bruce Miller, "'Boleros for the Disenchanted' Earns a Rave," *Barksdale Buzz* (blog), September 20, 2009, accessed April 17, 2023.
23. Patricia Herrera and Marci R. McMahon, interview with Nathaniel Shaw and Ben Miller (musical director of *In the Heights*), July 13, 2017.
24. Lin-Manuel Miranda, "The Room Where It Happens," *Hamilton: An American Musical* (Original Broadway Cast Recording) Atlantic Recording, 2015.
25. Virginia Rep also tried to make inroads with the Latinx community by helping to publicize *Nuestras Historias* in the lobby of the theatre during the production run, which included four panels on the exhibit.
26. Miranda, Hudes, Burns, Dacal, and Gomez, *In the Heights Original Broadway Cast Recording* (2008).
27. "There are two Latino protagonists that live in a New York City neighborhood. One of those characters is Abuela. You will identify with many of them. Perhaps you have a grandmother like her? The other protagonists: Nina is Puerto Rican and Benny is an African American man who wants to be part of her family. Usnavi is Dominican" (translation by authors).
28. Patricia Herrera and Marci R. McMahon, interview with Susan Davenport (director of communications), Nathaniel Shaw, and Oscar Contreras, July 17, 2017.
29. Lisa Jackson-Schebetta's "*In the Heights* at the University of Pittsburgh: Failures, Successes and Change" discusses the importance of not only developing community-university relationships and collaborations but also sustaining them through intentional and meaningful interactions that build cultural competency skills. Lisa Jackson-Schebetta, "*In the Heights* at the University of Pittsburgh: Failures, Successes and Change," ed. Stephani

Etheridge Woodson and Tamara Underiner, *Theatre, Performance and Change* (London, UK: Palgrave Macmillan, 2018), 145–54.
30. Since then, Virginia Rep has made changes in their leadership. More recently, they hired Katrinah Carol Lewis as the interim coartistic director, followed by the permanent appointment of Desirée Roots as coartistic director of Virginia Rep to offer a more inclusive season and create more casting opportunities for BIPOC performers. In 2020, the Virginia Rep board also created the "IDEA Taskforce: Inclusion, Diversity, Equity, Access." See "Social Justice: Anti-Racism Commitment & Accountability Statement," Virginia Rep Theatre (website), accessed April 17, 2023.
31. The group process of conducting oral histories was developed by Herrera and Browder's team-taught course in 2016. In that course, students examined the history of Latinx in the United States and the South, visited Latinx spaces in Richmond, and took part in the series of NEH-sponsored events. As part of this work, students conducted two oral history interviews with groups of five-to-seven community members.
32. Reverend Seidel conducted the first official Spanish masses at Sacred Heart and St. Augustine Catholic Churches on July 29, 1999. Less than a month later, he passed away.
33. WNET Group, "'Dear White American Theater,'" 2020.

The Actor's Life and State Funding for Theatre in France

"We Are the State"

—CYNTHIA RUNNING-JOHNSON

In an exchange that I had with French theatre director Guy-Pierre Couleau concerning the public funding of theatre in his country, I expressed a certain jealousy for what I saw as the generosity of the French government toward theatre professionals.[1] In the United States, in comparison, much less support is available, as American theatre practitioners can confirm. As one American journalist put it, in the United States the arts have historically been a "funding afterthought."[2] Government support for culture in France, including theatre, which has traditionally been in the vanguard of arts funding, is approximately ten times larger per capita than in the United States.[3] This statistic was on my mind, in fact, when I characterized the French state as generous in my discussion with the French director. His response to me was pointed: "We are the state." I understood him to be referring to the fact that, in France, funding of the arts, including theatre, is an accepted aspect of the *état providence* (usually translated as "welfare state"). The arts are one of the essential public services supported by the country's significant taxation of all, including theatre professionals themselves (the "we" in his statement). It is this "we" that I plan to examine here. I will describe the forces that govern the professional lives of theatre artists—actors in particular, as I will explain—including the role that public funding of theatre has played in their work over the past five decades in France.

In the director's statement, "We are the state," the word "state" of course has (at least) two meanings. In the context of French history, it implies popular sovereignty, the people as the state and the state as the people. The word also suggests the workings of government, the policies that it creates, and the application of them in everyday life, a more concrete aspect of the larger sense of "the state." Theatre professionals in France find themselves in a relationship with each. In one sense, they constitute an aspect of the state in its role as provider, in the functional meaning of the word, as they and their work serve the people of through the extensive system of government-funded theatre. At the same time, they are themselves part of the people, different only in that they are able to request funding for creation (simply to enable them to participate as workers in French society, of course) along with receiving their regular benefits. This difference, though, makes the theatre professionals' relationship with the public at large ambiguous as well, as they both belong to that whole and are positioned outside of it, or at least constitute a distinct division of it.

As Loren Kruger and David Whitton have each explained, theatre has occupied a special position in France since the Revolution in linking "the state" with the people. It has played an important part in the development of French democratization and nationhood.[4] Theatre professionals, in their role as part of the public, are in a position to critique and criticize government handling of public theatre and its workforce. They have done so throughout recent decades, including quite powerfully in the time of the pandemic. In this article, I will examine the position of theatre artists in their different roles, as providers of state services and as (at times) satisfied and (at other times) unsatisfied recipients of its benefits. I will examine the influence of larger societal forces as well as particular policy decisions on theatre professionals over the past fifty years and the changes that have taken place in the theatrical institution, some of which have occurred—and are occurring—through the actions of theatre artists themselves. What follows is generous in facts and statistics, in order to give a full picture of these creators, who are the heart of public theatre in France.

I will discuss the position of actors in France in part through the example and comments of individual performers whom I interviewed in 2018, while studying rehearsals for a French production. In addition, because the show was sponsored by one of the thirty-eight regional state theatres, the Centres Dramatiques Nationaux (CDNs, National Dramatic Centers), I was able to examine that institution and the interface between the CDN and the performers. During my discussions with the actors and creative team, I was struck by how often they made reference to state structures that were providing support for them and their work. They mentioned the publicly funded theatres, companies, and drama schools that employed them (or, in certain cases, that they themselves headed); public educational institutions that had nourished them in their younger years; and the government-provided unemployment insurance for theatre professionals. It was evident that state support was essential to their involvement in the production that I was observing and, indeed, to the show as a whole. I will concentrate upon the actors in particular rather than also including the set, costume, mask, and lighting designers and the composer, all integral to the production. I did this in part for practical reasons: I had greater opportunity to speak regularly with the ten performers, who were each present for every rehearsal of this ensemble show. Just as importantly, significant sociological and historical research that has been done in France in the area of workers in the theatrical arts, which informs my writing here, has itself often focused on actors, the largest professional group on the artistic side of theatrical creation. My article brings together this research with my own case study of working actors in the context of publicly funded theatre in France.

The show that I studied was *La Conférence des oiseaux* (The Conference of the Birds), directed by Guy-Pierre Couleau and produced by the Centre Dramatique National located in Colmar, in Alsace (the Comédie de l'Est [The Theatre of the East], in 2019 renamed the Comédie de Colmar). At the time, Couleau was also the director of the theatre itself, nearing the end of his third (and by law final) three-year term in that government-appointed position. The play was written by playwright and screenwriter Jean-Claude Carrière, based on an allegorical poem by twelfth-century Persian author Farid ud-Din Attar. It has a rich theatrical heritage: it was the fruit of Carrière's work with famed director Peter Brook and his company in the mid-1970s.[5] *La Conférence des oiseaux* chronicles the challenges faced by a heterogeneous flock of birds traveling to find their "true king," who, as they discover at the end of their long and arduous trip, is in fact themselves. Through the characters' discussions and enactment of illustrative though often enigmatic stories in the course of their voyage, themes of immigration, cooperation, and the search for self are developed. The resonance of these themes with contemporary issues in France and internationally made the play particularly attractive to director Couleau. For my discussion here of the professional life of actors, including its collective and collectivist aspects, the question of cooperative action in the play is especially appropriate. The bird characters that populate the play also resonate with the image of theatre artists that I will be presenting. Like the birds in the show, theatre professionals are on the move, from one engagement to the next (since virtually no theatre in France, public or private, has its own troupe[6]). They, too, are in an ambiguous relationship with authority, and they are on a journey of discovery, dealing with the vagaries of their voyage as artists.

When I discuss the system of public-funded theatre in which these artists work, in their double position as providers of a state service and beneficiaries of the state, it should be understood that virtually all theatre in France depends to one degree or another on government sponsorship. To best appreciate the position of actors within this system, it is helpful to review the various components of French infrastructure and their development. In order of greater to lesser support from the central government, there are, first of all, five Théâtres Nationaux (national theatres): the Comédie Française, the Odéon-Théâtre de l'Europe, the Théâtre de la Colline and the Théâtre National de Chaillot, all in Paris, and the Théâtre National de Strasbourg. They receive their funding (apart from income through sources including ticket and merchandise sales) from France's Ministry of Culture. The thirty-eight Centres Dramatiques Nationaux, which are next down as far as the degree of state subsidizing is concerned, are located around the country and in suburbs of Paris. They are funded by different levels of municipal and regional government in addition to receiving substantial amounts from the central state. In 2017, at the CDN in Colmar, for example, 72 percent of the budgetary needs of the theatre were paid through funding by various levels of government. Of that portion, 44 percent came from the French government through grants from the Ministry of Culture, 33 percent from the city, 17 percent from the region (the Grand-Est), and 6 percent from the *département* (the Haut-Rhin).[7] Throughout France, the different levels of government together cover approximately 80 percent of the CDN budgets, with the state requiring a minimum of 20 percent of self-financing. As French sociologist Serge Proust explains, the state wishes to make directors of the theatres assume what it sees as their financial responsibility in running these *entreprises* (businesses), expecting them to bring in an adequate number of spectators to cover their 20 percent of expenses.[8]

Other types of theatres make up the system of state funding outside of the five national theatres and the CDNs: the seventy-four Scènes Nationales (National Stages), which generally obtain 31 percent of their public support from the central government,[9] the fourteen Centres Nationaux des Arts de la Rue et de l'Espace Publique (CNAREPs, the National Centers of Street Theatre and Theatre in Public Spaces), the fourteen Pôles Nationaux du Cirque (PNCs, the National Circus Centers), the Parc de la Villette, a large cultural park northeast of Paris, and the 124 Scènes Conventionnées (Performance Spaces), a three-year funding opportunity from the state that generally makes up 10 percent of a theatre's budget.[10] Municipal theatres, independent companies, and even private theatres, most of which are located in Paris, can also apply for financial support from the state.[11] François Kergourlay, an actor and director who was a cast member of *La Conférence des oiseaux* and had previously headed a private theatre in Paris, wryly characterized this process as "going to battle."[12] Indeed, it is important to state that in the case of all types of theatre that obtain state support, the funding is not simply given but is the culmination of an intensive application process. This process is accompanied by regular in-person contact with local, regional, and central government officials on the part of the theatres' directors and administrators, as Couleau and his chief administrator at the Comédie de l'Est, Arnaud Koenig, explained to me.

The Centre Dramatique National in Colmar, the producer of *La Conférence des oiseaux*, occupies a significant place in the history of public theatre funding in France. It was one of the first two CDNs designated by the French government in 1947 as part of its new, postwar policy of theatrical decentralization. Provision for culture had increasingly been seen as part of the *état providence* for some years, after the time of the Commune, the working-class insurrection in Paris in 1871, and during the years of the Popular Front, the alliance of leftist parties that came to power in the 1930s. Following the Second World War, reconstruction of the country included the development of governmental cultural policy, much of it focused on theatre. Because dramatic production at the time was concentrated in Paris, regional CDNs were instituted under the direction of Jeanne Laurent, a senior government official for the arts, with the goal of making theatre available to people around France. The seeds of theatrical decentralization had been planted earlier on, for example, in the form of Maurice Pottecher's Théâtre du Peuple in Bussang (les Vosges) in the late nineteenth century (and still in existence today) and, beginning in the 1920s, in the troupes of important theatre artists such as Jacques Copeau with his company Les Copiaus in Beaune and Jean Dasté in Grenoble and Saint-Etienne, in the more popularly oriented work of the Cartel des Quatre, and in the founding of the Théâtre National Populaire (TNP, National people's Theatre) by Firmin Gémier, who had begun an ambulatory theatre a decade earlier. As Loren Kruger explains, these projects countered the dominance of Parisian theatre through their physical location outside of Paris, their presentation of works written in everyday language, and reductions in ticket costs or the granting of free admission.[13] The Théâtre National Populaire, restarted by Jean Vilar in 1951, remained an important element of decentralization and, as David Whitton has put it, "democratic theatre culture"[14] in the national theatre system into the 1960s. As far as the CDNs proper were concerned, they increased in number especially after the Ministry of Culture was instituted in 1959, with André Malraux as its first and extremely influential head, and later the equally important minister Jack Lang. Both of them cultivated mass culture, giving a special place to theatre, although they had diverging views on the role of art in the lives of citizens.

Many consider the system of CDNs as the "aristocracy" of French theatre,[15] since, through the efforts of their directors and staff who apply for funds, they are generally able to ensure an excellent working environment, appropriate salary, and specialized artistic support. (It is important to recognize, however, that there is significant diversity among the different CDNs. This is due to their particular histories and the choices and energies of the individual directors, in conjunction with changing government administrations over the years.) Most often, as was the case in Colmar, actors receive payment for rehearsal hours as well as performances, the creative team usually has separate set, costume, lighting, and sound designers, and an in-house administrative staff takes care of the creators' practical needs, with coordinators for contracts, housing, and transportation arrangements. The CDN in Colmar, for example, had a twenty-three-person administrative and technical staff. Usually in shows produced by the CDNs, again as was true for *La Conférence des oiseaux*, actors have their room, board, and transportation paid for as well as having the chance to participate in extended runs of shows through touring. *La Conférence*, for instance, originally played in June and October 2018 and then toured over the next sixteen months (coincidentally ending just before the pandemic shutdown) in France, Switzerland, and the island of Réunion, one of France's overseas *départements*. In most cases, the theatres on the tour were coproducers of the show with the Comédie de l'Est. The advantages listed above, which apply even more completely to the five Théâtres Nationaux, do not always exist in the theatres or companies that receive lesser amounts of central government funding. Payment of rehearsal time, most importantly, is not assured outside of the system of CDNs and the five national theatres.

In terms of who is chosen to act in productions by CDN, as well as in the field of theatrical performance as a whole in France, access is often limited, in ways that generally reflect larger societal biases and restrictions. Not all actors achieve a level of success that permits them to work regularly and thus obtain such state support. Sociologist Pierre-Michel Menger, who studies artists as workers, estimates that a relatively small percentage overall (20 percent) obtain most of the benefits (80 percent) associated with their profession.[16] He theorizes that the element contributing most importantly to the obtaining of these benefits, both artistic and financial, is the making of reputation in their profession. Menger describes an artistic hierarchy, created through competition, as the driving force behind innovation in the work of individual professionals in the arts, which ultimately helps determine their success: "Their place in the competition does not depend on the status attached to a job, as is the case in an organization, with its seniority and hierarchical position, but on the estimated value of their production and their possibility of maintaining themselves or rising in [that artistic hierarchy]." He details a dual process of self-evaluation and evaluation by the community that determines creators' positions in the hierarchy. This process is always evolving, "by gradual comparisons."[17]

In addition, casting choices are often made according to categories such as gender, age, and ethnicity, which therefore play a role in determining actors' position in a professional hierarchy. These restrictions are basic to performers' ability to work and take advantage of government support. They show the limits of the state to completely provide for this group of people—theatre professionals—who serve it and, in theory at least, the general public. (Later, I will discuss the eternal debate in France about who, exactly, that audience is, or should be, and how to reach it.) First of all, as far as gender and age are concerned, white men in early middle age predominate in the performing arts, as indicated in statistics from 2018 and as my own viewing of theatre in France confirms.[18] Women constitute a little over one-third of performance professionals (36.9 percent), a proportion that has not changed significantly over the past thirty years.[19] The numbers slant toward younger ages for women: those under forty represent two-thirds of the female population in the performing arts, while a smaller portion of the male population—half—is under forty.[20]

Certain of these statistics were reflected in the cast of *La Conférence des oiseaux*. Overall, the women in the ten-member cast were younger than the men, thus corresponding to national tendencies. (The women varied in age from their mid-thirties to early fifties, and the men from their forties to early sixties.) But there was a larger percentage of women than average, five women and five men. This was a deliberate choice by the director. The text of *La Conférence* was particularly flexible in this regard, with much of the dialogue being spoken by birds instead of people and all of the actors playing multiple characters. In addition, the director assigned roles such as "The Slave" or "The Thief" to women rather than following the masculine gender indicated in the text.

The percentage of female performers in France mirrors that of women in other capacities in French theatre, as well: playwrights, directors, choreographers, and set designers. Female-authored works are only 26 percent of the total number performed in national theatres, and the proportion of female directors of CDNs, for example, is currently at 37 percent.[21] In addition, pay levels as well as amounts of state funding allocated for projects proposed by women are, in their aggregate, less than for men.[22] Government efforts to increase *parité* (equality) between men and women in the performing arts, pushed by individual creators and arts leaders and spurred on more recently by the #MeToo movement (in French originally appearing as *#Balancetonporc* [#OutYourPig]), have focused on these roles of women in positions of responsibility, including directors, writers, administrators, and members of the cultural ministry's staff. Two Ministry of Culture reports, in 2006 and 2009, led by cultural specialist Reine Prat, documented the underrepresentation of women in decision-making positions in the arts, administratively and creatively.[23] President Macron stated that the issue of gender parity was one of the major concerns of his first term, and the Ministry of Culture has a *Diversité/Egalité* (Diversity/Equality) mission. To date, however, their efforts have had little effect on theatre. The state has increased its requirements for evidence of gender equity when awarding funding for the creation of music and works in the audiovisual sector, but it has not yet done so for theatre and the other performing arts.

As far as racial and ethnic diversity are concerned, the whiteness of the French stage has been a subject of concern and polemics over a number of years. In fact, several directors whom I interviewed brought up the continued lack of diversity in the course of our conversations.[24] It is a situation that they have been attempting to change through their own productions and that they see evolving to some degree. Indeed, efforts in this direction have been made mainly by individual directors, notable among them Peter Brook, in his project of bringing together actors from different nations and ethnicities in his company, and Ariane Mnouchkine and her multicultural troupe, beginning in the 1960s and 1970s, respectively. Single productions such as Jacques Nichet's groundbreaking 1996 show at the Festival d'Avignon, *La Tragédie du roi Christophe* (The Tragedy of King Christopher), by Aimé Césaire, with its entirely Black cast, have constituted important milestones in this evolution. (See Sylvie Chalaye, who provides a detailed accounting of productions featuring Black performers, the introduction of repertoire by African and Caribbean authors, and the formation of groups of theatre professionals that have pushed for change over the past decades.[25]) In the case of *La Conférence des oiseaux*, one can see director Couleau's choice of play and cast members as part of this endeavor, with different performers originating from Cameroun, Argentina, and Iran, having international heritage (Maghreban, East Asian, or Swedish), or coming from culturally distinct regions within France itself. The cast member from Cameroon was, in fact, the actor who had played the title role in Nichet's *La Tragédie du roi Christophe*, Emil Abossolo M'Bo. Another of the performers, Shahrohk Moshkin Ghalam, commented to me on what he saw as Couleau's brilliance in choosing performers who were so diverse in many ways, including in this respect.[26]

In recent years in France, in addition to work by individual directors and performers, there have been institutional efforts toward racial and ethnic inclusion, particularly as far as theatre training is concerned. Most prominently, the program 1er Acte (First Act), begun in 2014 by noted director Stanislas Nordey through the Théâtre National de Strasbourg in collaboration with the Théâtre de l'Odéon in Paris, the Festival d'Avignon, and the Centre National Chorégraphique in Grenoble, has as its goal the promotion of "greater diversity on the theatre stage."[27] They sponsor master classes for young actors and then support these actors through performance opportunities and professional mentoring. One of the cast members of *La Conférence*, Carolina Pecheny, who was also Couleau's artistic collaborator for the production, taught in a similar program at a regional theatre school, L'Ecole Supérieure Professionnelle de Théâtre du Limousin in Limoges.[28] During the performance period of the play in Colmar in October 2018, she was planning a *classe préparatoire* (preparatory course) to ready candidates from a number of overseas *départements* and territories including Martinique, Guadeloupe, Mayotte, Reunion, New Caledonia, and French Guiana. Later on, their course completed, nine of the ten class members were accepted into *écoles supérieures d'art dramatique* (schools for advanced study in the dramatic arts), four of them into the top national conservatory, the Conservatoire National d'Art Dramatique de Paris.[29] Such educational programs as the one in Limoges and 1er Acte find themselves at the crux of discussions of diversity in French theatre. Some theatre professionals and scholars say that reflected in these programs are the inherent racial biases of the theatrical institution and its inevitable connection with the country's colonial past. These initiatives, they say, assume a lack on the part of students of color—a lack of French culture—rather than addressing the issue of lack in French theatre tradition and practice themselves in this respect.[30] In my observation, however, such state-supported programs are pragmatic steps toward addressing these limitations and biases. Pecheny, for example, was helping to make participation in professional theatre available to a greater range of artists. Their work, in turn, can increase the richness of offerings to the public, widening and diversifying its concept of theatrical culture in France.

The issues of imbalance and bias regarding gender, age, ethnicity (and the intersection of these elements), as well as efforts to change French theatre, of course reflect wider social, economic, and political conditions. In addition, the initiatives of individual theatre professionals and groups to produce changes in public theatre structures and regulations can be frustrated by the inherently conservative nature of these government institutions, including their famously bureaucratic tendencies. (Public theatres and independent theatre directors with sufficient means most often hire special staff for the writing of applications and the reporting activities associated with obtaining grants.) At the same time, individuals within theatrical institutions, such as in the examples cited above regarding gender and ethnic diversity, are undeniably moving the system as a whole in more socially helpful directions.

Certain political decisions in France regarding government support for the arts over the past fifty years have to some degree counterbalanced the detrimental effects of the systemic social conditions described above. Principally, state budgetary regulations have made it possible for a larger number of performers to be active. Between 1980 and 1990, under the direction of Minister of Culture Jack Lang during the tenure of socialist president François Mitterrand, more actors were able to practice and develop their craft professionally, that is, to be paid a sufficient amount. During that decade, *les années Lang* (the Lang years), increased public funding was made available for culture, including the performing arts. Referred to as "*le 1% culturel*," or 1 percent of the federal budget, this arts funding still exists, constituting .97 percent of the proposed national budget in 2020.[31] According to the budget proposal for 2022, the portion for culture was to increase by 7.5 percent, passing the level of 4 billion euros for the first time in its history.[32] As one of the actors I interviewed pointed out, such percentages and amounts are not substantial in the larger scheme of things.[33] But, as I indicated earlier, state support of the arts overall compares favorably to that in the United States (an extreme example, to be sure), where approximately .003 percent of the federal budget is allotted to the National Endowment for the Arts and similarly small sums to the National Endowment for the Humanities and the Corporation for Public Broadcasting.[34] In France during the Lang years, as a result of the increased government subsidies, the performing arts grew. Between 1986 and 2007, the amount of work for actors and technicians, including both live performance and audiovisual production, was multiplied by 2.7, and the number of workers by 3.7.[35] In more recent years, the population of professionals in the performing arts has continued to rise, although at a slower pace. The number of workers specifically in live performance rose 35 percent between 2000 and 2016.[36] Currently, however, with the effects of the pandemic on theatre artists' lives (the long period of closure of theatre venues and, later, restrictions on the number of attendees), the size of future populations of performers is not clear.

In the case of *La Conférence des oiseaux*, most of the ten performers had benefited directly from the Lang years, when the cultural budget increased. The older two-thirds of the cast, the seven actors who were in their late forties to age sixty, had been in their teens or twenties when they experienced this surge in subsidies and the excitement that accompanied it. One of them, for example, actor and musician Nathalie Duong, who is on the younger end of that scale, explained to me the joy of discovering theatre as a teenager, in the early 1980s, through the opportunities that greater state support had provided. She did so through very active companies that had residencies in the *maison de la culture* (cultural center) in her *ville nouvelle* (new town, one of a series of new communities constructed near Paris in the 1960s and 1970s). Duong passionately described to me the importance of these experiences (which, she emphasized, were supported by the new government funding) in fostering her creativity as a young person and determining her decision to devote her life to performance: "I was in high school, totally hungry for social relationships, and I fought with my father to be able to go to a theater workshop [at the *maison de la culture*]. That is where I discovered the work of the troupe in residence. These are people who are really into street theater. They do performance brigades: we dressed up like crazy people and went into supermarkets to recite Michaux, Rimbaud, things that weren't at all planned, not at all 'nice,' and I loved it."[37] She was chosen to act and sing in large original productions by the Théâtre de l'Unité and Musiques de la Boulangère, the group of composer Nicolas Frize, and the shows included both professionals and nonprofessionals. The directors, Hervée de Lafond and Jacques Livchine, and Frize, all distinguished creators who work today, singled her out for her work and urged her to continue. "That was where I discovered the professional life of adults. When you have people like that who notice you, it's very gratifying, and then you want to go on. That's when I caught the stage bug (*le virus de la scène*)."[38] Other interviewees told me stories of their initiation into theatre in similar, state-supported contexts: at school, in cultural centers, or in new, experimental troupes. The three youngest members of the cast are the inheritors of work by that generation of enthusiastic theatrical creators.

One aspect of theatre policy and practice during the Lang years that enabled larger numbers of professional actors to work was a dramatic change in the average length of contracts. The use of short-term contracts for performers and technicians became predominant, increasing twelvefold between 1986 and 2007.[39] In 2016, two-thirds of workers in the performing arts were on short-term contracts: the CDD (*contrat à durée déterminée*, limited-term contract) and the later-added CDDU (CDD *d'usage*, standard limited-term contract), which is even more flexible and is now the main way of hiring temporary workers in the performing arts.[40] In fact, professions in the area of culture use such contracts twice as often as the whole of the private sector.[41] The overall amount paid to professionals in the performing arts rose during the twenty years after Jack Lang's first budget increase for the arts, growing by a factor of 2.9 between 1986 and 2000; but that unfortunately was not enough to keep pace with the rising number of workers.[42] As a result, the average pay for those hired on short-term contracts fell behind. There are attempts by some labor unions to bring long-term contracts for these workers into greater use, but the current preponderance of short-term contracts in performance, as well as the flexibility that they permit, work against that change.

For many theatre professionals, financial losses have been balanced by the special system of unemployment insurance for *les intermittents du spectacle* (temporary workers in performance). I consider this system to be an element of public funding of theatre, and it is one that theatre artists themselves have influenced through their political activity. It was first created in 1936 to support managers and technicians in the growing movie industry. In 1958, it was melded with the then newly created regular unemployment insurance in France. Later, in the 1960s, the system for *les intermittents* progressively expanded from cinema to include the wider audiovisual area, the stage (*spectacle vivant*), and performers as well as technicians. In 1979 and 1984, reforms of the overall unemployment agreement enabled its financing to operate by *solidarité interprofessionnelle*, which exists to this day: the contributions of all employers and employees in France to the compensation system are combined and available to all of the eligible unemployed, with the goal of ensuring equivalent access. (The director's remark "We are the state" again comes to mind.) Unemployment insurance for *les intermittents du spectacle* currently offers up to twelve months of coverage, once a minimum number of work hours per twelve-month period has been met (507 hours). However, with the advent of the coronavirus, workers in the performing arts saw their number of hours and therefore their eligibility for insurance payments decrease abruptly. This situation produced considerable political action on the part of theatre professionals, including actors. During the summer of 2021, the level of organized protests by theatre artists, along with other gig workers and students, initiated by the union of the far left, the CGT (Confédération Générale du Travail), was impressive: more than seventy state-funded venues were occupied by various combinations of the above groups, including three of the five national theatres. This collective action was not to be seen in the United States and indicates the relative strength of French theatre workers in demanding change for their working conditions. (It should be noted, however, that US theatre workers were part of protests around racial injustice beginning in 2020.) In France, the union of theatre professionals with other gig workers and students was attacking the wider problem of the CDD and proposed restrictions on the system of unemployment compensation, not simply its effect on the theatrical sector. This united action brought theatre squarely into the "public sphere," as theatre scholar Christopher Balme would term it.[43] After protests on the part of these activists, the government continued coverage of *les intermittents* in stage performance for a period of a year, until August 2021, with the requirement of an increased number of hours working in the schools.[44] That period was later extended to December 2021.[45] At the same time, however, more stringent rules for obtaining unemployment payments have been looming on the horizon.

In fact, the special unemployment compensation for *les intermittents* regularly receives pubic criticism. The overall unemployment insurance system has been in increasing deficit since 2008, and because *les intermittents* and other temporary workers put a heavier burden on the system than other unemployed workers, negotiation of their regulations is highly politicized. (Rules for *les intermittents* undergo periodic revision as part of the larger unemployment insurance negotiations between the *partenaires sociaux* [social partners], that is, between business groups and the various unions to which workers belong.) The part of the agreement for *les intermittents* underwent particularly significant reductions in 2003, when numbers of both existing and potential participants were excluded from coverage. Only years later, in 2016, after massive protests, did the system regain some of what had been lost.[46] Although it seems unlikely that the unemployment compensation for *les intermittents* will disappear, its specific provisions are never certain.

Over the years, more and more workers in the performing arts in France, actors and musicians, in particular, have relied on unemployment compensation to cover their expenses, to the point that they often consider it part of their earnings for the year. Sociologist Serge Katz explains, "In reality, unemployment payments have generally become complementary revenue, even the principal salary."[47] In 2019, for example, the gross monthly income for *les intermittents du spectacle* was 2,500 euros (about 2,800 US dollars), with 40 percent of that amount, 1,000 euros, coming from unemployment compensation. In 2020, as a result of the pandemic, the levels of salary dipped sharply but the amount of unemployment payments rose, to bring the total monthly income to 2,100 euros.[48]

Antonella Corsani and Maurizio Lazzarato undertook a major study of temporary workers in performance and found that for "the large majority" of the 833 professionals who were interviewed, "going from work to unemployment does not mean going from activity to non-activity, but from one activity to another."[49] In the interviews that I conducted with the actors in *La Conférence*, although I did not question the actors specifically about the unemployment system for *les intermittents*, six of the ten referred to it spontaneously, a sign of its integration into their lives. Nils Öhlund, for example, while discussing his and his colleagues' good fortune to be working with Couleau, spoke of the necessity of having the required number of hours of theatre-connected work in the year.[50] Luc-Antoine Diquéro described himself as "invested in the mission to arrive fueled by personal research" for each production, with "an enormous backpack full of ideas," and he sees the status of *intermittent* as clearly facilitating this essential aspect of his art.[51] At the same time, another of the actors believed that a system in which unemployment insurance does not play a major role produces artists who work harder and are more engaged in their profession. (He saw this as being the case in the United States.)[52]

In fact, although many performers' salaried work is regularly complemented by unemployment payments, this is not true for all actors. The providers of theatre are not all provided for. In 2015, the proportion of *les intermittents du spectacle* who received unemployment compensation was 40 percent.[53] According to Serge Katz, "ordinary" actors (that is, the greatest number) go through periods of access to unemployment insurance followed by a prolonged or even definitive loss of their right to compensation because they are not able to be hired for enough theatre-related hours.[54] Katz points out that these actors are the ones who are least able to find work in the most institutionalized areas of theatre, which principally means the CDNs. The further one goes from the public theatre structure, he writes, the less financial recognition of artistic activity there is. Theatre artists may go for long stretches without contracts and must find jobs that are "limitrophe," on the edge of professional theatre.[55] In the best case, this employment may consist of teaching or tutoring and, in less optimal scenarios, offering communication workshops for business, doing theme park entertainment, or working as extras for the audiovisual sector, for example. Some may need to take jobs outside the area of theatre altogether, as is so frequently the case for actors in the United States. According to Katz's findings, performers who need to do such work most often suffer from feelings of estrangement from the profession. More recently, the effects of the coronavirus have only exacerbated this problem.

When the actors in *La Conférence* spoke to me about work that they were pursuing outside of the production, it was evident that their activities were meaningful in terms of their art, as the earlier quote from Diquéro indicated. Five of the ten cast members were engaged in preparatory work for future productions as performer, writer, or director. Two others were planning courses that they would be offering, one in a private theatre school, the other in a conservatory. Four of the actors have worked in the audiovisual field as well, as performers in television shows or films or as voice-over actors dubbing international movies and television series into French. One cast member was an active professional musician as well as an actor, and another worked professionally as both an actor and a dancer. In speaking with the performers formally and informally, I found virtually no expression of the alienation that Katz had seen in his interviews with "ordinary" theatre professionals. On the contrary, it was striking to see the degree of investment that they showed in their work and how fulfilled they felt by it, in spite of difficulties that they might encounter. Emile Abossolo M'Bo echoed comments made by others in the cast when he described his passion for the profession, "where we are always in the process of discovering what we don't yet know, and improving what we know already."[56] These performers were evidently part of the 20 percent of arts workers who are able to make it, artistically and economically, according to sociologist Menger's theory. As I saw, however, persistent effort on their part was required: ongoing perfecting of their skills and constant searching for appropriate professional projects in between engagements that were offered to them.

As I stated earlier, a majority of the performers in the company had come up through the Lang years of increased government spending on the arts, including theatre. Unfortunately, over the past two decades, mainly because of budgetary limitations in France, there has been attrition of that support. Economic conditions have limited the state's role as provider. One indicator of the financial health of the country is its rate of unemployment, which in May 2022 was 7.3 percent. This compares to 7.1 percent just before the pandemic, its lowest point in years.[57] Although these figures are down from a high of 10.5 percent in 2015, they remain substantial. In this climate, subsidies from the central government have skewed somewhat toward the TNs and CDNs and less toward independent directors and theatres, a tendency noted by one of the actors I interviewed.[58] Funding from the regions, *départements*, and particularly cities have declined over the past two decades, although not in Colmar, which is an especially strong financial supporter of its CDN and its municipal theatre.

Even the larger institutions have not received sufficient subsidies from the central government in recent years to cover inflation and increased production costs.[59] This was evident in an interview that I conducted with Stéphane Braunschweig, head of the Théâtre de l'Odéon, one of the five national theatres. Braunschweig, mirroring information that Couleau and Koenig gave me concerning the Comédie de l'Est, said that although the amount of funding from the state had been stable over the previous ten years or so, the money available for artistic programming had effectively been shrinking. He mentioned the salaries of the Odéon's approximately 130 permanent employees, which increase yearly (according to laws governing state employees), in addition to the growing costs of maintaining their venues and hosting international troupes. This situation results in an increase in average ticket price, which, he said, is "a problem, in spite of everything, because it means that the goal of public service, which is to perform challenging works for a wide and diverse audience, is more difficult to maintain when seats are more expensive."[60] In this difficult budgetary context, the financial responsibilities of the Théâtres Nationaux and the CDNs and the tradition of hiring theatre artists to direct the CDNs (rather than people with a business background, as is often the case with the seventy-eight Scènes Nationales) have become important subjects of debate in the profession and at times in the popular press.[61] Government decisions on who directs state theatres and on the budgets for them then affect the number and kind of individual actors who are hired.

I mention the kind of actors—meaning their professional background, strengths, and interests—because the question of what type of theatre is to be subsidized is also a topic of lively discussion in France, as it has been for decades. The subject arose in my conversations with Couleau and others, including a former government arts official who spoke of *la crise des CDN* (the CDN crisis), and articles on the role of the CDN appear regularly in the press. As David Whitton has described, since the late 1960s, state-supported theatres and companies have manifested a tension between their founding purpose as disseminators of culture and an increasing movement toward commodification.[62] The CDNs stand out in this respect because of their role as the main government tool for theatrical diffusion across the country as a whole. Debate concerning the CDNs is part of a national discussion on the goals and management of public funding of the arts, in which the theory of *le ruissellement*, the trickle-down theory, has predominated for decades. This theory posits that "the richer the cultural offering, the more it will be shared by all."[63] Indeed, after decades of government investment in cultural infrastructure, personnel, and programming, the overall number of people participating in cultural activities (including visiting museums and attending theatre and music and dance concerts) has grown. However, the type of audience has not widened considerably from the group of financially comfortable, educated, mainly Parisian art aficionados that has constituted its majority for years.[64] This is not to discount work by the Ministry of Culture and individual directors of theatres, museums, and festivals to cultivate more economically and socially diverse audiences. This effort was evident in the various outreach programs at the CDN in Colmar, mainly to local schools as well as people of limited means, immigrant support groups, prison populations, people with visual or auditory impairment, and city groups and associations. Perhaps as a result of such initiatives around the country, there are indications that the number of first-time attendees of cultural events in France is increasing.[65] In the area of theatre in particular, spectatorship increased from 12 percent to 26 percent of the population over the last forty-five years. However, at the same time, among people of the most recent generation (those born between 1995 and 2004), the number attending theatre performances is smaller than among people of the previous one, corresponding to the emergence of the "all-digital" world.[66]

Social anthropologist Fabrice Raffin sees French cultural offerings as being very much linked to Malraux's 1960s vision of the role of the state: that is, to transmit major cultural works—traditional and modern classics—to the people. Raffin proposes a more expansive notion of culture, "defined by the esthetic experience that it provides," to be determined differently by different social groups.[67] His critique corresponds in some ways to that of Christopher Balme, who views contemporary theatre as being largely isolated from the general public, however "transgressive" it may be. As Balme writes, "The darkened auditorium has become to all intents and purposes a private place." Concerned with the "political and social efficacy" of theatre, Balme sees its engagement with the public sphere as happening through "reconnection with new media on the one hand and an increasing move outside theatre buildings on the other."[68] In France, a more liberal approach to the arts has appeared in government policy in recent years, with the formation of the new national centers for street arts and for the art of the circus, something of a shift of funding away from the traditional structure of theatres and companies. This is occurring much to the chagrin of some theatre directors and directors of state theatres, who see the issue as being more nuanced than a division between what is considered "high culture" and what it is assumed the general public desires. Prominent director Joël Pommerat, for example, has criticized what he sees as the "populist" approach, "(culture for all, not one culture but many), . . . pitting professional artists and amateurs against each other."[69]

In light of concerns about public-supported theatre truly serving the public and in the context of budget reductions, it is interesting and perhaps indicative of larger developments that the three youngest members of the cast of *La Conférence*, who are in their thirties and forties, have been orienting their theatre work toward community involvement. Actor Jessica Vedel cofounded a traveling troupe (perfectly named "Le Temps est incertain mais on joue quand même" ["The Weather is Iffy But We're Performing Anyway"]) with the purpose of bringing theatre directly to people—to an audience that does not necessarily attend theatre—in villages and outdoor public spaces as well as in the more traditional theatre network.[70] She and her colleague call their work *hyper-décentralisation* because of the small size of the communities that they visit. They also produce shows that include both professionals and amateurs, and they host residences, workshops, and productions for the Loire region. Cécile Fontaine, an actor, writer, director, and musician from the overseas department of Réunion, has produced theatre that foregrounds everyday people, including those from marginalized groups. She spoke to me at length about two productions that she had written and directed with her troupe, Rouge Bakoly, one based on interviews with local prostitutes and the other on interviews with prisoners.[71] More recently, her artistic work is of a more interdisciplinary nature, through Rouge Bakoly and her musical group La Sépia, focusing on the people, traditions, and cultures of Réunion.[72] Manon Allouch, having finished a Diplôme d'Etat de Professeur de Théâtre, has pursued teaching activities that address the needs of disadvantaged adolescents in addition to continuing her professional acting career.[73] These younger theatre artists belong to a generation of creators who seem newly connected to social concerns and inspired to respond directly to them. (This said, my interviewees who are part of the previous generation certainly are sensitive to the connection of their professional work with the current conditions and issues in French society.) The perspectives of the younger actors coincide with the government focus on the availability of arts to all (with all of the ambiguity and debate existing around that concept). In the projects of each of these women one can see, interestingly, the nonconsumerist spirit of the early-twentieth-century practitioners of theatrical decentralization before it became part of government policy, an approach that reflects some of the suggestions of scholars Kruger, Whitton, and Balme concerning the future of theatre in society.

Actors in France, then, are in an interdependent relationship with the state. They depend on receiving from the state—benefiting from their status as artists and as part of the public—in order to serve the state and their fellow members of the public. Their double existence, as belonging to the people and at the same time working in government structures that are providing for the people, corresponds closely with their profession: the doubleness inherent in acting, the bringing together of the bodily self and an imagined character. The theatrical body and its historical connection with the larger, assembled body of the people as well as with art, or perhaps located somewhere in between the two, as Loren Kruger has theorized about French theatre as a whole, has permitted French theatre professionals' contestation of state policies governing public theatre. The population of performers whom I have presented are the human actors in the space that Kruger has described, "the stage on which the contradiction between the [aesthetic and the political] can be enacted."[74] Performers, the lively center of the declaration "We are the state," assure continued connection between theatre and the public, and continued—though not always rapid—change in state-funded theatre in France.

FUNDING FOR THEATRE IN FRANCE

Notes

1. Guy-Pierre Couleau, email exchange with Cynthia Running-Johnson, June 29–30, 2019. Translations from French to English in this article are by Cynthia Running-Johnson.
2. Laura Collins-Hughes, "Dear Extremely Famous Friend of the American Theater," *New York Times, It's Been a Year*, March 14, 2021, AR14.
3. Jesse Green, "Should the American Theater Take French Lessons?" *New York Times*, March 17, 2021, C1.
4. See Loren Kruger, *The National Stage: Theatre and Cultural Legitimation in England, France and America* (Chicago: University of Chicago Press, 1992); and David Whitton, "Whatever Happened to *Théâtre Populaire*? The Unfinished History of people's Theatre in France," *European Studies: A Journal of European Culture, History and Politics* 17 (*Morality and Justice: The Challenge of European Theatre* [2001]), 55. Whitton cites government decrees from the 1790s, explaining the connection that was made in them between theatre and instruction, to which all citizens should be given equal access. In this context, he mentions the Revolutionary theatre festivals of those years. Kruger, as part of her larger project of developing the concept of "theatrical nationhood," or "staging the nation," discusses the role of Revolutionary festivals throughout the following century, as well, putting the emphasis on their assembling of the people as manifesting the interconnection of the theatre and the public.
5. Jean-Claude Carrière, *La Conférence des oiseaux* (Paris: Centre International de Créations Théâtrales, 1979). Dir. Guy-Pierre Couleau, Comédie de l'Est, Colmar, France, Oct. 2018.
6. There are several prominent exceptions to this statement, however: the Comédie Française, Ariane Mnouchkine's Théâtre du Soleil, and Peter Brooks' Théâtre des Bouffes du Nord.
7. Arnaud Koenig (administrator of the Comédie de l'Est), interview with Cynthia Running-Johnson, October 4, 2018.
8. Serge Proust, "La pluriactivité dans une économie administrée: Le théâtre public," in *l'artiste pluriel: Démultiplier l'activité pour vivre de son art* (Villeneuve d'Ascq, France: Presses Universitaires du Septentrion, 2019), 97.
9. *Rapport public annuel 2016: Les théâtres nationaux: Des scènes d'excellence, des établissements fragilisés* (Paris: Cour des comptes, December 3, 2018), 493.
10. "Création et diffusion," *Chiffres clés, statistiques de la culture 2018* (Paris: Ministère de la Culture, 2019), 159–89, 57. It should be noted that programming for these theatres often includes music and dance performances as well as drama, which therefore places them partially outside of the subject of public funding for theatre in particular.
11. Federal and municipal subsidies for private theatres are generally less generous than for public ones. About 18 percent of the budget of private theatres is provided by the central government and 20 percent by the municipal level (Serge Dorny, Jean-Louis Martinelli et al., *Financement du spectacle vivant: Développer, Structurer, Pérenniser* (Paris: Ministère de la Culture et de la Communication, February 5, 2018), 31–32.) Prominent exceptions exist, however, such as the Théâtre de la Ville in Paris, which, for example, had 59 percent of its budget in 2018–2019 covered by the city (Martine Robert, "Le Théâtre de la Ville célèbre ses 50 ans hors de ses murs," *Les Echos* (website), January 2, 2019, accessed April 14, 2023). Professional theatre companies, which in nearly all cases are not

{ 45 }

tied to a particular theatre and which number approximately twelve hundred, also can apply for public funding. About half of them receive it. For more details on these areas of funding, see Cynthia Running-Johnson, "What Is the Future of *la compagnie* in French Theatre?" *Text and Presentation* 14 (2018): 195–208.
12. François Kergourlay, interview with Cynthia Running-Johnson, October 5, 2018.
13. Loren Kruger, "The National Stage and the Naturalized House: (Trans)National Legitimation in Modern Europe," in *National Theatres in a Changing Europe* (UK and New York: Palgrave Macmillan, 2008), 40.
14. David Whitton, "Proliferation and Differentiation of National Theatres in France," in *National Theatres in a Changing Europe* (Houndsmill, UK: Palgrave Macmillan, 2008), 155.
15. Serge Katz, *Comédiens par intermittence: Le métier à l'épreuve de la disqualification professionnelle* (Paris: Presses du Châtelet, 2015), 162.
16. Pierre-Michel Menger, interview by Olivia Gesbert, "La création, à quel prix? avec Pierre-Michel Menger," *La Grande Table*, France Culture, June 7, 2018.
17. Pierre-Michel Menger, *Etre artiste: Oeuvrer dans l'incertitude* (Paris: Al Dante, 2012), 61.
18. *L'emploi intermittent dans le spectacle au cours de l'année 2018—Statistiques et indicateurs no. 18.036* (Paris: Pôle emploi, July 18, 2020), 3.
19. Pierre-Michel Menger, *Les intermittents du spectacle: Sociologie du travail flexible*, second ed. (Paris: Editions de l'Ecole des hautes études en sciences sociales, 2011), 237; *Observatoire: Métiers du spectacle vivant, Première Partie, Données 2016* (France: Commission Paritaire Nationale Emploi et Formation Spectacle Vivant [CPNEF-SV]), November 12, 2018), 58.
20. *L'emploi intermittent dans le spectacle au cours de l'année 2018*, 3.
21. *Observatoire de l'égalité entre femmes et hommes dans la culture et la communication.* (Paris: Ministère de la Culture, 2021), 10, 33.
22. *Observatoire de l'égalité entre femmes et hommes dans la culture et la communication*, 5.
23. See Reine Prat, *Arts et spectacle: Pour l'égal accès des femmes et des hommes aux postes de responsabilité, aux lieux de décision, aux moyens de production, aux reseaux de diffusion, à la visibilité médiatique* (Paris: Ministère de la Culture et de la Communication, May 2006 [Part I] and May 2009 [Part II]), Vie publique: Au Coeur du débat public (website), May 20, 2009; accessed April 17, 2023.
24. Guy-Pierre Couleau, interview with Cynthia Running-Johnson, October 10, 2018; Stéphane Braunschweig, interview with Cynthia Running-Johnson, May 18, 2018; Cynthia Running-Johnson, "Directing Crimp and Corneille in France: A Conversation with Brigitte Jaques-Wajeman," *Theatre Topics* (June 2015): 169–75.
25. Sylvie Chalaye, *Race et théâtre: Un impensé politique* (Arles: Actes sud, 2020).
26. Shahrokh (Shah) Moshkin Ghalam, interview with Cynthia Running-Johnson, October 15, 2018.
27. "1er Acte," Théâtre National de Strasbourg, January 31, 2021, TNS (website); accessed April 17, 2023.
28. Ecole Supérieure de Théâtre de l'Union (website), "La Plateforme Outremer," accessed April 24, 2023.
29. Stéphane Capron, "Les jeunes pousses de la classe préparatoire de l'Académie de l'Union font un tabac aux concours d'entrée des écoles de théâtre," *Scèneweb* (website), May 25, 2019; accessed April 17, 2023.
30. See Leïla Cukierman, Gerty Dambury et al., *Décolonisons les arts!* (Paris: L'Arche, 2018);

Aïssa Maïga, ed., *Noire n'est pas mon métier* (Paris: Le Seuil, 2018); and Chalaye, *Race et théâtre*.

31. "Projet de loi finances pour 2020: Culture," Le Sénat (website), August 2, 2020.
32. "Le Projet de loi de finances 2022 pour la culture," Ministère de la Culture (website), September 22, 2021.
33. Nathalie Duong, interview with Cynthia Running-Johnson, October 16, 2018.
34. "NEA Quick Facts," National Endowment for the Arts (website), June 1, 2021; accessed April 17, 2023.
35. Menger, *Les intermittents du spectacle*, 234, 370.
36. *Observatoire: Métiers*.
37. Duong, interview with Cynthia Running-Johnson, October 16, 2018.
38. Duong, interview with Cynthia Running-Johnson, October 16, 2018.
39. Menger, *Les intermittents du spectacle*, 234.
40. *Observatoire: Métiers*.
41. Pierre-Michel Menger, "L'emploi dans les spectacles et les paradoxes de sa croissance: Flexibilité des relations contractuelles et des protections assurantielles," *Communications* (2008/2 (no. 83)): 77–104, 2.
42. Menger, *Les intermittents du spectacle*, 234.
43. Christopher Balme, *The Theatrical Public Sphere* (Cambridge, UK: Cambridge University Press, 2014).
44. "Intermittents du spectacle: l'année blanche' a été officiellement actée au Journal officiel," *Franceinfo Culture* (website), July 26, 2020; accessed April 17, 2023.
45. "Mesures en faveur des intermittents du spectacle et de l'audiovisuel à compter du 1er septembre 2021," Ministère de la Culture (website), August 5, 2021; accessed April 17, 2023.
46. See Marion Bain, "Intermittents du spectacle: Les nouvelles règles d'indemnisation au 1er août," *l'Express* (website), August 1, 2016; accessed April 17, 2023.
47. Serge Katz, "Des comédiens exclus du métier," *Biens symboliques, revue des sciences sociales sur les arts, la culture et les idées* 1 (2017): 2.
48. Sandrine Blanchard, "Le revenue brut mensuel moyen a diminué de 400 euros en 2020, selon l'Unidec," *Le Monde* (website), April 9, 2021; accessed April 17, 2023.
49. Antonella Corsani and Maurizio Lazzarato, *Intermittents et Précaires* (Paris: Editions Amsterdam, 2008), 96.
50. Nils Öhlund, interview with Cynthia Running-Johnson, October 15, 2018.
51. Luc-Antoine Diquéro, interview with Cynthia Running-Johnson, October 11, 2018.
52. Emile Abossolo M'Bo, interview with Cynthia Running-Johnson, October 2, 2018.
53. Pierre Cahuc, "France: Social Protection for the Self-Employed," in *The Future of Social Protection: What Works for Non-Standard Workers?* (Paris: Organization for Economic Cooperation and Development, April 2, 2019), OECD iLibrary (website), accessed April 17, 2023.
54. See Katz, " Des comédiens exclus du métier."
55. Katz, "Des comédiens exclus du métier," 18.
56. Abossolo M'Bo, interview with Cynthia Running-Johnson, October 2, 2018.
57. "Au premier trimestre 2022, le taux de chômage est quasi stable à 7.3 %," L'Insee (Institut national de la statistique et des études économiques) (website), May 17, 2022, accessed April 17, 2023. Unemployment reached 9.1 percent in November 2020 during the height of pandemic-related shutdowns and quarantines.

58. Proust, "La pluriactivité dans une économie administrée," 98.
59. See "Subventions et spectacle vivant: La parole aux directeurs de lieux culturels," *Télérama, Arts et Scènes* (websites), June 7, 2016; accessed April 17, 2023; and Gilles Renault, "Centres dramatiques nationaux. Conflits en coulisse," *Libération* (website), February 1, 2018; accessed April 17, 2023.
60. Braunschweig, interview with Cynthia Running-Johnson, May 18, 2018.
61. See, for example, Renault, "Centres dramatiques nationaux."
62. Whitton, "Whatever Happened to Théâtre Populaire?"
63. Michel Guérin, "La thèse du ruissellement, selon laquelle plus l'offre culturelle sera riche, plus elle sera partagée par tous est illusoire," *Le Monde* (website), October 27, 2018, accessed April 17, 2023.
64. Guérin, "La thèse du ruissellement," *Le Monde*, October 27, 2018.
65. See, for example, Emmanuel Négrier and Aurélien Djakouane et al., *Les publics des festivals* (Paris: Editions Michel de Maule, 2010).
66. Philippe Lombardo and Loup Wolff, *Cinquante ans de pratiques culturelles en France, Collection Culture Etudes* (Paris: Ministère de la Culture, July 2020), 52.
67. Fabrice Raffin, "Débat: Trois idées (fausses) à l'origine des politiques culturelles françaises," *Conversation* (website), February 24, 2020; accessed April 17, 2023.
68. Balme, *The Theatrical Public Sphere*, 3, 14.
69. Joël Pommerat, "Grenoble, la déception de l'écologie culturelle," *Libération* (website), June 2, 2016; accessed April 17, 2023.
70. Jessica Vedel, interview with Cynthia Running-Johnson, October 15, 2018. In November 2020, when Vedel's codirector, Camille de la Guillonnière, became head of the Théâtre Régional des Pays de la Loire, the company integrated into the TRPL and now is known by that name.
71. Cécile Fontaine, interview with Cynthia Running-Johnson, October 12, 2018.
72. Cécile Fontaine, public interview with Cynthia Running-Johnson, "The Lives of French Theater Artists: A Conversation with François Kergourlay, Jessica Vedel and Cécile Fontaine," France-Florida Research Institute, University of Florida, Gainesville, February 18, 2022.
73. Manon Allouch, interview with Cynthia Running-Johnson, October 13, 2018.
74. Kruger, *The National Stage*, 187.

"She Is No Longer What She Was"

Charlotte Cushman, Melodramatic Femininity, and the Maidenly Mode of Singing in Daniel Terry's *Guy Mannering*

— ALEXANDRA SWANSON

Early on May 8, 1837, Charlotte Cushman received word that she was to play Meg Merrilies that evening in the New York National Theatre's production of Daniel Terry's melodrama, *Guy Mannering* (figure 1). Cushman had first been assigned a minor role in the National Theatre production, but she jumped at the chance to play Meg—an old, Scottish, Romani Queen and the play's heroine—when the production's original Meg fell ill.[1] About a decade later, Cushman would reach the lofty levels of acclaim that have led a substantial set of modern scholars to herald her as the "greatest American actress" of the nineteenth century.[2] Yet, in 1837, she was only beginning her acting career. Usually, Meg was played as an unfailingly acrimonious, harsh, and authoritative figure. It was a position so atypical for a female melodramatic character that Terry tried to cast a man for the role in his original 1816 production in London. But while Cushman was waiting for her entrance and listening to the play's dialogue, inspiration for a rather different approach to the role suddenly came; she listened to one of the minor characters onstage as he pronounced that the once-fearful Meg had gone soft: "She is no longer what she was. She doats [sic]." Cushman's romantic partner and biographer, Emma Stebbins, later reported, "with the words a vivid flash of insight struck upon [Cushman's] brain: she saw and felt by the powerful dramatic instinct with which she was endowed the whole meaning and intention of the character."[3] Fortified by this last-minute understanding of Meg as a woman who "is no longer what she was," Cushman hurried onto the stage.[4]

Due to the last-minute shift in parts, Cushman performed a lullaby that the

Figure 1. John Rice. *Charlotte S. Cushman as Meg Merrilies [in Terry's "Guy Mannering"]*. Folger Shakespeare Library Shelfmark: ART File C986 no.4 (size XS). Used by permission of the Folger Shakespeare Library.

character Meg does not usually sing, introducing a soft and gentle dimension to Meg. In Meg's first scene, a young military captain ambles into her camp. In proper melodramatic style, she recognizes him as the long-lost Henry Bertram, who was kidnapped on his fifth birthday and is now ignorant of his own identity. Meg had been Henry's childhood nursemaid, and, at this point in the play, she would usually instruct a young woman from her camp to perform the Bertram family lullaby to jog his memory. Originally, Cushman had played this young woman; but then, in the flurry of reassignment, no one was slated to replace Cushman when she stepped in as Meg. Hence, the first time Cushman took the stage as Meg Merrilies, she sang the lullaby (John Whitaker's "Oh! Rest Thee Babe") herself, as Meg.[5] In her many later performances in the role in both the United States and England, Cushman continued to sing "Oh! Rest Thee Babe" to great success.[6] I argue that this success was due to the fact that Cushman's performance of the lullaby made references to earlier moments in the play, Meg's character history, and Cushman's past career in which conventional femininity had been on display. Cushman's performance of "Oh! Rest Thee Babe" thereby momentarily contradicted Meg's otherwise unconventional and near-masculine feminine mode.

Choosing Cushman's lullaby as an object of analysis allows for several different interventions in melodrama studies. While the history of literary melodrama criticism has acknowledged the music underlying, comingling with, and occasionally interrupting the dialogue onstage, melodramatic music has yet to receive its full due in analytic attention. Following the work of critics such as Katherine Hambridge, Jonathan Hicks, Michael Pisani, and Sarah Hibberd, I have deliberately chosen a musical subject in this essay—"Oh! Rest Thee Babe"— in an effort to reach across the critical divide between musicological and literary melodrama studies.[7] One of the many things we miss when we fail to pay careful attention to melodramatic music is a musical score's potential to contradict its script. *Guy Mannering*'s music, for instance, not only emphasizes the emotions made explicit in the script but also, at times, counterpoints that emotional tone. Cushman's Meg and Terry's *Guy Mannering* are similarly understudied. Cushman's audiences clamored after Meg throughout her career. She was perhaps the most cherished melodramatic character in the oeuvre of America's most worshipped nineteenth-century actress, and yet a remarkably small amount of criticism has focused on Cushman's Meg or even more generally on Terry's *Guy Mannering*.[8] Finally, although critics such as Christine Gledhill, Katherine Newey, and Faye Dudden have produced excellent work that centers on unconventional femininity in melodrama, the phenomenon of female melodramatic characters playing in the margins of conventionality for subversive purposes remains severely understudied.[9]

Before Cushman came to the character, Meg's potential for subversion was curbed by her position on the very outskirts of the genre; she acted as a foil to the more conventional female characters of the play. When Cushman interpolated the lullaby into Meg's character, she created common ground that Meg and the more conventional female characters of the play could occupy together and diluted the border between conventional and unconventional femininity in the play. Within that common ground, Meg's character ceased to function only as an outlier, and the unconventional aspects of her femininity became more threatening. Cushman exhibited a feminine mode capacious and elastic enough to hold conventional and unconventional femininity simultaneously.[10] Cushman's success embodying seemingly contradictory femininities in *Guy Mannering* suggests that American and English melodramatic audiences may have been more receptive to nonnormative stagings of femininity, if slightly, than is generally assumed.

Meg Before Cushman

Before we can consider Cushman's contribution to Meg's character in detail, we must think at greater length about who Meg was in the several decades before Cushman took on the role. In 1815, Walter Scott published the novel *Guy Mannering*, on which Terry's theatrical adaptation is based, in Edinburgh and London. At the start of Scott's novel, before Henry's kidnapping, Meg is a maternal nursemaid, aligned with at least some conventional feminine standards. She "often contrived to waylay [Henry] in his walks, sing him a gipsy song, give him a ride upon her jackass, and thrust into his pocket a piece of gingerbread or red-cheeked apple," and when he was ill, "she lay all night below the window."[11] Her maternal characteristics largely fade after Henry goes missing early in the novel, and from that point forward, Meg more often appears "in all points of equipment, except her petticoats, rather masculine than feminine."[12] Although Scott's Meg feels a kinship with the adult Henry, enough to help him reclaim his rightful identity, she no longer acts as a mother to him.

As Terry composed his *Guy Mannering* theatrical adaptation, he relied on Scott as an advisor. The melodrama was an instant, abiding success. Scott scholar Annika Bautz estimates that in the first nine years of *Guy Mannering* performances at London's Covent Garden Theatre—and it was widely performed beyond the Covent Garden—the production attracted a cumulative audience of about 250,000 spectators.[13] In those nine years, *Guy Mannering*'s audience at the Covent Garden was, therefore, five times larger than the entire UK readership of Scott's novel.[14] Terry's *Guy Mannering* was so sensational that Scott began sending Terry proofs of his subsequent novels in advance to ensure that he could beat any and all competing playwrights to the stage.[15]

Terry's stage adaptation begins long after Henry's disappearance. The audience is made aware that Meg used to be Henry's nursemaid but they never see her in that role. From her first appearance in Terry's play, Meg is already "rather masculine than feminine." In an attempt to make obvious Meg's masculine features, Terry initially asked actor John Emery to play Meg, but as Emery "declined to put on petticoats," Terry had to make due with Sarah Egerton for the 1816 premiere.[16] Twenty-one years and many Megs later, Cushman's physical appearance fit well with Terry's initial conception of Meg as manly. Lisa Merrill notes, "Standing five feet six inches tall, with a large forehead and square jaw, even in her youth she looked powerful and substantial, not at all the diminutive, feminine part most women played in the cultural imaginary of the period."[17] In 1882, a reporter for the *Milwaukee Daily Sentinel* likewise claimed that "When the gods made Charlotte Cushman, they only just missed making a man."[18] Her supposedly unfeminine stature answered the call for a part that Terry would have preferred a man to play, a part that Terry never intended to include the performance of a lullaby.

Before Cushman interpolated "Oh! Rest Thee Babe" into Meg's performance, the play's female characters occupied fundamentally dissimilar feminine positions: characters Lucy Bertram, sister to Henry, and Julia Mannering displayed conventional femininity, while Meg embodied her unbound and unconventional feminine mode. When the audience first meets Lucy, she is singing a sorrowful air to lament her father's death, during which she self-identifies as a melodramatically typical heroine in a state of distress, innocence, and virtue: "A maiden friendless, desolate / With Heaven my innocence to guide."[19] Indeed, Lucy's and Julia's plots are stories of restoration to the patriarchal order. Just before the final curtain falls, Lucy and Julia are restored to the care of their brothers, and then the two women instantaneously enter into marital engagements with—in regular melodramatic fashion—one another's brother. Meg's initial lack of singing helped solidify her separation from Lucy and Julia, who sing often throughout the play. Bautz suggests that Meg's amusicality may have been part of Terry's attempt to "keep her as a character apart from the others."[20] To further explain why Terry affords Meg so much more autonomy than Lucy or Julia, Bautz cites race, class, and nationality: "For [contemporaneous] reviewers, it is only Meg who is allowed to be unconventional and unbound by the rules of female propriety because she is a Scottish gypsy, so twice removed from the reviewers' own lives."[21] In the nineteenth-century British imagination, Romani female characters were often seen as "implicitly threatening, perhaps over-assertive and conspicuous," lustful, and endowed with supernatural abilities.[22] To that end, non-Romani-identified European writers often associated Romani women with the wild.[23]

Further, Meg and her camp have used the Bertram estate in Scotland as a base for generations, and their residence carries a particular set of gender connotations. Maureen Martin argues that in the eighteenth century and especially in the documents surrounding the Acts of Union 1707, Scotland was regularly referred to as the submissive female partner in its union with England, but "Scotland had undergone a sex-change by the Victorian era with representations of Scotland as female scarce indeed." In the nineteenth century, Scotland came to represent "the primal male element of female Britannia."[24] Scott, as a Scottish author, intended *Guy Mannering*, and the *Waverly* series as a whole, to serve as "literary bridges between the various nations comprising Great Britain."[25] Indeed, the novel's first pages follow the English Guy Mannering as he crosses the border from England into Scotland, and a number of characters continue to cross that border for the book's duration. Terry's play, however, was written by an Englishman and premiered in England with the English Sarah Egerton debuting as Meg. In the play, Meg's Scottishness becomes an alienating and masculine feature. It is, then, partially through ventriloquizing Romani and Scottish stereotypes that Meg is able to embody an identity that reaches outside the conventional bounds of femininity. Meg modeled masculine, unbound femininity from behind a caricature of a Romani, Scottish woman.

Meg's performance of "Oh! Rest Thee Babe" momentarily disrupts this caricature by bringing forward a musical representation of conventional femininity. In his evaluation of Cushman's performance, nineteenth-century actor George Vandenhoff evaluated Meg as a "deep-shadowed, lurid-tinged character . . . half human, half demon,—with the savage, animal reality of passion, and the weird fascination of crime, redeemed by fitful flashes of womanly feeling."[26] "Oh! Rest Thee Babe" was just such a supposedly "redeeming" womanly flash. Vandenhoff's racialized and troubling review of Cushman's Meg suggests that the purportedly "savage" and "animal" persona she exhibited for the majority of the play was somehow offset, made palatable, and compensated for by Cushman's ability to *also* exhibit conventional femininity in the role. When Cushman adhered to the conventional mold for a melodramatic heroine for the length of the lullaby, she perhaps earned some clemency for her decision to act outside of tightly bound gender prescriptions for the remainder of the play. Cushman's addition of the lullaby to Meg's character revealed points of continuity between Meg and the other women of the play, not only insofar as Meg too became a musical character but also by creating an overlap of the women's feminine modes. This connective web perhaps made it more difficult to dismiss Meg's nonnormative mode of femininity outside the lullaby as an isolated outlier. The performance supplied Cushman's Meg with a couple of minutes in which she could travel between both ends of *Guy Mannering*'s spectrum of femininity, shrinking what formerly seemed like immeasurable distance between them.

CHARLOTTE CUSHMAN

The Lullaby's Maidenly Mode

In the most obvious sense, the character who pronounces Meg to be "no longer what she was" before her first entrance onstage intends for the audience to understand that the Queen has lost her edge. However, Cushman's performance of the lullaby is where the suggestion that "she," referring to both Cushman and Meg, "is no longer what she was" begins to collect depth and take on various gendered meanings. The lullaby occurs twice in *Guy Mannering*: sung first by the demure Lucy and second in the Romani camp, making Meg's performance of the lullaby a reprise. Lucy's performance of "Oh! Rest Thee Babe" occurs early in *Guy Mannering*, before Meg has even appeared onstage. When the scene opens, Guy asks Lucy to pick up singing the air she had been singing a moment earlier. He implores, "It was a beautiful thing! Wild,—yet so pathetic." Lucy replies, "It has borrowed its tone of feeling Colonel Mannering, from the situation of the singer! It is said, from a very ancient period, to have been sung in our family to soothe the slumbers of the infant heir!"[27] The lullaby recalls not only her own childhood but looks backward to "a very ancient period" and thereby links the song with a long genealogical line of maternal performances. At Mannering's entreaty, Lucy sings once again.

Formally, this lullaby meets conventional melodramatic standards for femininity, conjuring for the audience an image of a crooning mother. The time signature of "Oh! Rest Thee Babe," like so many lullabies, is in 6/8 time to mimic the rocking of a child to sleep. Then, each of the first four measures begins with another imitation of physical rocking: a dotted eighth note, followed by a downward-moving neighbor tone, then followed by a half-step back up to the original tone, bouncing up and down like one handles a child (figure 2). In an undated copy of the piano and vocal sheet music, published by G. Balls in Philadelphia, the majority of the lyrics, written by Walter Scott, are marked dynamically as *piano* to account for feminine reticence and delicacy, excepting one: the *forte* verse that details the responsibilities of manhood. The singer loudly urges an infant boy to sleep while he can, before the time "When thy sleep shall be broken by Trumpet and Drum ... For war comes with manhood, as light comes with day," after which the dynamics recede to *piano* again.[28]

As a rule of thumb in mid-century transatlantic vocal performance, the higher the vocal range, the daintier the role. As famed musical pedagogue François Delsarte remarked, "caressing, tender and gentle emotions find their normal expression in high notes. This is beyond all doubt."[29] The most traditionally feminine of vocal roles were, therefore, usually composed for soprano voices. Although most of the notes in "Oh! Rest Thee Babe" are in range for a soprano,

Figure 2. Measures five through ten of "Oh! Rest Thee Babe," N.D., Box 065, Item 081, Lester S. Levy Sheet Music Collection (website), Special Collections, Johns Hopkins University, accessed November 25, 2019.

alto, or contralto, the song's highest note is a G perched at the top of the treble staff. The vocal line, therefore, swells and stretches up toward or, at times, perhaps even beyond, the ceiling of a typical alto or contralto voice. The lullaby as a whole fits most comfortably in a soprano register; indeed, Catherine Stevens, Terry's original Lucy, was a soprano.[30]

We have no recordings of Cushman or other contemporary actresses singing the lullaby because she was singing in what turned out to be the final decades of the nineteenth century to exist without recording technology. Cushman died in 1876, a year before Edison's phonograph and about a decade before the enormously more reliable Berliner Gramophone. There are traces within the sheet music of what Roger Freitas has identified as a "maidenly mode" in nineteenth-century operatic singing, a mode he identifies with Adelina Patti's particular musical style.[31] This "maidenly mode" communicated womanly virtue by employing soft dynamics, rubato, and other musical imitations of speech.[32] Freitas includes rubato singing—"the expressive alteration of rhythm or tempo"—in his theory of maidenly vocal performance because the refusal to observe a strict and regular tempo gives off a speech-like impression in the music, thereby attenuating the extent to which a performance feels artful.[33] Nineteenth-century transatlantic female stage performance was, in many ways, an affront to domestically centered femininity insofar as female performers were working not only in public but onstage; in some cases they crossed oceans in the name of their careers. A musical style that mimicked quotidian speech—the sort of speech one might hear inside a home—seemed less ostentatious.

Figure 3. Measures eleven through thirteen of "Oh! Rest Thee Babe," N.D., Box 065, Item 081, Lester S. Levy Sheet Music Collection (website), Special Collections, Johns Hopkins University, accessed November 25, 2019.

With its embrace of demure and artless expression, "Oh! Rest Thee Babe" adheres to the maidenly mode. The delicate artlessness of the song becomes clear, in part, by cataloguing what is not present: there is no real opportunity for flashy virtuosity because the lullaby is largely devoid of vocal ornamentation, such as melisma or coloratura, complicated rhythms, key modulations, and accidentals. What is present is a pervasive sense of temporal malleability by way of rubato markings. To further signify the manipulability of the song's tempo, Whitaker marks several bars in "Oh! Rest Thee Babe" as "ad lib," signaling to the singer to progress at whatever tempo feels suitable. Fermatas often punctuate these ad-lib bars as additional instances in which note length and pace are left to the singer's discretion. The pickup function of the word "oh," as in the first set of lyrics, "Oh, slumber my darling" provides yet another space for the singer to slow down, lingering on the pickup note before falling back into tempo for the rest of the phrase. At some points, the word "oh" is stretched into an ascending triplet figure rather than one single eighth note (figure 3). Though not technically taking up any more rhythmic space, the presence of three notes where there was only one suggests a temporal elasticity and the potential for rubato. The lullaby's most evocative speech imitation lies in Whitaker's exhaling musical figures. Measures five and seven, for instance, mimic the sound of a sigh with descending major thirds that take place on the words "darling" and "lady." (figure 2).

Reenactments of Feminine Pasts

Guy describes Lucy's lullaby performance as "wild," and Terry's stage directions instruct that the second lullaby performance in the camp be sung "much more wildly."[34] Then, just before the lullaby, Henry adds to the mounting expectation that the performance in the camp will be unruly by asking Meg to perform magic. He offers to pay Meg to deliver a prophecy that will tell his future as well as his past, pleading, "Your manner is wild and oracular enough; come, give me proof of your art." She scoffs, "Offer it not. If with a simple spell, I cannot recall times which you have long forgotten, hold me the miserablest [sic] imposter."[35] Yet, the only "spell" she casts is singing the lullaby, or her instruction for a young woman to sing the lullaby, depending on the production. Although the script calls for a musical enactment of Romani wild stereotypes, the lullaby produces instead a sense of restrained domesticity by adhering to the maidenly mode. Whitaker's "Oh! Rest Thee Babe" even washes away some of the supposedly "wilder" elements that were once part of the lullaby. The lullaby includes several instances of the Scottish snap—a rhythm associated with Scottish music.[36] But Walter Scott's original lyrics for "Oh! Rest Thee Babe" featured a chorus in Manx Gaelic: "O ho ro, i ri ri, cadul gu lo / O ho ro, i ri ri," while, in contrast, Whitaker's theatrical version puts English lyrics in place of the Gaelic: "Oh rest thee babe, rest thee babe, sleep until day / Oh rest thee babe, rest thee oh sleep while you may."[37] This anglicization helps ensure that the lullaby is heard as a demonstration of English domesticity rather than Scottish wildness.

When Cushman sang as Meg, she reenacted Lucy's diminutive performance. Further, in this second lullaby performance, Meg reenacts an earlier version of herself. Because Meg sang "Oh! Rest Thee Babe" to Henry as his nursemaid, singing to him again recalls that early maternal station. Though Meg's lullaby is only a few minutes long, it is a major turning point in the plot. Meg offers the lullaby to Henry as proof of his true identity, and it spurs him to reclaim his family estate at the climax of the play. Contemporaneous accounts of Cushman's Meg attended carefully to the lullaby, often remarking that "Oh! Rest Thee Babe" was a touching, compassionate moment at odds with her otherwise masculine character. Actor Lawrence Barrett marveled that though Cushman's approach to Meg overall was "almost masculine in manner, there was a gentleness in her which only her intimates could know: The voice which crooned the lullaby of the Bertrams' so tenderly came from a heart as gentle as infancy."[38] Stebbins recorded that Cushman's Meg produced an assortment of reactions in audience members, including an admiration for "the soft, tender, loving notes of [Meg's] voice, as with the tremulousness of age it croons over the boy the songs of his infancy, or changes to ringing notes of ecstatic joy as she sees awakening in his mind the dim remembrances she is seeking to evoke."[39] All in all, this lullaby is an about-face for Meg: her sudden, but temporary embodiment of a more conventionally feminine mode.

O. A. Roorbach, in his 1856 *Actors as They Are*, spoke to the implied chronology of Meg's brush with conventionality as well as the impression of Cushman's physical voice: "That cracked and tremulous voice took a tone of that most exquisite of all melody, a mother's lullaby! And how the blood of youth itself seemed to swell up from the singer's heart, only to leave her in the next scene, what, in reality, she was—the crippled, poor old woman, with more than eighty winters on her head!"[40] For as long as the song lasted, Cushman's Meg was suddenly younger and bolstered by "the blood of youth," having time traveled backward to when she worked as Henry's nursemaid. The resurgence of that past, however, disappeared with the last note of the lullaby. Further, in characterizing her voice as "cracked," Roorbach called to mind a vocal injury that Cushman suffered early in her stage career. Before Cushman was an actress, she was a singer in command of a voice that spanned almost two full registers: that of the contralto as well as a not quite complete soprano register. For women on the transatlantic stage at mid-century, singing was nearly always considered a more suitable occupation than acting. We might recall that, at this time, actresses and sex workers were nearly interchangeable in both the American and English public imagination.[41] In comparison to acting, therefore, professional singing seemed unsensational and conventional. Sopranos, in particular, were wont to perform the most refined and docile of roles.

In this initial professional era, Cushman sang as a soprano almost exclusively, though the roles reached, and in some cases reached past, the uppermost limit of her vocal range. Cushman's later performances of "Oh! Rest Thee Babe," therefore, likely for many audience members called to mind Cushman's early—and more conventional—profession as a singer.[42] Two years before she would make her first appearance as Meg, Cushman made her musical debut as the Countess Almaviva in the opera *The Marriage of Figaro* in April 1835 to largely enthusiastic reviews. For the purposes of understanding Cushman's later success as Meg, her most remarkable early soprano role came soon after the Countess: *Guy Mannering*'s Lucy Bertram.[43] Lucy's role is far more musically demanding than Meg's; Lucy is singing when the audience first encounters her, and she continues to sing throughout the melodrama. Meg, in comparison, did not sing at all until Cushman started in with the lullaby business. Cushman cut her teeth on roles like the docile and soprano-pitched Lucy in her first stage career; and yet these soprano roles turned out to be only a professional dalliance. Her singing career lasted less than a year.

Later in 1835, Cushman reported an irreparable vocal injury and made a premature retirement from professional singing.[44] After Cushman became renowned on the theatrical stage, a number of her contemporaries reflected on her early career and, to make sense of her vocal injury, cited overstrain as the cause. Fellow actor James Murdoch suggested, "In consequence of the vigor of

Miss Cushman's efforts to carry the citadel by storm, rather than by cautious approaches, in a short time she broke down her voice and destroyed her prospects as a singer."[45] In this same incident, however, Merrill sees something more gendered: "Being forced to assume the highest-pitched, most 'feminine-sounding' role, [Charlotte] claimed, harmed her health . . . Charlotte could not be made into a soprano any more than she could be cast successfully in any traditionally feminine role on- or off-stage."[46] In the wake of the injury, Cushman asserted that she had little choice but to turn toward dramatic acting. Merrill questions how absolute the need for a professional pivot was, suggesting that, far from restricting Cushman, the injury may have served as justification to begin again onstage, this time in her preferred career as an actress.[47]

Whether or not Cushman exaggerated the injury's severity, the history of her ruined voice began to surface repeatedly in American and English newspapers as she grew more and more popular on the theatrical stage. An 1844 biography of Cushman printed in the *New York Sun* and reprinted in the *Leeds Intelligencer* reported on the "calamity" that was Cushman's early loss of her singing voice.[48] On the occasion of Cushman's farewell engagement in New York preceding her departure for Italy in 1858, the *New York Herald* likewise remembered the injury: "Her voice, which was a contralto, was seriously impaired by an endeavor to force it up to the soprano register."[49] Obituaries for Cushman, following her death in 1876, regularly referred to the early loss of her singing voice, both in American newspapers, as in the *Milwaukee Sentinel* and the *Daily Inter-Ocean*, and in English print, such as the *York Herald* and the *Western Daily Press*.[50]

Audiences heard the injury in Cushman's voice even decades after her retirement from professional singing. Nine years after Cushman damaged her voice, Stebbins cited an acquaintance of Cushman's on the subject: "Her singing, although the upper notes of her voice had disappeared, was excellent of its kind. . . . Nor was it less remarkable as a work of art, because the artist was, by consummate skill and knowledge, conquering the imperfections of an organ already almost destroyed, her great science enabling her to make use of what remained."[51] Clara Erskine Clement's 1882 biography of Cushman spoke more plainly to the permanence of the injury's sonic residue: "There *always* remained in Miss Cushman's voice a certain quality of tone which was probably the result of this early abuse of it,—a quality well suited to the deep passions portrayed in her strongest parts."[52] For many in Cushman's audience, the absence of the higher notes she could once sing was striking; the gap in her vocal ability became a critical part of her success on the stage.

As an actress, Cushman often instrumentalized her splintered voice to dramatic advantage, fabricating tortured or unnatural sounds. These vocalizations may have worsened the initial injury, as Merrill suggests in reference to Meg's spoken lines: "Late in her career, when she played [Meg,] Cushman would have to resort to constant gargles to keep her from losing her voice completely, a problem that had plagued her since her days as an opera singer. Her vocal work had always been a significant aspect in her performances, but the 'weird, prophetic, tones' she employed as Meg were achieved at the price of real physical pain. Charlotte forced her voice to express intense, sustained grief and anger or denunciation, making her voice thicken as though she were dying, crack with advanced age, or sound hollow and despairing."[53] If roles like Meg, for which Cushman pushed against the walls of her vocal capacity, did not exacerbate the injury, they at least accentuated the brokenness of her voice—and in a couple of different ways. When she spoke as Meg, Cushman's cracked voice was on display, contributing to her "wild" and acrimonious affect, but when singing "Oh! Rest Thee Babe," her voice worked as a callback to the more conventionally feminine occupation Cushman held when she was a singer. As Marvin Carlson has written, "The recycled body of an actor, already a complex bearer of semiotic messages, will almost inevitably in a new role evoke the ghost or ghosts of previous roles if they have made any impression whatever on the audience, a phenomenon that often colors and indeed may dominate the reception process."[54] For those in Cushman's audience who knew her vocal history—a percentage that rose parallel with Cushman's mounting fame in the 1840s and 1850s—Cushman's history as a ruined soprano haunted each performance of "Oh! Rest Thee Babe," her forfeit vocal ability conspicuous in her singing.

Cushman's lullaby, therefore, made a number of synchronized references to conventional femininity. The lyrics establish a long genealogical line of mothers singing to sleeping boys, and it temporarily restores Meg to her former days as Henry's nursemaid. Listening to Cushman sing, the audience heard a repetition of Lucy's lullaby from an hour or so earlier in the play as well as an echo that rippled back much farther, to Cushman singing as a yet uninjured soprano, performing "Oh! Rest Thee Babe" as Lucy Bertram herself. The composite of these layers allowed, and maybe required, Cushman and Meg to momentarily inhabit a conventionally feminine persona by stepping back into the past. Cushman's lullaby folded both Meg's and Cushman's histories onto themselves, offering a point of contact for their past and present feminine modes.

Meg abandons this conventional feminine persona as soon as the lullaby concludes, at which time Henry finds himself open to the idea that he may really be the long-lost Bertram heir. He begs of her, "Woman, speak more plainly, and tell me why those sounds thus agitate my inmost soul; and what ideas they are, that thus darkly throng upon my mind at hearing them."[55] The lullaby drags

Henry so entirely back to his long-forgotten childhood that he entertains the possibility of an identity unknown to him, one tethered to the melody. As Dudden contends, Meg's song is "the power of nurturing domesticity and motherly love before which men may in effect be reduced to the infants they once were."[56] In response to Henry's appeal for plain speaking, Meg stops singing and speaks to him in verse:

> Listen, youth, to words of power,
> Swiftly comes the rightful hour!
> They, who did thee scathe and wrong,
> Shall pay their deeds by death e'er long[57]

Cushman's shift from song to speech—and its signaling of a shift in her position from singer to actress—was in and of itself a curt step away from the lullaby's exhibition of conventional femininity: Meg does not sing again in the play, nor does she again so clearly occupy a conventionally feminine space. In her spoken verse, Meg commands Henry with the imperative "listen" and enjoins him to hear her "words of power." Her prediction of a future replete with deeds payable only by death strays further still from the reserved way of being that she so recently displayed in "Oh! Rest Thee Babe."

Shortly after reciting this verse, Meg explicitly articulates her masculine capabilities. She orders Henry to be on his way and assigns him a guide from her camp, cautioning them, "If you are attacked, be men, and let your hands defend your heads! I will not be far distant from you in your moment of need. And now begone!"[58] Meg publicly announces her capacity to assist the men should their own show of manhood prove insufficient. Then, as Merrill reports, Cushman made a spectacle out of Meg's more-than-womanly strength: "Suddenly doubting the guide's trustworthiness, Charlotte's Meg used her robust physical prowess to protect Bertram. Gripping the other Gypsy's arm, Meg literally threw him toward the footlights."[59] Immediately after the lullaby, therefore, Cushman's Meg abandoned the music that had allowed her to reenact her conventionally feminine pasts. She abandoned conventional femininity altogether and became, once again, no longer what she was.

Balancing the Conventional and the Unconventional in Public

In his 1996 essay "What the Heroine Taught," Léon Metayer proposes, "Playhouses dedicated to [melodrama] were hardly places where female spectators could take lessons in feminism."[60] He asks what "confused pleasure" female spectators might have garnered from melodramatic story lines, in which women are so often beholden to the authority of fathers, brothers, and husbands. Cushman's melodramatic performances, however, did produce pleasure, confused or otherwise, for her female spectators. Dudden goes so far as to claim that "no other American woman inspired such worshipful attention from women, young and old alike."[61] Clement's biography reproduced the testimony of one such Cushman-fanatic: "Dearly as I loved my mother and my home, if Miss Cushman had asked me . . . to go with her and be her slave, without even going back to say farewell to my friends, I should have consented. I would have given my life for her."[62] This extraordinarily popular persona was constructed in part by Cushman's publicly putting forth a self-presentation, especially during the 1840s and 1850s, that appeared sometimes boundary breaking and sometimes deferentially within the bounds of conventional expectations for female conduct. This public persona also allowed Cushman an exceptionally effective position from which to represent Meg as at once conventional and unconventional. Cushman's embodiment of Meg likely meant something different to audiences than did, for instance, Sarah Egerton's original approach to the role. To Meg, Cushman brought a carefully measured and legible irreverence for gender prescriptions and costuming; this careful irreverence complimented Meg's own.

Offstage and in public, Cushman's fashions garnered comment in both American and English newspapers. Merrill refers to an August 1851 column in the *Cleveland Plain Dealer* that reported a sighting of Cushman "in masculine attire, hat, coat, unmentionables, and all." The *Boston Atlas* picked up the story, adding, "Here was not . . . a mere desire to astonish the dinner table . . . No, she rode in it, fished, walked, ran, and romped in it; and for aught that we can learn, has determined to wear it for the remainder of her days—at least of maidenhood."[63] Later that same month, the story crossed the Atlantic. The *Lancaster Gazetter* reported, "A New York paper states that Miss Charlotte Cushman has adopted the male attire—hat, coat, and trousers—is [sic] is believed permanently."[64] These public appearances in men's clothing guaranteed that Cushman was not publicly pigeonholed as conventionally feminine and, for some, Cushman's sartorial choices also signaled her queer relationships with women. As Martha Vicinus notes, "[Cushman] and her partners wore matching jackets and dresses, so that they looked alike, but different from heterosexual women."[65]

There is some uncertainty as to how widely Cushman's relationships with women were known of and understood by her theatregoing public, but her audiences were aware that Cushman's offstage public life, in which she never legally married and in which she dressed frequently in masculine attire or clothes that matched those of her female partners, was not typical of an American actress.[66]

At the same time, as Merrill has argued, Cushman's lack of relationships with men did much to elevate her status as a reputable, virtuous actress: there was never a "hint of any emotional or sexual entanglements with men in her past to dishonor or distract her."[67] For some members of her audience, Cushman represented, in an odd twist, an insignia of heterosexual purity who had managed to escape the nearly inevitable acting-induced female fall from virtue.

Onstage, too, Cushman often dressed in masculine clothing. Indeed, she made a name for herself as an actress by playing male characters. A reporter for the *Daily Picayune* commented that Cushman was "well fitted naturally for work of this sort, her figure, her voice, and the features of her face being of a cast that favored the assumption of masculinity."[68] She performed a great number of "breeches roles" in her career and earned accolades in some of the most canonical male roles in English-language drama—roles such as Romeo, Hamlet, and Cardinal Wolsey. Of her Romeo, H. Barton Baker of the *Graphic* raved that Cushman was "not a woman masquerading in male attire, but in carriage, gesture, voice just such a man as we might conceive young Montagu to have been."[69] When Cushman played women, she rarely played anyone who was reticent enough to meet conventional melodramatic feminine standards; she was famous for her Meg Merrilies as well as her megalomaniacal Lady Macbeth.

Cushman was wary, however, that she not become overwhelmingly associated with unladylike roles, a cautiousness that factored into a deliberation over whether to continue playing Meg after she had firmly established her acting career. In 1845, Cushman was engaged at the London Princess Theatre opposite Edwin Forrest. As this was her first season in England, Cushman was disinclined to play Meg out of a concern that she was too ill-mannered and unrefined a character to play in front of English audiences—she was loath to tip the scales of her public persona too far toward feminine unconventionality. She agreed to an English debut of her Meg at the Princess in June 1845 only because her brother, acting as her booking agent, committed her to the part against her will.[70]

Despite Cushman's reservations, her Meg was the subject of wild acclaim in England, as she had been in the United States. Meg's at once conventional and unconventional feminine mode—that which resonated so vibrantly with Cushman's public persona—was a major component of her popularity. Merrill writes that 1845 London audiences delighted in finding Meg "both of them *and* otherworldly—given leave to assume unusually powerful dimensions *and yet* sympathetic as the 'foreign,' caring, maternal figure who watches over the hero."[71] Though Cushman was fairly consistent in her approach to Meg, Stebbins noted that audiences on either side of the ocean saw within the character a number of distinct feminine modes: she was "strong yet weak, full of the contrasts of matter and spirit . . . 'It is terrible,' says one; 'it tears one all to pieces.' 'It is lovely,' says another; 'it melts my heart,' 'She is a witch,' says a third."[72] As Meg, Cushman modeled feminine conventionality and something decidedly more masculine in one singular character. Many in Cushman's audiences were drawn to the incongruity of both the conventional and unconventional feminine modes present inside Meg.

An Alternative Ending for Cushman's Meg

The novel *Guy Mannering* concludes with Meg's protracted death scene. In aiding Henry to reclaim his rightful estate, Meg is shot and carried moaning back to her camp. Townspeople crowd inside Meg's home to hear her, with her dying breath, relate Henry's true history. Such an end for Scott's Meg calls attention to how very easily the mantra "she is no longer what she was" might have become "she is no longer" in Terry's theatrical adaptation. As Katherine Newey notes, "the restoration of class and gender hierarchy through the 'happy' ending of marriage—or the retributive deaths of transgressive female protagonists" were commonplaces in Victorian melodrama.[73] Terry's conclusion, however, veers from that set course. Lucy and Julia adhere to the compulsory marriage plot in the play, and yet Terry does not definitely sentence Meg to the usual retributive death—though she does come uncomfortably close to it.

In the stage version of *Guy Mannering*, Meg contemplates the possibility that she may die in an upcoming ambush of the play's villains: "That tree is wither'd now, never to be green again:—and old Meg Merrilies will never sing blythe songs more."[74] Because this old, withered Meg is no longer what she was—no longer a nursemaid singing blythe songs such as "Oh! Rest Thee Babe"—she seems to sense that she no longer fits into the conventional order of things and, therefore, risks expulsion from the play. Though some critics, both in Cushman's time and ours, have referred to Meg's final scene in Terry's adaptation as a death scene, what exactly happens to Meg is ambiguous.[75] Meg is shot in her last moments onstage, just as in Scott's novel. And yet, as Meg sinks to the ground under the weight of her injuries, Mannering shouts for assistance: "Let all care be taken of her support, and bear her gently away, she may yet recover."[76] Mannering's words are the last we hear of Meg, and they give the audience license to hope for her revival.

Though death scenes were fine opportunities for actresses to display show-stopping and ticket-selling exhibitions of agony, Terry holds back Meg's death from the audience. To be sure, that a character as unconventionally feminine as Meg would survive the length of an 1816 melodrama was anomalous. For that reason and others, critics like Metayer have long painted melodramatic audiences as strict sticklers for rigid gender roles. Meg's survival, however, is a telling indication that melodramatic audiences were, at least on occasion, absolutely willing and eager to root for boundary-breaking heroines like Meg.

Naturally, Meg's survival takes on additional meaning when we consider Cushman's approach to the character. Cushman dramatized Meg's willful, autonomous feminine mode as that which was not harshly oppositional but rather musically tied to the conventional standards for femininity that would have weighed heavily on the members of her female audience, who found themselves pressed to adhere to the Cult of True Womanhood.[77] Further, Cushman's lullaby drew a direct timeline between the comparatively conventional nursemaid who sang to Henry as a child and the quite unconventional Queen who sings once he is grown; so too did the lullaby remind audiences of Cushman's own timeline, in which she outgrew a conventionally feminine occupation as a soprano singer and aged into a quite unconventional actress. Cushman's portrayal of Meg, therefore, underscored a subversive chronology of feminine development, demonstrating how a reticent, Lucy Bertram-esque mode of femininity might ripen into a more masculine and unconventional Meg-like mode. Further, the absence of Meg's death scene in Terry's play meant that the audience could imagine this subversive chronology continuing beyond the play's end. Therefore, for any female audience members who felt dissatisfied with their prescribed roles as True Women, Cushman's addition of the lullaby to Meg's character may have resulted in a sort of blueprint—based, we should remember, on a racially charged and exoticized understanding of unconventional femininity—that modeled how one might outgrow such prescriptions.

Meg's range of feminine identities becomes fully legible only through careful study of *Guy Mannering*'s music. Attention to Cushman's lullaby, in addition to amending our understanding of how different feminine modes circulate and interact in the play, illustrates the potential contradictions in meaning between a melodramatic score and its script. When we listen closely to the lullaby, we are able to note the dissonance between Terry's stage direction that calls for the lullaby to be sung "wildly" and the maidenly mode to which the music adheres. We are able to note the dissonance inherent in Meg's near-masculine character performing a lullaby that clings tightly to conventional feminine standards. Meg's lullaby, in short, shows us what we risk overlooking when we neglect the role of music in literary analyses of melodrama.

Notes

1. Lisa Merrill, *When Romeo Was a Woman* (Ann Arbor: University of Michigan Press, 1999), 42.
2. See Faye Dudden, *Women in the American Theatre* (New Haven, CT: Yale University Press, 1994), 6; and Don B. Wilmeth and Tice L. Miller, eds., *The Cambridge Guide to American Theatre* (Cambridge: Cambridge University Press, 1996), 346.
3. Emma Stebbins, *Charlotte Cushman: Her Life, Letters, and Memories* (Boston: Houghton, Osgood and Company, 1878), 148. The dialogue that Stebbins quotes here is slightly altered from the printed dialogue in Terry's *Guy Mannering* as printed by Samuel French in 1893. For the remainder of this essay, I will cite from Daniel Terry, *Guy Mannering; or, The Gypsy's Prophecy* (New York: French, 1893).
4. Merrill also analyzes Cushman's first appearance as Meg and cites the phrase "She doats" in the play as Cushman's primary inspiration for the character. See Merrill, *When Romeo Was a Woman*, 42.
5. John Whitaker and Daniel Terry, "Oh! Rest Thee Babe" (Philadelphia: G Balls), Johns Hopkins University Libraries, Lester S. Levy Sheet Music Collection, accessed November 20, 2019.
6. Merrill, *When Romeo Was a Woman*, 100–101.
7. Katherine Hambridge and Jonathan Hicks, *The Melodramatic Moment: Music and Theatrical Culture, 1790–1820* (Chicago: University of Chicago Press, 2018); Michael Pisani, *Music for the Melodramatic Theater in Nineteenth-Century London and New York* (Iowa City: University of Iowa Press, 2014); Sarah Hibberd, *Melodramatic Voices: Understanding Music Drama* (Surrey: Ashgate Publishing, 2011).
8. Dudden, *Women in the American Theatre*, 88. For scholarship on Charlotte Cushman's portrayal of Meg Merrilies, see Merrill, *When Romeo Was a Woman*, 42–43 and chapter 4; Dudden, *Women in the American Theatre*, 86–88. For criticism on Daniel Terry's *Guy Mannering* more generally, see Annika Bautz, "The 'Universal Favourite': Daniel Terry's *Guy Mannering; or, The Gipsey's Prophecy* (1816)," *Yearbook of English Studies* 47 (2017): 36–57.
9. See Christine Gledhill, "Domestic Melodrama," in *The Cambridge Companion to English Melodrama*, ed. Carolyn Williams (Cambridge: Cambridge University Press, 2018), 71; Katherine Newey, "Melodrama and Gender," in *The Cambridge Companion to English Melodrama*, ed. Carolyn Williams (Cambridge: Cambridge University Press, 2018), 156–61; and Dudden, *Women in the American Theatre*, 71. Of the domestic subgenre of Victorian melodrama, Gledhill concedes that the conventional heroine usually weeps or faints at some point in the play but posits that these collapses signal forces of social inequity within the play: "While villains and heroes are volatile, succumbing to panic or derangement, it is the stoic endurance of the heroine, defending truth and resistant to corruption, whose eventual collapse registers conflicts inherent in patriarchy. . . . Heroines weep or faint not because they are weak or feeble but because they are sites of extremity—of anger, terror, pain." Newey focuses on the female melodramatic playwright Mrs Denvil and her centering of female agency in her play *Susan Hopley*. Faye Dudden contends that "although melodrama frequently is described as featuring a passive heroine who must be rescued, it is easy to find numerous examples in the genre of active women."
10. When I use "conventional" and "unconventional" as descriptors for femininity in this

essay, I refer to the conventions of American and English early-nineteenth-century melodrama that insist that the majority of female characters—white female characters especially—appear reticent, innocent, family-oriented, pious, dependent, frail, and obedient. These character conventions also have much in common with what being conventional may have meant for a number of women either performing or sitting in the audiences of these melodramatic productions—especially white, middle-to-upper class women—who may have felt pressed to adhere to what Barbara Welter has called the Cult of True Womanhood: a code of piety, purity, submissiveness, and domesticity. In referring to conventionality in this essay, therefore, I use the standards that early-nineteenth-century melodrama often applied to its female characters as an expansive mode, applicable not only to the characters onstage but also potentially to the women playing them and the women spectating from the audience.

11. Walter Scott, *Guy Mannering or The Astrologer* (London: James Ballantyne and Co., 1815), 54–55.
12. Scott, *Guy Mannering or The Astrologer*, 40.
13. Bautz, "The 'Universal Favourite,'" 42.
14. Bautz, "The 'Universal Favourite,'" 42.
15. Bautz, "The 'Universal Favourite,'" 42.
16. Mrs. Baron C. Wilson, *Our Actresses; or Glances at Stage Favourites Past and Present* (London: Smith, Elder and Co., 1844), 79.
17. Merrill, *When Romeo Was a Woman*, 16.
18. "Clara Erskine Clement's Effusive Biography of Charlotte Cushman" (*Milwaukee Daily Sentinel*, 1882), 2, Nineteenth Century Newspapers, accessed March 21, 2020.
19. Terry, *Guy Mannering; or, The Gypsy's Prophecy*, 14.
20. Bautz, "The 'Universal Favourite,'" 47.
21. Bautz, "The 'Universal Favourite,'" 56. It is perhaps important to note here that Bautz is considering Meg's character broadly, without significant analysis of particular actresses who played her.
22. Colin Clark, "'Severity has often enraged but never subdued a Gypsy': The History and Making of European Romani Stereotypes," in *The Role of the Romanies: Images and Counter Images of 'Gypsies' / Romanies in European Cultures*, ed. Nicholas Saul and Susan Tebbutt (Liverpool: Liverpool University Press, 2004), 232–34.
23. Judith Okely, *Own or Other Culture* (London: Routledge, 1996), 64.
24. Maureen M. Martin, *The Mighty Scot: Nation, Gender, and the Nineteenth-Century Mystique of Scottish Masculinity* (New York: State University of New York Press, 2009), 37–38.
25. Evan Gottlieb, "'To Be at Once Another and the Same': Walter Scott and the End(s) of Sympathetic Britishness," *Studies in Romanticism* 43, no. 2 (2004): 190.
26. William Thompson Price, *A Life of Charlotte Cushman* (New York: Bretano's, 1894), 99.
27. Terry, *Guy Mannering; or, The Gypsy's Prophecy*, 26.
28. John Whitaker, "Oh! Rest Thee Babe" (Philadelphia: G. Balls).
29. François Delsarte, L'Abbe Delaumosne, and Angelique Arnaud, *Delsarte System of Oratory* (New York: Edgar Werner, 1893), 415.
30. "Catherine Stephens, Countess of Essex" (Early Victorian Portraits Catalogue Entry) National Portrait Gallery (website), accessed March 18, 2020.
31. The music in Terry's *Guy Mannering* was central to the production. Especially in the ini-

32. Roger Freitas, "Singing Herself: Adelina Patti and the Performance of Femininity," *Journal of the American Musicological Society* 71, no. 2 (2018): 287–369. While Freitas writes of the maidenly mode specifically as a mode tied to Patti's musical style, I argue that traces of this mode can also be found in "Oh! Rest Thee Babe."
33. Richard Hudson, "Rubato," *Grove Music Online*, at Oxford Music Online (website), 2001, Oxford University Press, accessed April 17, 2023.
34. Terry, *Guy Mannering*, 41.
35. Terry, *Guy Mannering*, 41.
36. My thanks to Nicholas Chong for identifying the Scottish snap in the sheet music.
37. Walter Scott, *The Complete Works of Sir Walter Scott* (New York: Conner and Cook, Franklin Buildings, 1833), 690. Scott provides a footnote to the lullaby, clarifying, "These words, adapted to a melody somewhat different from the original, are sung in my friend Mr. Terry's drama of 'Guy Mannering.'"
38. Price, *A Life of Charlotte Cushman*, 99.
39. Stebbins, *Charlotte Cushman*, 150–51.
40. O. A. Roorbach, *Actors as They Are* (New York: O. A. Roorbach, 1856), 10.
41. For more on nineteenth-century perceptions of female acting as a profession, see Tracy Davis, *Actresses as Working Women: Their Social Identity in Victorian Culture* (London: Routledge, 1991), 107; or Merrill, *When Romeo Was a Woman*, 81. Davis notes that nineteenth-century actresses in British theatre circuits found themselves heavily identified with prostitution. The profession of the actress appeared in Victorian erotic literature more than any other profession. This association between the stage and prostitution was near-ubiquitous, notwithstanding the fact that actresses rarely engaged in sex work for fear that they would be dismissed from their stage positions. Merrill notes that the association of the actress with "sexual license and freedom" was prevalent in both the United States and England.
42. My insights here are indebted to Marvin Carlson's scholarship on how an actor's past roles and performances can affect the way audiences perceive their later roles and performances. See Marvin Carlson, *The Haunted Stage: The Theatre as Memory Machine* (Ann Arbor: University of Michigan Press, 2003).
43. Stebbins, *Charlotte Cushman: Her Life, Letters, and Memories*, 22. Cushman also sang the role of Julia Mannering in this early stage of her career. See Edward J Fletcher, "Charlotte Cushman's Theatrical Début," *Studies in English* 20 (1940): 174.
44. Merrill, *When Romeo Was a Woman*, 27.
45. James E. Murdoch, *The Stage: Or, Recollections of Actors and Acting from an Experience of Fifty Years* (Cincinnati: Robert Clark, 1884), 235–36, quoted in Price, 16.
46. Merrill, *When Romeo Was a Woman*, 27.
47. Merrill, *When Romeo Was a Woman*, 28.
48. "Miss Cushman" (*Leeds Intelligencer*, 1846), 2, British Library Newspapers, accessed March 20, 2020.
49. "Farewell Engagement of Miss Charlotte Cushman" (*New York Herald*, 1858), 5, Nineteenth Century U.S. Newspapers, accessed February 27, 2020.
50. "Death of Miss Cushman" (*York Herald*, 1876), 3, British Library Newspapers, accessed

February 27, 2020; "Death of Charlotte Cushman, the Great American Tragedienne" (*Daily Inter Ocean*), 2, Nineteenth Century U.S. Newspapers, accessed February 27, 2020; "Charlotte Cushman" (*Milwaukee Daily Sentinel*, 1876), 2, Nineteenth Century U.S. Newspapers, accessed February 27, 2020; "The Late Miss Cushman" (*Western Daily Press*, 1876), 7, British Library Newspapers, accessed February 27, 2020.
51. Stebbins, *Charlotte Cushman*, 87.
52. Clara Erskine Clement, *Charlotte Cushman* (Boston: James Osgood, 1882), 5, emphasis mine.
53. Merrill, *When Romeo Was a Woman*, 103–4.
54. Carlson, *Haunted Stage*, 8.
55. Terry, *Guy Mannering*, 42.
56. Dudden, *Women in the American Theatre*, 86–88.
57. Terry, *Guy Mannering*, 42.
58. Terry, *Guy Mannering*, 42.
59. Merrill, *When Romeo Was a Woman*, 101.
60. Léon Metayer, "What the Heroine Taught," in *Melodrama: Cultural Emergence of a Genre*, ed. Michael Hays and Anastasia Nikolopoulou (London: St. Martin's Press, 1996), 235–44.
61. Dudden, *Women in the American Theatre*, 77.
62. Clement, *Charlotte Cushman*, 73–74.
63. "Telegraphic Despatches" (*Boston Atlas*, 1851), Nineteenth Century U.S. Newspapers, accessed March 21, 2020.
64. "General Intelligence" (*Lancaster Gazetter*, 1851), British Library Newspapers, accessed March 21, 2020.
65. Martha Vicinus, "Lesbian History: All Theory and No Facts or All Facts and No Theory?" *Radical History Review* 60 (1994): 60.
66. See Sharon Marcus, *Between Women: Friendship, Desire, and Marriage in Victorian England* (Princeton, NJ: Princeton University Press, 2007), 191–222; Lisa Merrill, Robert A. Schanke, and Kim Marra, "LGBTQ Historical Scholarship: What Was It Like Twenty Years Ago," *Theatre Topics* 26, no. 1 (2016): 33–34; and Martha Vicinus, *Intimate Friends: Women Who Loved Women, 1778–1928* (Chicago: University of Chicago, 2004), 38–40. Marcus suggests that Cushman may have been concerned that her relationship with Emma Crow, which began while she lived with Emma Stebbins as her wife, would be harshly judged by the public. In her discussion of Cushman's romantic relationships with other women, Merrill emphasizes the meticulous care Cushman gave to keeping letters to her romantic interests private. Vicinus describes Cushman's relationship with Emma Stebbins as publicly acceptable and writes that Cushman was invested in gaining social approval for her intimate relationships.
67. Merrill, *When Romeo Was a Woman*, 241.
68. Lyman Horace Weeks, "Female Romeos and Hamlets" (*Daily Picayune*, 1893), 21, Nineteenth Century U.S. Newspapers, accessed March 21, 2020.
69. H. Barton Baker, "Famous Romeos and Juliets" (*The Graphic*, 1895), British Library Newspapers, accessed March 21, 2020.
70. Merrill, *When Romeo Was a Woman*, 99.
71. Merrill, *When Romeo Was a Woman*, 99, emphasis mine.
72. Stebbins, *Charlotte Cushman*, 150.

73. Newey, "Melodrama and Gender," 150.
74. Terry, *Guy Mannering*, 52.
75. Stebbins, for instance, wrote that early in the performance history of Terry's *Guy Mannering*, a musical performance followed "the death of Meg." See Stebbins, *Charlotte Cushman*, 152. See also Merrill, *When Romeo Was a Woman*, 101.
76. Terry, *Guy Mannering*, 58.
77. Welter, "The Cult of True Womanhood," 151–74.

Part II

CARE

Introduction to the Special Section

—MATTHIEU CHAPMAN AND MILES P. GRIER

On Friday, March 13, 2020, the then-president of the United States declared a national state of emergency regarding the novel coronavirus outbreak. Immediately, many states and counties went into lockdown to attempt to flatten the curve of a virus that had the potential to expand into a global pandemic. Many universities forced faculty to adjust their course modality from in person to online seemingly overnight with, in most cases, little training and no compensation. Two months later, on May 27, 2020, the grotesque video of George Floyd's murder at the hands of Minneapolis police officer Derek Chauvin spread across social media, causing protesters to break lockdown and take to the streets demanding justice for this heinous act, burning the third precinct's headquarters in the process. On January 6, 2021, thousands of white supremacists, stoked by the ousted president's big lie that the election had been stolen, stormed the US Capitol in an attempted coup to prevent the certification of his successor. While the police in Minneapolis met protesters with riot gear and military-grade armaments, some police in DC greeted armed thugs aiming to commit treason and violence against elected officials with hugs and handshakes.

Before we could catch our breaths, COVID mutated, and a new variant overwhelmed the miracle vaccine that science had delivered us. Meanwhile, Russia was gathering forces at the Ukrainian border for an invasion that would put the world on the brink of nuclear war. Rising food, housing, and transportation prices have the world on the verge of global economic collapse. And all the while, politicians continue to yield to fossil fuel companies in the wake of impending climate catastrophe.

And here we are supposed to edit a journal issue.

MATTHIEU CHAPMAN AND MILES P. GRIER

Everything I just named occurred between when Lisa Jackson-Schebetta first approached me to edit a special section of *Theatre History Studies* and when you are reading this. Hell, by the time this is printed, you may be reading this with a flashlight in the cold, dark of nuclear winter. Initially, I was hesitant to accept. Editing was never a part of academia that much appealed to me—I had had one too many disheartening experiences with the academic journal submission process to want to be on the other side. Sometimes, I got valuable feedback to help strengthen my work, but more often than not, reviewers would respond to my work in ways that they never would without the shield of anonymity that the peer-review process affords—dismissive, insulting, derogatory claims about both my work and the lens I choose to make my arguments. With my own experiences with the juggernaut of academic editor-as-gatekeeper seared into my brain, I didn't think I had the heart to tell other scholars who poured their hearts, souls, and minds into their work that the fruits of their labor were not worthy of publication. In other words, I cared too much about my colleagues and their labor to tell them no, and if I couldn't say no to some submissions, I didn't think I was fit to edit.

Upon further thought, however, I decided that the best way to establish a nurturing and approachable editorial apparatus was to take the reins myself. So, I told Lisa I would edit a section under one condition: that I could have a coeditor. She, of course, agreed to these terms, so I approached someone whose work I greatly admire and who was as familiar with the politics of publication as myself: Miles P. Grier.

Thankfully, Miles accepted and from there we set about crafting a call for papers for a special section on the materiality of racial performance between 1500 and 1815. *THS* wanted to stimulate more submissions on early theatrical periods, which do not generate as much scholarship as contemporary performance. What better way than to engage premodern critical race studies—a field that boasts a high public profile and earns a mention in nearly every MLA job advertisement in the period? Miles and I hoped for contributions that eschewed the history of race as an *idea* to see it instead as an effect of ritualized behavior, onstage and off. The theatrical repertoire might well serve as the model for the reproduction of social hierarchies over time, as a stylized set of persons interact in a way that establishes relations of dominance.[1] We thought it would be particularly wonderful if we received submissions that focused on race-making outside of Europe, perhaps even with Europeans as the *objects* and not the agents of racialization. The initial call received significant immediate attention: friends and scholars were sharing the call on message boards, social media, and LISTSERVs, often with enthusiasm for the subject matter and the editorial team.

INTRODUCTION TO THE SPECIAL SECTION

Then, a funny thing happened on the way to the deadline. Despite the fact that we knew a number of people working in this area, we received only two queries and zero full submissions in the eight months between the initial call and submission deadline. We tried to recruit colleagues we knew who work on early representations of race on the stage but kept receiving the same responses: "I want to contribute, but I already have four deadlines coming up, and I can't give this the care it deserves"; "Thanks for the invite, but I am not taking on new projects due to child care issues"; and the one that aligns most with my own feelings, "The world is on fire; I am finding it hard to care about scholarship right now."

Each of our colleagues who declined signaled, in one way or another, a deficit of care. When the COVID-19 pandemic hit, all aspects of both the academic and theatrical apparatus were turned upside down. The lockdowns and quarantines forced professors, contingent faculty, graduate students, independent scholars, artists, and theatre practitioners to immediately adjust to entirely new lives and ways of teaching, learning, and working while simultaneously grappling with mandates from institutional forces to maintain "business-as-usual" as much as possible. We were supposed to shift from spaces of intimate connection to mediated isolation at the drop of a hat and continue functioning as though every impending second wasn't rife with the risk of death. And even worse, we were supposed to do this within neoliberal institutions in which caring for people is not profitable—and, hence, the labor of doing so is not compensated. So while we in academia and in theatre were expected to care for our students and for our audiences, the institutions' care for us did not extend beyond time-consuming webinars and hollow advice—neither of which helped ease physical and emotional burnout.

We knew that the collision of the worsening climate emergency, the COVID-19 pandemic, and the still-deferred racial reckoning in the aftermath of George Floyd's murder had impacted our colleagues. But, until we started receiving these responses, we had no idea how much. We were now a full year into the pandemic, and the early optimism that the disease might be contained had deteriorated into a slow burn of exhaustion, anguish, and collective rage. Between lockdowns and curfews and travel bans and cancellations, people in academia and in theatre had become isolated from one another not only physically but also emotionally and intellectually. And while many organizations made valiant efforts to continue to provide times and spaces for collaboration and exchange, as the months dragged on, these opportunities became chores:. "I want to see this, but I can't handle another Zoom meeting," became the unofficial motto of the newly virtual teacher.

Well, we heard our colleagues, listened to their exhaustion and concern, and made a pivot. We moved away from the traditional ethos of academic editing as gatekeeping and asked ourselves these questions: How can we use this issue to care for our colleagues who are on the brink of exhaustion in a world on the brink of collapse? From here, we formulated a series of questions that would guide our new editorial approach: What if, instead of having the authors serve the venue, we made the venue serve the authors? What would editing an academic journal look like if peer review were defined as a form of fostering—of care—and not as an opportunity for dismissal? What does it mean to care in neoliberal institutions that treat workers as fungible commodities, and how can we subvert these institutions by incorporating the uncompensated labor of care into the practices for which the apparatus does pay?

These are big questions, and to fully solve these problems would require a revolution that cannot occur within these pages. Recognizing this, however, does not mean we cannot offer methods and practices for delivering, within the standard operating procedures of academia and theatre, small morsels of love and care that feed the humanity and empower the spirit of those trying to move beyond survival and find ways to thrive.

And that is what we decided to do with this section.

With these questions as our guiding principles, we began an entirely new approach. First, I crafted a new call for papers, this time focused on care. The aim of this second call was to allow the authors the freedom to explore and express their thoughts rather than restricting their output to a narrow topic.

The call was designed to serve authors in six specific ways that a typical call for papers does not. First, it is structured as an invitation. While many calls will use the phrase "we invite contributions," this phrase signals an open cattle call for submissions, not a targeted recognition that the editors value individual contributors and their voices. This call instead shows the authors that we are familiar with their work and care about what they have to say. Second, we didn't invite contributors to submit papers but rather asked authors to contribute to a discussion. This small turn of phrase makes any engagement that we as editors have with contributors a conversation and not a judgment. It also removes the pressure of writing in a voice that conforms to the racial-, gender-, and class-coded standards of scholarly writing and, in so doing, can defang the work. Third, we removed any restrictions on form, allowing authors to submit work that challenged or completely eschewed the traditional scholarly essay form. This freedom of form shows contributors that we are serious about reexamining and remaking the ways in which academia functions. Fourth, we allowed for submissions that are much shorter than the traditional journal article to accommo-

INTRODUCTION TO THE SPECIAL SECTION

date people's lives and current capacities. Fifth, we assured the authors that the peer-review process would be designed to move the piece to publication, not disqualify it from publication. Part of this step is to remove anonymity from the process: each reviewer agreed to work with the contributors directly to discuss the submitted work. Sixth, and most importantly, we assured the contributors that their voices, if they chose to contribute, would be shared in the journal. We did our best to craft the call for papers in a way that showed our potential contributors we cared, both about them and about their work.

Did this small practice in care have an impact? We can't say for certain, but reframing our editing practice as one of care certainly produced a positive experience for us as editors. The interactions were warm and generous—there was no tension or frustration, only sincerity and love. What follows is the result of allowing the academic editing process to account for the lives, voices, and humanity of those contributing as opposed to just their careers and their academic fields.

Matthieu didn't take full credit above, but the pivot to "care" was his brainchild. It never would have occurred to me. I would have continued trying to solicit traditional academic essays. In fact, that's precisely what I did (and I appreciate Cen Liu and Daniel Ruppel for their efforts in the limited time we had). But Matthieu's vision proved compelling and, indeed, practical. The section he envisioned has come to pass, and I've been surprised and moved reading the profound essays the contributors offer to artists, activists, and scholars. Under the circumstances, care was what we could—and apparently *should*—have been meditating on.

As our original CFP struggled to attract submissions to match the enthusiasm that accompanied the announcement, I began to wonder at the disjuncture. Four aspects of contemporary life for those who teach or stage early modern drama became starkly apparent: the dearth of time and research support facing an increasingly precarious faculty, the increasing quantitative analysis of scholarship as *output* for those lucky enough to make it to tenure-stream positions, the renewed desire for more diversity in all aspects of theatre (from playwrights and performers to directors, designers, and crew), and the sudden hunger for race scholarship in medieval and early modern European studies. The contributors address the first three ably; I'll tackle the last, since it determined the scope of this section.

Looking at job advertisements in the last four or five years, one would surmise that English studies suddenly *cares* about the study of racial formations from the fall of Rome to the rise of Napoleon. People insufficiently moved by any number of prior extrajudicial murders of unarmed people certainly seemed newly restlesss after the brazenly public murders of George Floyd and Ahmaud Arbery and the midnight seige on Breonna Taylor's home. The flurry of initiatives and invitations that followed stem from altruistic intentions, to be sure. The field now called premodern critical race studies (PCRS) is being summoned to offer explanations for centuries of violence and exploitation. Yet, some of these requests come from institutions without much prior relationship to—and, therefore, little practical knowledge of—the capacities of the scholars who make up the field.

Premodern critical race studies was unable to earn legitimacy at first, launching (and relaunching) with major publications in 1965, 1987, or 1995, depending on whom you ask. In those decades and since, the academic guild did not sow enough scholars to produce the harvest of race scholarship, pedagogy, and programming it would now like to reap. While some venues have indeed devoted time and resources, benign neglect and outright antagonism toward premodern critical race scholarship still reign in other spaces. Indeed, the very summer after the murders of Arbery, Taylor, and Floyd (an incomplete list, to be sure), a lengthy essay appeared that ends by positing scholars of race in premodernity as unwitting Orientalists who see the past as merely an underdeveloped version of the present.[2] It strains credulity to argue that attempts to fill the lacunae of colonizers' self-serving account of when they began to engage in racism are themselves a form of cultural imperialism. Yet, this essay was published to the surprise of the community of scholars who could have been consulted to challenge mischaracterizations and sharpen the argument—and to some positive response on social media from those outside PCRS. As I write, monographs by skeptics are under review at presses and a journal article just appeared that erroneously refers to the entire board of RaceB4Race as "junior scholars who did not have a forum for their work at national conferences." The author of that essay hopes to restore premodern race scholarship to "just proportions" by correcting its alleged tendency to "[reinforce] the bloated signification of race in the present, and thus . . . [lend] unwitting support to its regimes of truth."[3] In short, the backlash is underway, even at the moment when some speculate that the only new hires cost-conscious deans will approve in premodern fields will be race scholars.

If race scholarship serves as a target for some, it has another value for its well-wishers. Alongside the backlash, there has been an increased desire to include race scholarship among the variety of premodern approaches. It now ap-

INTRODUCTION TO THE SPECIAL SECTION

pears that every subfield in premodern studies would like a race contribution. Long deprived and disrespected, premodern race scholars are suddenly invited, like Shylock, to dine. But have we been invited to sup or to be consumed? Kind as they are, the invitations indicate a hunger that those of us trained to do the work cannot satisfy—at least not while producing work that advances the field by engaging questions of core importance. We can produce scholarship that confronts historical and theoretical tangles within the field—scholarship that also, therefore, confronts the political and ethical problems of the fraught present in which we work—or scholarship that turns the work of the field into digestible shibboleths that can be dished up to fulfill the lunch rush. Given those alternatives, I am glad that the initial forum Matthieu and I proposed could not find work that was ready to order.

The professors, graduate students, and adjunct faculty whom we hoped would contribute to our special section simply could not. They were tapped out. Our editorial transition to something more feasible reminded me that nothing—not brilliant ideas, profound sympathies, or the editors' minoritized identities—can override limitations on the capacities of people who are overextended or undersupported. Only the patience to develop an ongoing, accountable relationship will bring about a lasting restructuring, such that we don't have to keep reissuing these calls to *diversify*, *decolonize*, and so on every time the (unjust) status quo, normally tolerated, reappears in the harsh light of truth.

If there isn't enough scholarship to harvest this season, the time is ripe to sow the field. However, it must be understood: the (re)emergent fields of critical race, queer, disability, trans, and asexuality studies were not created to satisfy hunger for a sampler plate. The only way to increase the likelihood of attracting contributors from these subfields is to sustain an abundance of people working in them and critical approaches to the work. If journals, presses, academic institutions, and libraries *do* foster an uncapped number of scholars whose work stems from different locations and critical traditions, then the forum Matthieu and I envisioned—and so many other projects—will bloom with work that fulfills and even exceeds the critical agenda we set out.

In the meantime, we have a remarkable constellation of essays for the Care section. The contributions range from the personal to the theoretical and the lyrical to the historical. Yet, all the while, they keep a sharp focus on care as a material reality, not simply proper feelings. While neoliberal workplaces, including universities, were imposing a standardized version of care, these essays elude conformity and interchangeability. They embrace the anecdotal, the private, and the fragmentary as precisely the means to confront the isolation of this time. Although we offer no grand theory of care, the editors hope that the rich particulars of these essays can help chart new constellations, new formations of both theory and activism. When a frame coalesces prematurely or rigidifies, it becomes impossible to see injuries that do not accord with its own grand theory. Perhaps, from the shards of singular explanations shattered by events, we can begin to assemble provisional frames, kaleidoscopes, mirrors, scalpels: a cornucopia of tools and insights for the years ahead in which the only certainties are change, trouble, and human potential to face and survive them. One of the great surprises of this process was that even "care" itself did not emerge as the single solution at this moment. The essays that follow historicize and problematize care as much as they revise and redeploy it.

Robert Yates begins the collection with an essay in a recognizable scholarly form that nevertheless pursues a new genealogy of "care." Rather than simply celebrating the term, Yates revisits *The Tempest* to inform us that "care" can be mobilized as a *tool* of imperial patriarchy, the lament of a burdened white authority who feels unappreciated by the social subordinates in his care (and at his service). Jessica N. Pabón-Colón points to precisely this "carewashing"—a term she takes from *The Care Manifesto*—to identify ways in which the dominant attempt to legitimize their power by presenting themselves as caring. Pabón-Colón's meditation on organizing at her university pairs well with that of Katherine Gillen. Each contribution emphasizes keen political analysis, transformative vision, and fierce solidarity in the face of institutional aggression. Rejecting the false hierarchy that would subordinate the local to the universal, these two essays show that the local is a site where world-historical forces converge in a particular way. The activist academic must be attuned both to the specific inequalities within academia's social world and to the academy's relationship to the broader society (the local manifestation of which is often called "town/gown"). Rather than an object of mere theorizing, Pabón-Colón and Gillen show that academic care is about forging an ongoing relationship around a commitment that must remain open to revision and renegotiation.

Academic fields that confront the vulnerable body and the climate crisis undergird many of the essays in this suite, but it figures most prominently in the essays by Catherine Peckinpaugh Vrtis and Sherrice Mojgani, who envision theatre programs reformed by "access intimacy" and "emergent strategy," respectively. Vrtis argues that the almost universal experience of this pandemic as a time of enforced debility offers the time to implement "access intimacy," a term articulated in crip/disability theory to describe the goal of ensuring access, whether the impediments to it arise in disability or another vector of oppression. Mojgani imports "emergent strategy" from Black speculative fiction to re-

INTRODUCTION TO THE SPECIAL SECTION

negotiate relationships between part and system in ways that are responsive to change and move toward a just and equitable distribution of resources. These essays are particularly instructive in their applications for academic theatre.

Kara Raphaeli argues that the options of "male," "female," and "decline to state" in universities' demographic surveys and enrollment software operate as a method of violently erasing the presence of trans people to reinforce cisgender heteronormativity. As such, they argue that within a neoliberal capitalist society, care for one's gender interacts with market forces and is utilized only when profitable. Shane Wood's essay also engages with the idea of care as a mode of profiteering and challenges the notion by offering how he transformed the mediated space of the Zoom classroom into a space of caring and trauma-recognition to push back against the emotional detachment applauded by academia.

From a different angle, Kelly advocates that theatres turn their attention away from presenting likable characters. He argues that the nebulous criterion of likability perpetuates a conservative notion of propriety, thus inhibiting the capacity to stage progressive theatre that might contribute momentary glimpses of other possible worlds. Extending that imaginative work, Murillo lyrically traces a genealogy of Afropessimism's structural analysis of an uncaring world to Black feminist theory and praxis, which offer both healing and an eagle-eyed vision of a world constructed otherwise.

In their different modes and from their disparate premises, these essays converge not only in their content but, as Matthieu said, in the spirit in which they were offered. It is indeed true that the mode and content of scholarship, as well as the process used to create it, require rethinking in the face of a planet on the brink. However, this reconception does not entail any sacrifice of rigor: in fact, it demonstrates rigor as honesty, precision, and usefulness not oriented first toward capital accumulation. Rejecting care as a sentiment without action behind it—as well as uninformed resistance—these essays offer some of the essentials that are so desperately needed for thoughtful, creative, and effective action in the face of nationalists who would destroy the earth rather than have to live without the assurances of excess property, pleasure, or protection that the rest of us have been without during the modern era. If there will be a world to come, it will be because we manifest the ethical vision of essays such as these.

Notes

1. Readers may recognize this formulation as a blend of the discussions of materiality and ritual in two texts: Erika T. Lin, *Shakespeare and the Materiality of Performance* (New

York: Palgrave Macmillan, 2012); Karen E. Fields and Barbara J. Fields, *Racecraft: The Soul of Inequality in American Life* (New York: Verso, 2012).
2. Vanita Seth, "The Origins of Racism: A Critique of the History of Ideas," *History and Theory* 59, no. 3 (September 2020): 366–68.
3. Feisal G. Mohamed, "On Race and Historicism: A Polemic in Three Turns," *ELH* 89, no. 2 (June 2022): 377, 378, 379.

"Humane Care"

The Rhetoric of Premodern Care in *The Tempest*

—ROBERT O. YATES

Care is a flexible term that encompasses relations between self, other, and environment.[1] Etymologically, care links to notions of concern, trouble, pain, and action as well as those of love, nurture, and safety. The Oxford English Dictionary indicates that in the fifteenth and sixteenth centuries, "care" functioned as a noun and as a verb to express weighty passion. As a verb, "care" might mean "to feel concern (great or little), be concerned, trouble oneself, feel interest." As a noun, "care" suggests a spectrum of heavy feelings: on the one hand, it might reference "mental suffering, sorrow, grief, trouble"; on the other hand, it is "serious or grave mental attention; the charging of the mind with anything." Care also appears in moments of great loss and might facilitate pause and reflection or, like modern understandings of anxiety, might conjure up the "mental attention" necessary to avoid disaster by acting quickly. Additionally, it can mean "charge" or "oversight" with the intent to protect, preserve, or guide people or things.[2]

Why Premodern Care Studies?

I propose that care is an affective expression—a passion connecting kin, companions, and adversaries—that deserves closer attention because it can enhance our understanding of how early moderns imagined the interdependence of home and state governance. These intersections of home and state governance demonstrate that power operates through performances of care on the early modern stage. I argue that care relations reveal hierarchies of power across lines of race, class, gender, and ability in a world in which every character needs care, and many characters are obliged or forced to perform care in *The Tempest*.

Early modern English literary language around care frequently establishes relations of governance and ownership, which will matter to readers and scholars of early modern literature, particularly those concerned about colonialism and the study of premodern racial formation, as well as to those interested in the importance of liberatory forms of care in the present. The evidence I offer from William Shakespeare's *The Tempest* "presents and represents" care to make legible subjects across lines of race, gender, and class who might be turned into enslaved objects, if they have the potential to be Blackened.[3] *The Tempest* as a theatrical performance transforms the lexical uses of care into a form of what Karen E. Fields and Barbara J. Fields call "racecraft"—the sleight of hand and tongue work that imposes a racial logic on bodies despite the illogic of race itself.[4] By tracing one of care's genealogies, I invite us to think about the ways in which hierarchical understandings of care become so well-rehearsed as to continue down to the present day.

Lisa Lowe's "History Hesitant" offers a generative framework for considering what such a reading of *The Tempest* and care offers us in the history of the now of care. Lowe proposes that "to account for differentiated yet simultaneous colonial histories and modalities," we must think "differently—politically, historically, and ethically—about the important asymmetries of contact, encounter, convergence, and solidarity."[5] For Lowe, "intimacy" is a keyword. Intimacy conjures associations of bodies, individually and corporately, that are always-already political and feeling. Through this rubric, I read the care relations between Prospero, Miranda, Ferdinand, and Caliban to demonstrate that "care" in *The Tempest* shows some of the lasting effects of the asymmetrical nature of the colonial encounter, which is important in light of scholarship aimed at identifying dispersed agency within the specific historical context of hierarchical early modern England. I ask to what extent can the subordinates of the play challenge Prospero's rule through an analysis of care in *The Tempest*.[6]

Prospero('s) Cares

In *The Tempest*, the paterfamilias cares the most. Prospero speaks three of the seven instances of "care" in *The Tempest*—all three utterances occur in act 1, scene 2. He addresses Miranda with the first two—"I have done nothing but in care of thee" (1.2.19) and then "Here in this island we arrived, and here / Have

I, thy schoolmaster, made thee more profit / Than other princes can, that have more time / For vainer hours and tutors not so careful" (1.2.208). The third he directs to Caliban—"I have used thee / Filth as thou art, with humane care, and lodged thee / In mine own cell" (1.2.415). Prospero's cares reveal an important set of relational dynamics between Prospero, Miranda, and Caliban as a household unit containing sexual and racial anxieties, resonant with contemporary analysis of care.

Consider the preposition "of" in Prospero's characteristic: "I have done nothing but in care of thee." In a special issue of *Pedagogy*, Jay Dolmage and Alison Hobgood query the formulations "caring about," "caring of," "caring for" bodies because of the way such language either creates or sustains oppressive hierarchical relations between the care giver and the one receiving care.[7] Dolmage and Hobgood cite Foucault's "The Hermeneutics of the Subject," in which "care of the self [is] a certain way of considering things, of behaving in the world, undertaking actions, and having relations with other people." The authors suggest that an "ethical orientation towards others, could be useful for disability studies and for retheorizing care," arguing that formulations such as "caring from and caring through" level the hierarchy, by accepting that all bodies are in fact frail and will ultimately become disabled. Prospero's famous colonial "orientation" toward others stands against this "liberating disability politic," as Prospero's care renders him a full person and his subordinates as something lesser.[8]

Care becomes Prospero's central rhetorical strategy to enforce his dominance over the behaviors and even feelings of others to maintain his desired social order. Act 1, scene 2 establishes the play's plot through Miranda's witness of Prospero's power vis-à-vis the tempest he conjures. She says, "If by your art, my dearest father, you have / Put the wild waters in this roar, allay them" (1.2.1–2). Miranda is interceding on behalf of the strangers by seeking their well-being— what we might call a form of good care—but Prospero appears unconcerned with those on the ship. "I have done nothing but in care of thee" (1.2.19), he responds, implicitly arguing that even if he has caused harm (to others) everything has been in service of Miranda.

For Prospero, care requires attention and can be applied to only a limited circle. Indeed, as the scene proceeds, he claims he is Miranda's provider and protector, arguing that she really doesn't need to meet any other men—she has just exclaimed that she wishes she could see Gonzalo, the man who provisioned them in their distress—because Prospero has "made thee more profit" than other princes or princesses, who have more time for vain pursuits and who have less-caring tutors (1.2.208). The passage's rhetoric warrants closer examination:

> Now I arise.
> Sit still, and hear the last of our sea-sorrow.
> Here in this island we arrived, and here,
> Have I, thy schoolmaster, made thee more profit
> Than other princes can, that have more time
> For vainer hours, and tutors not so careful. (1.2.203–8)

Prospero narrates his actions—he stands!—and then he proceeds to make meaning of Miranda's experience on the island. Prospero elides any opportunity for Miranda to express her experience of the island and asserts his own dominance in the name of care. Because of her father's care, Miranda has not wasted time with "vain pursuits." Since he has served as schoolmaster, careless tutors have not impeded her learning. The conclusion? Miranda should not worry about knowing any other man but Prospero. Care, for him, is both an action and an affect that he possesses in excess, which—from his perspective—warrants the obedience of others, especially his daughter and slave.

Prospero's strategic invocation of "care" to encourage submission recurs in his relationship with Caliban, his slave. Before Caliban arrives on the stage, he figures as both a villain and a "profit" to Prospero and Miranda:

> MIRANDA: 'Tis a villain, sir,
> I do not love to look on.
> PROSPERO: But, as 'tis,
> We cannot miss him. He does make our fire,
> Fetch in our wood, and serves in offices
> That profit us. (1.2.370–76)

Notably, "profit" links Caliban and Miranda in terms of their use for Prospero—both produce and are of value to the lord of the island. Prospero indicates Caliban's value not only by directly declaring it but also through his invocation of care. Prospero uses the language of care and instructs Miranda to perform care in the form of education to Caliban, even if she does not "love to look on" him. Unlike contemporary notions of caring for bodies as sources of value production in the commercial market, and certainly unlike Foucault's notion of the "care of the self," care for Miranda rests in tension with her dislike of Caliban's appearance. As Prospero verbally abuses Caliban, he utters the third instance of care in the scene:

> PROSPERO: Thou most lying slave,
> Whom stripes may move, not kindness. I have used thee,

Filth as thou art, with humane care, and lodged thee
In mine own cell till thou didst seek to violate
The honor of my child. (1.2.411–18)

Given the violence of these lines—"lying slave," "stripes may move thee," and so on—what does "humane care" mean? It seems unlikely that Prospero speaks tongue in cheek. His rhetoric up to this point in the scene is direct, reflecting Prospero's confidence in his own sovereignty. Nonetheless, the lines' juxtaposition of expressions of violence and anger with the phrase "humane care" reveals a sovereign liberty that Prospero feels confident to exercise.

"Humane care" is Prospero's mastery of Caliban as the ruler of the home. Furthermore, "lodged thee" underscores Prospero's self-assurance of his ability to rule over others. Similar but not the same as with Miranda, Prospero "cares" for Caliban by covering him with shelter, which for Prospero warrants Caliban's gratitude, given that he is "filth," a word associated with dirt or soot. On the early modern stage, the transferability of filth such as soot and coal, as Morwenna Carr has demonstrated, "mimics their use in rhetoric to carry or enhance notions of race as connected with devilry, miscegenation, threat, and dangerously shifting identity."[9] Caliban, therefore, presents problems for the home's material and racial "cleanliness" or whiteness despite receiving Prospero's "humane care."

Caliban indicates an awareness of Prospero and Miranda's dislike of the sight of his "filth," indicating his knowledge of the discord between Prospero's disdain and "humane care." The first line Caliban speaks, for instance, is, "There's wood enough within" (1.2.314), which is ironic on a few fronts. First, Caliban's line expresses a desire to get out of Prospero's home. The home for Caliban is one of oppression and servitude. Miranda's severe language—"'Tis a villain . . . / I do not love to look on" (1.2.308–9)—suggests that she and her father do not receive much pleasure from the sight of Caliban, underscoring the dislike and even fear of what his "filth" might do to dirty them. And yet, their household requires Caliban's labor (1.2.310–14). Caliban's first line, however, reveals the porousness of the home—he is literally outside of it as he enters the scene and wishes to remain so. The porousness of the home, the ability of members to travel in and out of it, produces a need for Prospero to contain all necessary members of the home while also managing them. In the case of Prospero, he must manage Caliban's filth, which could spread to Miranda.

Such a reading of care informs another way of understanding an effect of Prospero's accusation that Caliban has attempted to touch Miranda. From Prospero's perspective, he has incorporated Caliban as a slave into his home;

thus, he has cared for Caliban. With this knowledge, Caliban should be grateful and more obedient like the ephemeral Ariel. Nonetheless, Prospero finds himself surrounded by what Frances Dolan calls dangerous familiars.[10] This domestic scene appears to be the source of his exasperation and repetition of the word "care." His daughter's sexuality and assumed fertility must be managed, as well as his slave's labor, sexuality, and race. Caliban immediately responds to Prospero's accusation of attempting intimacy with Miranda by exclaiming:

Would't had been done!
Thou didst prevent me; I had peopled else
This isle with Calibans. (1.2.347)

In one reading, Caliban possesses the desire and ability to become a paterfamilias and sovereign. Shift the view slightly and Caliban acknowledges Prospero's fears of blackening. Sexual relationships, Carr argues, serve as a "site of potential colour transfer, and familial and female 'discoloration' becomes a violent threat."[11] Caliban by his Blackness and virility, and Miranda by her sexual openness could ruin Prospero's family line. Prospero cannot permit their coupling, because preserving the racial purity of his line is central to his goal of returning to his previous status as Duke. Caliban's lines illustrate how the role of father might slide into the role of sovereign: the island would be "peopled" with Calibans. To prevent this future, Prospero persuades (or compels) his subordinates to follow his orders and trust his care of all domestic, political, and personal matters.

By siring children with Miranda, Caliban would produce people known as Calibans—a name that suggests that he would rule the island as father-sovereign. Prospero intervenes to prevent this future. The comic scene of act 2, scene 2 confirms Prospero's repeated claim that Caliban is naturally unfit for such a role. When Caliban meets Trinculo and Stefano, Caliban, believing that the men "dropped from heaven," almost immediately submits to them. Caliban ironically "kisses the Book" of Stefano, which, unlike Prospero's magic book, is a bottle of liquor. The scene ends with an intoxicated Caliban singing, "'Ban, 'Ban, Ca-Caliban / Has a new master: get a new man" (2.2.174–75). At this point in the play, Caliban, as Melissa Sanchez has demonstrated, rejects the role of subject to Prospero by becoming the subject of Trinculo and Stefano.[12]

Although Caliban understands that he is now under the service of Trinculo and Stefano, Prospero does not view Caliban as such. At the end of the masque in act 4, scene 1, Prospero remembers that Caliban plots against him and proceeds to reincorporate Caliban under his control:

CARE IN *THE TEMPEST*

PROSPERO: I had forgot that foul conspiracy
Of the beast Caliban and his confederates
Against my life. (4.1.139–41)

"Confederates," according to *The Oxford English Dictionary*, suggests mutuality, and it can refer to a person or a state.[13] How then does Caliban as beast align in some form of mutual alliance with Stefano and Trinculo? Does this make all three confederates beasts? The phrase "foul conspiracy" casts Caliban as a potential insurgent. A conspiracy might imply that Caliban is not a stupid beast but a cunning one with the potential to usurp Prospero. Prospero attempts to resolve this ambiguity by invoking Caliban's "filth." The magus does not know how to account for Caliban: he is a slave, beast, and political opponent. Prospero's provision of shelter for Caliban produces a dangerous familiar—a threat within the home. Another inflection of care contains the danger: Prospero is also able to subordinate Caliban by referencing his care of him.

The Tempest in its overall use of "care" suggests a deep meditation on the relationship between sovereignty and an ability to supply care, sometimes in ways—unlike most of the examples presented so far—that are, put simply, life-preserving and life-giving. As I've demonstrated, Prospero needs the household of Miranda and Caliban to regain his title as Duke, and he uses the language of "care" to establish those household social bonds and to produce a hierarchy that preserves his sovereignty. This is not the only instance of *The Tempest* asking its viewer to consider the relationship between care and sovereignty. Within the first ten lines of *The Tempest*, Alonso cries "Good Boatswain, have care. Where's the Master? / Play the men!" (1.1.9–10). The king of Naples, drenched by a treacherous tempest, seeks to motivate the sailors by telling them to "have care." The boatswain—the sovereign of the ship—responds with a shout, "When the sea is. Hence! What cares these roarers / for the name of king?" (1.1.15–16). "King" as a position of sovereign power and authority is rarely merely a name in this context. For a play presented in the honor of the marriage of King James's child—a literal instance of securing power through dynastic marriage—*The Tempest* titillates its audience as it flattens "king" to a "name." The effect, of course, is twofold: immediately, it offers an explanation to Alonso and the others of why the men of the ship will not "have care" in their duty as sailors during a deadly storm. The boatswain is sovereign over the ship's passengers, and, therefore, *cares for* all on board. "Have care" reveals Alonso's lack of power in his relationship with the boatswain in the context of a ship sailing through a storm. As Alonso, Antonio, and Gonzalo all begin adding to the noise, the boatswain in a fit of exasperation announces: "What cares / these roarers for the name of king? To cabin! /

Silence! Trouble us not" (1.1.15–18). In other words, the boatswain might feel and act with all the care possible for his crew and passengers, but that would be irrelevant, since the storm—or so it seems—is the absolute sovereign in this scene of man, kings, and nature. The rhetoric of care from this perspective indicates the frailty of human life while simultaneously clarifying social hierarchies. And, crucially, care distributes social responsibilities and accountabilities in particular situations. It's like an improvisational readjustment or renegotiation of the social hierarchy. The boatswain here, not the king, has more power over life and death. His care is an expression of his (temporary, improvisational) power but also a claim on his responsibility to those dependent on him. "Care" illuminates the social/political structure itself: the king has more power/privileges, but also an obligation to care for his people—the greater power gives him the ability to take care of his people. We see this principle shifted to the boatswain in this very specific situation—he has the greater ability/authority and duty to protect his dependents.

Indirectly but no less importantly, however, the line proves Prospero's claim to his sovereign title. Indeed, as a wielder of magic books, able to control the storm, Prospero seems superhuman and thereby unquestionably sovereign. He does not need the "name of king" to elicit the care of others; he proves his kingly power. He possesses the power to enforce the care of others, including Miranda and Caliban, as well as the language to shape Caliban, Miranda, and Ferdinand into their subject positions. In the final act, Stefano, drunk but now free from Ariel's charm, utters,

> STEFANO: Every man shift for all the rest, and let no man take care for himself; for all is but fortune. Coraggio, bully monster, coraggio! (5.1.259–61)

In an ironic reversal of "every man for himself," Stefano suggests that all men should "shift"—a nautical term that conjures images of rowing—for each other and not to care for oneself. Yet, Stefano's vision of mutual aid in a world shaped by fortune does not prevail. Instead, *The Tempest* offers a rather bleak picture of care, a practice intertwined with the head of house and state managing borders through the process of racialization.

Notes

1. In feminist philosophy, see Nel Noddings's *Caring: A Relational Approach to Ethics and Moral Education* (Berkeley: University of California Press, 2013). Also, see Jean Keller

and Eva Feder Kittay's "Feminist Ethics of Care" in *The Routledge Companion to Feminist Philosophy*, ed. Ann Garry et al. (Abingdon-on-Thames, UK: Routledge, 2017). Keller and Kittay, influential feminist philosophers, trace the development of care ethics since it was first articulated by Nel Noddings. Keller and Kittay highlight the growing importance of the "political and global dimensions of care" in this article. From a cultural studies angle, see Duke University Press's "Care in Uncertain Times Syllabus" (2020), Duke University Press (website), accessed April 17, 2023. Feminist philosopher Nel Noddings, the first to coin the phrase "ethics of care," argues for care as a feminine ethics counter to male prioritization of abstracted moral deliberation in Enlightenment and post-Enlightenment thought. Care, for Noddings, is a series of choices that form bodily experience and knowledge. As Talia Schaffer in *Communities of Care: The Social Ethics of Care in Victorian Fiction* (2021) writes, "care is an action, not a feeling." Such theories of care draw important distinctions between care feelings and care actions while noting that although they are "intimately intertwined, they are not the same, and we can't always predict which will produce the other" (8).

2. "care, v." *Oxford English Dictionary*. Oxford University Press, OED (website), accessed March 9, 2021.

3. Erika T. Lin, in *Shakespeare and the Materiality of Performance* (New York: Palgrave Macmillan, 2012), writes, "Interlocking puzzle pieces, representation and presentation are mutually constitutive citational practices that, taken together, impact the cultural attitudes and practices that give rise to the particular specificities of their relationship in the first place. Performance, then, 'materializes' (in Butler's sense of the term) in two spheres at once: it cites particular cultural discourses related to specific semiotic transformations occurring within a play, and it cites affective and experiential dimensions of social life in its presentational effects" (8–9).

4. Karen E. Fields and Barbara J. Fields, *Racecraft: The Soul of Inequality in American Life* (New York: Verso Books, 2012), introduction.

5. Lisa Lowe, "History Hesitant," *Social Text* 33, no. 4 (125) (December 1, 2015): 85–107, 90.

6. I cite parenthetically from William Shakespeare's *The Tempest* in *The Norton Shakespeare*, edited by Stephen Greenblatt (New York: Norton, 2016).

7. Dolmage and Allison P. Hobgood, "An Afterword: Thinking Through Care," *Pedagogy* 15, no. 3 (2015): 559–67, 563.

8. See especially: Kim F. Hall, *Things of Darkness: Economies of Race and Gender in Early Modern England* (Ithaca, NY: Cornell University Press, 1995); Frances E. Dolan, *Dangerous Familiars: Representations of Domestic Crime in England, 1550–1700* (Ithaca, NY: Cornell University Press, 1994); Melissa E. Sanchez, "Seduction and Service in 'The Tempest,'" *Studies in Philology* 105, no. 1 (Chapel Hill: University of North Carolina Press, Winter 2008): 50–82; Edward Said, *Orientalism* (New York: Pantheon, 1978); Stephen Orgel, "Prospero's Wife," in *Rewriting the Renaissance: The Discourses of Sexual Difference in Early Modern Europe*, ed. Margaret W. Ferguson et al. (Chicago: Chicago University Press, 1986), 50–64; and Ania Loomba, *Gender, Race, Renaissance Drama* (Manchester, UK: Manchester University Press, 1989).

9. Morwenna Carr, "Material/Blackness: Race and Its Material Reconstructions on the Seventeenth-Century English Stage," *Early Theatre* 20, no. 1 (2017): 91.

10. Frances E. Dolan, *Dangerous Familiars: Representations of Domestic Crime in England, 1550–1700* (Ithaca, NY: Cornell University Press, 1994). Dolan focuses on textual repre-

sentations of subjects—primarily the "murderous wife" and the "rebellious servant"—in moments of domestic violence. *Dangerous Familiars* asserts the importance of domestic subordinates by revealing how legal and literary discourses construct the contradictory and agential subjectivities of the wife and the slave. They must submit to the husband/master of the house "as the foundation of the domestic and civil order" (24); yet, the law not only acknowledges that they might act rebelliously but also provides a method of rebellion by the rubric of "petty treason." The same discourse that insists on the subordination of women and servants also acknowledges they do not "always cooperate" (24). When discussing Caliban, who attempts both high and petty treason against Prospero (62), Dolan claims that "Shakespeare's masterful manipulation of form in *The Tempest* results from his privileging the master's story over the slave's" (70). Caliban functions as a rebellious servant to the extent that we accept Prospero's assertion that Caliban is a bad servant and thereby sidestep "Caliban's construction of Prospero as the betraying father/master and usurper of the island" (64). Dolan acutely notes that as Prospero accuses Caliban of seeking "to violate / The honor of my child" and references "lodging," Prospero subjugates Caliban. But I would like to suggest, however, that the scene's particular invocation of "care"—lodging is an act of care, certainly, but Prospero uses the term itself, which suggests an excess of the idea—produces Caliban as a dangerous familiar and legitimate subject. Prospero's invocation of domestic care relations simultaneously makes him a member of the household—against Caliban's expressed will in act 1, scene 2—as well as a dangerous servant. I suggest that drawing a distinction between these two categories affords a more capacious explanation of Caliban's unfortunate subjectivity in this play.

11. Carr, "Material/Blackness, 88.
12. Melissa E. Sanchez, "Seduction and Service in 'The Tempest,'" *Studies in Philology* 105, no. 1 (Chapel Hill: University of North Carolina Press, Winter 2008): 50–82. Sanchez argues that because women introduce the possibilities of marriage, courtship, and sexual desire, the female figures of *The Tempest* remind us that politics are not reducible to purely rational calculation but driven in large part by desire, fantasy, and identification (52). Sanchez persuasively accounts for the role of the other—the daughter, slave, and servant—in shaping the action of the play. For Sanchez, historical context produces as much doubt as assurance that *The Tempest* aligns to the view that a sovereign king possessed the right to rule and expand dominion.
13. "confederate, adj. and n." *Oxford English Dictionary*. Oxford University Press, OED (website), accessed May 25, 2021. "A person or state in league with another or others for mutual support or joint action; an ally."

"Not *Another* Essay on Care Work in Academia!"

—JESSICA N. PABÓN-COLÓN

"they really do. not. care."
—LEIGH DODSON, 2022

I want my title to be a call to action for my fellow minoritized academic care workers: let's *not* write *another* essay explaining our oppression to our oppressors. But like all performative utterances, the call takes on a life of its own and I find myself writing against my own desires. I'm a forty-two-year-old first-generation academic; a tenured professor of women's, gender, and sexuality studies; a diasporic, white-bodied Puerto Rican; a mother who often takes care of her disabled mother; a spouse; a survivor of childhood sexual assault and intimate partner violence living with PTSD; a bisexual cisgender woman who grew up working-class and is now employed by a state university where I am paid to read, write, think, create, and share knowledge. I found feminism within the walls of academia and committed myself to sharing the liberationist perspective I was privileged to receive through my higher education. A tenured position within an academic institution was supposed to be my happy ending.[1] Instead, I've spent copious amounts of time and energy healing from pervasive institutional violence and trying to plan an escape.[2] I no longer wish to escape, but I also do not *care* for these institutions as I once did.

As a recovering academic care worker, I am drawn to Sara Ahmed's visualization that diversity work is akin to banging one's head against a brick wall.[3] My understanding of why we keep hitting this brick wall, knowing it will make us bleed, is animated by the late Lauren Berlant's conceptualization of "cruel optimism"—the heartbreak experienced when we are betrayed by the "objects or object worlds or forms of life" that we are optimistically attached to.[4] In my experience, no matter how often or how hard we hit the wall as academic care workers in the neoliberal university, the wall does not move. It will not move. It was not built to move. For me, accepting that reality has been a pathway to healing from the trauma of repeated blunt force to the head. Here, I use the example of a community of academic care workers that I built at the State University of New York at New Paltz (SUNY New Paltz) to consider how our collective capacity to care is appropriated and (ab)used under the neoliberal university's newfound commitment to diversity, equity, and inclusion in a (not quite) "post-pandemic" world.

SUNY New Paltz is a public university with a reputation of being a "liberal haven"; this reputation, I would discover after being hired in 2014, regularly obscures a profound culture of white supremacist cisheteropatriarchy. I founded the Women of Color Network in 2016, hoping that we could provide the practical, social, and emotional tools necessary for women of color to thrive at a predominantly white institution. My priority was for self-identified women of color faculty and staff to feel that they belonged in their workplace, to have a space to celebrate successes or share challenges "confidentially," and to just be with one another without the expectation of work. That said, over time we built a reputation for action due to the visibility of our interventions (teach-ins, lectures, and statements calling others to action). I imagined that visibility meant that the network had gained some power and influence, despite being a "free entity" neither funded nor managed by the administration. We performed an immeasurable amount of care work advocating for an anti-racist, anti-sexist campus between 2016 and 2021—work on and in the institution, but not (*I thought*) of or *for* the institution.

Every fall semester, I sent an email to the faculty and staff LISTSERV inviting new members. The last recruitment email I sent announced that we are now called the People of Color Network (POCN), a move that marked our expansion as an activated community that doubled in the wake of the 2020 #BlackLivesMatter summer. As the individual sending our messages to the broader campus community, I am often the target of backlash from colleagues or administrators. I consider it a part of my anti-racist work, using my white-body privilege to absorb some of the institutional and interpersonal violence directed at my Black and Brown colleagues. And though I'm the only woman of color in women's, gender, and sexuality studies at SUNY New Paltz, I have the privilege of departmental support that too many of my POCN colleagues in other areas of the college simply do not have. The POCN is a manifestation of my activism and scholarship, which are both sutured to my capacity to care for my community and my desire to be in good relation with other marginalized peoples and their specific struggles for liberation.[5]

The POCN was built to be what is referred to as a "caring community" in *The Care Manifesto: The Politics of Interdependence.* The queer, feminist, antiracist, eco-socialist members of The Care Collective wrote the manifesto in the early months of the COVID-19 pandemic, arguing that "we are in urgent need of a politics that puts care front and centre," a caring politic that dismantles neoliberalism and embraces "our interdependencies."[6] In the manifesto, they define a caring community as one that is "beyond immediate kinship networks" and is instead based on "mutual support, public space, shared resources and local democracy."[7] While our in-person gatherings certainly offered the space for mutual support, resource sharing, and democratic decision-making, the vast majority of our care work for one another is done on an email LISTSERV that is and is not a public space; you have to be an employee in our system to be added to the LISTSERV by a moderator. Our space is "private" for protection, though this privacy hardly spares us from the bigotry, willful ignorance, and white male entitlement that travels through our inboxes every day. Judging by the touching farewell emails I receive when members leave SUNY New Paltz, the POCN positively impacts members. Perhaps this is because our care work with one another is exchanged in what disability justice activist Leah Lakshmi Piepzna-Samarasinha calls a "fair trade emotional labor economy"—our care for one another is reciprocal, consensual, acknowledged, and appreciated.[8] We practice care abundance, engaging in what The Care Collective refers to as "promiscuous care"—the kind of care rooted in alternative kinship structures that "enable us to *multiply* the number of people we can care for, about and with" within a systematically uncaring university system.[9]

I have always understood the POCN to be a labor of love, but because it was something I made without institutional input or support, I never considered how that labor was work, specifically diversity, equity, and inclusion (DEI) work *for* the neoliberal university. I convinced myself that all that labor was about making our workplace a more hospitable environment for our racialized, feminized, bodies. A—dare I say—"safe" (-ish) place to work and learn.[10] I considered myself lucky that I was able to "choose" university service I was passionate about and proud of, but I understand now that our caring community is tolerated by the institution because our external interventions are appropriated by the university as diversity, equity, and inclusion (DEI) work *for* the university. One recent and prominent example of how our care work is turned into DEI work is the January 15, 2021, "Note from the POCN regarding the Insurrection, Impeachment, and Inauguration Panel." Our note read:

JESSICA N. PABÓN-COLÓN

    We, the people of Color Network for Faculty and Staff, are writing this brief note to express our shock and dismay at the majority white, majority male makeup of the "Insurrection, Impeachment, and Inauguration" panel. We hope that the colleagues who organized this event consider the voices that they have chosen to amplify in the midst of a white nationalist insurrection in the wake of Black Lives Matter summer of 2020. We acknowledge that as a campus community this is an important conversation to have, but firmly believe that an effort needs to be made to include multiple voices and perspectives, to engage staff on these panels who represent non-white centric lived experiences.

    In particular, we believe it is entirely inappropriate to amplify the voice of Gerald Benjamin. It seems the institutional memory of his racism is short and/or there is the assumption that the people of color, and in particular the Black members of our community, were satisfied by his apology. How are we to believe that he will not offer up his opinion about "people like us" once more? Please consider the harm this choice in particular has already caused.

    We recognize our limitations as a predominantly white university. We recognize that some may be hesitant to repeatedly tap the same people of color for this kind of unpaid (often unrecognized) labor. We recognize that we are on the verge of a new semester, still in a pandemic, and that we are all working our best despite the lack of time, energy, and focus during this unprecedented time.

    We also recognize that as a community, **SUNY New Paltz simply must do better**.

    In collegiality,

    POCN[11]

The note was a result of our collective frustration; we felt that *something* "had" to be done. The panel organizers—two white women moving forward with the approval of their dean, also a white woman—responded to our note by: adding one woman of color to the panel (a member of the POCN who consented after collective discussion), closing the WebEx chat function during the panel, attempting to shame us for calling Benjamin out by name, and essentially locking down any further resistance. Our note set off a series of backlash emails followed by meetings with the administration, a BIPOC community check-in (prompting a new wave of backlash) and *one* "restorative justice" circle facilitated by our chief diversity officer with only the dean and I in attendance.[12] Eight months of uncompensated, emotionally taxing, thankless care work that cost some of us professional and personal relationships—done for *nothing*.

    In their 2021 essay "Housekeeping: Labor in the Pandemic University," Rebecca Herzig and Banu Subramaniam focus on care work in the "pandemic university," calling us to consider how "caring has assumed new status" and why "the affective work of academe [. . . has moved] front and center."[13] They use the term "housekeeping" as shorthand for the "invisibilized, undercompensated, and utterly indispensable labor" that is care work.[14] "In the pandemic university," they argue, "labor is merely extracted even more efficiently and surreptitiously via the sentimental imperatives of love and commitment."[15] Despite our intentions, the POCN has acted and been treated as "housekeeper"—expected to routinely clean up the institution's anti-diversity, anti-equity, anti-inclusion mess. The university *takes* our care work without returning care to us; it's an exploitative and abusive relationship. "To be clear, what 'caring community' does not mean is using people's spare time to plug the caring gaps left wide open by neoliberalism."[16] When we act as a collective, caring members of the POCN are "volunteered" to plug those gaps for the institution. "Advice for how to rectify these inequities, echoing the victim-blaming bromides delivered to overwhelmed housewives, often is reduced to individual behavioral modification, as when 'senior female professors' are encouraged to 'model self-restraint' for untenured faculty members by 'learning how to say 'no.'"[17] I've been told to stop caring *so much* because enactments of white supremacist cisheteropatriarchy at my university are "not my problem to solve"—as if caring about the learning and working conditions of minoritized students, faculty, and staff is something to be avoided, as if individual preservation is the answer to systemic oppression. Academic care workers have described this feeling as "burnout," but that word doesn't hold the correct entities accountable for the burn. The phrase "burnt out" implies that individuals have hurt themselves by doing too much, by caring *too much*. The ubiquity of the sentiment leaves the institution free to continue caring *too little*. If our institution truly *cared* for and about minoritized faculty and staff, we wouldn't have needed to form the POCN as a salve for the daily burn.

In fall 2021, my mental health plummeted. The university demanded that we all go back to work face-to-face, unvaccinated children and immunocompromised loved ones be damned. To receive administrative permission to teach remotely, I engaged in a months-long battle with human resources, my United University Professions union representatives (UUP), the ADA office, my therapist, and my doctor. There was rigorous discussion among members of the POCN and the UUP as to why the administration thought the ADA office was the appropriate one for handling remote teaching requests when the large majority of those asking *were not doing so because of a disability* (which is not to say they are not disabled), but because they wanted to avoid contracting COVID-19 in the classroom. In my case, as a person with invisible disabilities, the language of accommodation here is complex. I live with anxiety and depression, but that's not why I needed to teach online. I feared contracting COVID-19 and giving it to my then unvaccinated child and my disabled immunocompromised mother, but that was not what triggered my alternating states of panic, anxiety, and depression. In a stunning performance of institutional ableism, the university forced everyone who wanted to teach remotely to disclose our disabilities (an indignity regularly experienced by disabled people), as if their demand that we go back into poorly ventilated buildings with windows that don't open wasn't itself the disabling condition.[18] That semester, I cried—a lot. In (online) class. In (remote) meetings. And as a cursory look at how many women and people of color took to our campus-wide faculty and staff LISTSERV with harrowing personal stories of loss and anxiety proves, I was not alone. I went into a dangerous depressive mental state that made the most basic of executive functioning impossible on most days. I was simply unable to metabolize any more *uncaring* from my employer. I was disabled *by* the institution claiming to care. Despite repeated calls by members of the communities most impacted by COVID-19, it was crystal clear that the university truly *did not care* about those of us suffering from the racial and gender disparities of and in the pandemic.[19] Like many others, I received no accommodation. I refused their suggestions to use my sick days (I wasn't sick!) or use FMLA (I wanted to work, just from home) and instead exercised my tenure privilege and taught online, adding another source of anxiety as I am the primary source of income and health insurance for my family. And though I love my career in academia, all I could do was focus on leaving.

Early in the pandemic, SUNY New Paltz adopted a "We Not Me" slogan. For some, the "we" may be obvious, but I am still wondering: "We" who? Who is this sentiment meant for? The same semester many of us were unsuccessfully battling the administration and desperately requesting to teach online to keep our families safe, SUNY New Paltz announced a new *online* bachelor's degree in general studies. The financial effects of the pandemic exacerbated our institution's pre-pandemic multimillion-dollar budget crisis, so the move was clearly profit-driven, though it is marketed as though it was designed specifically because they *care* about "underserved population[s] in our society."[20] Meanwhile, faculty continued to receive emails threatening disciplinary action should we teach remotely without permission. The administration went so far as to develop various mechanisms for students to report disobedient faculty. Without any change in our working conditions (beyond the temporary mask mandates), "We Not Me" is just a carewashed directive meant to extract from our individual affective capacities for institutional financial gain.[21] The term "carewashing" appears in *The Care Manifesto* to describe "corporations trying to increase their legitimacy by presenting themselves as socially responsible 'citizens,' while really contributing to inequality and ecological destruction [. . . and capitalizing] on the very care crisis they have helped to create." "We Not Me" is now positioned as "essential" work at SUNY New Paltz, but we know what happens to essential workers in a racial capitalist economy: the essential worker is always-already the disposable one.

In 2018, the POCN and our accomplices invited Dr. Dana Cloud to campus to address the right-wing idea that free speech is under threat on college campuses by "leftist" demands for safe spaces and political correctness.[22] In her lecture, she stated that "making campus safe for capitalism, requires making campuses safe for white supremacy."[23] The POCN is situated within a neoliberal institution that *will not* become anti-capitalist and therefore will not become anti-racist, anti-sexist, or anti-ableist for that matter. The institution is not going to change. So we must change. We are the uncared-for "citizens" of the neoliberal university, the ones whose well-being is sacrificed to the demands of the capitalist world order. The burden of care work is not on the institution but instead on individual workers who are expected to be "endlessly resilient."[24] We are done being resilient. I am done being resilient. I will no longer care *for* the university.

University care *takes*—institutions of higher education claim to *care*, but they *take* our care. The university extracts care labor from feminized, minoritized workers—uses us like plugs—and when our staying power fades they replace us with new plugs (read: new faculty, new staff). Where we place the emphasis matters. When the social-institutional expectation is that we will care, perhaps the real care work is refusing to caretake on behalf of a university that has no intentions of caring for us. I titled this essay "Not *Another* Essay on Care Work in Academia!" because we—those most affected—have been sounding the alarm on the issues of racism, sexism, classism, and ableism in/for academia for decades—perhaps for as many decades as we've been granted access to academic institutions.[25] It is a cruel optimism indeed that we continue to do the majority of the academic housekeeping, knowing that a lifetime of institutional abuse kills women of color in the academy. It's not that I don't want to read another essay on care work in academia, I just don't want us to have to write them anymore.

Notes

Epigraph. Leigh Dodson, "They Really Do.Not.Care.," text with Jessica N. Pabón-Colón, March 21, 2022.
    1.   Sara Ahmed, *The Promise of Happiness* (Durham, NC: Duke University Press, 2010).

JESSICA N. PABÓN-COLÓN

2. Lorgia García Peña, *Community as Rebellion: A Syllabus for Surviving Academia as a Woman of Color* (Haymarket Books, 2022), 10–12.
3. Sara Ahmed, *On Being Included: Racism and Diversity in Institutional Life* (Durham, NC: Duke University Press, 2012), 26.
4. Paul Rand, "Why Chasing the Good Life Is Holding Us Back, with Lauren Berlant," November 4, 2019, *Big Brains* (Podcast), *University of Chicago News*.
5. Sarah Nickel and Amanda Fehr, *In Good Relation: History, Gender, and Kinship in Indigenous Feminisms* (Winnipeg: University of Manitoba Press, 2020), 2.
6. Andreas Chatzidakis et al., *The Care Manifesto: The Politics of Interdependence* (Verso Books, 2020), 5.
7. Chatzidakis et al., *The Care Manifesto*, 47, 46.
8. Leah Lakshmi Piepzna-Samarasinha, *Care Work: Dreaming Disability Justice* (Vancouver, BC: Arsenal Pulp Press, 2019), 144–48.
9. adrienne maree brown, *Emergent Strategy: Shaping Change, Changing Worlds* (Chico, CA: AK Press, 2017); Chatzidakis et al., *The Care Manifesto*, 33–34.
10. When serving on the university's DEI council, I was told that at SUNY New Paltz we practice "brave spaces." And while the rhetoric of safe spaces is itself an object of queer feminist critique (see Hanhardt 2013), the notion that people of color need to be brave in spaces of knowledge production centers the fragility of white campus members. Historically underrepresented people in academia can't "choose" to be brave in spaces built to perpetuate our destruction; we are "brave" under duress and never by choice. Christina B. Hanhardt, *Safe Space: Gay Neighborhood History and the Politics of Violence* (Durham, NC: Duke University Press, 2013).
11. For more background on the Gerald Benjamin reference, see Teghan Simonton, "A College Administrator Told 'The New York Times,' Rap Is Not 'Real Music.' His President Called the Comment Disappointing," *Chronicle of Higher Education* (website) July 18, 2018; accessed April 17, 2023.
12. Jessica N. Pabón-Colón, "On White people Upholding a Culture of White Supremacy at SUNY New Paltz . . . ," *Jessica Nydia Pabón, PhD* (blog), April 28, 2021; accessed April 17, 2023.
13. Rebecca Herzig and Banu Subramaniam, "Housekeeping: Labor in the Pandemic University," *Feminist Studies* 47, no. 3 (2021): 503–17, 504.
14. Herzig and Subramaniam, "Housekeeping," 503–4.
15. Herzig and Subramaniam, "Housekeeping," 504.
16. Chatzidakis et al., *The Care Manifesto*, 11–12.
17. Herzig and Subramaniam, "Housekeeping," 514–15.
18. I don't have the space here to fully explain this aspect at length, but it seems that the university situated our requests to be cared for as ADA accommodations in order to make it that much easier to bury the denials in a pile of "status quo" denials of accommodations to disabled folks.
19. Bob Brigham, "New Study Shows White Americans Cared Less about COVID Once They Learned It Was Hurting Minorities Even More," *Raw Story* (website), March 30, 2022; accessed April 17, 2023.
20. "Bachelor of Arts: General Studies," State University of New York at New Paltz (website), accessed April 17, 2023. The full paragraph reads "This new General Studies program provides a flexible, high-quality educational opportunity for an underserved population in

our society: former college students, often working adults, for whom a residential, on-campus experience is not a realistic option."

21. Chatzidakis et al., *The Care Manifesto*, 11–12.
22. For transparency, her lecture was one of a three-part series funded by the university president's office after our public intervention (and proposal-writing labor).
23. Dana Cloud, "Responding to the Right on Campus as Social Movement: Putting Struggles Over 'Free Speech' and 'Academic Freedom' in Historical and Material Context" (Whose Free Speech Speaker Series, SUNY New Paltz, February 22, 2018), SUNY New Paltz's Mediasite (website), accessed April 17, 2023.
24. Chatzidakis et al., *The Care Manifesto*, 12.
25. Sami Schalk and Jina B. Kim, "Integrating Race, Transforming Feminist Disability Studies," *Signs: Journal of Women in Culture and Society* 46, no. 1 (September 1, 2020): 31–55.

Responding to Crises of Racial Capitalism with Care and Resistance

—KATHERINE GILLEN

In the summer of 2020, the Texas Legislature passed laws prohibiting educators in public schools from teaching the full history of systemic racism and its social impact in the United States. In October 2021, Texas State Representative Matt Krause circulated a list of books, mostly addressing race, gender, and sexuality, that he wanted removed from public schools. Bills have been introduced in the 2023 legislative session seeking both to revoke tenure from the state's faculty and to ban critical race theory and diversity, equity, and inclusion (DEI) policies. In February 2022, Lieutenant Governor Dan Patrick expressed his desire to revoke tenure from faculty who teach critical race theory. Shortly thereafter, Governor Greg Abbott issued a directive criminalizing parents who seek gender-affirming care for transgender children, encouraging doctors, social workers, and teachers to report on their trans students and their parents. These recent events are simply the latest in a line of injustices in Texas, including the incarceration of migrants and family separation at the border, the criminalization of abortion after six weeks, and restrictions on voting rights. As many activists have pointed out, Texas is witnessing a backlash against the Black Lives Matter movement as well as struggles for the rights of immigrants and LGBTQ2IA+ people. Much of this backlash has been targeted at educational spaces, particularly after Mexican American studies and African American studies were integrated into the high school curriculum. All of this has come amid the COVID pandemic, which has disproportionately affected Black, Latinx, and Indigenous communities and which Texas politicians have exacerbated through their hostility to mask and vaccine mandates. Educators of all levels, therefore, have struggled during these overlapping crises while at the same time justifying the value of our profession and our disciplines.

In 2018, faculty in the Language, Literature, and Arts Department at Texas A&M University–San Antonio, which I currently chair, committed to building an interdisciplinary department that is responsive and accountable to our community on the Southside of San Antonio and that, therefore, centers anti-racist and decolonial approaches. A Hispanic-Serving Institution (HSI), our university is situated on or near the ranchlands of the former missions San Francisco de la Espada and San Antonio de Valero (the Alamo). Many of our students, approximately 80 percent of whom identify as Latinx, are descended from the Indigenous peoples that have long lived in the region, including from Payayan and Coahuiltecan communities. On our campus and in our city, histories of colonization and white supremacy are palpable, lived realities. As Gina Ann García argues, "coloniality of power is what plagues HSIs, inhibiting their ability to fully serve Raza students from enrollment through graduation."[1] García calls, therefore, for HSIs to ground their work in decolonization "for the empowerment and liberation of racially minoritized students."[2] As my colleagues and I began to revise our curriculum and pedagogies to align with decolonial imperatives, we quickly recognized that we would need to address administrative structures, as well.[3] We simultaneously found that doing such work required a multipronged approach if we were to improve access, redistribute resources extracted from minoritized communities, mitigate systemic and intersectional inequities among faculty, and protect ourselves from blowback and forces of reaction, both within and beyond the university.

The pandemic and intensifying racist, anti-immigrant, and heteropatriarchal violence in Texas has compelled us to deepen these commitments and to prioritize care work in our efforts. The pandemic has underscored Ruth Wilson Gilmore's point that systemic racism involves "the state-sanctioned and/or extralegal production and exploitation of group-differentiated vulnerability to premature death," limiting access not only to resources and power but also to life itself.[4] The sense that Black, Brown, queer, trans, and disabled lives are disposable is a hallmark of "corona capitalism," a term that Marc Lamont Hill uses to describe "how centuries of racial capitalism and decades of neoliberal economic policy not only created the conditions for the COVID-19 pandemic but also informed our legal, economic, medical, ecological, cultural, and social responses to it."[5] For these reasons, COVID has devastated our community, with its most acute effects felt in Black and Mexican American areas of San Antonio. According to a recent report by the *San Antonio Express News*, residents of the 78224 zip code, which is home to Texas A&M University–San Antonio, were sixteen times more likely to die from COVID than residents in the zip code on the north side of the city, where the University of Texas at San Antonio is located.[6] In 2020, the San Antonio City Council declared racism a public health crisis, recognizing inequities and discrimination within the health care system as well as the health disparities that result from the city's history of segregation and redlining.

Like most universities, our courses moved online during the Spring semester of 2020, but in-person classes quickly resumed as the pandemic wore on, under pressure from the state and the Texas A&M University System to return to business as usual. The return to campus seemed dangerous to many of us, especially as Governor Abbott worked to make mask mandates illegal at public institutions. Many of our students, faculty, and staff—already affected by racialized health disparities—had conditions that put them at greater risk of severe illness or death from COVID. Many members of our campus community hold jobs as frontline workers; many live in multigenerational households; and many serve as caregivers for unvaccinated children or for immunocompromised or elderly family members. At convocation in Fall 2020, we learned that eleven students had died since the start of the pandemic.

Resisting this politics of disposability necessitated an ethic of care that recognizes ourselves, our colleagues, our students, their families, and our communities as invaluable. Our department, therefore, pushed back against the statewide effort to return to in-person classes, insisting that we see one another as more than consumers or laborers who could be sacrificed in the pursuit of tuition dollars. Our advocacy was often public facing, as it included an open letter in August 2020 to the A&M University System that garnered nearly one thousand signatures as well as appearances by faculty on the local news. But we also found that we needed more direct ways of protecting ourselves and each other when the university refused to. Internally, we worked to ensure that faculty who were uncomfortable returning to campus could teach online—without demanding that they document their personal vulnerabilities or caregiving situations. We also sought, though often informally, to account for the care work we were doing ourselves, especially as many of our faculty members were caring for young children who could not safely attend school or daycare. As Angela Davis writes in *Freedom Is a Constant Struggle*, "we have to encourage that sense of community particularly at a time when neoliberalism attempts to force people to think of themselves only in individual terms and not in collective terms. It is in collectives that we find reservoirs of hope and optimism."[7]

These pandemic experiences sharpened our resolve to rethink business as usual within our department and to center care in our anti-racist work. This effort is ongoing and has taken several forms. We have, for example, developed a process by which we can pool and distribute our professional development funds more equitably and communally, in ways that ensure that those with lower salaries and less institutional power can access resources they need to meet their professional goals. Along similar lines, we are establishing nonhierarchical modes of assigning offices and summer teaching opportunities, seeking alternatives to the traditional prioritization of the longest-serving or highest-ranking faculty members. For us, it has been important to include non-tenure-track faculty in our governance structure and to recognize the many ways in which systemic inequities shape faculty status. In so doing, we refuse the meritocratic logics that obscure these inequities and take small steps toward harm reduction. Fundamental to this work is reconceptualizing faculty evaluation in order to resist the white-centric standards of the academy and to account for the intertwined labor of care and resistance. How can we account for the additional labor undertaken by Black, Indigenous, and Latinx faculty to mentor BIPOC students? For the labor of caring for families and communities, often with little support? For the work of establishing anti-racist approaches to academic administration, instruction, and evaluation? For the advocacy work of faculty members with visible Senate and AAUP roles? And how do we account for the toll taken by the backlash inevitably provoked by this work, as it challenges the instrumentalist and racist modes of relationality fostered by the neoliberal university?

As a white faculty member and department chair working in this context, I draw from social movements that privilege care in the abolition of unjust systems. As Bettina L. Love explains, care is central to "the practice of working in solidarity with communities of color."[8] An abolitionist approach to teaching, she suggests, encompasses elements of "mattering, surviving, resisting, thriving, healing, imagining, freedom, love, and joy," especially for those who are often treated as disposable.[9] In decolonizing aspects of the university system that are harmful, abolitionist perspectives demand replacing the risks to life named by Gilmore with sustaining care. I have also learned a great deal from the disability justice movement. In her book *Care Work: Dreaming Disability Justice*, activist Leah Lakshmi Piepzna-Samarasinha enumerates the ways in which care work has been devalued precisely because it is typically performed by those most oppressed within the hierarchies of racial capitalism, and she recommends that we look to BIPOC, queer, trans, and disabled communities in our efforts to reconceptualize care and to acknowledge the "next-level genius of skill" shown by care workers.[10] As state systems fail, Piepzna-Samarasinha suggests, "we have the opportunity to dream and keep dreaming ways to build emergent, resilient webs of care."[11] Such models can guide efforts to foster an ethic of care, mutual aid, and resistance within neoliberal academic institutions that rely on the personal investments of workers but are ultimately accountable not to students, faculty, or communities but to state legislatures and private donors.

Our department still has much work to do, and it remains to be seen whether our efforts can be sustained within the current political climate and in the neoliberal university. As we strive to mitigate harm and foster communities of care, though, we can look to long histories of mutual aid and care work in Black, Latinx, and Indigenous communities and in communities of disabled, queer, and trans folks. Examples of this work abound in our communities. During the 2021 Texas ice storm, which turned deadly because of price gouging and because energy companies had not weatherized the power grids, people expanded networks of care to share resources. In response to the recent ban on abortion, reproductive rights activists have been providing underground abortion care as well as other forms of medical care, often drawing on Indigenous and womanist healing practices. Teachers and parents are forming educational collectives to provide the culturally sustaining education not available in schools, even as they advocate for public schools to better serve community needs. While our department is not, and cannot be, an activist organization, we can learn from communities that have long resisted the violences of racial capitalism and settler colonialism to create spaces in which to care for one another.

Notes

1. Gina Ann García, "Decolonizing Hispanic-Serving Institutions: A Framework for Organizing," *Journal of Hispanic Higher Education* 17, no. 2 (2018): 133.
2. García, "Decolonizing Hispanic-Serving Institutions," 133.
3. For more on our curricular and pedagogical efforts, see Jackson Ayres, Katherine Bridgman, Scott Gage, Katherine Gillen, and Lizbett Tinoco, "Toward Decolonization: Integrating the English Studies Curriculum at Texas A&M University–San Antonio," *ADE Bulletin* (forthcoming); Lizbett Tinoco, Sonya Barrera Eddy, and Scott Gage, "Developing an Antiracist, Decolonial Program to Serve Students in a Socially Just Manner: Program Profile of the FYC Program at Texas A&M University-San Antonio," *Composition Forum* 44 (2020); Lizbett Tinoco, Scott Gage, Ann Bliss, Christen Barron, Petra Baruca, and Curt Meyer, "Openings, Risks, and Antiracist Futures: Labor-Based Contract Grading at a Hispanic-Serving Institution," *Journal of Writing Assessment* 13, no. 2 (2020); and Katherine Gillen and Lisa Jennings, "Decolonizing Shakespeare? Toward an Antiracist, Culturally Sustaining Praxis," *Sundial*, November 26, 2019.
4. Ruth Wilson Gilmore, *Golden Gulag: Prisons, Surplus, Crisis, and Opposition in Globalizing California* (Berkeley: University of California Press, 2007), 247.

5. Marc Lamont Hill, *We Still Here: Pandemic, Policing, Protest, and Possibility*, ed. Frank Barat (Chicago: Haymarket Books, 2020), 21.
6. Laura Garcia, "A Broken System Got Worse: How COVID Ravaged San Antonio's South Side," *USC Annenberg Center for Health Journalism*, April 20, 2022.
7. Angela Davis, *Freedom Is a Constant Struggle* (Chicago: Haymarket Books, 2016), 49.
8. Bettina L. Love, *We Want to Do More Than Survive: Abolitionist Teaching and the Pursuit of Educational Freedom* (Boston: Beacon Press, 2019), 2.
9. Love, *We Want to Do More Than Survive*, 2.
10. Leah Lakshmi Piepzna-Samarasinha, *Care Work: Dreaming Disability Justice* (Vancouver: Arsenal Pulp Press, 2018), 141.
11. Piepzna-Samarasinha, *Care Work*, 35.

Access Intimacy as a Philosophy of Care in Post-Pandemic Academic Theatre

—CATHERINE PECKINPAUGH VRTIS

Among disabled and chronically ill communities, one observation has been repeated since March 2020: COVID time is crip time on a mass scale. The capitalist regimentation of time, which Michel Foucault places at the heart of the disciplinary project, has gracelessly given way to the reality of pandemic and its manifold disruptions to what Elizabeth Freeman calls "chrononormativity."[1] Crip time, for those who have not previously had bodily betrayal forcibly restructure their lives, is a flexible term, encompassing all the ways that debility defies scheduling, from the devastating—years lost to surgeries, brain fog, and pain—to the liberatory and even inspiring, as the rhythms of life and work are reshaped to the needs of people instead of the authority of clock and calendar. The slow process of learning to live in, and even embrace, crip time is often a lonely one, part of the broader isolation that comes with failing to perform "wellness" as expected. The experience of the coronavirus shutdown is different, in that it has been collective; it's a shared trauma granting empathic solidarity in spite of physical distancing. We, who have been living in crip time since before the slow realization of crisis overtook the world two years ago, have been sharing our hard-won knowledge of managing quarantine, skills of maintaining relationships virtually, and mastery of equipment and programs designed to allow access when working from home. Unfortunately, as the broader population looks forward to getting "back to normal," the crips, the mad, the disabled, and the otherwise debilitated are once more being left behind.

As an example of this phenomenon, consider the shift to online work from home. To maintain productivity, corporations and academic institutions have suddenly found that the necessary accommodations, previously considered impossible when requested by disabled workers, are in fact both highly effective and easily implemented. However, too many institutions are already—still deep in the pandemic—demanding a return to in-person work regardless of actual need so that those who can only work online from home are once more being forced out of employment for no reason other than bias toward normative models of labor. This broad rejection of the lessons in crip wisdom forced by the pandemic is incredibly harmful. It is not, however, inevitable. This ongoing moment of pandemic time provides the perfect opportunity to completely rethink the exclusionary cultural norms of the twenty-first-century United States—and to embrace the radical inclusivity of access intimacy as a philosophy for increasing interpersonal, academic, and professional care in post-pandemic life.

Crip theorist Mia Mingus devised the term "access intimacy" to describe the specific experience of having one's needs met in a way that is affirming of the dignity and humanity of the disabled individual. As she explains in the 2011 blog post that first describes the experience, "access intimacy is that elusive, hard to describe feeling when someone else 'gets' your access needs. The kind of eerie comfort that your disabled self feels with someone on a purely access level." Access intimacy provides a deep sense of welcome into a shared community, in sharp contrast to the degrading experience of merely being tolerated in a space. Per Mingus: "Access intimacy is not just the action of access or 'helping' someone. We have all experienced access that has left us feeling like a burden, violated or just plain shitty. Many of us have experienced obligatory access where there is no intimacy, just a stoic counting down of the seconds until it is over. This is not access intimacy."[2] Expanding on Mingus's writing on the topic, Desiree Valentine explains, "Access intimacy centers recognition of the *impact* of inaccessible environments on disabled (and non-disabled) people and the norm of abled-existence, instead of taking access *achievement* as its main goal."[3] As a philosophy of care, access intimacy shifts the labor of inclusion away from the formerly excluded individual and onto the individual or collective to be joined.

While originally defined in terms of the experience of disability, access intimacy provides a language and a philosophy for creating full inclusion for all participants, in which all aspects of their bodyminds are supported and all needs, whether from experience due to marginalization or minoritization of identities or individual characteristics, are met. Mingus, who self-identifies as "a queer, physically disabled, transracial and transnational Korean adoptee raised in the Caribbean," expanded on the multivalent anti-oppression and pro-justice potential of access intimacy during her Paul K. Longmore Lecture on Disability Studies on April 11, 2017:[4]

Disabled people get told we must shrink ourselves and our desires to settle for living in the wake of an able bodied parade. And especially if we are part of other oppressed communities, we are expected to be grateful for whatever crumbs are thrown our way . . .

Queer people of color to-be-parents want to spend hours talking about how they will support their will-be children to explore their genders and sexualities outside of binaries, but when I ask them how they will support their child if they are or become disabled the conversation abruptly stops or I am told I am being "negative." Or Asian, Korean or Korean adoptee communities don't make their gatherings accessible and then I am asked, "why aren't you more connected to those communities?" Or disabled communities who have no interest in talking about race, sexuality or gender and respond with hostility that you are being divisive when you explain that you cannot separate your disability from your other identities . . .[5]

In contrast to the painful, isolating experience of this balkanized approach to identity, justice, and inclusion, access intimacy offers a holistic model of mutual access and support. As Valentine explains:

Fundamentally, I propose that access is not a practical and isolated thing or event. It is not about what one person or institution can do for another person but involves an ongoing, interpersonal process of relating and taking responsibility for our inevitable encroachment on each other. At base, access intimacy invites attention to our fundamental intersubjectivity, our inherent vulnerability, and the asymmetries of power in any relationship. Beginning from these assumptions, the question of whether access needs are met cannot fully be answered via attempts at equalizing or accommodating (though these are nonetheless necessary elements of access in our present moment). It must be answered through the development of individual and collective (re)orientations, ways of being responsive to our primary interdependence.[6]

By embracing this understanding of access, academic theatres can move away from the official university committee model of checking off equity and inclusion for each kind of diversity, instead embracing a fluid, individually focused, and multivalent approach to ensuring the program provides for the unique matrix of needs held by each student—and each faculty and staff member.

The access intimacy model is particularly relevant given the high degree of intimacy involved in both education and performance and the fact that both the theatre and academia have historically been particularly hostile to temporal and other forms of flexibility in labor. Colleges and universities are rigidly scheduled from the ground up; Freeman and Ellen Samuels, writing together, note, "As academics, we knew that our lives were structured by time as a vector of power, from minutiae, such as class schedules, through annual reviews and milestones, such as merit steps and promotions, through the larger temporal systems that govern invisibly."[7] The theatre, meanwhile, is known for its unforgiving schedule. Performers are not paid for the hours spent attending auditions and memorizing lines, and paid work days can be as long as ten hours out of twelve during technical rehearsals. Technicians work even longer hours, with tech rehearsal work blocks lasting twelve hours out of fourteen, with only eight hours of "turnaround time" from the moment work ends to when it begins again—and these already exhausting hours can be extended further into what technicians call "golden time," when pay is doubled. No other consequences are levied for productions that make these demands. Of course, these rules apply only to union productions, and nonunion show scheduling can be even more arduous. In addition to the long hours, insufficient breaks, and other demands, the performing arts are built around an ideology of hypercapacity and virtuosity that considers disability an intolerable flaw; this is why 95 percent of disabled characters are played by abled performers.[8] When these two fields—both already habitually ableist—intersect, the results are devastating for disabled students and faculty. Physical spaces—the classrooms, stages, shops, and rehearsal halls—are difficult or impossible to access; discrimination is rampant; and, of course, flexibility around student or faculty needs for rest, for extra time to complete work, and for other accommodation, temporal or otherwise, is rarely available.

Sivert Das, writing about his experience as a disabled student at a major Canadian theatre school, found the experience so devastating that the COVID shutdown was a relief: "For me, the pandemic provided an escape from a traumatic and brutal experience: I got to go back to my family in Toronto and have a fresh start. . . . Disabled artists have yet to gain significant space and respect in the performing arts. The abuse that I suffered and the cruelty that disabled artists face in the arts need to be addressed. . . . The people who tortured and abused me continue to perform in their community. . . . There has been no accountability for their actions, and I don't think there ever will be."[9] Das's experience was not atypical, particularly in the school's decision to eliminate his accommodations after his classmates complained, mischaracterizing them as unfair advantage. As in this case, equity efforts are all too often framed as granting "special" privileges rather than accommodating specific needs, the result of a culture that defines "fairness" as "maintaining the advantages of the normative population." Even when accommodations are granted and remain available, the experience of negotiating with disability offices and academic administrators too often results in the degrading experience of being subjected to the barely concealed resentment referenced by Mingus, in sharp contrast to the access intimacy approach. Bureaucratic inconvenience is mapped onto the bodies of disabled students, making their existence a "problem" to be solved, rather than treating accommodation as an opportunity to ensure the highest degree of student success. However, there is no reason for this besides enculturated acclimation to existing power structures.

Access is not a fixed, binary state, either available or not. The ideal of complete inclusion is asymptotically approached yet forever out of reach. It is also an intersectional issue, as issues of race, gender, class, sexuality, language mastery, immigration status, and more all affect students' abilities to participate in the academic structure and social culture of a department. In terms of concrete actions, standard accommodations need to include not just wheelchair access and American Sign Language interpretation but also considering whether our handouts are compatible with screen readers and are in dyslexia friendly fonts, whether deadlines are truly necessary for all assignments, and if required doctors' note policies are creating undue stress for sick students. Access includes picking texts that accurately reflect the makeup of our programs while simultaneously actively recruiting so that BIPOC, disabled, immigrant, and other historically excluded populations are genuinely welcomed into the higher education theatres—and are provided culturally appropriate work to study and perform once matriculated. Providing access intimacy includes proactively offering these accommodations and more, but fundamentally access intimacy as a care philosophy means the humility to respond to our students' evolving needs on a continuing basis; maintaining a respectful and mutually supportive environment that honors all aspects of student identity; and adjusting assignments, courses, and curricula to ensure each individual can fully participate without being treated as disruption, distraction, or burden. It means releasing defensiveness when discovering an overlooked access issue, and never choosing standardization of material or method over individuation.

The bureaucracy of higher education innately pushes for the documentation and individual accommodation model of access, yet by consciously choosing the access intimacy approach, even in conjunction with the standard model, educators can create a safer, more welcoming community for all students. This is particularly valuable in theatre and performance, given the personal risks of creative sharing required in group art making. COVID has brutally revealed that the hard-earned wisdom of the disability experience has value for all people in times of crisis, and as we—hopefully soon—leave this historical moment, we should continue to draw on that knowledge and reject a return to a flawed normal. Access intimacy will make our shops, classrooms, rehearsal halls, and performance spaces all a bit safer and more welcoming for students as we determine the shape of the post-pandemic future. So let's take a moment, while the pandemic still prevents an unthinking return to the normative way of doing things, to create a more equitable future for all the individual bodyminds who make up the current and future academic theatre collective.

Notes

1. Ellen Samuels and Elizabeth Freeman, "Introduction: Crip Temporalities," *South Atlantic Quarterly* 120, no. 2 (April 1, 2021): 245.
2. Mia Mingus, "Access Intimacy: The Missing Link," *Leaving Evidence* (blog), May 5, 2011, accessed March 30, 2022.
3. Desiree Valentine, "Shifting the Weight of Inaccessibility: Access Intimacy as a Critical Phenomenological Ethos," *Puncta: Journal of Critical Phenomenology* 3, no. 2 (2020): 82.
4. Mia Mingus, "About," *Leaving Evidence* (blog), accessed May 23, 2022.
5. Mia Mingus, "Access Intimacy, Interdependence, and Disability Justice," *Leaving Evidence* (blog), April 12, 2017, accessed May 23, 2022.
6. Valentine, "Shifting the Weight of Inaccessibility," 78.
7. Samuels and Freeman, "Introduction," 245.
8. National Disability Theatre (website), "Mission," accessed February 8, 2022.
9. Sivert Das, "Tales from a Disabled Theatre School Grad," *Intermission Magazine* (website), May 21, 2021; accessed February 8, 2022.

There Are No Small Parts, Only Fractals

—SHERRICE MOJGANI

In the winter of 2021, I was teaching an advanced stage management class for undergraduates at George Mason University in northern Virginia. The School of Theater at Mason taught the majority of our courses online during the 2020–2021 school year. I serve as the head of the design/tech area—my primary focus is lighting design, but I also teach courses in collaboration and stage management. We had a number of upper-division students who had served as stage managers on our productions, and we offered this class to serve their need to delve deeper into stage management studies. As part of the course, we read and discussed adrienne maree brown's *Emergent Strategy: Shaping Change, Changing Worlds* as a set of guiding principles for organizing and leading a company through a production. My goal was to present an alternative values structure to the capitalist-based business model lurking only slightly below the surface of the standard "love for the art form."

In the United States, commercial theatre is given the most media attention and our highest awards often correlate with a production's ability to entertain and sell tickets: "good" theatre becomes defined as that which nets the biggest box office receipts, and the goal of entertaining the audience is enshrined as a value. Young folks are then drawn into the industry by the feeling of admiration and attention from the audience. They are taught that that good feeling should outweigh the amount they are paid or the way they are valued, that their only value is in how they contribute to making a production popular, and that this exploitation is justified by their love of the art. This elevation of commercial theatre runs counter to the ideal that we make theatre to contribute to community problem-solving and building our collective empathy. In brown's work, I saw a robust tool kit for exposing and exploring this tension.

In the class, we used the principles of *Emergent Strategy* to ask questions of our current policies and systems in order to reflect on how we might do better and create a more equitable and just rehearsal room. For example, consider the old adage "There are no small parts, only small actors." What does this mean, exactly? To whom does it give power? Why say it? In my experience, I most often hear the phrase in response to an actor complaining about a chorus or ensemble role. It is an attempt to reprimand and silence the actor, to shame them into ceasing to ask questions of authority. It whispers to the actor, "If you weren't being so petty, you wouldn't complain about not having a larger role—you would just be glad to have a part at all!" It blatantly ignores the entire concept of power dynamics. If we hold on to the first part ("There are no small parts") and view it through the lens of *Emergent Strategy* ("Everyone's part is important"), then we might be able to construct a value worth keeping in 2022.

Introduction to *Emergent Strategy*

Emergent Strategy: Shaping Change, Changing Worlds was published by adrienne maree brown in 2017. In the text, we learn from nature's systems how to better organize, survive, and thrive as humans.

There are six elements of *Emergent Strategy*:
Fractal: The relationship between small and large
Adaptative: How we change
Interdependence and Decentralization: Who we are and how we share
Non-linear and Iterative: The pace and pathways of change
Resilience and Transformative Justice: How we recover and transform
Creating more possibilities: How we move toward life[1]

"There are no small parts" aligns most closely with "Fractals." The element of fractals highlights that large organizations are often built on the replication of small relationships. brown says, *"this may be the most important element to understand—that what we practice at the small scale sets the patters for the whole system."*[2] There are also a number of principles of *Emergent Strategy* that are themselves loosely associated with the elements. These are the five that I find most useful when thinking about "there are no small parts:"

- Small is good, small is all.
- There is a conversation in the room that only these people at this moment can have. Find it.
- Never a failure, always a lesson.
- Trust the people.
- What you pay attention to grows.[3]

There Are No Small Parts, Only Fractals

As an exercise, the stage management students and I imagined the following situation and how we would approach it using *Emergent Strategy* as our guide: "You hold a position of power, and you are directing a college production, or perhaps you are the stage manager of the production. A student actor comes up to you after the cast list has been published, and they are upset about their ensemble role."

How can we use this moment to center the element of fractals and focus on building a relationship with an actor? Fractals teach us that what we practice is scalable. That strengthening our relationship with one ensemble member strengthens the bond of the company, as long as we center the needs of the student and approach the interaction with honesty, care, and integrity. We will be using the element of fractals as our guide.

First, I asked my students to consider a question for themselves: do you need the unhappy student in the role? Is it necessary? Do you have work for them to do? Will they learn and grow? If not, maybe it's okay for them to not accept the part. Maybe the director made a mistake and cast too many people.

If yes, start with "Trust the people" and "There is a conversation in the room only these people can have." This student has come to you with a concern; hear their concern as legitimate, understand their grievance, and absorb why they are disappointed in the role. Offer to help them understand why the casting decision was made and what they might do to improve in the future. Recognize that no one likes to tell anyone that they are not "good enough," but they need you to be as honest and transparent as you can be, so work on pushing the limits of what makes you comfortable. Offer to connect them to people who can help answer their question or help them do better. Remind them of "Never a failure, always a lesson." Work with the student to generate an ideal outcome of the experience and ask what support you can give to help them achieve this outcome and further their growth.

Then let them know that you believe that "small is good, small is all" and the ensemble is critically important to the whole production. Follow this up by treating the members of the ensemble with as much respect as you treat your principal actors. And remind yourself that "What you pay attention to grows." You can't know what your investment in care and time with this one student will lead to or how they might improve as an actor, but if you dismiss their concern, it might breed resentment on their part.

The students came out of the exercise with a better understanding of how to apply both the element of fractals and the principles of *Emergent Strategy* to their theatre practice and to the way they move through life. I have found that "There are no small parts, only fractals" is a value that is easy to extend into design, tech, and support roles. It helps inform interactions with board operators and ushers. It helps me stay calm in conversations with the dean or a wealthy donor.

By exploring the hypothetical situation of "There are no small parts" with students, I was able to demonstrate a few things to them. Most importantly, I am willing to change the system to make it better for all of us. Running a low-stakes scenario with people you trust is a great way to practice acting on your values in difficult situations. You can be in a position of power, have your authority questioned, and still use your power for good. And I hope it helps them trust me and learn that they can come to me with their issues—that I will not dismiss them but hear them out and help them work through their challenges.

We are all a part of adjusting the culture of how we care for each other in this industry. Some might say I am not preparing my students to deal with the "real world." But that "real world" is a system that I am actively trying to dismantle; I will not simultaneously prop that system up by "preparing my students" to conform to its harmful pressures. Instead, I choose to teach them how they should be treated and how to seek out employers that are moving forward in our collective work of changing the culture. Even this work with the students is fractal in nature: if we change the culture for our students, they can help us scale it accordingly.

Notes

1. adrienne maree brown, *Emergent Strategy: Shaping Change, Changing Worlds* (Chico, CA: AK Press, 2017), 50.
2. brown, *Emergent Strategy*, 53.
3. brown, *Emergent Strategy*, 41.

Beyond Polite Words

Understanding Trans Erasure and Exploitation in Academe

—KARA RAPHAELI

In November 2018, UC San Diego announced that it would be unveiling a trans-inclusive name option for students on the university's online system. I was excited to be able to set my preferred name on the system so that I would no longer have to see a name that makes me uncomfortable next to each comment I leave on student work on Canvas. But when I logged into the online system, the tool was not there. You see, they rolled the system out for students only. As I was a graduate teaching assistant, the university excluded me from the change, just as they excluded staff and faculty.

I had grown used to institutional neglect, being used by the university to teach undergraduates rather than the university being concerned with my education, mental health, and well-being. But this was the first time that differential treatment, that institutional neglect, was related to my gender. Would there be a phase 2, when graduate teaching assistants, faculty, and staff would also have this gender-inclusive option? There was no indication either way anywhere on the UC San Diego website.

This made me wonder: does the administration think that transness is a youth phenomenon? That these "preferred pronouns" are a teen trend born of Tumblr and Snapchat rather than the articulation of a sense of self found in some form across cultures and over centuries? Or does the modern university view diversity, equity, and inclusion (DEI) work less as an ethical commitment than as a tool for student recruitment and a source of university revenue? One might optimistically assume that the new trans-inclusive IT infrastructure was achieved through student-driven campaigning. But it had little to do with student activism and everything to do with California's Gender Recognition Act coming into effect on January 1, 2019. The law requires all organizations gathering demographic information in California to provide a nonbinary option, in alignment with the X option on state driver's licenses and birth certificates. And so, the university announced this change without specifying that it was being rolled out for students first. It was more than a year later that UC San Diego provided the preferred name and pronoun option for faculty and staff, as well.

I've been on the job market since 2019. In that time, I've submitted 166 applications, which constitute approximately half the advertised positions that I am qualified for. The first thing I do when I see a job posting is research the surrounding environment. If the presence of trans resources and community both on- and off-campus are sufficient to make the university's location seem safe for me and my partner (who is a trans woman and therefore in greater danger of transphobia than I am), then I look into the department and consider if I am a good fit for the position. In one instance, I discovered early on an article about a trans staff member's discrimination lawsuit against the college I was considering. Negative results like these, as well as a dearth of resources on university webpages or evidence of queer presence in the surrounding community, cause me to move on without even researching the department or position. As queer and trans people, our physical safety and mental well-being limit where we can live.

This is old hat for me by now, as is the small act of self-erasure I take part in at the end of nearly all applications: lying about my gender. You see, at the end of each application is the page for the EEO survey—the gathering of information about applicant gender, race, and disability status for the Equal Employment Opportunity Commission (EEOC). How gendered information is collected depends on state law, such that some states require there to be an opt-out option beyond male and female: "I decline to state" or "I prefer not to say." Each time I reach the demographics section of the application, I wonder, "Will there be a 'prefer not to say' option?" All too often there is no such option. Other times, the "prefer not to say" button is available, so I lie and click it. It is a lie for me to claim that I prefer not to state my gender, because I'm dying to state that I am nonbinary—an opportunity that so far only the University of California employment system and Reed College have given me. Recently, Interfolio.com has added an "Other" option, which is perhaps the most literal form of Othering I've encountered in academia.

This might seem like a minor complaint, especially since the demographics survey is a voluntary portion of job applications. Yet the reason it irks me is that the very purpose of gathering demographic data is to better understand the composition of the workforce as well as help the EEOC investigate discrimination charges. When applications allow people to state gender along a triptych of male, female, or decline to state, these categories are trans-exclusionary, rendering those who do not fit into cisnormative categories invisible. Furthermore, when a nonbinary category is not provided, the nonbinary portion of the trans community becomes doubly erased.

This invisibility, as well as that of other historically marginalized groups, functions to reinforce white, able-bodied, cisheteronormative men as the default identity in academia. Those of us who manage to exist within academia must remember that our presence is exploited but not cared for and is tolerated only as long as it remains undisruptive. When the wider community becomes aware of us and the structural oppressions we face, the university engages in DEI work to insulate itself from criticism. As Kalwant Bhopal and Clare Pitkin write in relation to higher education in the UK, the "identification of significant racial inequalities across all parts of university life has become a 'policy issue'; which, in the context of marketised universities competing for students has to be addressed in order that institutions continue to be economically viable."[1] To be sure, DEI can improve our circumstances, just as Title IX can provide recourse for students, staff, and faculty who experience sexual harassment. Yet as tools of human resources, both DEI and Title IX are self-protective, not self-reflexive; the university cannot undo systemic oppressions, because it is invested in and dependent on capitalism, white supremacy, and patriarchy.

Do universities place the same institutional barriers on prospective students? Of course! Trans students face significant structural oppression, but they are less likely to experience erasure through the EOO survey, as many universities use the Common App, which provides options for preferred pronoun and identifies "sex" as "legal sex" for the sake of trans students—a distinction that allows more visibility but bears its own complications; the laws governing legally changing sex designation vary by state, with some states requiring no medical certifications, others requiring proof of surgical interventions and/or amended birth certificates, and only twenty-one states providing the X gender option.[2]

The irony is that while many universities increasingly position themselves as accepting of and friendly toward trans students, in part through encouraging self-identification in the admissions process, by failing to support trans faculty, including job seekers and new hires, they diminish the amount of care and support available to those students. Despite infrastructural changes like preferred name and pronoun IT systems, the work of supporting trans students almost inevitably falls first and foremost on friendly faculty, especially trans faculty. In 2014, I came out as nonbinary within my department and started using they/

them pronouns in the classroom. While that choice was due to my personal desire to live authentically in all areas of my life, another result was that I provided a safe space for the trans and gender nonconforming students in my courses. I have had several students privately come out to me as trans and/or nonbinary before being ready to be out more publicly. When the university makes a career in academia oppressive to trans scholars, there are fewer visibly out trans faculty, leaving trans students more isolated.

Trans scholars generally endure more precarious economic circumstances than cis scholars. Many are trapped cycling between adjunct positions. The isolation of being contingent faculty is compounded by the isolation of transness in a cisnormative scholastic environment, and the lack of inclusivity in faculty application processes is a continual challenge to escaping adjuncting and finding a secure position within the academy.[3]

If universities want to be serious about trans inclusivity in their communities, they need to support us rather than exploit us. A few first steps would be: include an expansive list of genders on their applications regardless of the state requirements for their EOO demographic surveys (the Common App can serve as a model for how to do this); allow name changes on all internal records, student ID cards, and diplomas regardless of legal name change; provide easy to understand instructions for name changes on the university website; provide trans-focused DEI training to all faculty in leadership positions and for staff employed in admissions, the registrar's office, residential life, student health, and campus facilities; and provide a map of all the campus's gender-inclusive bathrooms on the university website. These reforms are the bare minimum universities should enact; they would lessen, not end, trans oppression in academia. A more radical approach to trans inclusivity would require critical examination of cisnormativity, sexism, racism, and ableism within the university; trans people often have multiple marginalized identities. But until the neoliberal university receives greater incentives from a capitalist structure, universities will continue to engage in performative DEI reforms that may or may not offer any real-world benefits to us.

Notes

1. Kalwant Bhopal and Clare Pitkin, "'Same Old Story, Just a Different Policy': Race and Policy Making in Higher Education in the UK." *Race Ethnicity and Education* 23, no. 4 (2020): 530–47.

2. National Center for Transgender Equality (website), "ID Documents Center," February 2023; accessed April 17, 2023.
3. Nicolazzo, Z., Kristen A. Renn, and Stephen John Quayle, *Trans* in College: Transgender Students' Strategies for Navigating Campus Life and the Institutional Politics of Inclusion* (Sterling, VA: Stylus Publishing, 2017).

A Path Out of the Desert: Enduring and Educating in the Time of COVID

—SHANE WOOD

After the events of the last two-plus years, few can say that they walk a trail free of ghosts—ghosts of family and friends, of careers, of selves past and projected. We are collectively living through a process of trauma and loss while being expected to continue with life as if we aren't in the midst of a global event that will have countless pages dedicated to it in the works of future historians. To compound this dissonance is the uncanny lived experience of trying to navigate two paths at once: the best laid plans of isolation, social distancing, and masking alongside the mass media narratives and capitalist forces declaring business as usual through repeated waves of infection. The system that repeatedly shows us it doesn't care about us bombards us with messages of self-care as a remedy for the daily horrors we've endured, partially due to their actions and inaction. But within this new world of trauma and dissonance, self-care becomes yet another responsibility laid at the feet of our already overwhelmed bodies. COVID-19 has brought with it increased instances of both acute and prolonged grief, further exacerbated since COVID has interrupted the grieving rituals that might bring closure. For over two years now, people have been unable to participate in funerary rituals without risk to those still alive. We've found ourselves isolated and working for employers that could not and would not acknowledge the increased personal and professional pressure the pandemic put on us. Those in fields such as education and medicine were asked—and often ordered—to give more of their time, to be more flexible and understanding, and to further delay their own processing of grief and trauma in order to serve a society that repeatedly failed to recognize their need for protection. This ultimately resulted in increased burnout and many leaving the professions, which further compounded the strain put on those remaining.[1]

While grief has a negative connotation in American society, it creates opportunities to seek resolution and salvation from the traumatizing events. After the initial trauma, one still has to contend with the loss that has occurred because of it. This loss can be material in the form of people, jobs, money, homes, or it can be existential as in losing a sense of self with all of the devastation that one witnessed. Acknowledgment of this loss comes in the form of grief. Bruno Latour described grief as a desert in which people learn how to "seek and foster new humanities."[2] This desert is vast, and once humans enter it, we are bound to get lost. As scholars Casper and Wertheimer theorize, "trauma as a mode of being violently halts the flow of time, fractures the self, and punctures memory, and language." But while navigating the loss brought about by trauma, people can also find what they are looking for. The desert blends social reality and imagination to help people face their trauma, open their world, voice out pain, mend fences, and heal.

Over the course of several lockdowns, many of us were isolated in our homes and forced into new lives free from anything deemed inessential. As one lockdown led to another and another, our isolation created moments of both suffering and solace as we navigated this new, almost fully mediated, world. As public spaces became off-limits, our screens became our sole source of nourishment, work, community, and entertainment. We were alone together, processing and adapting through this cultural trauma. In the technology-assisted bubbles, we built oases that allowed us to shut out the horrors of the pandemic-ravaged world outside. If we were not one of the "essential workers" forced to continue working in the midst of this disease, we could begin to convince ourselves that things were settling into a new normal. We could believe this was something we could survive and learn to live with. However, when we peered from our oases, we saw that we were not safe from the trauma; we were only coping, by distracting ourselves from it. Many of us were working so hard to distract from the trauma we were experiencing that we didn't even realize we were also grieving. In our attempts to return to normalcy, we wandered deeper into Latour's desert of grief, deeper into desolation and hollowness. We had lost so much, but politicians bent to the will of capitalists and forced us to continue to move forward while not allowing ourselves the loss rituals that have sustained mourners for generations. So we pushed forward: alone together, with no roadmap for how to resolve the trauma and exit the desert.[3]

As my university began to coerce faculty and students back to business as usual, I became acutely aware of how our classrooms intimately interact with trauma. Instead of proceeding with the university's mandate, I adapted my pedagogy to analyze our changing conditions and provide space for students to confront and alleviate some of their trauma. Instead of pushing through our grief or outright dismissing it, we explored and engaged the trauma and grief we were all dealing with by making the analysis of trauma part of the class. To do this, my class used literature and film to explore the trauma and its effects on characters. Some pieces explored in this class included the films *Osama*, *Water*, *Precious*, *Doubt*, *Room*, *Us*, and *Persepolis*. As such, our readings and discussions became a form of group therapy that offered students a chance to process their own trauma through the safety of a double-mediated experience: both the Zoom screen and the characters' lives. By doing so, we created a space that recognized the humanity of students and put care at the forefront of our collective experience. My classroom became a safe space for students to process their individual and our collective trauma, which led to a community built on personal, emotional, and intellectual breakthroughs that challenged students to grow as both scholars and human beings.

An example of these breakthroughs came while exploring William Shakespeare's *The Winter's Tale*. In *The Winter's Tale*, Paulina creates a space for the scarred king Leontes to recover from his wounds, reflect on his mistakes, and evolve. Paulina's role in the play intersected with contemporary discourse on the role of women in the midst of trauma. It is no coincidence that many of the occupations deemed essential during the pandemic, including nurses, retail workers, and teachers, each skew heavily female. As such, the students were seeing the women in their lives burdened with more and more responsibility for the health of society while simultaneously being told that this work didn't merit the pay and prestige of colleagues with much less responsibility. With this discourse undergirding our everyday experience, Shakespeare's Paulina became a favorite case study, as the students can see in her the responsibility for holding together an entire kingdom while the sovereign mourns the events he solely is responsible for creating. His grief paralyzes him to the point wherein he can no longer function as a ruler. For Leontes to mend, Paulina utilizes her magical voice to be the king's consult and voice of reason amid blinding pain. She capitalizes on grief by constructing a graveyard of those who died due to Leontes's actions. Confronting the results of his actions allows the king to regain his sense of self and humanity. Although he has a duty to rule, the king chooses to isolate himself and spend time repairing his brokenness.

The breakthrough the class made when discussing this play altered how the class functioned. The students saw their own situations reflected in Leontes's choice between fulfilling his duty and prioritizing grieving so that he could heal himself and lead effectively. The students experienced this in a multitude of ways, such as precarious living situations where they are separated from others but may not have the equipment available to them to fully participate or attending class in their rooms at home where they are never fully separate from family life. Many students were in positions where they had to help manage their households alongside their parents as their younger siblings were now home from school, as well. So along with their responsibilities as students, they had newfound responsibilities as caretakers and homemakers while navigating the instability and uncertainty of the pandemic.

To help address this ever-changing social and academic landscape, the students and I used the lessons from the text to influence the construction of our classroom environment. We saw that Leontes needed time away from some responsibilities to more effectively tend to others and recuperate in a manner that would allow success. So we agreed to create ways for students to succeed even if they stepped out of the rigid expectation of active attendance at two predetermined times per week to contend with the challenges this new reality gave them. The only requirement was that they come back better equipped to continue learning. In our classroom, we re-created the transformative space of Paulina's graveyard, the desert that Latour describes in which there is "representation and experience" that heals people over time.[4]

In a play dealing with loss brought about by selfishness, the character of Paulina is essential for the turn from tragedy to reconciliation at the end. The lessons learned through an exploration of this work in the time of COVID clearly demonstrate the continued relevance of literature as a tool of education and care. We see how Paulina creates a reality separate from the one she finds herself in and so doing creates a path through the desert and what may be our only chance at healing from the trauma inflicted upon us.

At first, students distanced these works from the trauma they were experiencing. Yet, as we discussed how these characters dealt with loss, heartache, and abuse, discussion of the reality of their own lives began to enter the space. So conditioned had they been to just push through to some undefined "normal" that they had not afforded themselves the opportunity to examine the circumstances in which they found themselves. Once students connected the trauma on the page to their own lives, we explicitly worked to implement a practice of generosity with one's self, especially concerning one's supposed shortcomings in work, school, and life. I encouraged students to allow themselves forgiveness and to take breaks, the only requirement for doing so being that the student must articulate what they believed to be the cause of their disruption or lack of motivation. Through the exploration of trauma, both outer and inner, we began to create a vocabulary for how to identify and therefore rectify the issues with completing any given task under the traumatic circumstances we found ourselves in.

People often ignore wretched feelings of grief for fear of being perceived as weak. The work begun with these students in this course has altered my perceptions of myself, as well as my pedagogical practices moving forward. I found myself being much more open and honest with my students about how difficult teaching was in this time. No longer am I willing to suffer through the triggering light of my laptop while enduring a blinding migraine. I gave myself slack and came up with contingencies for when class needed to be cut short, start late, or be cancelled, and I encouraged my students to openly communicate with me about the struggles in their own lives that don't just go away for the two hours we spend together twice a week. Together, we agreed to strive to do our best work but also to hold space for the uncertainty that we live with every day, and by doing so we enabled students who normally would disappear, never to be heard from again, to openly discuss the issues they were facing. And once the discussion began, we were able to work together to find solutions and successfully navigate to the end of the course.

Recalling traumatic histories can be unsettling for society, but it paves the way for people to understand injustices and the darkness that surrounds people. In understanding the value of naming our trauma, we can move past the binary of trauma = bad and no trauma = good and explore what it means to live through these experiences and be better for them. In discussion posts after the weekly watching and reading, I encourage students to relate what they've taken in that week to their own lives and traumas. They acknowledge that what they've studied may not mirror their own experience perfectly, but by creating space to openly discuss trauma, they are able to better analyze the trauma they've encountered through these characters.

Much like Paulina, the individuals who have created these spaces for our students will have their work mostly overlooked by those in power, but the impact will be invaluable on the students who are given the chance to collectively grieve and find solace in the shared experiences of a global trauma. Together, this class began to blaze a path out of the desert. In doing so, we hopefully continue the slow, often infuriating path toward a more inclusive and human-focused academic community, not with yet another committee meeting but with the day-to-day work and struggle of our graduate students, young faculty, and students.

Notes

1. Michael W. Rabow, Chao-Hui S. Huang, Gloria E. White-Hammond, Rodney O. Tucker, "Witnesses and Victims Both: Healthcare Workers and Grief in the Time of COVID-19," *Journal of Pain and Symptom Management* 62, no. 3 (2021): 647–56; Nisha Sajnani and David Read Johnson, *Trauma-Informed Drama Therapy: Transforming Clinics, Classrooms, and Communities*, ed. Nisha Sajnani and David Read Johnson (Springfield, IL: Charles C. Thomas, 2014).
2. Bruno Latour, "Why Has Critique Run Out of Steam? From Matters of Fact to Matters of Concern," *Critical Inquiry* 30 (2004).
3. See Michel Foucault, *Architecture, Mouvement, Continuite: Pavillon, l'architecture De La Maison* (Paris: Société Française des Architectes, 1980); Peter Johnson, "Unraveling Foucault's 'Different Space,'" *History of the Human Sciences* 19, no. 4 (2006): 75–90.
4. Bruno Latour, "Why Has Critique Run Out of Steam?"; Monica J. Casper, ed., *Critical Trauma Studies* (New York: NYU Press, 2016); and Yochai Ataria, David Gurevitz, Haviva Pedaya, Yuval Neria, eds., *Interdisciplinary Handbook of Trauma and Culture* (Cham, Switzerland: Springer, 2016).

Who Cares if We Like Them? The Problematics of "Likability" in Production and Progress

—JOSHUA KELLY

"What does it *matter*?" I'm bellowing to a friend across the table, a fellow playwright. "I don't give a good *goddamn* if they're dislikable."

We're several pints in. I've just read a critique of Simon Woods's debut play at the Lyttleton Theatre, *Hansard*, which I watched on the National Theatre at Home streaming service. There was much to criticize despite the fact I loved it: the conflict inescapably reminiscent of Albee's *Who's Afraid of Virginia Woolf?*, the somewhat predictable (if moving) subject of the couple's schism, the political divisions being resolved just a bit too easily in deference to the personal. The review, however, used a phrase that incensed me: "The sometimes vicious sarcasm throughout makes both characters dislikable, at least until the final ten minutes or so."[1] It should be said that, by this time, I had developed a sensitivity about this word from overexposure. Mr. Omaweng's observation was innocent enough and not even incorrect.[2] Yet this bizarre criteria for acceptable drama has been chewed in the industry like grass in the bovine gastric system: regurgitated and congealed into an indigestible cliché. The likability of characters is now an opening consideration in professional criticism and is inconsistent from one writer to the next. For the purposes of this essay, the term "unlikable" is in no way related to something like "problematic," in which the *unintended offensiveness* of a character is the result of tone-deafness, dehumanizing politics, or social myopia on the part of the playwright, director, or performer. Critical rejection of those characters is necessary. It refers rather to the necessarily distasteful or horrifying—or even innocently unappealing—nature of characters whose charisma or bonhomie aren't the point: antiheroes, villains, arguably tragic figures, or simply those who are flawed past the point of magnetism. In other words, I mean the opposite of "likable" that is too often awarded in theatre reviews as an arbitrary gold star for good writing and performance.

"Well, yeah," my friend responded at last. "You have to like a character if you want them to succeed or want to get to the end of the story."

I contented myself with finishing my pint, but inside I was shouting *Attica!* After all, who the hell ever *liked* the child-murdering Richard III? Find me the person who wanted to give Willy Loman a cuddle while he abused and neglected Linda? Shall we grab a drink with Arturo Ui after the curtain? Invite Jimmy Porter along? Who was rooting for either George *or* Martha, come to think of it—the play that *Hansard* echoed so strongly no review failed to reference Albee somewhere in the first graph? I hate to begin with obvious axioms, but plays have been written about unlikable characters since . . . ever. Dislike occurs often enough without forcing us to slip away at intermission or causing us to detest the play afterward. This, too, must have been the case for audiences throughout history, as the lengthy walls of drama are positively graffitied with characters worthy of revilement well beyond those in *Hansard*, yet still they're produced, sold out, and have found their place in anthologies.

But this word is now a badge of discernment. Ben Brantley diminishes the antihero (there might have been a clue, there) of *The Low Road* as "nowhere near . . . likeable."[3] Bruce Weber makes this his thesis headline in his review of *The Butterfly Collection*.[4] Brigid Delaney's reaction to *Jack of Hearts* even recognizes that "it's a satire, the characters are not meant to be likeable" but bemoans this very fact as though it were a failure of the text—they're *too* unlikable.[5] Playwright Ruth Fowler's television show *Rules of the Game* has recently been "slammed by viewers for 'unlikable characters.'"[6] A major contention in Sophie Gilbert's review of the movie adaptation of *The Last Five Years* was that Jamie's "character [was] rendered so unlikeable it's hard not to imagine Brown himself wanting to sue for having his stage avatar interpreted as such a consummate asshole."[7] The list goes on.[8]

The danger of using "likability" as a metric is devastating to stories and characters whose objectives, situations, tactics, and conflicts upset and destabilize hegemonic tranquility. This is what interesting, progressive, and transformative theatre does: no one invested in the status quo is going to "like" the characters who even passively criticize it, so these are the stories we should care about the most and give the most care. Furthermore, "likability" has established itself as a dog whistle for heinous considerations in other fields as well, from politics to literature.[9] In the theatre, "likability" too easily translates into a passive consumption on the part of a hegemonic audience (largely white, educated, and neoliberal), which in the worst of cases can contribute to the dehumanization of the character and rejection of the (often lived) experiences being portrayed. By extension, "dislike" of a character is a psychological warning that some piece of our ideology is being threatened; rather than consider the logic of the experience being played for us, it is easier to write off the given circumstances and conflict as being, inherently, a consequence of the flawed character experiencing them. Viola Davis identifies this in regard to gender in her response to the "unlikability" of her character in *How to Get Away with Murder*: "It's really only women that you want to be pretty and likeable. . . . They'll put it on the actor. And me, as an actor, that's not my responsibility. If I make her likeable, then I'm pushing an edit button and that's not what you're supposed to do as an actor."[10] Understanding how women are one class of people undermined by this conceit, the renowned comedy company the Second City points out the disparity between likability and hegemonic bias in a satirical article on their website listing ways to make female characters "likable," including making them hot, quiet, agreeable, weak, and uncomplicated.[11] Wrestling with an audience's ideological expectations of likability in an honest way complicates the work of presenting fully realized characters with all their flaws and complexities, leading directors like Cathy Yan to reject the standard and assert, "Women have to be real, not likeable."[12]

Yan's framing of the likable against the real is revealing. "Likability" has proven to be such a strong reaffirmation for audiences that even their expectations of relatable *humanity* can be swayed by its execution, as a study that explored the likability of robots using theatre theory found. In this experiment, likability was discovered to depend on "creating aesthetically coherent representations of character, where all the parts coalesce to produce a socially identifiable figure demonstrating predictable behavior."[13] It logically follows, in a very dangerous implication, that a character who is found *unlikable* either in rehearsal or in performance is being read as *socially unidentifiable* by refusing to follow *predictable behaviors* prescribed by mass expectation. In other words, unlikability is not only counter-hegemonic but can predictably be the stuff of dehumanization for audiences who do not recognize the reality being offered.

Because the victims of likability are so often members of marginalized communities, producing and performing dislikable characters demonstrates an ethic of care for the text *and* the audience; it forces us to dissect objectives and tactics that render unlikable people and desires into a logic of ideological intercession. Audiences are encouraged to confront their own lack of care for people and ideas that deserve such care and have been denied it in favor of representations more affirming of hegemonic biases. The fact that sometimes such lack of care is completely unconscious until pointed out makes those productions (and production practices) all the more urgent.

Offstage, some realization of this phenomenon is gaining traction. In an essay by Broadway stage manager Narda E. Alcorn and UCSD professor Lisa Porter, it's explained that a commitment to anti-racist stage management education includes the tool of "Dismantling Perfection," a key practice of which is to "recognize and redirect working exclusively to attain the approval of systems and people. Aspiring to be likable can interfere with anti-racist action."[14] Onstage, likability can even be dramatized as an attempt to make palatable characters that proliferate malingering ideologies—as in a review for David Mamet's *Race*, wherein Jack Lawson was seen as having an "aggressive cynicism . . . so extreme that he becomes not just likeable but adorable too."[15] This of a character who receives his just desserts on the final pages of the play for having been so entrenched in certain ideas of white supremacy that a Black character must spell out the mistaken assumptions he's made during the course of the action—mistakes that many audience members were well aware he was making. That some find this character likable is why they follow his arc, sure, but that many *don't* for his obvious myopia is another excellent reason to stay until the end: to see someone suffer the defeat he deserves and to (hopefully) witness an audience critically consider it.

Reconsidering "likability" in this way shows that the language of reviews is a microcosm of the unspoken dynamics at play in theatre institutions—from professional productions to academia. Actors and directors who see "likability" as a metric for "producible" or "successful" (even if they aren't consciously thinking this way) are incentivized to make performances appeal to the broadest common receptor. During auditions, directors are conditioned to consider subjective magnetism at least as much as the originality, insight, or commentary a certain performer brings to a reading. The more such an invisible, hegemonic force pervades the professional sphere, the more it becomes ossified in definitive performances that are awarded, recorded for posterity, canonized, and studied within theatrical disciplines. (Productions that engage hegemonic conceits of leading type like the 2019 Broadway revival of *Oklahoma!* And the 2022 revival of *Funny Girl* demonstrate how such conceits become ideologically disseminated and require radical practice to reveal to an uncritical public.) In this way, "likability" has perpetuated itself by invisibly asserting that to be likable is *to be of like kind to those watching*. Or even more perilously, as the study in sociable robotics suggests, it is a requisite simply *to be*.

THE PROBLEMATICS OF "LIKABILITY"

Likability, then, is part of a semiotic language of dominant taste and hegemonic comfort—its gatekeepers and its uncritical adherents perpetuate a subtext every time this metric is invoked to pass judgment on a character or is considered in the creation of one. As academics and practitioners, we are doubly likely to pass on this dangerous assumption in our work—the myths of meritocracy, accessibility, and equity that pervade our professional lives are dependent on concepts as ephemeral as, and related to, likability. Consider how many times "likability" was even an *implied* metric for which student is accepted to the program, who gets funding, who gets cast, and thus who goes into the professional world with the resources for success and continues to reaffirm those rarely self-critical standards as institutional common sense? How we accept certain assumptions of character in theory and practice is undoubtedly at work in the re-creation of major works as carbon copies in regional, community, and academic productions and in the prevailing decisions of who gets seen, what gets read, and what choices get to be played. Whether a character (or the performer portraying them) is "likable" may be only one of those unreflexive assumptions, but the logic of this essay should illustrate the ways in which it is deeply connected to the oppression of marginalized artists and stories and—less impactfully—makes the act of simply producing texts for entertainment likely to create facsimiles of earlier productions.

So, what do we *do* with this? How do we begin to reconcile the dramatic, personal, and political problems that "likability" foists onto writers, actors, audiences, and critics? Its nebulous conception, its contradictions, and its implications impede our ability to produce and consume art with honesty and nuance. We should avoid invoking conceits of likability from script selection, character creation, casting, and criticism. If for no other reason, refusing to fetishize and reify the insubstantial concept of likability leads us to produce theatre that is more honest, diverse, and dialectic and less constrained by ideological conceit—more interesting to produce and more interesting to consume. For practitioners with more radical goals, we should continue the progressive work of reducing hateful re-performances onstage while at the same time acknowledging that our capacity for "likability" is limiting to progressive performances and texts; it hardens our already-calcified notions of good character, conflict, and plot, revealing our often unconscious propagation of white supremacist and misogynist "taste." We should selectively engage who and what we like onstage and reconcile that likability to a *useful* end, remember that some people aren't *supposed* to be liked, and produce theatre that tempers unlikability with purpose. The characters we care about are our responsibility as much as they are the playwright's, and we should treat them with the same care. Because who we care about onstage ultimately defines who we care about in the world outside the theatre.

Notes

1. Chris Omaweng, "Review of Hansard—A New Play by Simon Woods at the Lyttleton Theatre," London Theatre 1 (website), September 3, 2019; accessed January 20, 2022.
2. Though his despair is consistent. He was also disappointed in the Hope Theatre's production of *Darling*, in which "dramatic tension finally erupts, but not until well into the second half. By this point, one wonders whether the wait was really worth it, particularly in a show whose characters are all dislikeable." Chris Omaweng, "Darling by Kathy Rucker at The Hope Theatre," London Theatre 1 (website), November 12, 2021; accessed January 22, 2022.
3. Ben Brantley, "Poking Fun and Punching Holes," *New York Times*, March 8, 2018: C4
4. Bruce Weber, "Theater Review; Like Father (a Writer), Like Son (an Actor), and Neither Is Likable," *New York Times*, October 4, 2000: E5.
5. Bridget Delaney, "Jack of Hearts Review—Star Power Fails to Save David Williamson's 50th Play," *Guardian* (website), February 8, 2016; accessed April 17, 2023.
6. Eve Watson, "BBC One Rules of the Game Slammed for 'Unlikable Characters,'" *Plymouth Herald* (website), January 12, 2022; accessed April 12, 2023.
7. Sophie Gilbert, "How to Lose a Guy in 1,825 Days," *Atlantic*, February 20, 2015; Yahoo!-Finance (website), accessed April 17, 2023.
8. Indeed, the idea of characters needing to be "likable" is now so pervasive it has gained satirical potential: *The Prom* is a musical whose primary characters suffer from finding out their performances simply aren't likable in their new Broadway show. See Norah Dick, "Theatre Review: 'The Prom' at the Kennedy Center," *MD Theatre Guide* (website), January 8, 2022; accessed April 17, 2023. Furthermore, "dislikable" in reviews too numerous to cite is used as a cautionary mark of a great performance—a character that could have been despicable is thankfully spared (as is the audience) by the charm of a gifted actor. Even when this fails, some reference to the likability of a character seems unavoidable, as in Charles Isherwood's review of *Plaza Suite*, in which Matthew Broderick and Sarah Jessica Parker "are immensely likable and talented performers" yet ultimately miscast. If miscast, why does their likability matter at all, especially if it's not so momentous as to save the production for one influential critic? See Charles Isherwood, "'Plaza Suite' Review: Entertainment Checks Out," *Wall Street Journal* (website), March 31, 2022; accessed April 17, 2023.
9. Alisha Haridasani Gupta, "The Likability Trap Is Still a Thing," *New York Times* (website), November 22, 2019; accessed April 17, 2023.
10. Lisa Weidenfeld, "Viola Davis Says Her 'HTGAWM' Character Shouldn't Have to Be Likeable," *Metro*, (website), September 23, 2015; accessed April 17, 2023.
11. Sam Bailey, "5 Steps to Making Your Female Characters Likeable," Second City (website), June 3, 2015; accessed December 12, 2022.
12. Alaka Sahani, "'Women Have to Be Real, Not Likeable': Cathy Yan," *Indian Express*, (website), February 28, 2021; accessed April 17, 2023.

13. Louise LePage, "The Importance of Realism, Character, and Genre: How Theatre Can Support the Creation of Likeable Sociable Robots," *International Journal of Robotics* 13 (2021): 1427–41.
14. Narda E. Alcorn and Lisa Porter, "We Commit to Anti-Racist Stage Management Education," *Howlround Theatre Commons* (website), July 28, 2020; accessed April 17, 2023.
15. Lloyd Evans, "Race Is 'Ingenious. . . . Shocking and Hilarious," *Spectator* (website), June 10, 2013; accessed April 17, 2023.

When We Gather in the Clearing, A Cardinal Croons

—JOHN MURILLO III

A few days before your birthday, in this, the nineteenth year since your departure, Mom and Auntie Rita arrive at about the same time while I'm soaking up the sunshine in the small clearing behind the house, writing what will become these lines to the tune of a crooning cardinal, its bold red plumage barely obscured by the thick fronds of the pine tree leaning over Claudia's fence into our yard. On the table, I've made the arrangements for this act of conjuring, gathering what I can hold: a thick book with a worn, faded, red cover and the words *Natural Healing* embossed in big, gold letter on the spine; the hand-carved wooden box you gave me, the one you told me to write my name on and that currently stores all the notes and poems I wrote for Chinyere when I proposed; and the warped, crimson copy of Toni Morrison's *Beloved* I borrowed in high school, then kept so long that "borrowed" became "stole." I grab my *Beloved*, grasp it in my (large) talons, and take flight toward the front door.

My *Beloved* is precious. A stolen thing, it is precious plunder.

I stole it after it sang its red song of power from its perch on the shelf in Mrs. Moreau's bungalow. It intoned a cardinal's croon in crimson-toned notes, and its breath smelled sweetly of roasted corn. In my mind, I fractured and flew through gold skies, grasping at the jewel of its red star.

They say the philosopher's stone is red. Yes, the philosopher's tome is red. The philosopher's stone is a red tome calling to be held, unbound, and read. Really read. It is a crystalline bird pining for real flight.

Softly, deftly, I enclosed its gemstone wings in both hands. I opened it up, let fly its pages. And we stole away—together.

I read the red book. I devoured its contents. I flew. I was filled. I did not know how hungry I was for the lift of the philosopher's words, the salve of her stories, or the transformative anointing of genius, care, and defiance breathing and booming between the lines.[1] Only after my *Beloved* lifted me, asked me to sit, hush, and listen for a minute, and fed me did I understand the kind of nourishment I once thought was exclusive to Mom's cooking, Dad's cooking, and your laughter. Toni Morrison's insistence upon offering we who fracture and fall the medicinal, spiritual, lyrical, political, narrative sustenance for which only she knew the recipe filled and fills me with a shard of that same insistence. Thus, I insist on carrying my *Beloved* with me. I need to hold my Beloved closely, clutch it with both claws, wholly behold it in thought and in dream. And I must hold out the red book as an offering, a question, and an opportunity.

In a few weeks, Auntie Rita will gift me a leather bookmark and leather notebook for my birthday, and in their ornateness they will feel totemic in the drag and press of my fingers across their surfaces. Which is to say they will feel heavy and immediately precious. I will take two more weeks before writing my name in the space provided on the inside cover of the notebook, and three more months before arriving at words that feel weighty enough to inscribe on the notebook's pages, but I will take only a few moments to decide where to stake the bookmark, what destination in lyrical prose I will want to return to first. I will open my *Beloved* to the sermon in the Clearing without having to fan through the pages and will wedge the bookmark there tenderly but with intent. I will not close the book right away—this will seem disrespectful, misaligned with the auspice of this sacred way-marking; instead, I will read the passage to myself aloud, to remind myself where I have arrived.

"Here," she said, "in this here place, we flesh, flesh that weeps, laughs; flesh that dances on bare feet in grass. Love it. Love it hard. Yonder they do not love your flesh. They despise it. They don't love your eyes; they'd just as soon pick em out. No more do they love the skin on your back. Yonder they flay it. And O my people they do not love your hands. Those they only use, tie, bind, chop off and leave empty. Love your hands! Love them. Raise them up and kiss them. Touch others with them, pat them together, stroke them on your face 'cause they don't love that either. You got to love it, you! And no, they ain't in love with your mouth. Yonder, out there, they will see it broken and break it again. What you say out of it they will not heed. What you scream from it they do not hear. What you put into it to nourish your body they will snatch away and give you leavins instead. No, they don't love your mouth. You got to love it. This is flesh I'm talking about here. Flesh that needs to be loved."[2]

JOHN MURILLO III

Here.
In the flesh.
Of the flesh.
Love your flesh.

Like a cardinal's song, like batter in the pot or skillet, the words stain the air.

Toni Morrison chooses the word "flesh" (as opposed to "body") here, and in doing so exposes a resonance between herself, Baby Suggs's sermon, and Hortense Spillers's "Mama's Baby, Papa's Maybe: An American Grammar Book." The three women—Baby Suggs, Morrison, and Spillers—stand in the Clearing conjured by Black feminist theory. Baby Suggs's is a sermon delivered as an untimely spiritual, political, and theoretical collaboration, and the three women in the Clearing imbue its every imperative with a radical Black feminist regard for the way Black flesh bears both profound vulnerability and intimate care.[3] Black flesh knows unimaginable suffering, and Black flesh hungers for intentional tenderness; Black *flesh* is at the center.

Amid the splendor Spillers gifts us in "Mama's Baby," she proffers an indispensable distinction between the Black body/Black bodies and Black flesh.[4] The violence and violations of chattel slavery and its aftermath strip Black bodies of any human dimension, that third or fourth dimension of existence that affords humanity its purportedly singular depth and value. To echo scholar and creator Dionne Brand: slavery tore open the world, rupturing Black folks' kind and quality of being, and reducing our bodies to this flattened, fleshy, one- or two-dimensional state of existence onto which the world scrawls out its whims, desires, and needs and with which the world sustains itself.[5] "Take and eat; this is our body": This is the "primary narrative" of our flesh. It is the story of irreparable, bodily breaking, of obliterated being, and of countervailing hungers: the world's insatiable hunger for our flesh and blood, our lives and deaths; and our *being* hongry for that which this world cannot offer—double emphasis on being.

We bear this breaking, this
hunger, in the flesh,
as our flesh

The weight of the word "flesh" throughout Baby Suggs's sermon becomes heavier as we understand what's stewed into that word: on the one hand, a Black feminist regard for the specificity of Black women's flesh "ungendered," or Blackly gendered, and the way this specificity functions as the urtext for understanding the relationships between violence and being and vulnerability and care; and, on the other, an Afropessimistic basis for understanding what care for Black being(s) might look like when we can only approximate the kind of violence to which we are vulnerable with words like "atomization," annihilation, or obliteration.[6] Spillers, who disavows the "pessimist" label but whose work often offers pessimistic insights, transforms how we receive Baby Suggs's sermon by compelling our congregation to think about the *scale* of difference between the violence that paradoxically unmakes and constitutes Black flesh and the care we must and are able to provide for that flesh. We must attend to both the facticity of *and* difference between the haptical intimacies of touching your flesh tenderly in the Clearing, of both the singular and collective "you" in the smallness of "here," and the oceanic broadness of "they," the structures and purveyors of antiblackness out yonder, *as all of yonder*, who embody and practice the most violent kinds of disregard.

When I hear Baby Suggs's insistent invocation of "flesh" in this Clearing conjured by Afropessimism and Black feminism, I hear Suggs, Morrison, and Spillers performing the important labor of calibration. By compelling us to consider the smallness of the intentional, if fleeting, magic we might call "care" *in relation to* the magnitude of terror and domination we most broadly describe as "violence," Afropessimism does not disavow Black feminist theory's regard for the insistence, resistance, and tenderness of the kinds of care defiantly cobbled together in the Clearing, throughout the rest of *Beloved*, across the works of Morrison and Spillers, and beyond the bounds of these sentences; rather, Afropessimism *calibrates* that care in relation to the violence that necessitates it to begin with. Here, in this Clearing conjured by Afropessimism, Black feminist theory, and Black women's regard for Black folk, we heed their call comprehending that it is the absoluteness of the violence that unmakes us that makes tending tenderly to our fractured and flayed flesh imperative. It is because the world is built on the total disavowal of Black mattering that we must love our flesh, raise and kiss our hands, tend our hearts, stroke our necks, and breathe and hold and keep our breaths. It is because of the abyssal void where our Human being never was that our attempts to love ourselves must aspire for greater—even hadalpelagic—depth. It is because our lives are lived in intimate proximity to death that we must summon and seek out the satiation that may not save us but that will sustain us here, in our flesh.

> *I/we hear it louder, feel it stronger. We live our Blackness here, in this antiblack world, and here, in the flesh. We are of the flesh. "This is why we must love our flesh."*

Let us recollect, revise: I stole the red book because I identified a resonance between the sermon in the Clearing I'd yet to hear and the loneliness in me that I knew needed to be rocked, a rocking I could not bear on my own. Peering into the Pensieve, this me believes that the yawning maw devouring my feeble attempts at joy, love, and faith moaned an unintelligible pain that, in 1987, Toni Morrison, through Baby Suggs in 1860-something, knew to tend to, protect, care for, and wholly regard as vital. Like the thunderous drumming of the Jumanji games heard by those destined to play them, the feel of the sermon on loving the flesh breathed and boomed from the book in my hands. In the dancing silver filaments of rememory, I spy with my mind's eye why I still shudder to the cadence of the novel's final refrain: for me, selfishly, this would not be a story to pass on.

Not long before your birthday, in the Clearing behind our house, amid magenta and canary hibiscus flowers springing into bloom, crows cawing in the neighbors' too-tall ancient palm, and a cardinal crooning its crimson tune in the nude chestnut tree, four women gather—together.

In my mind, I
clutch my Beloved
close, hold it up to my eyes
and bear witness
through blood-colored lenses.

Mom cups her hands over her eyes to contain the tears overtaking the levy of her black mask. Her stress, and worry, and fear, and pain flow oceanic. Auntie Rita rises and moves to clutch her close to help bear the outpouring of saltwater. Their love for each other is oceanic, too. Held there, Auntie holding Mom around the shoulders and Mom holding Auntie's hands, they ride the waves of a wordless thing, a known but unsayable sibling sense. They hold one another at the edge of the maelstrom of loss that whirls around your birthday in a few days' time. The cardinal croons and you loom large as loss and love over the sisterly Pietà.

My wife, Chinyere, shifts the tableau, taking down Mom's hair, taking up twin bunches between her fingers, and rhythmically twisting it into a new geometry of tenderness. Mom is tender-headed, and always has been, Auntie says, and her eyes betray a smile and a wince at once that her mask cannot mask.

My mother-in-law, Celine, laughs from across the open circle and sympathizes. She, too, is tender-headed. She, too, knows oceanic loss: the loss of independence, stolen by the stroke from years back, after decades of working as a registered nurse, dancing tirelessly at parties, and tending her lush garden; and the loss of her home to fire that devoured so much time, and space, and feeling, and life. Her voice on that 5:00 a.m. phone call wailed grief and disbelief vaster and deeper than this metaphor can bear. But, and, here, now, in the Clearing, she laughs while her daughter holds my mom's hair in her hands, and they all behold each other.

Chinyere tends Mom's hair, and Mom is both child and woman, daughter and mother, seated there in the chair. Chinyere's fingers, raw from bearing her own water, weave pain and faith into flat twists. Her hands tug and twist, tug and twist, until love's labor is done and my mom's hair fully tended. Its sheen in the sun is glory.

They are all bodies of water. They are an outpouring. They bear and bend oceans. I bear blood witness to the water-bearing-bending Black women in the Clearing while the cardinal croons. As they hold and behold one another, I hold and behold them in the frame of the red book.

Can you see what I see? Oh, the scene and seas I see. I see through the jewel of the philosopher's tome how they bend and bear boundless, extraordinary loss and love in the small, ordinary vessels of the circle, the moment, and the flesh.

Here,
in the flesh. We,
flesh and blood. We,
water and want. This is why
we must love
our flesh.

Notes

1. A reference to *Breath, Boom*, a play by Kia Corthron, to which I was introduced by longtime friend and colleague Jaye Austin Williams (Dr. Jaye) when she presented an analysis of it at the Afropessimism Symposium held at UCI in 2012.
2. Toni Morrison, *Beloved* (1987; repr., New York: Vintage International, 2004), 103–4.
3. "Untime" is the name I gave "Black time" in my first book, *Impossible Stories: On the Space and Time of Black Destructive Creation* (Columbus: Ohio State University Press, 2021).
4. Hortense Spillers, "Mama's Baby, Papa's Maybe: An American Grammar Book," *Diacritics* 17, no. 2 (1987): 67.

5. Dionne Brand, *A Map to the Door of No Return: Notes to Belonging* (Toronto: Doubleday Canada, 2001), 5.
6. Spillers, "Mama's Baby, Papa's Maybe," 68. I'm gesturing toward Patrice Douglass's argument in "Black Feminist Theory for the Dead and Dying," *Theory and Event* 21, no. 1 (2018): 106–23, which presents the most compelling take on what "ungendered" does for Blackness. Spillers, "Mama's Baby, Papa's Maybe," 68.

Part III

ESSAY FROM THE CONFERENCE

The Robert A. Schanke Award-Winning Essay, MATC 2022

Present Perfect Tense

Revolutionizing Dramatic Narratives through Living History at the Oconaluftee Indian Village

—HEIDI L. NEES

"Story, like culture, is constantly moving. It is a river where no gallon of water is the same gallon it was a second ago. Yet it is still the same river. It exists as a truth. As a whole. Even if the whole is in constant change. In fact, *because* of that constant change."
—DEBORAH A. MIRANDA

Tense: Present Perfect—"Designates an Action That Started in the Past but Which Continues into the Present or the Effect of Which Still Continues"

Revolution (n.): "Process of Turning Over in the Mind, Consideration, Reflection [. . .]"

The *Egwanulti*—also known as the Oconaluftee River—cuts through Cherokee, North Carolina, a small tourist town on the Qualla Boundary, home of the Eastern Band of Cherokee Indians.[1] Meaning "by the river," the tributary is also the namesake of a living history site, the Oconaluftee Indian Village, which contributes to educational, cultural, and economic lifeways of the area by providing (re)presentations of Cherokee life in the past and present tenses. As I offer these categories—past and present—I am confronted with their shortcomings. To be honest, I find myself in a "temporal tangle," to borrow Rebecca Schneider's phrase.[2]

Craig Howe, founder and director of the Center for American Indian Research and Native Studies, points to the museum exhibition as a form that lends itself to relaying tribal histories more than writing does because of its ability to "incorporate multiple media that may be accessed in a nearly infinite variety of sequences."[3] Living history sites have the potential to engage audiences in sensorial experiences that allow room for self-determined sequencing through mixed media–laden spaces, thus possibilizing Howe's vision for tribal perspectives. But *how* does a site like the Oconaluftee Indian Village achieve and communicate tribal perspectives given its foundation in linear notions of time presupposed on notions of progress? How do attendant issues involving representation, sovereignty, and economics further complicate epistemological and material implications of *living* history?

To help me untangle (or maybe further tangle?) this knot of questions and quandaries, I turn to scholars whose own explorations inform the way concepts such as temporality, history, presence, stasis, and (re)vision revolve around a central query in my mind. That is, how do living history sites such as the Oconaluftee Indian Village create conduits for intergenerational sharing of knowledge, as well as educate non-Native audiences about tribal culture, all while maintaining tribally specific ways of knowing and being, as well as a fiscal bottom line?

In this exploration, I call upon ways in which Mark Rifkin and Rebecca Schneider consider the modes by which we (re)create and (re)enact history. These scholars call into question Euro-American, settler society's assumption of progress-driven temporal constructs as "natural." Schneider intervenes on the normalizing of such linear abstractions while also calling attention to non-hegemonic groups who embrace modes of thinking that do not align with Western models. Rifkin more explicitly engages *Indigenous* temporal frameworks. He seeks "to pluralize temporality so as to open possibilities for engaging with Indigenous self-articulation, forms of collective life, and modes of self-determination beyond their incorporation or translation into settler frames of reference" such that he can "open conceptual room [. . .] for engaging expressions of temporal sovereignty."[4] In other words, Rifkin suggests that the recognition of value and validity of multiple temporal frameworks creates space for sovereignty. In the brief time we have today, I invite you to work this temporal tangle with me, grappling with the ways in which we might decolonize the present(ing) of the past tense in living history sites.

LIVING HISTORY

Tense: Past Progressive—"Past Action That Took Place Over a Period of Time."

Revolution (n.): "A Recurring Period of Time, a Cycle; an Epoch." Obsolete.

Paul Chaat Smith points out that "no history is complete without knowing the history of the history."[5] To understand how the Oconaluftee Indian Village (re)presents history in the twenty-first century, we must consider its origin story. The village exemplifies the type of museum that accompanies outdoor historical dramas as an addendum designed to buttress the drama's claims of "historical accuracy." These auxiliary attractions range from one-room displays to extensive exhibits, and in most cases, the notions of history that formed these touristic sites were based on Euro-American views of the past steeped in claims of objectivity and positivism.

Though the village did not open until after the premiere of Kermit Hunter's *Unto These Hills* in Cherokee, discussions of its creation predate the drama, thus distinguishing it from similar spaces. Furthermore, the village has continuously proved more successful than the drama in terms of attendance. While people often couple the village and *Unto These Hills*, the former stands on its own in terms of reach and impact. Millions of people, mostly non-Native and mostly white, have visited the village since its opening in 1952.

In 1950, the Cherokee Historical Association (CHA), the producing entity of both the village and the drama, began developing plans to create a Cherokee village "as it was in the old days."[6] Joe Jennings, a member of the CHA board of trustees and superintendent of the reservation, was tasked with researching the best way to approach such an endeavor. In his 1982 history of the CHA, William P. Connor Jr. reports, "Jennings had been advised that a research excavation would be necessary to discover the archaeological data on which a truly authentic town could be based."[7] Given the expenses of such an effort, Jennings suggested partnering with three "outstanding" universities.[8] Connor's chronicle indicates the CHA's emphasis on "authenticity," considering the number of times the word appears in the source. Of course, also apparent is the irony that the CHA pursued "authenticity" through archaeology and the academy, rather than the knowledge and expertise of the Cherokee people around it.

The CHA formed an offshoot called the Tsali Institute of Cherokee Research to "provide leadership and expertise necessary" for the creation of an "authentic replica" of an eighteenth-century Cherokee village.[9] The organization's charter identified its mission thusly: "To engage in scientific research into early Cherokee Indian History, customs, and modes of living. To study, collect data, publish information and in every way practicable to sponsor projects of investigation and education, including the excavation of archaeological sites of supposed Cherokee occupation, and anything calculated to inculcate a wider public understanding and appreciation of the early Cherokee Indian customs and traditions."[10] This passage indicates two key attitudes that shaped the inception of the village: (1) Historical research should be an empirical pursuit, based on scientific methodologies, and (2) the goal was to foster "wider public understanding and appreciation of the *early* Cherokee Indian," as opposed to contemporary Cherokee culture. These foundational mindsets, adopted and enacted by a group consisting primarily of white men, shaped the village's dissemination of history for decades.

CHA funding requests from this time outline early plans for the village: "The village must come alive if it is to serve the purpose of giving the public knowledge of Cherokee life as it existed shortly after the Cherokees had established permanent contact with the white people, and give the Cherokees of the present an insight into their own past way of life, of which they have now only a vague knowledge. In order to provide an atmosphere of reality, Indian families are expected to live in the village. Their household utensils will be like those of long ago, and they will wear clothing such as is described by the travelers who visited the Cherokee towns of that period. They will work at the same tasks and use the same tools as their ancestors."[11] This excerpt demonstrates other key assumptions integral to the creation of the village, among them the belief that (1) the Cherokee lack cultural and historical knowledge, (2) authenticity rests in the "realistic" portrayal of a past moment, and (3) "factual" information about the past is extracted from white-authored primary sources. To validate the history, the CHA brought in John Witthoft of the Pennsylvania State Museum to teach an anthropology class and train the Cherokee demonstrators. The CHA regarded Witthoft, who was white, as "perhaps the best-informed man on the culture of the Eastern Cherokees."[12]

Clearly, racist and white supremacist logic that esteemed white understandings of the past, time, and groups of people framed these approaches and fueled harmful perceptions. The premise that insists on "realistically" rendering the past as a means to perform "authenticity," especially in light of the proposal that Cherokee demonstrators *live* at the village, contributes to the widely held view of Native Americans as relics of the past. A 1954 *New York Times* article notes that the village "is all *authentic,* and so artfully done that a vivid image of *real* Indian life is left to modify the stereotypes of the movie Westerns."[13] While the authors' impressions of "authenticity" and "realness" caused them to question Hollywood stereotypes, the implication of such association is nonetheless insidious. By viewing the performance of the past at the Oconaluftee Indian Village as "authentic," thereby validating Cherokee demonstrators as "real," visitors may perceive Native Americans as "past"/"passed."[14] The bifurcation of time as past/present creates a binaried impression that freezes Native Americans *in* and *of* the past.

Rifkin identifies an implication of such thinking; "To be authentic means to preserve forms of tradition that emanate from the past in pristine ways; the performance of stasis is the condition of possibility for being accorded status as proper Indians."[15] In other words, the perceived preservation of pure traditional practices can satisfy dominant society's criteria for qualifying as "real" Indians. The trade-off? Paralysis. Rifkin continues: "Such enactments of aboriginality explicitly and implicitly serve as the basis for (grudging, partial, and circumscribed) governmental acknowledgment of Native sovereignty. From this perspective, being recognized as Indian means staging a version of pastness that disavows the 'complexities' of Native life."[16] To be acknowledged as sovereign, tribal nations must adhere to the US government's criteria, much of which depends on performances of "pristine" pastness. Such dictates create an impossible situation: Native communities, as with any community, must change and adapt to survive. To process the continual ramifications of settler colonialism, tribal nations must be able to respond in ways that enable healing and survivance.[17] And yet, doing so risks the settler colonial state's refusal to recognize the identity and self-determination of the tribal community. Change, revision, revolution becomes the purview and privilege of white communities but is not afforded to Native communities.

Tense: Present Progressive—"Activity in Progress."

Revolution (n.): A Convolution; a Twist, a Turn; a Loop. Obsolete.

In the last twenty years, many sites that feature Native American histories have attempted to combat the persistent trope that casts Native peoples as living in the past, disappearing, or vanished. These efforts include calling attention to Native presence in the present, though this sometimes rubs against the sites' settler temporal frameworks. Scott Magelssen calls attention to discord between the use of interpretative tenses at Plimoth Plantation, where the Pilgrim interpreters strictly adhered to first-person interpretation, widely considered the industry gold standard.[18] The Wampanoag interpreters used third-person tense, opting to separate themselves from the seventeenth century by using "they" to refer to past figures. An employee informed Magelssen of resulting "negative experiences" reported by guests and strategies to address the perceived dissonance, including first-person tense for the Wampanoag interpreters.[19] Magelssen identifies the use of third-person interpretation as a choice by Wampanoag employees to address harmful stereotypes and notes that the exclusive reliance on first-person prevents "a radical shift in mode of interpretation that would allow for alternative voicings."[20] Magelssen further asserts that this use of third-person tense, as well as the inclusion of present-day issues that Indigenous peoples face, "continuously put into question the status quo of a singular narrative comprised only of events provable via factual evidence, delivered through first-person interpretation."[21]

While efforts to accentuate the present-ness of Native Americans challenge the long-propagated relegation of Indigenous peoples to the past, a binaried configuration persists as an either/or.[22] This dynamic remains firmly rooted in settler temporal frames that depend on segregated articulations of past or present and subscribes to the belief that this temporal model is "neutral, universal, and inherently shared."[23] Rifkin advocates going beyond "arguing for temporal recognition, being seen as equally 'modern' or part of a shared 'present'" for Indigenous peoples and instead recognizing temporal sovereignty of Native peoples among a multiplicity of temporal formulations. Doing so can "open the potential for conceptualizing Native continuity and change in ways that do not take nonnative frames of reference as the self-evident basis for approaching Indigenous forms of persistence, adaptation, and innovation."[24] Oftentimes, Native Americans who work with and at these sites must translate (or jettison altogether) their temporal realities to accommodate Western sensibilities of time. While present-ing Native cultures in living history sites is a significant endeavor, what potential could be opened if these sites intentionally marked Western constructs as one of many understandings of temporality while also incorporating Indigenous frames of reference?

Tense: Future Continuous—An Action That "Will Occur in the Future and Continue for an Expected Length of Time"

Revolution (n.): "Change, Upheaval."

According to a 1952 "White report" to the CHA, "Some visitors [to the village] thought the guides were occasionally uncomfortable and seemed to be reciting memorized information."[25] Given that the guides were reciting information that had come from white-authored scripts based on research from white-generated sources and shaped by positivistic conceptualizations of time, it is unsurprising that Cherokee guides may have felt uneasy with or did not seem invested in these narratives. While there are many ways in which the Oconaluftee Indian Village continues to operate within linear frameworks, changes in the last two decades have offered new approaches to the (hi)stories present-ed by the site. As Rifkin notes, rigidly differentiating settler temporalities from Indigenous temporalities or linear versus circular models tends to "freeze the terms into a static opposition that denies internal forms of difference as well as meaningful relation."[26] Falling into binaried systems of logic denies the ability to conceive of time within a matrix of temporal considerations. Thus, the village connects with visitors using multiple temporal perspectives that encourage visitors to, in Schneider's terms, "suspend ingrained sociocultural approaches to time as singularly linear and try to think outside of well-worn habits of thought."[27]

One way this is accomplished is through the mode of interpretative tense adapted by the Cherokee guides and demonstrators. Rather that strictly adhering to first- or third-person, they often shift between the two while introducing an additional dimension: "we." The guides often say "We would" when referring to the past or use the simple present tense to describe present-day practices.[28] The choice of this identifier elides a model that conceives of "past" and "present" as two points on a line. Instead, "we" centers people and community, thus collapsing the separation. Fred Wilnoty Jr., who continues his family's legacy at the village, describes this collectivity as an alternative to the "HIStory" taught in schools; "[Guests] come here and they're learning OURstory.... Rather than learn it from a book, a textbook, they can learn it from us and what's passed down to us from our grandparents."[29]

When shifting tenses, the guides call attention to changes in Cherokee traditions and practices, and they identify reasons for adaptations, such as the incorporation of cotton into attire because of its convenience and weight or the impact of Euro-American gender expectations on Cherokee women and society. This latter point came up during a village tour I was on during the summer of 2021. While in the Council House, the guide discussed contemporary issues the Eastern Band of Cherokee and other tribal nations face, including the role of women in Cherokee governance, Missing and Murdered Indigenous Women (MMIW), local elections, outsider leasing of commercial real estate on the reservation, and the lasting effects of Indian boarding schools. The contextualization of these issues revealed the complicated and difficult circumstances that tribal nations and Native individuals endure every day.

Ecological effects also force change across various aspects of Cherokee life, as explained by Laura Blythe, the current CHA program director. Blythe shared an adaptation that the village and tribe may be facing in the future: "Another challenge will be getting the proper materials to do our traditional crafts. Rivercane is getting scarce and finding people who harvest and make white oak splints is hard. There are only a few elders that remain who know how to do it."[30] Blythe's remarks point to the ways in which tribal nations have had to adapt to changing landscapes, oftentimes because of settler colonial impacts on environments. The effects on the community are far-reaching. Craig Howe describes the relationship between landscapes and a tribal community as one that is "often encoded in stories about particular past events that their ancestors experienced."[31] The scarcity in not just the rivercane but also the elders who work with it threatens the relationship Howe describes. This situation highlights the ways in which change is necessary for survivance, as well as the role living history sites can play in creating and maintaining opportunities for intergenerational knowledge transfer.

In 2012, Blythe created the Oconaluftee Indian Village Mentoring Program, which serves as a Youth Internship Program for Cherokee teenagers. Blythe conceived of the initiative as a way to address the "dwindling" number of master artisans and regards it as her "hope for the future."[32] The program offers opportunities to develop life and work skills and was "built around learning [Cherokee] culture; crafts, lectures, and Cherokee studies."[33] The CHA sees a 90 percent return employment rate of the young people who have completed the program.[34]

These (re)visions speak to the importance of change and tradition. On Indigenous interpolation of settler colonial intrusion, Rifkin remarks: "Modes of settler invasion, intervention, regulation, dispossession, and occupation become intimate parts of Indigenous temporalities, but they do so as part of Native frames of reference, meaning that they are encountered through a perceptual tradition and a set of material inheritances that includes ongoing Indigenous legacies of landedness, mobility, governance, ritual periodicities, social networks, and intergenerational stories. Together, these various aspects of being and becoming give historical density to the engagement with settler policies and everyday presence, orienting Native perception and action."[35] This being and becoming are the acts of survivance that generate adaptive change. The Oconaluftee Indian Village offers examples of implementing such (re)visions into living history programming.

While the village introduces visitors to Cherokee temporalities, much of its outreach relies on Western-based temporal frameworks. While suggesting that sites like the village pivot to formats that exclusively feature Indigenous temporal sovereignty may seem ideal, it is also idealistic. The economic implications of turning away from non-Native timelines can negatively burden sites and surrounding communities, especially those for whom tourism is the major industry. In the case of the Oconaluftee Indian Village, that surrounding community is the Eastern Band of Cherokee. Beth Caper and Rebecca Schneider astutely recognize that "performance and performativity are, as such, centrally implicated in the larger mandate to reproduce ourselves, others, and the social world according to the hegemonic organization of labor, time, citizenship, and identity that keep the machinery of capital running."[36] Blythe relayed that the past two seasons have been fiscally difficult, given the pandemic, but that attendance had been down prior to its onset.[37] For the village, supplying visitors with histories aligned with "hegemonic organization of time" and "identity" can aid in maintaining the "machinery of capital."

Tense: Future Conditional—"A Structure Used for Talking about Possibilities in the Present or in the Future"

Revolution (v.): "To Revolutionize (in Various Senses)."

Rifkin claims that "in the absence of a mutual frame of reference . . . between Natives and non-natives, non-natives engage in forms of translation, not primarily to understand Native temporalities but to insert them within settler timescapes."[38] What would happen if non-Natives committed to translation, but not to manipulate Native temporalities into settler timescapes? Rather than operating as places that subscribe to settler time or Indigenous time, what would happen if living history sites and similar spaces that orient to settler frameworks were to dismantle and lay bare the constructedness of such a paradigm? By revolutionizing in this manner, might settler-centric institutions take on the labor and thus relieve Indigenous communities of some of the burden and economic risk? Might we, in Will Daddario's terms, become We+ and thus, "be[come] more than we think"?[39] Might our (hi)stories be(come) more than we think?

Notes

Epigraph. Deborah A. Miranda, *Bad Indians: A Tribal Memoir* (Berkeley, CA: Heyday, 2013), xvi.
1. Throughout this piece, I pair English verb tenses with definitions of "revolution" in order to explore variations on the 2022 MATC conference theme and the ways in which the English language (spoken within a US context) semantically packages Western-based

temporal notions. I recognize, however, that this is in some ways counter to my central arguments, given that the tenses I provide do not align with Indigenous languages (and thus temporalities). Donald L. Fixico describes Indigenous telling of (hi)stories as "transcending past-present-future" such that "time does not imprison the story." I do not mean for my framing device to enact such imprisonment but rather hope that the variations on tense and definition encourage a (re)examination of the ways that (in this case, English) language shapes one's thinking and speaking about "time." Donald L. Fixico, *The American Indian Mind in a Linear World: American Indian Studies and Traditional Knowledge* (New York: Routledge, 2003), 22. See "Introduction to Verb Tenses," Purdue Owl (website), Purdue University, accessed April 17, 2023;; "revolution, *n.*," *Oxford English Dictionary*. Oxford University Press, OED (website), accessed February 3, 2022. See also "The Remapping of America—From an Indigenous Point of View" by Gregory Smithers, *New Republic*, January 17, 2022.

2. Rebecca Schneider, *Performing Remains: Art and War in Times of Theatrical Reenactment* (New York: Routledge, 2011), 10.
3. Craig Howe, "Keep Your thoughts Above the Trees: Ideas on Developing and Presenting Tribal Histories," in *Clearing a Path: Theorizing the Past in Native American Studies*, ed. Nancy Shoemaker (New York: Routledge, 2002), 164.
4. Mark Rifkin, *Beyond Settler Time: Temporal Sovereignty and Indigenous Self-Determination* (Durham, NC: Duke University Press, 2017), ix–x.
5. See "Introduction to Verb Tenses," Purdue Owl (website), Purdue University, accessed April 17, 2023; "revolution, *n.*,"*Oxford English Dictionary*. Oxford University Press, OED (website), accessed April 17, 2023. Paul Chaat Smith, *Everything You Know about Indians Is Wrong* (Minneapolis: University of Minnesota Press, 2009), 53.
6. At the time, most of the trustees were white men, though two spots were reserved for the chief and chairman of the EBCI Tribal Council. William P. Connor Jr., *History of Cherokee Historical Association 1946–1982*, Historical Association Board of Trustees (1982), 29.
7. Connor wrote the history at the behest of the 1982 CHA Board of Trustees. Connor 29.
8. Connor, *History of Cherokee Historical Association*, 29.
9. Connor, *History of Cherokee Historical Association*, 29–32.
10. Qtd. from the "Certificate of Incorporation of the Tsali Institute for Cherokee Research, Inc. (May 1951)," in *History of Cherokee Historical Association 1946–1982* (1982), 30.
11. Connor, *History of Cherokee Historical Association*, 32. These descriptions are reminiscent of World's Fair exhibitions. The insistence that the families live at the site and conduct quotidian life as if in the past is also reminiscent of Larissa FastHorse's play *Average Family* (Minneapolis: Plays for New Audiences, 2007).
12. Qtd. from a 1952 CHA report in *History of Cherokee Historical Association 1946–1982* (1982), 33.
13. Sue Meyer and Henry Meyer, "Visiting the Cherokees on a Tour of the Great Smokies," *New York Times* (August 22, 1954), X15. (Emphasis added.)
14. I include "passed" to highlight the situation of these notions along a progress-based timeline. Within this realm of thinking, Native Americans are not just relegated to the past but are seen has having been "passed" by Western society. Note the passive tense required for both syntactical and hegemonic construction.
15. Rifkin, *Beyond Settler Time*, 6.
16. Rifkin, *Beyond Settler Time*, 6.

LIVING HISTORY

17. I am invoking Gerald Vizenor's sense of the term, which combines "survival" and "resistance." See Gerald Vizenor, *Manifest Manners: Postindian Warriors of Survivance* (Middletown, CT: Wesleyan University Press, 1994), and *Survivance: Narratives of Native Presence*, ed. Gerald Vizenor (Lincoln: University of Nebraska Press, 2008).
18. See "Introduction to Verb Tenses," Purdue Owl (website), Purdue University, accessed April 17, 2023; "revolution, n.," *Oxford English Dictionary*. Oxford University Press, OED (website), accessed April 17, 2023. This site is now called Plimoth Patuxet Museum.
19. Notably, shifting the Pilgrim interpreters to third person was not mentioned as an option.
20. Scott Magelssen, *Living History Museums: Undoing History through Performance* (Lanham, MD: Scarecrow Press, 2007), 19.
21. Magelssen, *Living History Museums*, 20.
22. In looking at Plimoth Patuxet Museum's website, it seems that they have made many changes to their programming, including the production of a short video, *The Wampanoag Way*, which follows young Wampanoag sisters as they vacillate from their present-day lives to performing the past at Plimoth Patuxet Museum.
23. Rifkin, *Beyond Settler Time*, ix.
24. Rifkin, *Beyond Settler Time*, ix–x.
25. See "Introduction to Verb Tenses," Purdue Owl (website), Purdue University, accessed April 17, 2023; "revolution, n.," *Oxford English Dictionary*. Oxford University Press, OED (website), accessed April 17, 2023. The "White report" is referred to thusly in the original source because it was composed by Carol White, the CHA general manager. Quoted from "White report, CHA Records, 1952," *History of Cherokee Historical Association 1946–1982* (1982), 35.
26. Rifkin, *Beyond Settler Time*, 17.
27. Schneider, *Performing Remains*, 41.
28. These observations are based on my numerous visits to the village, the most recent in June 2021.
29. Fred Wilnoty Jr., personal interview, June 16, 2011.
30. Laura Blythe, email correspondence with Heidi L. Nees, January 31, 2022.
31. Howe, "Keep Your thoughts Above the Trees," 165.
32. Blythe, email correspondence with Heidi L. Nees, January 31, 2022.
33. Blythe, email correspondence with Heidi L. Nees, January 31, 2022.
34. Blythe, email correspondence with Heidi L. Nees, January 31, 2022.
35. Rifkin, *Beyond Settler Time*, 33.
36. Beth Capper and Rebecca Schneider, "Performance and Reproduction: Introduction," *TDR* 62, no. 1 (Spring 2018): 10.
37. Blythe, email correspondence with Heidi L. Nees, January 31, 2022.
38. See "First Conditional," English Language Centre, Continuing Studies @ UVIC (website), University of Victoria, British Columbia, accessed April 17, 2023 See "revolution, n.," *Oxford English Dictionary*. Oxford University Press, OED (website), accessed April 17, 2023. Rifkin, *Beyond Settler Time*, 25–26.
39. Will Daddario, "Here We Go Again: On Revolution," Mid-America Theatre Conference Theatre History Respondent Notes, distributed via email, January 12, 2022.

Part IV

BOOK REVIEWS

BOOK REVIEWS

Marginalized: Southern Women Playwrights Confront Race, Region, and Gender. By Casey Kayser. Jackson, MS: University Press of Mississippi, 2021. pp. xii + 204. $99.00 cloth. $30.00 paper.

In *Marginalized*, Casey Kayser turns her attention to female authors identified as multiply marginalized due to their gender, genre, sexuality, race, and region. Of the shared identity categories (gender, genre, region) among all writers featured, Kayser's analysis is primarily focused on region and the particular "prejudice and problems" faced by southern women playwrights who attempt to portray the South in drama (5). She argues that these women have employed a pattern of conscious strategies to confront and negotiate these difficulties, strategies Kayser has categorized within a framework formulated as "*placing, displacing*, and *re-placing*" the South (5). She considers plays from the modern and contemporary periods that combine southern authorship (authors who were born in or spent considerable time in the south) and subject matter (plays in which region is an important factor).

Following a brief introduction, Kayser provides a detailed contextual chapter in which she outlines the unique challenges of depicting the South onstage, including its geographic and ideological distance from the nation's theatrical center, New York City (17). Borrowing Una Chaudhuri's term, Kayser discusses the South onstage as a form of "geopathology," constructed from conflicting perceptions of the South as backward, racist, and violent—yet fetishized, romanticized, and mythologized. She devotes considerable attention to how regional identity intersects with other categories, offering a succinct overview of the historical devaluation of drama among literary genres and the long-standing gender inequity in the theatre industry, an inequity intensified by homophobia and racism.

Kayser devotes her second chapter to Lillian Hellman, reading three of Hellman's plays (*The Little Foxes* [1939], *Another Part of the Forest* [1946], and *The Autumn Garden* [1951]) as ones that *place* the South by employing an explicitly southern setting, presenting characters identified as southern, and drawing on familiar southern tropes and themes. Kayser views Hellman as "the foremother in the tradition of southern women playwrights," arguing that Hellman's vision of the South "acts as a place of departure for her successors," especially given Hellman's concern with "discrimination based on gender, racial, and sexual identity," in her use of satire and irony to critique the South, and her portrayal of white women's complicity in patriarchy (41, 66). Kayser reads all three plays as manifestations of geopathology, depicting characters who experience their current home as a problem and long for departure (64). In this chapter, Kayser also underscores Hellman's perception that critics and audiences frequently failed to see her satire, therefore missing her critique of traditional southern ideology.

In chapter 3, Kayser looks at three playwrights who explicitly placed the South through an overtly comic frame, a strategy Kayser credits Beth Henley with developing to "ensure satire will not be overlooked" (73). Kayser's examination of Henley's *Crimes of the Heart* (1980) in juxtaposition with the lesser-known *Flesh and Blood* by Elizabeth Dewberry (1996) is an enlightening choice. Kayser sees both plays as satirical critiques of white southern womanhood, noting how both use absurd juxtapositions to illustrate serious themes of familial dysfunction, adultery, and death. In *Crimes*, Babe coerces a fifteen-year-old Black boy into a sexual affair and shoots her husband. In *Flesh and Blood*, Dorris feeds her philandering husband a fatal dish of potato salad, and Charlotte stabs her sister in the back with a kitchen knife. Sandra Deer's *So Long on Lonely Street* (1986) is also set in the Gothic South, taking an unconventional approach to the depiction of familiar southern tropes, including incest, death and dead bodies, land disputes, and interracial relationships. Kayser argues for substantial misreadings of these plays, a circumstance she blames on lack of interpretive skills on the part of critics and audiences.

Chapter 4 explores the strategy of *displacing* the South (using the South as a peripheral physical setting or as present only in characters' memories) in Paula Vogel's *The Oldest Profession* (1981) and *How I Learned to Drive* (1997) and Pearl Cleage's *Chained* (1992). Kayser's reading of *How I Learned to Drive* views the contradictions in Peck's character as illustrating the complexity of southern identities and sexual mores. In both *The Oldest Profession* and *Chained*, characters have relocated from the South to New York City, a strategy that calls attention to how these two locations have been constructed in the popular imagination as polar opposites, a circumstance specifically relevant to southern playwrights presenting southern plays to New York audiences and critics. In its depiction of aging prostitutes who have been transplanted from the legendary red-light district of Storyville, Louisiana, to New York City, *The Oldest Profession* critiques nostalgia for a southern past that exists mostly in the imagination. *Chained* centers on the migration of a Black family from Alabama to Harlem, and both locations are experienced entirely through the voice of the play's single character, a young girl whose parents have chained her to a radiator in their apartment in a desperate attempt to keep her from accessing crack. Rosa embodies the two warring identities—the innocence and "backwardness" of the south, the sophistication and "corruption" of the city—and Cleage's ambiguous conclusion allows audiences to interpret which identity will dominate Rosa's future.

BOOK REVIEWS

Chapter 5 examines two plays by contemporary African American lesbian playwrights: Shay Youngblood's *Shakin' the Mess Outta Misery* (1988) and Sharon Bridgforth's *loveconjure/blues* (2007). Both works exemplify Kayser's concept of *re-placing* the South, as both works employ southern settings (a small southern town and a rural southern blues bar, respectively) but "break genre, temporal, and spatial constraints to redefine notions of belonging in southern communities" (6). As Kayser observes, the expanded belonging depicted in both works encompasses an embracing of African American lives in the South and of the African roots of their cultural traditions, the presence of first southerners (Native Americans), and nonbinary gender and sexual identities. Youngblood is a native Georgian, and in an interview with the author, Bridgforth reveals an interesting identity replacement, situating the South, from which her LA community had migrated, as a moveable feast and herself as "urban-raised and southern spirited" (146).

In her conclusion, Kayser exhorts readers to further study of southern female playwrights, identifying several possible lines of inquiry. Her study is a valuable contribution to many fields, including theatre studies, literary studies, gender studies, southern studies, and African American studies. It is authoritatively and engagingly written, and Kayser's focus on "southernness" and the intersection of region with gender, genre, race, and sexuality is timely. In recent years, there has been a surge of interest in this region of the United States and a growing conviction among political and cultural leaders that understanding the South, in all its complexity, is crucial to understanding America. Kayser's study may be seen as part of that larger project.

—CHERYL BLACK
University of Missouri (emerita)

Earth Matters on Stage: Ecology and Environment in the American Theater. By Theresa J. May. New York: Routledge, 2020. pp. xvi + 294. $44.95 paperback.

It's an understatement to say that things have changed since the advent of what could be called "environmental theatre studies." Most cite the publication of a special environmental issue of *Theater* magazine in 1994 as the formal emergence of a theatre studies interested in questions of the natural world—and humanity's place in it. Theresa J. May also cites this moment as the beginning of ecodramaturgy as a critical discourse, a scholarly conversation that has reached its next stage with May's most recent volume, *Earth Matters on Stage: Ecology and Environment in the American Theater*. In *Earth Matters*, May builds on her earlier formative work to offer a history of the US American theatre in service of her theory of ecodramaturgy: a roughly chronological "braided history and play analysis" (2) that includes the frontier myth in late-nineteenth-century US American theatre, the golden age US American musical (*Oklahoma!*) and canonical dramas (*Death of a Salesman*), theatre of the civil rights movement (*A Raisin in the Sun*; El Teatro Campesino), and contemporary climate change plays (*Burning Vision*; *Sila*), among others.

This historical excavation, May asserts, is critical to fostering a form of theatre that responds to climate change, one that reaches the form's potential to be "a potent force for social change and environmental awareness" (xii). The concept of ecodramaturgy is the main theoretical tool May deploys to this end. The volume lacks a clear definition of this term—or rather, it offers several conflicting definitions. Early in the book, May defines ecodramaturgy as "theater praxis that centers ecological relations by foregrounding as permeable and fluid the socially-constructed boundaries between nature and culture, human and nonhuman, individual and community" (4). To me, this is the most useful aspect of ecodramaturgy in the face of climate change: a self-reflexive shift in praxis that changes perspectives, thoughts, and ways of living. Also on page 4, May also presents ecodramaturgy as an interweaving of three strands: "(1) examining the often invisible environmental message of a play or production, making its ecological ideologies and implications visible; (2) using theater as a methodology to approach contemporary environmental problems (writing, devising, and producing new plays that engage environmental issues and themes); and (3) examining how theater as a material craft creates its own ecological footprint and works both to reduce waste and invent new approaches to material practice." Indeed, despite analyzing a wealth of examples that demonstrate the power of theatre to perpetuate *negative* social change and promote *anthropocentric* environmental awareness, May remains steadfast in her commitment to the possibilities of the theatrical form as a site of civic engagement.

As an example of the first strand of ecodramaturgy, May offers a nuanced analysis of the ways *Oklahoma!* not only appropriated an Indigenous story—*Green Grow the Lilacs* by Cherokee playwright Lynn Riggs—but also promulgated the violent and dangerous frontier myth that continues to influence US culture and politics. Through detailed attention to the text of the musical and the historical, social, and political context surrounding its first productions, May shows how "the musical offers up a whitewashed Oklahoma history that un-

BOOK REVIEWS

derscores the white supremacy implicit in U.S. nationalism" (122). As a reader, I hoped for more acknowledgment of or conversation about why such a play continues to be produced, the historical/social/political contexts that enable and are impacted by those productions, and how these affect environmental consciousness. In Hansberry's *Raisin in the Sun* and El Teatro Campesino's farmworkers' theatre, as examples of theatre during the civil rights movement, May sees precursors of later explicitly environmentally activist plays.

The case studies May treats in the book's final chapter, *Burning Vision* by Métis playwright Marie Clements (2003) and *Sila* by Chantal Bilodeau (2015) are arguably examples of the second type of ecodramaturgy, as both texts explicitly engage with environmental issues in their content. *Sila*, a kaleidoscopic story of climate scientists, Inuit families, and polar bears, is the first in Bilodeau's eight-play *Arctic Cycle*. Clements's play takes a single historical event—the detonation of atomic bombs over Japan—and expands outward to include the many different lives (human and nonhuman) touched by it: the Indigenous Dene workers who carried the radioactive black ore from the mine; radium girls who contracted cancer from their work in factories; Japanese families decimated by the bomb. *Burning Vision* appears often in May's ecocritical work; she repeatedly draws on it to demonstrate "theater's innate capacity to bend time and space into the hyper-present of the stage, making imaginative connections between temporally and spatially disconnected effects of climate change. In this way, theater serves as a kind of collective imaginative research into the lived experience of climate change" (241). In the book's conclusion, May reiterates that "ecodramaturgy is both a stance from which artists might proceed as well as from which to conduct dramaturgical analysis and historical study" (280). By engaging in the multiple aspects of ecodramaturgy, those of us in the theatre can "take a stand where we stand" (279) to "strategically animate" (280) the nonhuman world.

May consciously does not address the third strand of ecodramaturgy, namely how the material practice of theatre affects the environment and ways to reduce its impact, in this text. She has previously addressed this area, namely in her 1994 work *Greening Up Our Houses: A Guide to a More Ecologically Sound Theatre*, coauthored with Larry K. Fried. Yet, I found that the separation of the messages of theatre from the methods of their creation in *Earth Matters* made May's advocacy message less powerful. If theatre truly is to be a force for shifting environmental consciousness, it must also shift its own consciousness, including material practice.

Scholars and students of US theatre will find in *Earth Matters* both a reframing of canonical theatrical events and an important theoretical tool for writing new histories. But we must also, to borrow the title of May's earlier work,

BOOK REVIEWS

green up our own houses. This consideration applies not only to theatre practice but also to theatre studies. May argues that "we cannot proceed without understanding the ways in which theater has already participated in shaping social behavior and national policies" (1). I would add that we cannot proceed without understanding the ways theatre *studies* has participated in these same ideological movements. Just as theatre production cannot be environmentally sustainable without significant material changes, neither can theatre scholarship contribute to shifting ecological attitudes without significant changes to our practices: to truly cultivate change, our methods need to change as much as the content of our work does.

—SHELBY BREWSTER
Michigan State University

Carrying All Before Her: Celebrity Pregnancy and the London Stage, 1689–1800. By Chelsea Phillips. Newark: University of Delaware Press, 2022. pp. xi + 287. $120.00 hardback, $34.95 paperback.

When England's famed "Tragic Muse," Sarah Siddons, stepped onto the Drury Lane stage in the fall of 1785 as Lady Macbeth, she was pregnant with her sixth child. Siddons had premiered her Lady Macbeth in London in February of that year to critical acclaim; returning to the character three times during this pregnancy (and during several pregnancies that followed), Siddons's gravid body invited audiences to read Shakespeare's infamous Lady M not as "unsexed" and masculine but as reproductive and maternal. In *Carrying All Before Her: Celebrity Pregnancy and the London Stage, 1689–1800*, Chelsea Phillips mines the theatrical archive for signs of expectant mothers taking to (or temporarily vacating) the stages of London's premiere theatres. Employing a wealth of primary sources—company documents, newspaper reviews, satirical cartoons, memoirs, correspondence, and medical and parish records, among others—Phillips constructs a nuanced history of celebrity pregnancy that counters extant depictions of childbearing as almost always injurious to women's acting careers in the long eighteenth century. Phillips's is the first book to "address pregnancy as a specific and significant phenomenon in its own right" on the stage (6), complementing discrete studies of eighteenth-century motherhood, theatrical celebrity, actresses, and women's social roles, including those by Felicity Nussbaum, Helen Brooks, Joseph Roach, Marvin Carlson, and Lisa Freeman. With

{ 166 }

chapters detailing six performers whose reproductive lives coincided with their well-documented careers, *Carrying All Before Her* powerfully resists the historical erasure of Georgian-era actresses' pregnancies and the company accommodations that enabled them to keep working.

Phillips begins her introduction with Tony Award–winning performer Audra McDonald, whose 2016 pregnancy was blamed by producers for the premature closure of George C. Wolfe's *Shuffle Along, or, the Making of the Musical Sensation of 1921 and All That Followed* on Broadway, despite there being a contingency plan for covering her maternity leave. In attempting to recoup their investments through an insurance claim, producers positioned McDonald's (Black and pregnant) body "as having autonomously acted, disrupting and destroying the commercial viability of an artistic project" (2). The *Shuffle Along* debacle, Phillips argues, only partly resembles the workplace arrangements made between eighteenth-century pregnant celebrities and their employers, both of whom did not "resume a fundamental conflict between reproductive and economic labor" (3). Acknowledging that the accommodations proffered to celebrity actresses were likely not given to all pregnant performers, Phillips asserts that "pregnancy affected celebrity identity, impacted audience reception and interpretation of performance, changed company repertory and altered company hierarchy, influenced the development and performance of new work, and had substantial economic consequences both for women and for the companies for which they worked" (7). In four chapters, Phillips investigates the reproductive lives of actresses Susanna Mountfort Verbruggen, Anne Oldfield, Susannah Cibber, George Anne Bellamy, Sarah Siddons, and Dorothy Jordan, locating at the intersections of pregnancy, celebrity, and labor public performances of expectant maternity that ranged from the subtle to the spectacular.

Chapter 1 centers on the pregnancies of Mountfort Verbruggen and Oldfield, who, as Phillips suggests, "capitalized on different readings of the pregnant body to the same end: career advancement" (34). Whereas Mountfort Verbruggen made use of her pregnant body within a successful series of grotesque comic character parts, Oldfield expanded her lines of business to include tragic heroines "whose stoic natures enabled her to construct her pregnant body as classically contained" (31). The chapter's pairing of Mountfort Verbruggen and Oldfield also allows Phillips to chronicle a natural (though unfortunate) consequence of performers' reproductive lives: when Mountfort Verbruggen died from childbirth complications, Oldfield inherited a number of her roles. The book's next chapter focuses on Cibber and Bellamy, whose public scandals—an adultery trial for Cibber, counterfeit marriages and accusations of child neglect for Bellamy—affected how their extramarital pregnancies were read by audiences and critics. Throughout the chapter, Phillips situates the women's reproductive lives and the extreme passions they embodied onstage within the century's culture of sensibility. Whereas Cibber carefully curated a public image by obscuring aspects of her private life from view, a process Phillips labels as "tenebrism" after the Italianate painting technique (76), Bellamy combatted her declining reputation by embracing maternal roles onstage and sentimentalizing her life choices through a published memoir.

Sarah Siddons and Dorothy Jordan each receive their own chapters, owing both to the extensive source materials (archival and secondary) dedicated to them and the performers' many pregnancies. These chapters are the book's brightest; Phillips ably contrasts Siddons's capacity to "synthesize her on- and offstage performances of maternity into a powerful celebrity persona" with Jordan's disparate and shifting theatrical and social roles (32). Phillips's reading of Siddons's visibly pregnant Lady Macbeth is absorbing, as is her assessment of the fluctuations in Jordan's public identities over her thirty-year stage career, from celebrated actress to disparaged royal mistress to respected mother. As she did with Cibber's courtroom trial and Bellamy's memoir, Phillips usefully extends her thesis beyond the stage proper by analysing how satirical cartoons depicting Jordan with William, Duke of Clarence participated in the construction of Jordan's celebrity identity. Any redundancies found across the six case studies do little to hamper *Carrying All Before Her*'s compelling narrative, and Phillips is a confident and careful historian who suggests rather than pronounces what eighteenth-century audiences would have thought and felt while watching pregnant actresses at work.

I held *Carrying All Before Her* in my hands the very day that radical justices installed on the US Supreme Court overturned *Roe v. Wade* and revoked citizens' constitutional right to obtain abortions. It is perhaps unsurprising that Phillips's work felt weighty to me that day. If I had read the book even six months before, I might have taken for granted the pragmatic accommodations made for pregnant celebrities or mistakenly regarded Phillips's project as more niche than it actually is. Documenting the entangled, simultaneous nature of the eighteenth-century pregnant celebrity's many labors (reproductive, theatrical, economic, social, maternal), Phillips plots theatre workplace accommodations for reproduction and caregiving not on a strong upward curve toward the present day but on an irregular line that leaves in doubt the future trajectory of such critical arrangements.

—MEREDITH CONTI
University at Buffalo, SUNY

BOOK REVIEWS

The Chinese Atlantic: Seascapes and the Theatricality of Globalization. By Sean Metzger. Bloomington: Indiana University Press, 2020. pp. 274. $25.00 paperback.

In *The Chinese Atlantic: Seascapes and the Theatricality of Globalization*, Sean Metzger considers how artworks across multiple mediums challenge established paradigms of globalization to situate viewers' thoughts on the relationship between China and many Atlantic nations. The author scrutinizes "seascapes," an inherently dramatic genre of artworks primarily connected to the Dutch masters. He asserts that a seascape, while a stagnant painting, "captures a moment" in an ever-changing environment (20), with angular images and dramatic scenes that together infer the theatrical nature of the painting. Though the artworks he deems as seascapes eventually go beyond the medium of static oil paintings, Metzger begins his study there after a brief prologue, wherein the author declares that his book is *not* autoethnographic. Unlike many of the artists he considers, Metzger is uninterested in tracing his own familial oceanic crossings. While this formidable tome may not be a work of personal history, the "archaeology of seaways" crafted by Metzger within the pages of his book refracts tiny glimpses of the author's own (his)story (3).

Metzger's analysis begins by connecting the Dutch artistic tradition of seascapes with the global efforts of the Dutch East India Company, contending that the beginning strands of globalization emerged with the Northern European country's maritime sojourns to and from China. Metzger compares the pelagic "flow" of spices, ideas, and people from centuries ago to today's flow of migrants, information, and manufactured goods on a circular global scale, situating the sites and seascapes he discusses as "caught" in the flow of economic and political gains. It is from these notions that Metzger draws his methodology for this book: analyzing how perceptions of Chinese individuals and "Chineseness," or "the forces that construct the term *Chinese*" (5), have drifted over the last five hundred years, especially from a Western point of view. While the Dutch masters painted their seascapes in the seventeenth century, the artworks examined in this book were created throughout the twentieth and twenty-first centuries.

In each of his chapters, Metzger focuses on what he calls "logics" of "Chinese circulation in the Atlantic world" (38), or ideas that underlay the system of Chinese diaspora throughout Western civilization. The chapter titles reflect the dynamic nature of seascapes by using aqueous active verbs that indicate each chapter's central "logic." The first three chapters examine seascapes of the Caribbean Sea. In chapter 1, "Reeling," Metzger articulates his thoughts on the Chinese Atlantic as seen through narrative documentary films, viewing a broad swath of selections from 1988 to 2016, even including one that was still in production at the time of the book's publication. The chapter title is a play on "reeling" in fish, part of the fisherfolk occupation, and film "reels," or pre-digital cinematic apparatuses. The author notes that the dozen documentaries he critiques attempt to illustrate something "real," in this case "factors of family, history, labor, and migration" that specifically navigate the Chinese Caribbean, to archive the Chinese Atlantic experience (39).

For his second chapter, "Incorporating," Metzger discusses abstract representations of seascapes, including murals, installations, and sculptures. Focusing solely on the island of Trinidad, known for its rich deposits of fossil fuels, the author asserts that artists Nicole Awai, Carlisle Chang, Willi Chen, and Christopher Cozier reframe globalized economic notions of Chinese-Atlantic economic and political ties in works created between 1964 and 2018. This chapter's title alludes to "incorporated" businesses alongside the emulsifying nature of spilled oil and seawater in the myriad Caribbean-based capitalist ecological disasters. Metzger's chosen artworks utilize processed materials like construction foam and nail polish and hang in centers of Trinidadian commerce, all while commenting on the history of "coolies," or indentured workers trafficked from China to the Caribbean for commercial pursuits during the nineteenth century, whose descendants still populate the island today.

With chapter 3, "Flowing," Metzger surveys corporeal artistic practices on the island of Martinique. Unlike the coolies of Trinidad, many individuals with Chinese heritage on this island are merchants, with an income that allows for freedom of movement. Nodding in the chapter title to the "flow" of tai chi, Metzger interprets "living seascapes," or movement works combining traditional Chinese martial arts. In this chapter, Metzger takes up the work of tai chi artist Michel Assouvie, whose embodiment practices span more than thirty years, beginning in the late 1980s. Assouvie's performances mirror the Chinese Atlantic networks of migrants and families that stem from Martinique, a hub for Chinese immigrants to the Caribbean.

Chapters 4 and 5 take the reader from one side of the Atlantic to the other, homing in on two British ports-of-call and the Chineseness found among them, particularly Morecambe Bay, in England, and Cape Town, South Africa. The two pieces (Nick Broomfield's 2006 film *Ghosts* and Isaac Julien's immersive film experience *Ten Thousand Waves*) dissected in the fourth chapter, "Ebbing," concern the drowning of Chinese migrant workers in Morecambe Bay, with the titular verb indicating how the bodies of the individuals were discovered on the sands after the receding tide. With this chapter, Metzger capitalizes on the dialectical nature of "flow" and "ebb," recognizing the potential coercive nature of migration in a globalized society. The author notes echoes of stagnation, mortality, and erasure found in these disquieting pieces. "Eddying," the last chapter in the book, recognizes the circular nature of ocean currents. In Cape Town, Metzger reencounters Julien's *Ten Thousand Waves* alongside other artistic seascapes that comment on the spiraling reality of post/colonization and highlight the impacts of English and Dutch occupation on the southernmost tip of Africa, a reflection of Chinese-inflected globalization. From Chinese-heritage characters onstage in Pieter-Dirk Uys's 2015 play *African Times* to audiovisual reverberations of the Chinese Cultural Revolution and South African apartheid found in William Kentridge's 2015 video installation *More Sweetly Play the Dance* and several pieces of street art by DALeast crafted between 2011 and 2014, these artworks push against dominant currents of postcolonial thought and frame Cape Town as a transtemporal nexus point of Chinese Atlantic trade.

Metzger's epilogue completes the circuit, bringing the Atlantic to China. The author considers the voyage of Cai Guo-Qiang's 2014 sculpture *The Ninth Wave*, a title invoking Aivazovsky's 1850 oil-on-canvas opus. The New York–based artist's sculpture of an animal-filled wooden vessel à la Noah's Ark sailed from his home province to Shanghai, where it was installed. The exhibit, housed in the heart of a city that embodies China's economic achievements, features several artistic experiences of industrial waste, crude accumulation, and ecological devastation, situating the climatic (and climactic) impacts of commercial globalization.

As his book closes, the author acknowledges the potentially disorienting nature of his ambitious monograph, suggesting a true politics of form. Indeed, readers are submerged in a sea of theories, ideas, and analyses. Undertows pull readers into carefully constructed case studies deftly helmed by the author. Thus, with the book's churning and circular structure, indicative of global currents both political and oceanic, Sean Metzger has crafted a seascape himself.

—ZACH DAILEY
Lamar State College—Port Arthur

Lying in the Middle: Musical Theater and Belief at the Heart of America. By Jake Johnson. Urbana: University of Illinois Press, 2021. ix + 159 pp. $24.95 paperback.

Lying in the Middle, by Jake Johnson, represents a remarkable approach to "post-truth" era performance, providing theories on how, why, and where musical theatre is having its greatest cultural impact. Johnson's title refers to three main dimensions, "place, centrality, and duplicity," and *Lying* is made up of seven chapters in which Johnson examines the cultural, geographical, and narrative place of contemporary US musicals (Johnson 2021, 14). One of Johnson's central arguments is that the representations of the world that musicals offer are both inherently dishonest (massive song-and-dance interludes do not pepper our daily lives) and also point the way to larger, simpler truths. Johnson insists that moving beyond the lies musicals tell us about ourselves leads to a kind of truth telling that limits the theatre's ability to be poetic or imaginative. This "post-truth" moment is not a time for brutal honesty, Johnson argues, but rather an opportunity to gently shift our community values through easy lies. In this way, musicals can give audiences the false confidence necessary to be optimistic about the flexibility of our reality. As Johnson argues, musical theatre's widespread appeal and power to suspend our disbelief—it's "lying"—has profound implications for its ability to expand our imaginations, leading to real-world changes.

Johnson focuses his investigation around four case studies of performances that occur in the "middle" of the United States that also "fulfill a central role in identity formation," via duplicity, for various communities (14). The internal chapters range in their focus, including a close examination of a 1994 Mormon adaptation of *The Sound of Music*, a study of Sight & Sound Theatres' work in Branson, Missouri, ethnographic research into the Oklahoma Senior Follies, and a field-wide criticism of what Johnson calls the "Broadway voice," a cookie-cutter type of singing that relies on a mimicking of other Broadway cast recordings (96). Because the case studies are so different and range so widely in their scope, they occasionally feel like they do not belong in the same book. What ties the book together instead are Johnson's theories about the importance of musical theatre performance as a tool for bringing communities together via its emphasis on poetic lying rather than truth telling.

Common criticisms of a "post-truth" society highlight the ways in which lies explode in their potency, laying the groundwork for demagogues in public spheres and gaslighting abusers in private ones. Johnson, conversely, sees value in the ways that musical theatre's white lies can "dislodge [us] from the ennui of neoliberalism, corruption, social inequity, impending climate disasters, and so on" (7). Johnson's focus is the work musical theatre performance can inspire—or, in a less generous sense, *trick*—communities and individuals into doing in service of the egalitarian possibilities shown to them onstage. For example, in chapter 4 Johnson describes the work of Sight & Sound Theatres in Branson, Missouri, a theatre that originates spectacular musicals based on biblical stories. By creating enormous, high-production musicals, Johnson argues that Sight &

Sound enables its audiences to "see and hear themselves in ancient stories" (67). The experience leads audiences to a blending of their biblical understanding and contemporary lives, facilitating greater faith and a sense of belonging with their fellow pilgrims. Johnson refers to Jill Dolan's 2010 book, *Utopia in Performance: Finding Hope at the Theater*, but Dolan's utopian performatives are different in action from the mendacity that lies at the center of Johnson's book. For Dolan, utopian performatives create real moments of utopia that lift us beyond the present in a mutual exchange between the artist and audience. For Johnson, "theatrical deception" is an important tool artists use to showcase and explore new society-changing ideas (1). Perhaps the difference in these two approaches reflects the markedly different political climate of the United States in 2010 and in 2021, and Johnson is providing a post-Trump tool kit for artists looking to have a direct impact on their audience members.

Those familiar with Johnson's 2019 book, *Mormons, Musical Theater, and Belonging in America*, might think this book would also have much to say about theological connections to musical theatre within the contemporary United States. Rather, while Johnson's first two case studies explore versions of faith-based (Christian) performances, thereafter his attention turns secular. His fifth chapter, which examines the Oklahoma Senior Follies, attempts to portray the troupe's use of mash-up songs as a theological invention, which is a stretch given the limited religious focus of the group's work. As the book's title suggests, Johnson is more interested in belief than in religious faith. This focus reveals a great deal about the impact of musical theatre in the United States outside of traditional urban centers, in particular the formation of specific community identities through musical performance. With most musical theatre scholarship focusing on the activity of Broadway and Hollywood, Johnson's work criticizes that focus and offers an extended portrayal of the impact musicals have in places whose performance habits are not often preserved in scholarship.

Johnson's book itself is written in a poetic and commanding style that does not overly rely on his audience's familiarity with concepts in performance studies. Admirably, his work seems ready to engage with many of the audiences he writes about in his case studies: amateur theatremakers from the Middle of America. Sometimes Johnson depends on clever turns of phrase more than is helpful, particularly at the beginnings and ends of chapters. Johnson's prose begs for attention in these moments rather than solidifying his argument, but it also succeeds in maintaining this reader's interest. Overall, students and practitioners of community-based performance and musical theatre scholarship would be well-served in examining *Lying* as a tool for experimentation and well-intentioned deception through performance. The book is written in a very approachable style, making it a good fit for undergraduate or graduate curricula. In particular, educators interested in applied theatre, US theatre, community-based theatre, and the evolution of musicals will find a deliberate post-truth perspective here for students and continuing research. *Lying in the Middle* has perhaps too much to say, what with its two separate introductory chapters, and spends too little effort providing evidence for its theories in a relatively short 159 pages. *Lying* proves, however, to be a book that empowers musical theatre as an aspirational and inspirational force for community cohesion and transformation, especially outside of coastal and über-professionalized spaces.

—MICHAEL DEWHATLEY
University of Texas at Austin

Pure Filth: Ethics, Politics, and Religion in Early French Farce. By Noah D. Guynn. Philadelphia: University of Pennsylvania Press, 2020. pp. 272. £56.00/$69.95 cloth.

The front and back covers of Noah Guynn's *Pure Filth: Ethics, Politics, and Religion in Early French Farce* may at face value be taken as a silly and lewd depiction of two acrobats farting in each other's faces, but the image is expertly unpacked as an example of the subtlety that can be found in farce. Guynn argues that the essence of medieval French farce performance (approximately 1050–1450 CE) is more than just "low" ribald humor; rather, it is a subversive thread of aspirational purity woven through the plays. In service of this thesis, a series of primary documents and texts are put in conversation with a plethora of scholars and sources: some drawn from ancient times, such as the Bible and Thomas Aquinas, and some from modern scholars like Sandy Bardsley and Jason A. Josephson Storm. The four lengthy chapters are broken into several sections, which allow for the reader to be guided in the analysis of the various farces discussed in the manuscript. *Pure Filth* is a welcome addition to the scholarship on medieval theatre broadly (and farces specifically) and really shines when it demonstrates how applying theory to historical material can allow for a plethora of interpretations.

The introduction and first two chapters put forward an anthropological interpretation of performance that goes against the predominant idea that medieval French farce operated much like a "pressure release valve" (12) for society, allowing a little dissent to escape via performance in order to keep the unruly underclasses happy. However, Guynn asserts that instead of being seen as a naughty "allowed fool," the performance of farce is a powerful and subversive act of theatre that is "a highly intricate, deeply self-conscious cultural form that can accommodate . . . conflicting modes of interpretation" (6). As evidence of this, he brings up records of farceurs being arrested and prosecuted in court for their performances. Chapter 2 is dedicated to "the unquestioned masterpiece of the genre . . . *Maistre Pierre Pathelin*" (71) and uses a deep textual and linguistic analysis of the play to further a theory of the work as a "sacred parody" (82) where humor arises when the ludicrous actions of the characters are contrasted with stories from the Bible. The chapter is rounded out with a survey of the production history of *Maistre Pierre Pathelin* (and its sequels), offering proof of its enduring popularity through referential parodies in later plays.

Guynn's claim that farces, like medieval mystery and miracle plays, engage with Christian morality forms the core of chapter 3, which takes up Andrieu de La Vigne's *Mystère de Saint Martin* (1496 CE). In looking at the aforementioned mystery play and the secular farces written around it, Guynn brings attention to the two medieval performance traditions, which are usually examined separately, by pointing out how farces ask audiences to question established norms, a practice similar to what theologians and scholars do on a regular basis. The juxtaposition of Christian morality with scatological humor may seem incongruous, but Guynn argues that farces "bring blasphemy and heterodoxy into play as the irrepressible others of sacrament and dogma" (115). The French playwright La Vigne's farce *Le meunier*, in which a wife commands her husband, who is dying of an intestinal illness, to "extend his ass over the side of the bed" so that his final defecation can also release his soul (116), is perhaps the best example of how the scatological mixes with the holy. Guynn questions whether farce functions as a means of resistance against the ethical dogmatism of the church or as a way of confirming Christian morals through the performance of bad behavior.

Perhaps the most engaging section of the book is chapter 4, "Making History: Misbehaved Women, Well-Behaved Women, and the Sexual Politics of Farce," which takes up a feminist and gender studies perspective on the subject matter. The "woman on top" metaphor is the driving theme of the chapter with Guynn looking behind the standard domesticity in the plot of *Serre Porte et Fin Verjus* (early 1520s CE) to cite scholars of kink in the discussion of the power exchange between submissive and dominant characters in the household, a positionality that is then upended by characters tricking each other through disguises. Guynn discusses cross-dressing, an enduring trope of farce, in the context of the depiction of domestic gender dynamics. The stage directions of one comic scene call for a cross-dressed husband to "respond to his wife as a wife: *en femme*" (169), which serves to trouble the monolithic perception of husbands as both masculine and dominant. In *Le poulier à six personnages* (early 1500s), linguistic and textual analysis of the upended gender identities in the dramatis personae leads to a confusion of sexual difference as two of the characters are described as "the two wives of the two gentlemen, who are clothed as ladies" (192). Other farces showcase female characters in positions of economic and spiritual power, such as in *Quatre Femmes* (early 1500s), where a woman purchases a papal bull and the robes of a priest in order to earn money hearing confession. The chapter provides an extensive refutation of the submissive feminie form in farce and instead proposes that a specific kind of subversive agency for female characters was present in performance.

A short afterword, "Against Protoforms," begins with a discussion of "protofeminism" before developing into an insightful exploration of the historiography of modern theoretical terms as applied to historical subjects. Guynn points to the past struggles of "peasants, clerks, women, queers, and subalterns" as a guide for the future (226). The dramatic cover illustration offers a much-needed visual aspect to the discussion of medieval farce; although perhaps difficult to find, more imagery throughout the volume would have allowed a deeper appreciation of the historical conditions of live performance. Interested readers would benefit from the inclusion of an appendix of primary sources to ease the finding of documents, rather than embedding them in the lengthy works cited at the end of the book. Likewise, footnotes rather than endnotes may serve to put additional information at readers' fingertips, especially considering the manuscript's concise endnotes. While the heavy engagement with theory may drive off undergraduates looking for an easy summary of French farces, the deep reading of performance texts and their analysis, using the works of current medieval and performance studies scholars (and the author's own crisp wit), are the most enjoyable aspects of the book. In short, even a medieval theatre scholar familiar with all the plays discussed will find something new to consider in this work. This book would no doubt be useful for graduate students and other scholars who are interested in medieval performance, the history of comedy, historical feminism, or Christian ecclesiology in secular performance.

—WHIT EMERSON
SUNY Oswego

Emily Mann: Rebel Artist of the American Theatre. By Alexis Greene. Guilford, CT; Applause Theatre and Cinema Books, 2021. Pp. vii + 391. $29.95, paper.

BOOK REVIEWS

Alexis Greene's comprehensive biography of Emily Mann confirms her as an icon of late-twentieth and early-twenty-first-century US American theatre and provides a window into the struggles Mann encountered as she became a titan of both not-for-profit and commercial theatre landscapes. Greene reveals what it took for Mann to ascend the hierarchical theatre industry in the 1980s and 1990s. To Greene, Mann embodies the notion that "resistance can reside in defying preconceived assumptions of what a woman of the theater can stage or write or, finally, achieve" (ix). Greene's captivating biography divulges Mann's immense impact on theatre as a director, playwright, translator, adaptor, and innovator of form, as well as her long tenure as artistic director at the McCarter Theatre. The book provides an all too rare but important insight into the working methods and creative mind of a female theatre director.

The first several chapters illuminate how Mann's parents and education influenced her as an artist. Mann's father was a history professor at Smith College and then at the University of Chicago and was active in the 1960s civil rights movement. Her mother created opportunities for Mann to explore her artistic side through music and theatre. Mann began high school at the University of Chicago Lab School, which "provided an ideal place for encouraging Emily's self-esteem and self-reliance, her imagination and empathy, and an independent way of thinking" (34). The traits cultivated at this pedagogically innovative school became the foundation for Mann's directing and playwriting. Her devotion to theatre was made permanent at Radcliffe, where she studied as an undergraduate and explored experimental ways of directing at the Loeb Drama Center on Harvard's campus. Greene's insights into Mann's artistic process illuminate Mann's capacity for intellectual rigor and artistic obsession. For example, Greene reveals that "during most of her career, Mann would fill pocket-sized notebooks with ideas about the plays she was directing or writing" (59). Mann's early ability to develop high-concept productions and themes is evinced by her Artaud-influenced concept for Tennessee Williams's *Suddenly Last Summer*, which she proposed for an undergraduate modern American drama course at Radcliffe (60).

The next chapters explore Mann's professional beginning when she received the Bush Fellowship in Directing at the Guthrie Theater. This provided her an entrée into the not-for-profit theatre establishment. Mann worked with the "esteemed artistic director Michael Langham," received her Equity card, and after the second year was awarded an MFA in directing from the University of Minnesota (73). Simultaneously, Mann was developing her artistic voice as a playwright with her first "testimonial drama" based on the oral history interviews of Annulla Allen, who rescued her husband from Dachau in World War II (79).

Greene, perhaps unwittingly, reveals the enormous privilege influencing Mann's rise to theatrical stardom. From her Ivy League education and summers tramping about Europe to her first attempts at playwriting presented on the experimental Guthrie 2 stage, Mann had inroads to success that were embedded in the opportunity afforded by her race and social class.

Greene goes on in the next chapters to detail the ways in which Mann paved a creative path for herself as both a director and a playwright, and she also reveals details of her personal life. Mann met her first husband, actor Gerry Bamman, at the Guthrie and eventually moved into his East Village apartment when she moved to New York City in the summer of 1979. Bamman was already an established New York actor and had worked with André Gregory in his renowned 1970 production of *Alice in Wonderland*. Mann's opportunities came fast and furious in New York, and she was quickly hired to direct at the newly formed BAM Theatre Company. Then and throughout her artistic career, Mann seemed to have several projects brewing at all times, and her energy and enthusiasm for artistic detail appeared to be boundless. She honed her writing skills developing two additional documentary dramas that were workshopped and developed at the country's top regional theatres: *Still Life* had premiered at the Goodman Theatre in 1980 and *Execution of Justice* premiered at the Actors Theatre of Louisville in 1984 for the influential Humana Festival (182). Greene's biography gives the reader a glimpse into the long and arduous process of birthing a play and Mann's dogged determination in bringing works such as these to fruition.

Greene spends several key chapters describing Mann's tenure as artistic director of the McCarter Theatre in Princeton, New Jersey. Mann was awarded the position on December 4, 1989, and Greene reminds us that "out of LORT's sixty-eight theaters in 1989, she was the eleventh woman to lead a member theater" (224). There were many challenges when she arrived, and Mann hadn't been informed about the theatre's dire financial situation. Chapter 12, "By the Scruff of the Neck," describes the determination Mann brought to her role as artistic director when she saved the McCarter from economic and artistic ruin. Mann never shied away from risky theatrical endeavors and brought racial and artistic diversity and politically challenging productions to the McCarter, like 1991's *Betsey Brown*, which she cowrote with Ntozake Shange. Mann's inclusion of David Rabe's three-and-a-half-hour play *Those the River Keeps* in her 1991 inaugural season, which was accompanied by a caution to the audience that "the play had tough content and rough language," alienated longtime subscribers (210). Mann is quoted in her interviews with Greene about navigating those waters as a new artistic director with no prior experience managing budgets, personnel, boards, or a subscription base: "I definitely lost most of the old, established Princeton audience during my first few seasons. It wasn't for them. And I was very happy to wave goodbye. And a new group did come in" (247). Indeed, Greene reports that Mann had entered her second season with a $900,000 deficit but by its end had balanced the books and increased the subscription base by 30 percent (247).

Greene's biography will appeal to a broad audience of both theatre scholars and theatre afficionados, as she reveals both the personal and professional sides of Emily Mann the artist. The book offers practical guidance for theatre students hoping to carve an artistic path for themselves as directors, playwrights, or arts administrators. Greene reveals the personal sacrifice and cost of a life in the theatre, as she discusses the heartbreaking loss of Mann's father, her divorce, and diagnosis of multiple sclerosis, none of which hindered her artistic production. Through hundreds of hours of interviews leading up to Mann's recent retirement as artistic director of the McCarter Theatre, Greene provides an intimate portrait of Emily Mann's determination and persistence as well as her artistic achievements and influence across a generation of US American theatre makers and spectators.

—NANCY JONES
University of Kentucky

Shakespeare in Montana: Big Sky Country's Love Affair with the World's Most Famous Writer. By Gretchen E. Minton. Albuquerque: University of New Mexico Press, 2020. Pp. xviii + 196. $19.95, paperback.

Gretchen E. Minton ardently evokes the interplay of Montana's vast, gorgeous, and even threatening landscape with "the imaginative expansiveness" (111) of "the 'largest' of authors" (xvii). That theme pervades her six chapters and five shorter interlude sections covering the history of Shakespeare in Montana, the role of women, the Western theatrical context, minority groups, academia, and miscellaneous artistic endeavors, along with a special focus on Montana Shakespeare in the Parks (MSIP). Minton's enthusiasm extends to her captions for the thirty-four black-and-white illustrations. Another delight is the surprising pertinence of the quotations from Shakespeare chosen as epigraphs for each section.

The prologue, "Waiting for the Shakespeare," zeroes in on the remote south-eastern Montana town of Birney (population seventeen in 1980), where MSIP has performed on tour every season since its founding in 1973. Eagerly awaited by people from the surrounding area as much as a hundred miles away, the company finds a welcoming community with volunteers to help them set up the stage on Poker Jim Butte ten miles from town. The community raises funds, arranges lodgings in homes, and offers potluck meals for their annual visitors. The reminiscences from multiple sources intertwine references to specific plays with awe at the panoramic views in "this wild and beautiful place" (9).

Minton casts a wider net in her historical survey chapters, asserting Shakespeare's early importance to Montana by noting that his works accompanied the Bible as the books most often carried and discussed around the campfire by mountain men or cowboys. Although he was illiterate, Jim Bridger, through his obsession with Shakespeare, gave rise to a wealth of colorful anecdotes; an endnote attests that on at least one occasion, he visited what is today Montana. Another 1860s pioneer, Granville Stuart, traveled more extensively in Montana, including a 150-mile jaunt on horseback to buy five books, including Shakespeare. Figuring among many additional examples of early bardophilia was Sacagawea's son, described by a contemporary as "the Shakespeare-quoting half-Indian trapper" (25).

Montana became a territory in 1864 and a state in 1889. With an increasing population, it attracted theatrical touring companies like that of Colorado-based Jack Langrische and later of Frederick Warde. With towns large enough to support newspapers came published records of Shakespeare performances. For example, Laura Honey Agnes Stevenson's 1879 solo burlesque of the balcony scene in *Romeo and Juliet* won rowdy applause for her declarations of love to a dummy mannequin Romeo. By 1900, many mining communities had become ghost towns. Minton concludes chapter 2 with one of her frequent enthusiasms: "In the restless movements of these settlers during the 'golden age' of mining, Shakespeare symbolized permanence, for his cultural legacy was more stable than the boom and bust economies of mineral extraction" (51).

Women became the driving force for culture around the turn of the century. Numerous towns saw reading circles like the Shakespeare Club that formed in Dillon in the 1890s. Some of these clubs sponsored lectures and even ventured into amateur production. Minton's research is at its most thorough in gleaning these stories. Butte held the most noteworthy activities for the Shakespeare Tercentenary in 1916. Jumping ahead one hundred years, we learn of 2016 events in Missoula and Bozeman. The historical record of African American and Native American performance in Montana is sparse, but Minton has collected some impressive documentation. She goes on to assess Shakespeare's place in Montana's schools.

Minton's final chapter returns to focus on MSIP, which originated at Montana State University (MSU) in Bozeman. She traces its evolution and cultural contributions to the state through its three artistic directors: Bruce Jacobsen, 1973–1980; Joel Jahnke, 1980–2013; and Kevin Asselin. That coverage is excellent, but the omission of Shakespeare in Missoula is unfortunate, especially since many of the book's other cursory connections to Shakespeare are in the realm of "might have" or "must have." Having earned my BA at the University of Montana in Missoula, I wanted more on its ties to the renowned Daniel E. Bandmann, to whom Minton does devote six pages, as well as an endnote on the Daniel E. Bandmann Achievement Award for Outstanding Success in All Phases of Theatre (which I am proud to have been awarded in 1962). Our chair, Firman (Bo) Brown, regularly directed Shakespeare; I had the pleasure of playing Miranda in his *The Tempest* and touring with Montana Masquers as Lady Percy in *Henry IV, Part 1*. Given my experience in playing small towns, as well as Great Falls, on that extensive tour, Minton's evocative details about touring Montana ring true and nostalgic for me. Yet I would expect some mention of Bo Brown and Montana Masquers.

As a side note to Frederick Warde's comment on the low dressing-room ceilings in the Bozeman Opera House (91), I recall asking to see that stage when I lived in Bozeman and the building had become the police station, although the decorative glass panel over the entrance still proclaimed "Bozeman Opera House." I was shocked at the smallness of the stage (where they were storing bicycles) and an auditorium the size of a living room. The story I recall about the remodeling is that a delegation traveled to New York to learn about the latest in theatre architecture. They saw that raked stages had given way to flat stages in New York, and yet the Bozeman committee voted to keep a raked stage!

Gretchen Minton's book joins important regional studies like *The Bard in the Blue Grass*, *Shakespeare on the American Yiddish Stage*, and *Shakespeare in the South* that demonstrate Shakespeare's relevance through time to a specific place. Endnotes, a bibliography, and index complete the book. It is worth noting that Minton has established an online presence for her environmentally focused work with Shakespeare, including a 2019 production of *Timon of Anaconda*, which adapts *Timon of Athens* to Butte's copper-mining saga and its aftereffects.

—FELICIA HARDISON LONDRÉ
University of Missouri-Kansas City

BOOK REVIEWS

Children, Childhood, and Musical Theater. Edited by Donelle Ruwe and James Leve. New York: Routledge, 2020. pp. xiii + 254. $48.95 paperback.

In *Children, Childhood, and Musical Theater*, editors Donelle Ruwe and James Leve have brought together a diverse group of scholars from musicology, ethnomusicology, theatre studies, and literature studies to examine the various ways that children are involved with musical theatre: as the subject or characters of a musical, as child performers, and as viewers of musicals. The emphasis of the collection on children and musical theatre is in that order, with more concern for how children and childhood are portrayed onstage than on how actual children interact with musicals. Of primary concern is how musical theatre portrays attitudes toward childhood and how children are used to further narrative functions, ethical stances, and aesthetic goals.

The editors consider the definition of the "children's musical" in three broad categories: the children's musical (intended for amateur or noncommercial performances, usually focusing on education), the family musical (commercial theatre or musical films for children and adults), and the young adult musical (highly commercial, often foregrounds concerns of teens and young adults). The authors in the collection primarily focus on the family musical, including *The Sound of Music*, *Mary Poppins*, *Chitty Chitty Bang Bang*, *Bedknobs and Broomsticks*, *Annie*, *Oliver!*, *Newsies*, and *Matilda*. Unfortunately, there is only extensive consideration of one young adult musical in the collection, *Newsies*, and two chapters on children's musicals, which should be further explored as genres.

Ryan Bunch's opening essay on *The Sound of Music* (1959 stage, 1965 film) proceeds from his own childhood fascination with the film to investigate the ways that the film aligns with cultural expectations of the musicality of children and the role that music plays in portraying maturation. His essay touches on many themes that are central to the volume, including the emotional and narrative function that children provide in musicals and the crossover appeal that musicals have for children and adults. While considering the ways that music and children forward Rodgers and Hammerstein's limited narrative goals and moral norms, Bunch also challenges this reading by claiming that music, separated from the narrative, "provides access to a utopian space where resistance to linear narrative and upward growth is possible" (33–34).

William A. Everett and Raymond Knapp, in separate chapters, also investigate the portrayal of child-rearing and the nuclear family in mid-century musical films and their later stage adaptations. Everett describes the ways that Walt Disney actively advocated for contemporary theory on child development and child-rearing in his films, including *Mary Poppins* (1964, 2004 stage) and *Bedknobs and Broomsticks* (1971), and also the non-Disney *Chitty Chitty Bang Bang* (1968, 2002 stage), which all have scores by the Sherman brothers. Central to these films were Dr. Benjamin Spock's theories on the importance of having both an active father and an active mother figure. While Everett considers the roles that the songs of these films played as "a means through which the moral messages of the films could be reinforced" (42), Knapp takes a closer look at how music, particularly, helps fathers connect with their traditional family roles by becoming more connected to their children or allowing fathers to express romantic love. Knapp also explores the theories of Dr. Spock but examines how these theories are continued or challenged in later musicals, in which father figures are often not redeemed.

Marc Napolitano examines the use of narrative and music in the adaptation of two Charles Dickens novels, *Oliver Twist* (as *Oliver!* [1960, 1968 film]) and *David Copperfield* (as *Copperfield* [1981]). Napolitano considers how the conventions of musical theatre prove problematic for adapting literary works that are reliant on their literary and narrative styles, especially with child narrators or protagonists. Also focusing on narrative and adaptation, editor Donelle Ruwe explores the musical revue *The Me Nobody Knows* (1970). Ruwe succeeds at examining the bifurcation between the "fleshy" or "real" child and the "imaginative construct of 'childhood'" (96), which is aided by her source material. Adapted from a book of children's writing from the "ghetto," *The Me Nobody Knows* failed to credit the creative input from the real children behind the stories as it transformed their experiences to meet musical theatre's utopian tendencies. Ruwe also elucidates the reactions of the real child and young adult performers to being continually cast as "street kids" after appearing in the show (110).

In their chapters, James Leve and Marah Gubar bring two different perspectives to the narrative of *Annie* (1977) and its hold on the public imagination. James Leve explores the "aesthetic paradigm shift" (117) of belting in *Annie*, the dramaturgical implications of belting, and the legacy of belting for later musicals and for the real child performers tasked with singing this score. While Leve considers the ways that music supports the unification of Annie, Daddy Warbucks, and Grace into a family unit, Gubar extensively criticizes the politics inherent in *Annie* and offers *Newsies* (1992 film, 2012 stage) as a political antidote. Gubar explains how the cultural trope of the "Teflon Kid," like Annie, who is immune to the dangers of the world, invites "adults to indulge in the fantasy that we can embrace a sentimental vision of childhood as vulnerable and precious while simultaneously refusing any civic, ethical, or economic responsibilities that might naturally be expected to go along with it" (149). Conversely, the narrative of *Newsies* (on stage) advocates that "the individual is not strong enough to change the world; collective action is necessary to force the self-interested powers-that-be to share the wealth that working-class labor helps to create" (139).

In returning to the interaction between children and adults, Helen Freshwater explores the idea of the "inner child" from self-help literature and how the creators and viewers of *Matilda the Musical* (2011) engage with its ethos. Freshwater asks what adults want or demand of the child, arguing that the story and casting "suggests that adults are still children on a fundamental level, still anticipating the moment when they will be fully adult and hoping to find the strength to manage the challenges of adulthood" (171). Freshwater helpfully supports this claim by bringing in the real voices of adult audience members and online commentators.

Lauren Acton and Stacy Wolf focus on noncommercial children's theatre to close out the volume. In her rather introductory chapter, Acton discusses the tradition of children's musicals for elementary school children and their curricular goals. Acton draws on interviews with educators and composers of these musicals to discuss the ways in which they are created and used for young children, employing the primary example of Philip Kern, Susan Kern, and Eric Jacobson's *When the Hippos Crashed the Dance* (1988). This historical overview mainly covers the amateur musicals from the 1980s and 1990s, which have been largely supplanted (though not entirely) by Broadway Junior, a series of young adult adaptations of Broadway musicals published by Musical Theatre International. Stacy Wolf examines these musicals and children's engagement with them through her ethnographic study of the Junior Theatre Festival, offering an extensive portrayal of the interaction of actual children with musical theatre. Wolf also discusses how important amateur rights have become for musical theatre publishing.

Overall, this collection is an excellent introduction to the world of children, childhood, and musical theatre, though the editors concede that "our collection barely scratches the surface" (16). To this reviewer, more engagement with real children would help illuminate how musicals help children navigate their worlds. Other future considerations include questions of race and class, mostly absent from this collection of essays. And of course, this collection addresses the musical theatre output of only two countries, the United States and the United

BOOK REVIEWS

Kingdom. A broader geographic range would give broader insights into how musical theatre helps us construct and understand a variety of childhoods.

—BRET MCCANDLESS
  Rutgers University

Blue Song: St. Louis in the Life and Work of Tennessee Williams. By Henry I. Schvey. Columbia, MO: University of Missouri Press, 2021. Vii + 236. $25.95 paper.

Henry I. Schvey's *Blue Song: St. Louis in the Life and Work of Tennessee Williams,* introduces a needed perspective on a familiar writer. Williams is a playwright emblematic of the twentieth-century US theatre. His life spanned the heart of the century (1911 to 1983) straddling many contradictions that characterized the times. His works capture internal experience expressed through the external forms of poetry, theatricality, and emotional performance. Beginning with *The Glass Menagerie,* Williams linked his own identity to the fictitious characters of his plays. It has therefore always been difficult to separate the artist from the art, and in the case of Tennessee Williams, understanding the biographical details of his life enriches our appreciation of his work.

Somewhat like the playwright, Henry Schvey draws expressly from his own personal experiences as they intersect with those Tennessee Williams and St. Louis. For twenty years, Schvey chaired the Performing Arts Department at Washington University in St. Louis, one of the three institutions where Thomas Lanier Williams studied. Recognizing the famous author's connection to "Wash U.," Schvey organized a celebration of Williams's brief period of study featuring an unproduced play, *Me, Vashya.* This led to deeper research and the chance discovery of an unpublished poem, "Blue Song," also connected to Williams's student days in St. Louis.

Many of Williams's unknown poems, plays, essays, letters, and journals have been published since his death, and Williams has been the subject of much curiosity in the past thirty years, but like his nom de plume, "Tennessee," the popular understanding of Williams's identity has been fabricated and mythologized. Central to the myth, says Schvey, is that Williams was the product of "a romanticized childhood 'unshadowed by fear' in the deep South" (33). The twenty formative years in St. Louis between 1918 and 1938 "were virtually expunged" from this narrative (33). St. Louisans also hold on to the dogged myth

{ 185 }

that Williams hated the midwestern river city. As a corrective, Schvey sets out "to clarify the importance of a city [St. Louis] in the life and works of Tennessee Williams" (5). Besides making the case for St. Louis's significance to Williams, Schvey also does what has been needed since the introduction of so much previously unpublished work: he offers critical discussion of the early plays written during Williams's St. Louis years: *Candles to the Sun* (1937), *Fugitive Kind* (1937), *Not About Nightingales* (1938), *Spring Storm* (1938), and *Stairs to the Roof* (1936–1941). He references material from the author's letters and journals illuminating the circumstances surrounding these early plays and approaching them respectfully as works that deserve thoughtful evaluation, not as juvenile curiosities. The term "juvenilia," Schvey says, "is really not a meaningful or helpful distinction in examining the work of Williams. His writing follows a thematic continuity from first to last, irrespective of his age" (47). Schvey's readings of these plays incorporate them fully into the playwright's serious output.

Blue Song is structured chronologically, first introducing the Williams family's move to St. Louis and the author's childhood, then "Tom's" experiences in college, at the shoe company, and finally as a young playwright. Next, Schvey introduces the works written before *The Glass Menagerie*. After Williams left St. Louis for other cities and themes, Schvey stretches a bit to make connections back to St. Louis, finding elements in *A Streetcar Named Desire* and *Suddenly Last Summer* that recall the author's past. Schvey uses Williams's traumatic period of professional rejection that culminated in confinement to a St. Louis psychiatric ward to examine *In the Bar of a Tokyo Hotel* (1969), the negative reception of which may have accelerated Williams's decline. Returning to works more directly related to St. Louis, Schvey examines *A Lovely Sunday for Creve Couer* (1975) and the teleplay *All Gaul Is Divided* (possibly written in the 1950s, copyrighted 1978) within the context of his waning reputation. In the final chapter, Schvey considers the teleplay *Stopped Rocking* (1977) and the full-length plays *A House Not Meant to Stand* (1982) and *Clothes for a Summer Hotel* (1980), relating all three to Rose Williams, the playwright's sister, whose mental illness and lobotomy necessitated lifelong institutionalization. Although none of these works are directly connected to St. Louis, Schvey uses the works to return to the familial circumstances that colored the author's feelings about the city.

A challenge in any discussion of Tennessee Williams's life and work is the volume of material. Many books that take up the writer's biography and output include a chronology to assist readers in keeping it all straight. Though Schvey's book keeps its focus modestly on St. Louis, a timeline would help to clarify the connection of events. References to Williams, his father, and the shoe company as well as mention of his sister's mental illness become repetitive as Schvey makes the connections to various works.

In sum, not only does Schvey do a service in his critical discussion of the early works Tennessee Williams initiated in St. Louis, but he also draws attention to lesser-known later works. He successfully challenges the mythology that Tennessee Williams was the indisputable product solely of the Mississippi Delta as he makes the case to consider how Depression-era St. Louis impacted the playwright's development. There are still aspects of Williams's story that remain mythical, and Schvey does not address them fully. He perpetuates the characterization of Williams's mother Edwina as a prudish nag without considering the complexity of her circumstances. Likewise, he only hints at the life of Rose Williams as a young woman of the 1920s. Finally, the mythology of Williams's addictions and confinement to the "psych ward" are due for more complete reassessment. Hopefully these aspects of the Williams myth may yet be addressed by scholars who follow up on the material Schvey has provided. *Blue Song* is written in a voice that is accessible and clear, filled with the assurance of historical research along with thoughtful critical assessment. By resituating Tennessee Williams in the context of his prewar St. Louis household, Schvey shakes up our understanding of this very familiar playwright, poet, and author.

—TOM MITCHELL
University of Illinois—Urbana-Champaign

Radical Vision: A Biography of Lorraine Hansberry. By Soyica Diggs Colbert. New Haven, CT: Yale University Press, 2021. Pp. $30.00 hardcover.

Conversations with Lorraine Hansberry. Ed. by Mollie Godfrey. Jackson: University Press of Mississippi, 2020. Pp. xxv + 224. $25.00 paperback.

Celebrated and well-known dramatist, essayist, and intellectual Lorraine Hansberry left behind a legacy far beyond the era in which she lived. While her history-making play *A Raisin in the Sun* was foundational to the critical attention, access, and fame that Hansberry experienced in her short life, studies of her archive are often relegated to that one piece. Soyica Diggs Colbert's *Radical Vision: A Biography of Lorraine Hansberry* and Mollie Godfrey's edited collection, *Conversations with Lorraine Hansberry*, endeavor to disrupt this narrow engagement with Hansberry. These two books are part of a much-needed shift in theatre history that critically attends to Black female theatre makers' artistic, intellectual, and political histories and reshapes the additive model of scholarship that merely includes one chapter on Black women among a host of men. Distinct in their form and approach to Hansberry, each book expands a deeper understanding of the considerable breadth of her theatrical oeuvre.

Soyica Diggs Colbert's *Radical Vision: A Biography of Lorraine Hansberry* is an artistic and intellectual biography of Hansberry that examines how Marxism, existentialism, and Black radicalism shaped her writing and thought. Theoretically rich and infused with rigorous archival research, Colbert argues for the importance of Hansberry's writing both published and unpublished as invested in the act and process of freedom. As Colbert writes in the introduction, "A central concept of this book, 'becoming free,' names the processual nature of Hansberry's work, the ideas that underpin it, and its place in a long history of emancipation" (7). Colbert grapples with a decades-long tension of doing and writing theatre history, especially when your subject is not a cis white man. *Radical Vision* offers a useful methodology for negotiating the tensions that may arise when doing archival research by approaching the slippages of the archive as an opportunity, as "a space of both evidence and invention" (8).

In chapter 1, "Practices of Freedom," Colbert examines Hansberry's 1950s writing, including her poems, short stories, letters, and periodicals, arguing that these oft-overlooked Hansberry writings cultivated her practice of writing as a practice of freedom. Chapter 2, "The Shaping Force of *A Raisin in the Sun*," toggles between Hansberry's private and public lives prior to and immediately after the success of *A Raisin in the Sun* (1959). As Colbert argues, Hansberry's domestic drama led to the public perception of her as a young middle-class married housewife, thus obscuring her radical leftist ideals. Supplementing her reading of *Raisin* with interviews with Hansberry, Colbert also illustrates how she clarified the stakes of *Raisin* beyond the liberal platitudes that were often ascribed to it, instead reiterating the commitment of *Raisin* to depicting everyday forms of liberatory practices.

The third and fourth chapters continue to examine how Hansberry's public and private lives influenced her writing. Colbert crystallizes how Hansberry's writing was anchored in Black radicalism and feminism through critical exploration of her unproduced screenplay *The Drinking Gourd* (1960), her essays, her unpublished play *Toussaint* (1961), a photo essay she created in collaboration with the Student Nonviolent Coordinating Committee (SNCC), and her self-portraits. The book's third chapter is where Colbert argues that Hansberry's writing, what Colbert dubs the "origins," were informed by practices of looking, whether it be "observing, being observed, [or] witnessing" (97). In chapter 4, Colbert offers collaboration, not coalition, as the ethos of Hansberry's writing. As Colbert puts it, "Collaboration necessitated foregrounding the good of the whole over individual achievement" (137). Chapter 5, "From Liberals to Radicals," pairs Hansberry's dramas (*Sign in Sidney Brustein's Window* [1964], *What Uses Are Flowers?* [1964], and *Arrival of Mr. To Dog* [1964]) with her theatre criticism to trace how Hansberry's public debates with Norman Mailer shaped her thinking and writing. These encounters, both written and conversational, served to model working across differences. Colbert contends that these debates "served as an extension of her artistic work" and illustrate her deep engagement with the field of existentialism (166).

In the subsequent sixth chapter, Colbert takes up Hansberry's 1960 drama, *Les Blancs*. In her analysis, Colbert reveals Hansberry's investment in the "global movement for freedom" (101). In so doing, she argues that *Les Blancs* depicts the connection between political participation and the personal. Both past and present contexts of freedom movements receive focused attention in this chapter, leading to a larger consideration of how Hansberry used her dramatic work to deconstruct imperialism globally. In the epilogue, Colbert leaves the reader with a launching point to reconsider the importance of writing as crucial to "becoming free." Colbert does not end on the tragedy of Hansberry's premature death but rather takes aim at considering her steadfast investment in the uplift of Black life, both domestic and international, through her writerly practice.

Theoretically rich and infused with rigorous archival research, Colbert illustrates how Hansberry's radical vision was embedded in her various genres of writing. Colbert's scholarly biography ensures that theatre historians understand Hansberry as a radical, a dramatist, and an intellectual who found the utility of theatre in the project of Black freedom. With a fresh and compelling approach to Hansberry, *Radical Vision* is a valuable contribution to theatre history, Black studies, and critical theory. Colbert models how to engage historical subjects with care, ensuring that the complexity of their lives is not lost.

If Colbert identifies the radical visions of Hansberry's life and writings, the volume *Conversations with Lorraine Hansberry*, edited by Mollie Godfrey, reveals the depth and breadth of Hansberry's archive. The first comprehensive collection of Hansberry's interviews, essays, and public conversations, Godfrey's curation allows Hansberry's perspective to be primary. In so doing, readers are provided with Hansberry's insight on universality, the American theatre, racism and the role of the Black writer, her own formulations of what *A Raisin in the Sun* was accomplishing, and a host of other topics. Ranging from 1958 to 1964, in the twenty-one interviews, essays, and conversations, Hansberry's radical politics is on full display throughout the volume.

In her framing of the collection, Godfrey notes that her "hope [is] that these interviews will open a small window into the eloquence, intensity, and insight" of Hansberry's thinking (xiv). Godfrey prioritizes the most substantive pieces of Hansberry's archive and those harder to find in print, including three interviews of Hansberry by Mike Wallace, Eleanor Fischer, and Patricia Marx that were either fully or partially unaired. Additionally, Godfrey has taken great care in preserving the nonverbal components of the radio and television interviews by including in her transcriptions laughter, frustration, and pauses. In the introduction, Godfrey provides a salient overview of Hansberry's speeches, interviews, and essays; what is clear is that Godfrey is interested, like Hansberry was, in disrupting the biases that white audiences may have of Black drama.

Each piece highlights Hansberry's intellectual and social prowess and the wide-ranging audiences that she reached. For example, in an unaired interview with Mike Wallace in 1959, Hansberry refuses Wallace's formulation that there have been few Black novelists, dramatists, or poets of note. In a masterful reversal, Hansberry turns the statement on its head and probes Wallace to consider the material conditions that exclude Black writers from mainstream notoriety. Across multiple interviews, the question of naturalism versus realism arose for Hansberry, and she insisted that realism was the form by which the truth of Black life could be told. Additionally, a common thread of Hansberry's interviews and editorials is her critical position on the Black middle class. Over numerous pieces in this volume, Hansberry labors on the specificity of her middle-class upbringing and insists on the importance of depicting the Black working class onstage. Hansberry cautions against the Black middle class desiring acquisition and affluence over liberation. Moreover, the questions and framing by some of the interviewers and editors provide insight into their limited views of Hansberry. A frequent talking point was Hansberry's husband at the time, Robert Nemiroff—many interviewers were interested in how he felt about her success and how she balanced her role as wife and writer.

Godfrey's excellent curated collection of Hansberry's thinking makes readers feel as if they have been catapulted into dialogue with Hansberry. The range of topics that these selections include also illuminate the depth and breadth of Hansberry's social and political commitments and the ability for theatre to be one of the vehicles by which all oppressed people could unite. This collection would be a valuable teaching tool to pair with any of Hansberry's dramas. For scholars of theatre and performance, this collection offers a reintroduction to Hansberry's commitment to realism and places many of her oft-repeated quotes within a larger context. If I could offer any critique of this collection, it is that at moments I craved for the selections to be divided by theme to create a more cohesive understanding of how they fit within Hansberry's life and work. Nonetheless, Hansberry's interviews often addressed a large scope of topics, and I also understand the difficulty in attempting to categorize the rich insights she provided. Overall, I was struck by my own surprise at the foresight that Hansberry displayed in many of her public conversations.

Colbert's and Godfrey's contributions add to the recent influx of critical attention to Lorraine Hansberry, including Imani Perry's 2018 memoir *Looking for Lorraine*, the 2017 documentary *Sighted Eyes/Feeling Heart*, by Tracy Heather Strains, and the forthcoming book *Lorraine Hansberry: Am I a Revolutionary?*, by Margaret Wilkerson. Within this collective, Colbert's *Radical Vision: A Biography of Lorraine Hansberry* and Godfrey's edited collection, *Conversations with Lorraine Hansberry*, model fresh and compelling approaches to a major figure. Overall, these books' depth and breadth would be valuable across a host of academic disciplines including but not limited to Black studies, theatre and performance, women and gender studies, and English. Beyond the traditional academy, Colbert's and Godfrey's books are written in such a way that would also appeal to general audiences interested in learning more about the life and legacy of Lorraine Hansberry.

—LETICIA L. RIDLEY
University of Toronto—Mississauga

Working Backstage: A Cultural History and Ethnography of Technical Theater Labor. By Christin Essin. Ann Arbor: University of Michigan Press, 2021. pp 286. $80.00 cloth.

Working conditions, labor rights, and equity in the workplace have roared into focus in the American theatre in recent years. Long-established norms have been questioned, power structures challenged, and representation (and the lack thereof) vehemently critiqued. From the excoriating criticisms of We See You, White American Theatre to the calls for "no more 10 out of 12s," theatre makers are fervently calling for dignity, respect, and justice for those laboring in this craft. With her timely book *Working Backstage: A Cultural History and Ethnography of Technical Theater Labor*, Christin Essin foregrounds the experience and expertise of laborers whose work and lives have heretofore been largely invisible. The last decade has seen the publication of several texts that focus on the history of the material conditions of production, yet technical theatre workers have largely remained nameless and unseen. Essin's paradigm-shifting book provides long overdue recuperative work, centering the humanity of those who for centuries have been hidden in the wings, shops, booths, dressing rooms, lighting coves, and fly rails.

Working Backstage explores genealogies of theatrical production, tracing lineages among and between theatrical families—real and symbolic. While theatrical families have been a regular feature of *on*stage theatre histories for centuries, Essin shines a spotlight on the workers who are backstage to reveal myriad surprising connections. Multiple generations of a family have become International Alliance of Theatrical Stage Employees (IATSE) members (and in some cases worked together on the same production). "Orphans" speak of the care and support they receive from their fellow union members and coworkers as being like that of family, tracing their connections to each other through something of a theatrical union family tree. In the prologue, Essin situates herself within a lineage of technical production, recounting her own short career as a theatre technician. Essin is necessarily and delightfully present throughout the book, since one of the chief methodologies deployed in this study is ethnography. Her professional experience no doubt helped open (stage) doors. Her high regard for the people she met and enthusiasm for their work radiates off the page. She recounts her interviews, phone calls, and observations with such clear and lively prose that readers may feel as if they are accompanying her on these encounters. Essin also undertook complex archival work, mining collections of personal papers and IATSE records, viewing hours of video recordings, parsing newspaper clippings, and deciphering the gaps, erasures, and revisions of the few written records that exist. Additionally, Essin explicates metatheatrical representations of backstage laborers in plays, solo performances, films, and one not-to-be-missed YouTube video. This trifecta of methodologies paints a vivid and dynamic picture of the laborers in backstage positions, including spotlight operators, dressers, carpenters, and child guardians.

The book is divided into three sections, each deploying a slightly different approach. Part I: Backstage Narratives offers a strong foundation by explicating the various categories of backstage employment and a cogent explanation of what is really at stake with union membership, especially within IATSE. What makes this study deeply human, however, are the profiles that share the unique stories of several technicians in a variety of jobs from across an array of identities and professional backgrounds. This focus on real people and the complexity of their jobs and stories is a hallmark of the entire book.

Part II: Backstage Histories comprises three chapters, each of which could be used as a case study for innovative theatre historiography. In the first, Essin skillfully unravels the history of IATSE through the papers and writings of "laborer historians," the workers who dedicate personal time to documenting the history of their trade. She traces the revision process for the official histories, which were created as part of the commemoration of auspicious anniversaries for the union, and highlights elements that were erased or reframed. The second chapter in this section analyzes the media bias toward union theatrical labor that has long persisted in newspaper accounts, especially during heightened moments of fraught contract negotiations. Essin deftly upends a recurring disparagement of stagehands as merely sitting backstage playing pinochle, to contend that perhaps the card game could be read as a way to keep their intellect engaged and their response time swift. The final chapter in this section uses three iconic musicals to forge connections between the thematic elements of the scripts and the embodied labor of technicians. Thus, the choreography of the lighting technicians mirrors the dance choreography in *A Chorus Line*, the camaraderie and solidarity of the striking newspapers boys in *Newsies* is paralleled by the teamwork of the light and sound technicians, and the metaphors of protection and support in *Matilda* are made manifest in the wildly unsung heroics of the child guardians.

The final section of the book, "Backstage Dramaturgies," shifts its methodology to dramaturgical analysis, but the real-life experiences of backstage theatrical workers are still woven throughout. Here Essin crafts essays instead of chapters, using fictive and documentary texts to explore the ways in which laborers outside the purview of IATSE Local One in New York City have been depicted onstage and screen in contemporary theatre. These essays are compelling, offering vivid performance reconstructions tempered by critiques of representation of backstage workers. However, I found their placement at the end of the book, following the virtuosic archival-ethnographies, to be challenging. On the one hand, it was exciting to read these essays with the newfound knowledge of the intricacies of backstage jobs, union membership, and individual lives. On the other hand, however, several of the examples, as Essin argues, gloss the complexities of the work or fixate on the celebrity performers. This results in concluding the book on a relatively somber tone. Perhaps this was intentional as a means of illustrating how much more work there is to be done to recognize and celebrate backstage labor. How might the essays have landed differently, however, if placed near the beginning of the book? There is no simple answer, but in a study that so gloriously foregrounds un- and underrepresented theatrical labor, concluding with how these workers represent themselves, rather than how others (namely playwrights) represent them, might have shifted the tone at the end. Essin concludes the book with a brief and inspiring coda, galvanizing theatre educators to reassess the ways that technical theatre labor is taught and deployed within university theatre programs.

Any one of the chapters in this book would make for excellent reading in theatre history, stagecraft, or design courses. Read as a whole, this book is a tour-de-force exemplar of methodological innovation. But this book may also have appeal beyond academia, partly due to the accessibility of Essin's vibrant writing and partly to the fascinating level of detail with which she animates the work and workers. This may also be a necessarily humbling book for many readers. You may think you know what transpires backstage, but Essin's study reveals that most scholars and onstage theatre workers have barely glimpsed the performances and players behind the scenes.

—CHRISTINE WOODWORTH
　Hobart and William Smith Colleges

BOOKS RECEIVED

* indicates a title assigned for review

Baird, Bruce. *A History of Butô*. New York: Oxford University Press, 2022.

Boffone, Trevor, and Carla Della Gatta, eds. *Shakespeare and Latinidad*. Edinburgh: Edinburgh University Press, 2021.

Brietzke, Zander. *Magnum Opus: The Cycle Plays of Eugene O'Neill*. New Haven, CT: Yale University Press, 2021.

*Bryer, Jackson R., Robert M. Dowling, and Mary C. Hartig, eds. *Conversations with Sam Shepard*. Jackson: University Press of Mississippi, 2021.

Cermatori, Joseph. *Baroque Modernity: An Aesthetics of Theater*. Baltimore, MD: Johns Hopkins University Press, 2021.

*Conti, Meredith, and Kevin Wetmore, eds. *Theatre and the Macabre*. Cardiff: University of Wales Press, 2022.

*Cruz, Gabriela. *Grand Illusion: Phantasmagoria in Nineteenth-Century Opera*. New York: Oxford University Press, 2020.

D'Alessandro, Michael. *Staged Readings: Contesting Class in Popular American Theater and Literature, 1835–75*. Ann Arbor: University of Michigan Press, 2022.

Farfan, Penny, and Leslie Farris. *Critical Perspectives on Contemporary Plays by Women: The Early Twenty-First Century*. Ann Arbor: University of Michigan Press, 2021.

Forsgren, La Donna L. *Sistuhs in the Struggle: An Oral History of Black Arts Movement Theater and Performance*. Evanston, IL: Northwestern University Press, 2020.

Franks, Matthew. *Subscription Theater: Democracy and Drama in Britain and Ireland, 1880–1939*. Philadelphia: University of Pennsylvania Press, 2020.

Gjesdal, Kristin. *The Drama of History: Ibsen, Hegel, Nietzsche*. New York: Oxford University Press, 2020.

Guzzetta, Juliet. *The Theater of Narration: From the Peripheries of History to the Main Stages of Italy*. Evanston, IL: Northwestern University Press, 2021.

BOOKS RECEIVED

*Lee, Esther Kim. *Made-Up Asians: Yellowface During the Exclusion Era*. Ann Arbor: University of Michigan Press, 2022.

Leichman, Jeffrey, and Karine Bénac-Giroux, eds. *Colonialism and Slavery in Performance: Theatre and the Eighteenth-Century French Caribbean*. Liverpool: University of Liverpool Press, 2021.

Lipton, Emma. *Cultures of Witnessing: Law and the York Plays*. Philadelphia: University of Pennsylvania Press, 2022.

Liu, Siyuan. *Transforming Tradition: The Reform of Chinese Theater in the 1950s and Early 1960s*. Ann Arbor: University of Michigan Press, 2021.

Magelssen, Scott. *Performing Flight: From the Barnstormers to Space Tourism*. Ann Arbor: University of Michigan Press, 2020.

Morgan, Cecilia. *Sweet Canadian Girls Abroad: A Transnational History of Stage and Screen Actresses*. Montreal: McGill-Queens University Press, 2022.

Mujica, Bárbara, ed. *Staging and Stage Décor: Early Modern Spanish Theater*. Malaga, Spain: Vernon Press, 2022.

Ndiaye, Noémie. *Scripts of Blackness: Early Modern Performance Culture and the Making of Race*. Philadelphia: University of Pennsylvania Press, 2022.

Pahwa, Sonali. *Theaters of Citizenship: Aesthetics and Politics of Avant-Garde Performance in Egypt*. Evanston, IL: Northwestern University Press, 2020.

Persley, Nicole Hodges. *Sampling and Remixing Blackness in Hip Hop Theater and Performance*. Ann Arbor: University of Michigan Press, 2021.

Peters, Julie Stone. *Law as Performance: Theatricality, Spectatorship, and the Making of Law in Ancient, Medieval, and Early Modern Europe*. Oxford, UK: Oxford University Press, 2022.

*Rogers, Bradley. *The Song Is You: Musical Theatre and the Politics of Bursting into Song and Dance*. Iowa City: University of Iowa Press, 2020.

Schweitzer, Marlis. *Bloody Tyrants and Little Pickles: Stage Roles of Anglo-American Girls in the Nineteenth Century*. Iowa City: University of Iowa Press, 2020.

Valente-Quinn, Brian. *Senegalese Stagecraft: Decolonizing Theater-Making in Francophone Africa*. Evanston, IL: Northwestern University Press, 2021.

Walker, Julia. *Performance and Modernity: Enacting Change on the Globalizing Stage*. Cambridge, UK: Cambridge University Press, 2021.

Winkler, Kevin. *Everything Is Choreography: The Musical Theater of Tommy Tune*. New York: Oxford University Press, 2021.

*Wolf, Stacy. *Beyond Broadway: The Pleasure and Promise of Musical Theatre Across America*. New York: Oxford University Press, 2019.

Wood, Katelyn Hale. *Cracking Up: Black Feminist Comedy in the Twentieth and Twenty-First Century United States*. Iowa City: University of Iowa Press, 2021.

CONTRIBUTORS

MATTHIEU CHAPMAN is an assistant professor of theatre studies at the State University of New York at New Paltz and the literary director of New York Classical Theatre. His creative writing and essays have appeared in *Pithead Chapel, Prose Online, Beyond Words*, and the *Huffington Post*. His books include a memoir, *Shattered: Fragments of a Black Life*, and a monograph, *Anti-Black Racism in Early Modern English Drama: "The Other Other."* He is the coeditor (along with Anna Wainwright) of *Teaching Race in the Early Modern World: A Classroom Guide*. He has also published articles in *Medieval and Renaissance Drama in England, Theatre Topics, TheatreForum, Theatre History Studies*, and *Early Theatre*, and he has chapters in *Race and/as Affect in Early Modern England* (edited by Carol Mejia-LaPerle) and *Shakespeare and Atrocity*.

KATHERINE GILLEN is an associate professor of English at Texas A&M University–San Antonio. She is the author of *Chaste Value: Economic Crisis, Female Chastity, and the Production of Social Difference on Shakespeare's Stage*, and several essays on Shakespeare appropriation and race, gender, and economics in early modern drama. She is working on a monograph that examines Shakespeare's use of classical sources within the context of emerging racial capitalism. With Kathryn Vomero Santos and Adrianna M. Santos, she cofounded the Borderlands Shakespeare Colectiva and coedited *The Bard in the Borderlands: An Anthology of Shakespeare Appropriations* en La Frontera, Volume 1.

MILES P. GRIER is an associate professor of English at Queens College, City University of New York. He is the author of a monograph about *Othello* and the formation of white interpretive community during the seventeenth, eighteenth, and first half of the nineteenth centuries and is coeditor of *Early Modern*

CONTRIBUTORS

Black Diaspora Studies. His essays on Shakespearean material have appeared in *William and Mary Quarterly* and the volumes *Scripturalizing the Human*, *The Cambridge Companion to Shakespeare and Race*, and *Shakespeare/Text*. Essays on more contemporary North American topics such as racial profiling after 9/11, Joni Mitchell's blackface pimp alter ego, President Obama's Beyoncé-style approach to Black voters, and a review of the film of *Ma Rainey's Black Bottom* have appeared in *Politics and Culture*, *Genders*, the *Journal of Popular Music Studies*, and the *LA Review of Books*.

PATRICIA HERRERA, professor of theatre at the University of Richmond, is the author of *Nuyorican Feminist Performances: From the Café to Hip Hop Theater*. Since 2011, Patricia has engaged with the city of Richmond on a community-based public history project titled *Civil Rights and Education in Richmond, Virginia: A Documentary Theater Project*, which has led to the creation of a digital archive, *The Fight for Knowledge*, as well as four museum exhibitions and a series of seven docudramas about gentrification, educational disparities, HIV/AIDS, segregation, and Latinos in Richmond.

LISA JACKSON-SCHEBETTA is an associate professor and the chair of theatre at Skidmore College. She is the author of *Traveler, There Is No Road: Theatre, the Spanish Civil War, and the Decolonial Imagination in the Americas*. Her scholarship has been published in *Theatre Journal*, *Modern Drama*, *Journal of American Drama and Theatre*, *Theatre History Studies*, and *New England Theatre Journal*, among others.

JOSHUA KELLY is a PhD candidate at the University of Wisconsin-Madison, where his work is primarily in performance philosophy, gender theory, and political theatre. His scholarly work has been accepted to and presented at numerous conferences including SETC, MATC, ATHE, and more. As an artist, he is a freelance director, actor, dramaturg, and playwright, and his plays have been short-listed, long-listed, and performed in a number of theatre festivals, including Forward Theatre's Wisconsin Wrights, Activate: Midwest, the Garry Marshall New Works Festival.

MARCI R. MCMAHON, a professor of literatures and cultural studies at the University of Texas Rio Grande Valley, is the author of *Domestic Negotiations: Gender, Nation, and Self-Fashioning in US Mexicana and Chicana Literature and Art*. Some of her publications appear in *The Chicano Studies Reader:*

CONTRIBUTORS

An Anthology of Aztlán, third and fourth editions; *Aztlán: A Journal of Chicano Studies*; *Chicana/Latina Studies: The Journal of MALCS*; *Frontiers: A Journal of Women's Studies*; *Journal of Equity and Excellence in Education*; and *Text and Performance Quarterly*.

SHERRICE MOJGANI is an assistant professor at George Mason University, a DC-based lighting designer, and activist. She strives to disrupt white supremacist culture and transform a capitalist society to support a theatre industry that celebrates and welcomes BIPOC communities. Sherrice has designed for Arena Stage, Round House Theatre, Baltimore Center Stage, the Old Globe, and La Jolla Playhouse. Sherrice is a proud member of United Scenic Artist Local 829. Sherrice holds a BA in theatre arts from UC Santa Cruz and an MFA in lighting design from UC San Diego.

JOHN MURILLO III is an assistant professor of African American studies at the University of California, Irvine. His primary research interests include twentieth-century and contemporary Black literature, speculative fiction, Afro-pessimism, critical theory, and theoretical physics. He is the author of *Impossible Stories: On the Space and Time of Black Destructive Creation* and a "mythological memoir" titled *Orbitals*.

HEIDI L. NEES is an assistant professor of theatre at Bowling Green State University. Her research interests include historiography, Native American drama, and representations of the American frontier in performance, and her work has appeared in *Theatre Annual*, *Theatre Topics*, *Theatre Journal*, and *Theatre History Studies*, among others. Heidi is also the cofounder, with jenn stucker (an associate professor at Bowling Green State University School of Art), of In the Round: A Speaker Series Featuring Native American Creatives at BGSU.

JESSICA N. PABÓN-COLÓN is an associate professor of women's, gender, and sexuality Studies at SUNY New Paltz. She is an interdisciplinary performance studies scholar engaged in teaching and research at the intersections of women's, gender, and sexuality studies, performance studies, critical ethnic studies, cultural studies, and the digital humanities. In June 2018, she published her first book, *Graffiti Grrlz: Performing Feminism in the Hip Hop Diaspora*. Her research appears in *Signs: Journal of Women in Culture and Society*, *Women and Performance: A Journal of Feminist Theory*, *Performance Research*, and *TDR: The Journal of Performance Studies*.

CONTRIBUTORS

KARA RAPHAELI is a theatre historian and trans performance scholar. Currently a visiting assistant professor of theatre arts at Simpson College, they received their PhD in theatre and drama with a specialization in critical gender studies from the joint program between UC San Diego and UC Irvine. Their dissertation, "The Clothes Make the Man: Theatrical Crossdressing as Expression of Gender Fluidity in Seventeenth- through Nineteenth-Century Performance," explores cross-dressing and male impersonation through a transmasculine lens. Kara has been issue editor and managing editor of *TheatreForum*, an international journal of innovative performance. They are also a community organizer, director, and producer.

CYNTHIA RUNNING-JOHNSON is a professor of French emerita at Western Michigan University. In her research, inspired by participation in theatrical productions at the University of Wisconsin and work with French theatre companies, she has focused on questions of gender and culture in literature and performance. Dr. Running-Johnson's work has appeared in publications including the *French Review*, *L'Esprit Créateur*, *French Forum*, the *Journal of Dramatic Theory and Criticism*, *Theatre Topics*, *Contemporary Theatre Review*, *Plays by French and Francophone Women: A Critical Anthology*, and *Modern French Literary Studies in the Classroom: Pedagogical Strategies*. In recent years, she has studied the development of individual theatre productions in France and has researched the institutional structures that influence the lives of French theatre artists.

ALEXANDRA SWANSON earned her PhD in English literature from Washington University in St. Louis. Her research focuses on nineteenth-century melodrama and its afterlives, as well as the intersection of music and literature.

CATHERINE PECKINPAUGH VRTIS is an independent scholar of theatre and performance studies, specializing in Black theatre, theatre and disability, performances of medicalization, and monster and freak studies. Recent articles include "Proletarian Plays for Proletarian Audiences: Langston Hughes and Harvest" in the *Journal of African American Studies* and "Defending the Patriarchy: The Monstrous (Queer) Other and the Anti- Carnivalesque" in the anthology *Monsters in Performance: Essays on the Aesthetics of Disqualification*. Dr. Vrtis led in the creation of the emergent ATHE Disability, Theatre, and Performance focus group and also serves as the Accessibility Officer for the Mid-America Theatre Conference.

CONTRIBUTORS

SHANE WOOD is an award-winning educator, director, and designer. He studies drama and theatre at University of California, Irvine. He lives in Southern California and balances his time between his study of early modern religious women and teaching high school English full time in the Los Angeles area.

ROBERT O. YATES is a doctoral candidate at the City University of New York, Graduate Center, where he is a Mellon Humanities Public Fellow. In the 2022–2023 academic year, Robert held the Lillian Goldman Law Library Rare Book Fellowship at Yale Law School. He writes on early modern literature and culture.